MIDNIGHT DUET

OTHER TITLES BY JEN COMFORT

The Astronaut and the Star

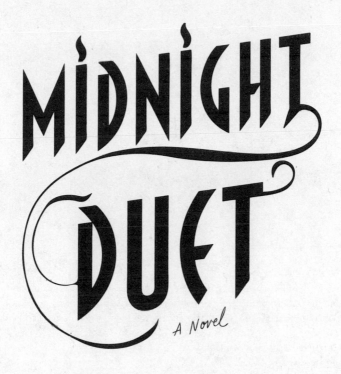

MIDNIGHT DUET

A Novel

JEN COMFORT

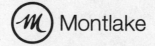

Montlake

Published by Montlake, Seattle

www.apub.com

Amazon, the Amazon logo, and Montlake are trademarks of Amazon.com, Inc., or its affiliates.

ISBN-13: 9781542038515 (paperback)
ISBN-10: 1542038510 (paperback)
ISBN-13: 9781542038508 (digital)

Cover design and illustration by Philip Pascuzzo

Printed in the United States of America

This book is for the former theater kids, the unapologetic divas, the "more is more" crowd, and those who live for melodrama—keep being your fabulous selves.

CHAPTER 1

"You know, they say you should never do prologues."

Misty's chipper little stream of consciousness from the next stool over had been a constant irritation ever since Erika Greene had staggered into the dressing room fifteen minutes ago, abominably late for dress rehearsal. It was also several decibels louder than what Erika's hungover brain had patience for.

"No one cares about your musical screenplay, Misty," Erika said under her breath. She pressed her index fingers into the puffy bags beneath her eyes to test whether the purple might magically disappear. It didn't.

I look like shit. Whose idea had it been to go out drinking last night with a full dress run-through scheduled for eleven the following morning? Oh, right—hers.

"Did you say something?" Misty pulled back from the dressing room mirror and squinted at Erika with one eye, a half-glued eyelash strip dangling from the other.

Erika tried mustering a polite smile. It came out more like a grimace. "Nope."

"Huh. Well, anyway, I know they can be kind of tacky, but I think it's necessary to reveal my antiheroine's origin story. I want the audience to *see* how awful and unlikable she is, you know? I want them to absolutely despise her . . ."

As Misty blabbed on, Erika once again considered the merits of moving to the private dressing rooms reserved for soloists, rather than this communal one, where the understudies and general chorus vied for space around overcrowded mirrors. There was also a pigeon nesting on one of the storage shelves that ran along the ceiling's perimeter, and it occasionally shat on anyone who was unlucky enough to choose the wrong mirror. Erika didn't like sharing space with the city's menagerie of vermin, which was why her modern two-bedroom apartment was located on the twenty-fourth floor of a high-rise, and she planned to upgrade to the penthouse when she won her first Tony. But the soloist rooms were dull and quiet, and Erika thrived in vibrant, chaotic settings full of people.

Besides, what was the point of being a Broadway star if one couldn't bask in the fawning admiration of the less talented? There was nothing quite like the feeling of gliding through the door over an hour past call time and knowing every soul in the room was watching her, wondering where she'd been and thinking with equal parts spite and envy, *How dare she?*

And how *did* Erika dare? Well, it wasn't like they could very well do *Les Misérables* without their Fantine. Their *Tony-nominated* Fantine, no less, one an article in *Playbill* had lauded as the heiress to Sutton Foster's throne. Erika regularly fielded inquiries about whether so-and-so was writing an original musical as a vehicle for her rising star power, but her demure reply had always been the same: she was delighted to continue doing Fantine's tragic character justice. No one else could possibly fill her shoes.

Although there was always Carla.

Erika wrinkled her nose at her own reflection. Her understudy was to Erika's looks and skill what Lea Michele was to Streisand.

There was simply no substitute.

Carla. Somewhere in the back of her head, a warning light went off. There was something she needed to remember about Carla. Something Jackson had mentioned last night, before they'd left the club. The second club, not the third. Or was it when they'd gone back to his place and—

Oh.

That's right; Erika had fucked Jackson Weatherfield last night. Ugh. Jackson, with the blue-white teeth and enormous . . . Liberty Bell. How had she forgotten?

Gin martinis, her brain helpfully supplied. Or maybe it was because she'd desperately wanted to forget having discovered the man kept a to-scale replica of the Liberty Bell in his living room. The plumbing empire heir's Benjamin Franklin obsession was well known amid Manhattan's social set, and he often monologued about *Hamilton*'s "insulting exclusion" . . . but an entire bell? If there was a line that one should never cross, it was intercourse with a man who owned a Liberty Bell.

Misty went on, ". . . the abysmal *depths* she'd sink to prior to the main story line . . ."

Though the rest of the night was blurry, she distinctly remembered the sound of ringing every time he'd thrust into her. Memory was a cruel mistress.

She did not like Jackson. Not before the bell reveal and not after. But he was talented and attractive, and everyone else in Manhattan wanted him. Therefore, Erika had wanted him.

Why? Who knew. Her brain hurt too much for self-reflection. Then again, it usually did. Cue gin martinis and self-destructive affairs with unavailable men; rinse and repeat.

"Places in ten!" called a stagehand.

"Ugh," Erika muttered as she yanked her hideous wig down over her bald cap. She wouldn't have time to finish her stage makeup, but who cared? The circles under her eyes suited the role, and besides—Erika could perform unconscious and still outshine everyone else in the cast.

Misty paused, eyelash curler still attached at the base of her lid. "You don't like it?"

"Like what?" Her head throbbed. Normally, Erika found Misty's sycophantic company oddly soothing; the woman never seemed to stop talking, and her inane musings kept Erika from sinking too deeply into her own head. For some reason Erika could not explain, she'd recently decided to take this woman who played her grown-up stage daughter, Cosette, under her metaphorical wing. Misty had the spark, but she needed direction from someone wiser and more experienced, Erika had decided. And though Erika wasn't yet thirty and only had five years on Misty, shouldn't all great performers nurture a devoted court of talented protégés, no matter their age? Today, though, Misty's devotion was beyond intolerable.

Was there still Midol in her makeup kit? Any painkiller would do.

"The title. *Sporeceress.* I wanted to convey that they were sorceresses but also organic mushrooms. Is it too on the nose?"

Erika shook out four pills and crammed them in her mouth. She swallowed them dry, forcing the whole lot down her throat with sheer willpower.

"It is! I knew it." Misty whimpered in dismay. "I'll never be the next Andrew Lloyd Webber."

"Absolute tragedy," Erika muttered.

"I know, right?"

If she tipped her head back and closed her eyes, maybe the painkillers would work faster.

A crash sounded, and everyone in the room gasped—except for Erika, who had long ago achieved the implacable demeanor of a jaded Manhattanite although she wasn't a born New Yorker. Erika's mother had married up and moved to the city when Erika was a toddler.

Consequently, Erika had grown up on the Upper East Side back when it had been exclusive to the kind of moneyed families who didn't *need* convenient subway access, and her years in elite private schooling had forged titanium shielding around her public persona, which conveyed at all times an outward air of vague ennui. Should a street performer's sneaker kick perilously close to her perfect little ski slope of a nose, she wouldn't so much as flinch.

Still, the sound was startling, and Erika was deeply interested in dramatics—she'd gone into theater, hadn't she?—so she allowed herself a discreet glance in the mirror. The view revealed that someone had swung the door to the shared dressing room open so hard it had slammed into the wall, causing a cloud of plaster dust to puff up around it. (Open Carefully: Broken Doorstop, warned a handwritten sign taped to the other side of the door.)

"You . . . *bitch*!" declared a familiar voice. Then . . . four beats.

Four beats to let the words sink into the air.

Four beats to let your audience drink in the stillness of *antici* . . .

The actress seated at the closest dressing table let out a tinny cough as she flapped at the dust cloud. The performer to the cougher's left whispered in a reedy voice, "Oh my God, is this asbestos?"

And in that four-beat moment, Erika suddenly remembered what she'd needed to remember about Carla.

. . . *pation.*

Carla was dating Jackson Weatherfield.

Oh fuck. A crescendo of guilt and shame swelled in her mouth, and it tasted kind of like bile mixed with the nonfat mocha she'd had on her way in. She forced it back down. Down, down, down, along with the rest of her conscience. Guilt made one weak, and we couldn't have that, could we? The audience could sense weakness. They'd go for blood.

No, misdeeds like these required the fine art of doubling down. A dash of indignation, even. How dare they assume she'd knowingly sleep with someone's new boyfriend? She couldn't possibly have known!

Unless Erika had heard the rumors going around backstage that Carla was dating Jackson. *Secretly* dating, of course, because Jackson had convinced Carla that subterfuge would be best—a paper-thin excuse that Erika had known even then was due to the fact that Jackson was a slippery, multiwoman-fucking eel. But that was none of Erika's business, was it? In fact, if the rumors *were* true, Erika had reasoned that getting one's heart broken by a Jackson Weatherfield type was simply a rite of passage that every starry-eyed ingenue must undergo—especially if one hoped to play Fantine.

Not that Erika was threatened by Carla. Not one bit. For one, Carla was profoundly boring and far too pretty (not compared to Erika, of course, but in that blandly inoffensive department-store-catalog way that made one think of settling down, developing undue interest in power tools, and then acquiring children and a golden retriever to train poorly and subsequently neglect).

The girl was from Oklahoma, for fuck's sake, and that wasn't even the worst of it! Carla was the winsome daughter of a poor farmhand who'd fallen in love with a wealthy rancher's rebellious and subsequently disowned daughter, and she'd once tearfully revealed her parents had saved for years to bring her on vacation to Manhattan for her fifteenth birthday, whence she'd fallen in love with Broadway and declared her intention to become a *star*!

If Carla somehow snatched the role of Fantine from Erika, it would further reinforce the outrageously misleading myth that any fresh-faced country bumpkin could hop on a bus to the Big Apple and get cast in a Broadway show within a week of arrival.

Which was, in fact, what Carla had done.

Carla's movie-perfect backstory was a slap in the face to someone like Juilliard-educated Erika, who had been assigned a classical singing tutor at age four, begun competitive tap dance at five, and begged for and been gifted a grand piano at six (in exchange for her silence regarding one of her stepfather's latest mistresses, of whom there were, conveniently, enough to ensure musical funding for the rest of Erika's childhood).

Nevertheless, Erika hadn't intended on sleeping with Carla's beau. That part was . . . regrettable. A mistake.

One of many.

Erika whirled in her seat and stood. "Carla, honey, whatever you heard—"

"We were in love," Carla cried, her mascara-streaked cheeks trembling. She stormed across the room to stand in front of Erika, crumpled tissues clutched in her fists at her sides. "In *love*!"

Even without tearing her eyes away from Carla's face, Erika could feel every eyeball in the room fixed on them. It was probably wrong to feel a thrill at that, but she couldn't help it. A craving for the spotlight was in her blood.

Erika drew her eyebrows together. If she concentrated, she could hear genuine innocence in her voice as she asked, "Who are you talking about?"

"Don't play games with me! I'm talking about *Jackson*." Carla bit his name out on a sob. "How could you? Stefano told me he saw you two kissing at that speakeasy on Canal Street last night."

Erika couldn't suppress a shudder at the returning memory of it. He'd taken her to the LES. And a speakeasy, no less. What was this, the early 2010s? How tacky. No wonder she'd had so many drinks—the experience would have been unbearable sober.

"Stefano is a petty gossip. I wouldn't trust anything he says."

From the hallway, there was an audible gasp of affront.

"He showed me pictures, Erika. Pictures! You went to second base with my boyfriend in front of *everyone*."

Well, shit. Erika's bubble of pretend popped, and just in time too. This was exhausting. "Not everyone, Carla. Don't exaggerate."

Carla gasped and recoiled in disgust. The reaction was a touch too drastic for such a small stage, but Erika sensed now wasn't the time to be doling out acting tips.

"So you admit it, then?" Carla asked.

Erika shrugged. "I did you a favor. Jackson is a sleazebag. He sure as hell wasn't acting like a man in a relationship when he invited me back to his place."

Carla's tear-glossed eyes widened. "You went back to his place? You slut!"

"Excuse me?" Well, *now* Erika was insulted. *Now* this was personal. And she'd been about to apologize too. "Are we slut shaming now? Are you really coming in here with your prissy, antifeminist Oklahoma values and acting like I'm not allowed to have casual sex before marriage because I'm a woman?"

"You slept with my boyfriend! That's a slutty thing to do!" Carla accused, her voice cracking with emotion. "And I am too a feminist! You don't know me at all. You think you're sooo—"

A stagehand knocked on the doorframe, sparing the soap opera before her only the barest glance. "Places, everyone."

No one moved.

"Like, now?" the stagehand added. No doubt the director had sent her to find out why half the cast was missing.

Erika decided to be the bigger person and gave everyone a wave of dismissal. "All right, show's over. Let's go have a revolution, shall we?"

Groans of disappointment sounded as half her audience disbanded, gathering their shoes and accessories as they went. The rest—cast members who weren't in the upcoming few scenes—shifted back to whatever they'd been doing before the interruption. But ears were most definitely still perked.

Erika moved to sweep past Carla, but to her surprise, the understudy's arm shot out, blocking her path.

Erika raised a brow. "I thought we were done."

Carla leaned in close enough that the cloud of her birthday-cake-scented perfume enveloped them both, and Erika suppressed a gag. "You'll pay for this," Carla hissed.

Despite her splitting headache, she snorted. "Are we in a Lifetime movie?"

Erika drew back then to see if Carla recognized how ridiculous she'd sounded, but the other woman's gaze was deadly serious.

"You're a bad person, Erika, and bad things happen to bad people. You'll see."

If only that were the way the world worked. If it were, people like Jackson Weatherfield would be getting shat on by pigeons on a daily basis, greedy financiers would be penniless, and her stepfather would have been eaten by a crocodile by now. But it wasn't Erika's job to educate Carla about how unfair the world was.

"I sure will. Now may I . . . ?" Erika gestured to the arm blocking her path.

Carla let her pass, but the weight of her vengeful stare left burn marks on Erika's back.

She made her way to the main stage.

When it was her turn to go on, she performed beautifully. No one who observed her would know that self-recrimination gurgled in her belly or that her palms were icy from the anxious moisture she didn't dare wipe on her costume skirt. Fortunately, the director wasn't happy with their new Valjean's take on the number, so Erika was given a short break before she had to be back onstage for her solo.

She found a folding chair in the stage left wing and plopped into it. The back of her neck itched with sweat.

Bad things happen to bad people.

No, they don't. Stop it.

You'll see.

Erika spied an unopened bottle of water tucked behind a set piece and leaned forward to grab it. They weren't supposed to drink anything in costume, but she was suddenly thirsty. So thirsty.

When she cracked the lid open, her hand trembled, and water spilled onto her lap. "Shit," she whispered, frantically brushing away the droplets. The lead costumer would *kill* her.

Bad things happen to bad—

"Fantine! You're up!"

Bad things happen—

She rescrewed the cap and jumped out of her seat. Swallowed a wave of nausea. Strode to her mark in relative darkness and settled into a defeated heap. The blue spotlight slowly came on above her. When the first strains of "I Dreamed a Dream" reached her ears, her tension began to drain away.

Booze was all right, but being onstage was her drug of choice; here, she sloughed off reality and transformed into her most powerful and impervious self. Even in a rehearsal like this one where there was no audience, the magic of the stage was undeniable. Everything beyond the stage lights' reach was dark and blurry, as if the shadows beyond the edge of the stage were held back by an impenetrable force field.

She began to sing as Fantine, a woman who'd once been full of hope and romantic idealism but was now exhausted from all the bullshit. Her voice was heady, the resonance wispy with exhaustion.

Bad things—

No.

As long as she was singing, she'd be safe.

This awful day would be over soon. And when she was done with rehearsal, she'd go back to her maid-cleaned apartment, shower to rinse her shame away, and pass out in her pillow-bedecked bed with its imported mattress. When she awoke from her nap, her hangover would be gone, and everything would be fine. She'd buy expensive shoes online to brighten her mood, have a nip of gin for fortitude, pop into some party around midnight, distribute air-kisses and accept compliments, and be back home before dawn with renewed confidence in herself.

Erika stood and began a slow procession toward her next mark, where the lighting would change. As she warned the audience about tigers in the night, her voice grew louder, its resonance more pronounced.

She had a good life. Everything she'd ever wanted. One little slipup couldn't take that away from her—her mistakes had never caught up to her before, had they?

It was better not to dwell on past misdeeds.

Finding her place, she gazed out into the audience, holding the poignant moment. Summoning her breath to deliver the next line.

About how, for Fantine, it had all gone wrong.

Something thumped in the rafters above her, but she ignored it. Ever since she'd been a girl, she'd dreamed of playing Fantine. This was only a rehearsal, but Erika was giving it her all.

She turned to the audience. Spread her arms wide and opened her mouth to release her voice's might.

Crack!

"Watch out!" someone screamed, but it was too late. Erika had smelled burning plastic, had already jerked her head back to locate its source.

The last thing she saw was the blur of the falling stage light.

CHAPTER 2

Two years later
Paris, Nevada

"Come see one of Paris's original buildings with a scandalous past. It was here at the infamous Paris Opera House that I, the beautiful and tragic proprietress of the most famous burlesque venue and brothel in the Old West, was murdered by my treacherous lover in the gruesome chandelier incident of 1922!" Erika called out, swirling her cloak behind her in dramatic fashion. A bead of sweat dribbled down her chest and slipped into the crevice where her breasts were crammed against the too-small costume corset.

It was two o'clock in the Nevada desert in late May, and Erika was wearing multiple layers of crepe and satin. She wanted to melt into the faux-cobblestone street and die. Instead, she held her poster board aloft and tried to make eye contact with the tourists ambling by. "The Paris Opera House and Haunted Brothel is a titillating tour you'll never forget!"

Nearly everyone in the large family taking photos in the picturesque plaza across the street ignored her. Except for the young teenage boy in the group, who dragged his gaze away from his phone long enough to snicker, "Heh heh, titty-lating."

His father hushed him—then did a double take. "Hon, look, a historical tour."

From the look on the mother's face, Erika wasn't about to get any customers. As the woman ushered her precious family away from Erika's corrupting influence, Erika muttered under her breath, "Whatever. I didn't need your forty bucks anyway."

Except she did. She really, really did.

"Excuse me?" came an accented voice from behind her.

Erika's heart leaped as she turned to face a pair of sunburned British tourists. *Customers?*

"Will you take our picture, love?" one of the men asked, thrusting his cell phone at her. He barely glanced at her as he grabbed his partner by the wrist and bounded into the plaza. "Get the fountain in the background, will you?"

As Erika dutifully complied, she clenched her teeth behind her smile, grateful for the mask that hid the left side of her face and made it harder to tell she was grimacing.

In another life, these tourists would have been clamoring for her autograph. Now, they didn't even glance at her long enough to recoil in horror at her partially hidden scars.

Fourteen shots later, Erika was allowed to return the phone. "How about a tour of a haunted theater that was built at the height of the western gold rush?" she offered. When the couple glanced at each other, as if to wordlessly coordinate an excuse, Erika rushed to add, "There's a special on tickets today. Buy one, get one free!"

"Ohhhh, lovely."

"Absolutely lovely," chimed in the man's partner, looking frantically around the plaza. "It's just we have—"

"Reservations," filled in the first man with a moue of regret. "Back at La Rose. For din—"

"Massages," came the quick correction. "At three. And we've got to catch the shuttle back."

The pair shuffled off in the opposite direction of the shuttle stop. La Rose was the closest resort and spa—a desert oasis nestled in a secluded valley beneath the shadow of defunct gold-mine-dotted mountains. Paradise for the posh Vegas set who wanted to retreat from the big city and relax in a "Parisian-inspired" town less than an hour away.

Erika had fallen for Paris's cutesy allure, too, back when it had seemed like inheriting an old theater was a serendipitous opportunity to escape her former life.

An earsplitting grinding sound rang out from the construction site two blocks down—a reminder that Paris's days as an idyllic retreat were numbered. Las Vegas's newest casino magnate, Raoul Decomte, was building his third flagship property, Magnifique!, at the edge of town.

Problem was, Paris was penned in by mountains, and there was only so much space for a megacasino. Erika eyed the **OUT OF BUSINESS** sign on the billboard of the town's only other hotel, Le Meilleur Ouest. It was only three businesses closer to Magnifique!'s construction zone than the Paris Opera House.

As if summoned by her thoughts, Dee, the hotel's former owner—and town's self-appointed Empress of Gossip—came out of the nearby bar. When she spotted Erika, she waved and hurried over as if they were bestest of friends.

"Any luck today, hon?"

Erika fanned herself with her billboard and gave the woman a beatific smile. "Tons. I've already had three full tour groups today. Plus, I've gotten lots of interest from that venue rental site I listed the theater on last week."

Well, the last part wasn't a lie. She *had* gotten two email inquiries from that pay-to-play tourism website, which supposedly matched small-town performance venues to younger indie bands looking for "quirky" spots to hold practices and jam sessions. Except the first email she'd gotten was from a guy named Kilroy-Bot83, who'd inquired as to whether she'd be willing to send him pictures of her feet, and the second email was from a weird German guy named Christof Daae, who'd claimed to manage a popular European hair metal band called Nachtmusik. A quick internet search had proved that his band was legitimate (even if its style of music was very much not Erika's type), and his email had been very polite and charming—until she'd gotten to the part where he'd wanted to know exactly how many ghosts lived in the opera house and whether she kept dossiers on them.

Neither lead seemed promising. But she'd emailed them back anyway. Two thousand dollars—per week or per photo—the price was high enough to discourage anyone who wasn't serious.

"That so?" Dee gave her a pitying look. Erika didn't miss how Dee's gaze kept snagging on her face, like a passing driver trying not to look at the accident on the other side of the freeway, even though she'd seen Erika's scars plenty. "Well, don't you worry. I'm sure that you'll get an offer from Mr. Decomte any day now. Bobby and I bought an RV with all that money."

"The Paris Opera House has been in my father's side of the family for over a hundred years," she reminded Dee. But Dee already knew that. Dee had loved telling Erika that the Greene family tree was abundant with small-time crooks, con artists, and professional whores and that it was a good thing Erika's mother had ditched town for a rich New York City financier when Erika had been born. If only Erika's paternal grandmother hadn't stuck around to continue scandalizing the locals with her burlesque theater for another three decades; now that Grandma Meg was dead, the responsibility fell upon Erika to offend all of Paris.

"Well, maybe you'll change your mind. Oh! I almost forgot why I came on over here," Dee said, pulling an opened envelope out of her purse. "This got misdelivered with our mail, and we accidentally opened it before realizing it wasn't the right address."

Erika thanked Dee and waited until the other woman ambled off before looking at the letter, which had been very obviously opened on purpose.

The text on the page made blood rush to her head, where it pounded loudly enough to drown out the beeping of construction trucks. *Loan overdue . . . foreclosure imminent . . . minimum payment due . . .* Erika crumpled the notice in her fist.

Where was she going to get $10,000 in thirty days?

The urge to run away came like a swelling tide, smothering her. Instead, she did the next best thing and stormed back up the steps of the theater and chucked her sign into the cobweb-laden umbrella stand by the door. She paused in the foyer, with its ornate domed ceiling from which the infamous murder chandelier hung, its once-beautiful metalwork dull with age, the defunct bulbs coated in dust. The grand entryway was two stories high, with dual flights of marble steps sweeping down both sides from the second-story balcony- and box-seating areas. The decorative carpets were worn and stained, the paint on the walls peeling. Wall-hung AC units, installed during Grandma Meg's reign for what had to have been the cheapest price possible, chugged helplessly against the oppressive heat outside. The building was hideously beautiful . . . and in dire need of repair and maintenance.

For some reason, Erika *liked* this place. If she let her vision go unfocused, she could imagine how it had looked in its heyday, with well-dressed theatergoers mingling with glittering dancers as a French chanteuse sang a bawdy ditty to warm up the crowd.

If she could finish paying off the theater's debt, she might have enough free capital to return it to some semblance of its former glory.

She was definitely *not* trying to redeem herself and undo a not-curse (since curses didn't exist) by saving the Paris Opera House.

Erika tugged her phone out of the hidden pocket in her skirt. Neither Kilroy-Bot nor Christof Daae had responded to her offer yet. Great.

She wondered if there was still a good market for hair and teeth. The thought of selling the theater to Raoul so he could tear it down to build a water park made her stomach revolt. Begging for money from her stepfather was out of the question; thank goodness for Actors' Equity insurance and the theater's lump sum settlement, the combination of which had procured the best plastic surgeons available in New York, because Stepdaddy Dearest hadn't wanted to cough up a spare dime to help her after the accident.

There had to be something else.

Erika made her way to her lair in the brothel's basement—and saw the door of her two-story rat castle had been jimmied open. Again. The remaining rat inside looked up from his seedcake when she entered and gave her a look of pure innocence.

"God damn it, Javert!" she groaned, dropping to her knees in front of the bed, but there was nothing underneath but a century of caked dust and a cardboard box full of magazine issues featuring mentions of her Broadway performances.

Erika flopped onto her back on the threadbare carpet, letting her arms and legs starfish in exhausted defeat. The mold spot on the plaster above her stared back. Was it getting bigger? It was probably cause for concern. She'd read somewhere that black mold could cause lung damage. Not that she'd ever sing publicly again, but still.

"Alexa, play 'Memory' from *Cats* the musical."

Again? she imagined the computerized voice chiding her. But it didn't say that. Maybe Alexa understood; Erika's life was shit. A certain amount of wallowing was required.

What had she ever done to deserve this miserable existence?

Before her brain could supply several helpful answers, Erika squeezed her eyes shut and began to sing along with the song.

Moving to Nevada was supposed to have been a fresh start. Erika had been lying in her deluxe recovery suite after the skin graft surgery, drowning in self-pity and loneliness and the depressing realization that her beauty was marred forever and she might never perform on Broadway again, when she'd gotten the notice about Grandma Meg having left her the theater and a small home in Paris.

At the time, it had seemed like serendipity. Not that Erika *believed* in fate—or curses, for that matter—but it had coincidentally seemed like a good idea to get as far away from the source of her not-curse as possible.

Besides, owning a charming, historic little theater had seemed like the perfect side hobby to engage in while getting back on her feet. *I'll be that glamorous city girl in a Hallmark movie who comes to a quaint desert town to rescue a small business, and the rugged bachelor sheriff will fall in love with me. We'll live on his sprawling ranch estate, raising horses and drinking whiskey at sunset under Pendleton blankets in oversize porch chairs.*

Ha ha ha. Never mind that the town sheriff was a happily married man in his late sixties. The lack of eligible sheriffs was far less of a narrative hurdle than the fact she was missing half her face. That sort of thing tended to thin the herd as far as interested parties went.

And the cute little home and business she'd inherited? Well, Erika had arrived in town and discovered the house had been repossessed by the bank months ago, and the Paris Opera House was a bottomless money sinkhole that was on the verge of encountering the same fate. Bonus: the theater building came with a defunct, ostensibly haunted brothel! What more could a girl ask for?

Something small and furry nudged her left hand, and without looking, Erika uncurled her fingers and flattened her palm to allow Javert to hop aboard. "There you are, you little escape artist."

Relief sank in as, after a moment of hesitation, the temperamental rat stepped into her hand and allowed her to move him onto her corseted belly. Javert spent most of his days plotting escape, and her greatest fear was that someday he'd leave her and never come back.

Good thing he seemed to like her voice; whenever she sang, Javert—and sometimes his brother, Jean—would draw toward her for comfort.

Which was nice, since the rats were her only reliable company these days.

If Erika had been less bitterly determined to prove that she was *not* cursed and that she could be a good person by rescuing this crumbling family legacy she'd inherited, she might have tucked tail and gotten right back on a plane to New York after day one. It might have also helped if she'd been less confident in her ability to run a theater (she'd been in theater her whole life; how hard could it possibly *be?*) and had sought legal and financial advice on the matter before committing. Instead, she'd "temporarily" moved into her great-great-grandmother's basement room in the brothel, which had been used as a sex dungeon and was not zoned for residence but happened to be the least sweltering room in the un-air-conditioned place, and poured her remaining savings into turning the Paris Opera House around.

That choice had been another excellent decision in Erika's flawless history of excellent decision-making.

The song ended, and she forced herself to get up and return Javert to his palatial prison. She'd done this to herself, after all. Wallowing was only allowed for three minutes and fifty-six seconds per day.

Jean, her brown-and-white rat, was unfazed by Javert's return. Jean had one interest and one interest only: eating. Erika sometimes wondered if he was depressed or if she was projecting. These days, Erika was thrilled that she didn't have to starve herself for that perfect Broadway body anymore. That was the only reason *she'd* gained weight.

Erika caught a glimpse of herself in the floor-length dressing mirror on the wall. A sweaty, bedraggled, sad-eyed stranger seemed to look back at her. The Old Erika Greene—Broadway's premier rising star and Manhattan's most desirable, sample-size, designer-clothes-wearing party girl—wouldn't recognize this person she saw. The Erika in the mirror had generous curves, and they were clothed in chintzy burlesque attire topped with a cobwebbed cloak she'd repurposed from a discount Halloween wall hanging. Even now, after two years to get used to it, her reflection still felt . . . unfamiliar. Like she was wearing someone else's body.

The changes weren't all unwelcome, of course. Doubling her cup size had been a welcome improvement; the clothing and scars, not so much.

She took off her costume mask and rubbed at the itchy patch of skin on her left cheek, careful not to smudge the thick foundation she wore during the day. The skin graft still felt wrong on her face: the wrong texture, the wrong elasticity, the wrong *everything*.

They'd told her she'd been lucky—had she missed her mark by a few inches, the falling stage light would have obliterated her. Instead, a chunk of searing-hot glass had landed on her face and melted right through the skin, down to her cheekbone. Thanks to the most expensive plastic surgeons in Manhattan, she'd been able to keep her eye. And they'd been able to reconstruct most of her cheek with the help of a cheese-slice-size square of skin from the back of her thigh.

Lucky? Yeah, sure.

Even her voice had changed after the accident—not enough for the untrained ear to notice, but now there was the slightest rasp to it that still threw Erika off whenever she sang.

Under her breath, she repeated aloud, "It's not bad. It's different." She squared her shoulders and forced her chin up. The show had to go on.

Tours had to be run.

Bills had to be paid.

And eventually, Erika would finish paying off the Paris Opera House's debt, prove that she wasn't a bad person anymore, and—*somehow*—return to the charmed life she'd lived before the accident.

Her phone chimed the two-note bell that theaters used to remind guests that intermission was ending. She had a new email. Erika swiped to her inbox, even though it was probably another ad for clothing she couldn't afford—

Erika's eyes bugged. She read the email twice.

The German band had accepted her offer. And they were booking the venue for *two months* while they developed their first English-language album.

"Yes!" she cried out, bouncing on the balls of her feet. Javert dashed to the corner of the cage and pressed his peach hands up to the bars, concerned. In a soothing tone, Erika assured him she wasn't being mauled, and Javert resumed his attempts to dig an escape tunnel through the metal-bottomed enclosure.

The money wasn't *quite* enough to meet that minimum loan payment, but it would cover most of it if she requested the first four weeks up front as a deposit. She'd double her tour frequency in the meantime and pray it covered the rest. Maybe she could negotiate with the bank. That was a thing, right?

Then she froze, remembering the small impediment to her plan. The theater was not exactly in operating order yet. This included but wasn't limited to the giant hole in the middle of the stage, a broken railing in Box Five, what might very well be quicksand in the rear parking lot, and the fact that she'd been putting off renewing her venue-occupancy permit due to the small but rather dangerous issue of the electrical-wiring situation in the main theater, which was—if one wanted to be precisely accurate—a catastrophic fire hazard.

She could fix that stuff before they arrived. How soon could a band get their travel plans set and send all their musical equipment halfway around the globe, right? A week or two, at the very least.

Plenty of time to dress the decrepit monstrosity she'd inherited in an air of legitimacy.

CHAPTER 3

Meanwhile, in Berlin . . .

"We leave tomorrow," Christof announced. He looked around the lofted living room at each of Nachtmusik's band members. When he got to the empty cup chair where Gillian usually perched, his brain quickly skipped past—a glitch. He forced a bright smile that he hoped masked the fact that he was in the deepest trench of shit imaginable.

Sibylle—who lay draped across his pristine white sofa with her platform leather boots still on—didn't bother to look up from her sketch pad. "We haven't even finished unpacking from the tour."

"Precisely! It's more efficient to depart before we're settled. Efficiency is key to success," Christof reminded everyone.

Sibylle grumbled something under her breath.

"I did verify this place is truly haunted, like you asked. 'Five confirmed ghosts, several others unconfirmed,'" Christof read aloud slowly, translating into their native German as he went. He lowered his phone and gave Sibylle an exasperated look. "Is that haunted enough for you?"

"Dossiers?"

"Yes, ten-page profiles on each one. Would you like to see?"

Sibylle finally looked up.

He gave her the finger.

"Stupidhead," she muttered, returning to her work with a sneer. She scratched something hard into the paper. Probably a rendition of him dying gruesomely with . . . spikes . . . or something.

What was it like to have a little sister who wasn't a pain in the ass? Did that type of little sister exist?

Christof threw up his hands. "Why does everyone look so miserable? With this album, we are finally going to fulfill our dreams of becoming international rock stars. And I found a place to conceive this album that meets our desires. This location claims to be haunted by unhappy spirits, per *your* request, Sibylle. It is also authentically 'American,' as you wanted, Waldo . . . I can't imagine a place more authentic than an Old Western bordello, yes?"

Waldo nodded eagerly. In English, he replied, "I hope I will meet a cow rider!"

"Cowboy," Sibylle corrected. Christof and Sibylle had been raised in a bilingual household; Waldo had learned most of his English from a free phone application called How To Sound Like A Coolest American!!!, and his translations were often questionable.

Christof continued, "And for you, Sergei, I have been reassured that the acoustics are superb."

Sergei looked up from polishing his guitar's neck and silently nodded his approval.

"And per request of our incredibly handsome front man, who is also our band manager—me—this venue is within our budget." Christof tossed the venue's website printout onto the coffee table for everyone to look at. "Yes, this is what you all wanted?"

Sibylle scribbled harder. The shaved sides of her pale-skinned head made it easy to see her jaw clenching furiously. "What I *wanted* was some time off between our eight-month European tour and recording a new album."

In fact, what Sibylle had requested was a month to travel to the Arctic Circle with three women she'd met at a tour stop in Trieste for an occult ritual that Sibylle had claimed was "absolutely imperative" in order to return "icon and savior" Mary Shelley from the dead. Why was Christof the bad guy for denying this venture in favor of the band's collective success?

Waldo gazed at him mournfully from beneath the long brown hair flopping over his forehead. "I wish Gillian was coming too. She's still coming, right?" From the suspicious sheen coating the drummer's eyes, Waldo had ignored Christof's warnings and eaten the entire edible he'd purchased during the Amsterdam tour stop, and he was now on a doomed path to discovering how much more potent real marijuana was relative to the bags of quite-possibly-tarragon their naive teenage selves had occasionally purchased from Sketchy Czech Guy in their sleepy hometown of Hemer.

Not that anyone could have talked Waldo out of the endeavor. If there was a thing that could be consumed, a niche skill to be learned, or a highly dangerous activity to be undertaken, not only would Waldo be first in line, but he'd buy everyone else he knew tickets to join him. Christof adored Waldo, but he didn't adore being Waldo's emergency contact—a full-time role he'd played ever since they'd become best friends in ninth grade.

"Yes! Well." Christof made his voice cheery. "Gillian has promised to join us as soon as her aunt is feeling better. Which we all hope will be very soon."

It was only a very, very small lie, but it still made his gut spasm like he was trying to digest rocks. What was he supposed to tell them—the truth? They'd never agree to go to America for two months if they found out he'd lost their keyboardist and second vocalist right before they were to begin recording their second album.

And it was technically his fault, which was a problem, because Christof was supposed to be the responsible one. That was why the band let him make all the important decisions.

She's going to come back, he reminded himself, carefully sucking in a controlled breath through his nose. *I didn't ruin everything. Once she returns my calls, I can explain it was a simple misunderstanding. There was a guitar pick on the ground, you see, and while it* looked *like I was intending to propose when I knelt to retrieve it, I assure you that was the last thing I was thinking—*

No. No, that didn't sound right at all. How to assure his girlfriend of over ten years that although he loved her, her panicked response to what had *not* been a proposal had made him realize that he didn't want to marry her either? And that, perhaps, she felt the same way, which was wonderful, because then she could stay in the band and they could continue being friends, because *surely* this breakup didn't have to happen *now*, when Nachtmusik was poised at the precipice of achieving their collective dreams?

Christof forced himself to stop thinking about it. The important thing was rallying the band and getting them on a plane to America before anyone found out the truth about Gillian—which they *wouldn't*, because he was going to convince her not to quit the band. Especially since he'd promised the record label they'd have an album recorded by September, which was only a little over three months away.

Behind the couch that Sibylle was sullying with her dirty boots, the window's partial view of Berlin's skyline taunted him. They'd recorded their first album in German, and it had been a surprise hit in Europe, propelling their band, Nachtmusik, to the top of the rock charts. They'd made a great deal of money off that album—enough that he and Gillian had moved out of their ground-level studio and into this spacious two-bedroom in a cooler neighborhood. Many musicians would be happy with modest fame in Europe and a comfortable life, but not Christof.

He wanted the world. And the world, as far as rock music was concerned, began with name recognition across the Atlantic.

"This next album," he'd promised the band, "will make us international superstars!"

25

Not only would he and Gillian sing both German and English versions of every song, but the plan was to write and record the tracks on US soil, to "fully absorb the culture" of their target audience. That part had been Waldo's idea, and despite Waldo's track record of pitching terrible ideas, it had been a rare gem that had solicited unanimous agreement from all five band members.

Even Christof was on board with the expensive venture, and that was saying something, since he prided himself on budgeting their chart-topping windfall with a ruthlessly tight fist. "We won't be superstars forever" was his new favorite mantra.

"You are so lame," Gillian would tease him.

"What's lamer than rock stars who don't blow all their money on booze, drugs, and black-opal-inlaid Ouija boards?" Sibylle would add, more directly.

"And hookers!" Waldo would always chime in. Waldo's excitement was contagious, and it made Christof feel far older than his thirty years.

Still, he'd always say something like, "I can assure you all it will be incredibly 'lame' if at forty we all have to go back to our town with tails between our legs and beg my mother for jobs at the food mart."

Because that was the worst fate, wasn't it? Having to rely on one's parents to hire one at the family's discount supermarket, where he might suffer the humiliation of ringing up a head of lettuce for his mean secondary school literature teacher while she looked at him smugly and croaked, *I told you you'd never be famous. Should have listened to me and done your schoolwork!* And given that Sibylle had stated she'd rather *die* before engaging in a boring profession and Waldo was still unclear on how the concept of gainful employment worked at all, Christof didn't have high hopes for their post-Nachtmusik careers should they fail to make it big. Hence his attempts to find a location to create their forthcoming album that would make his bandmates want to go so badly that they'd overlook Gillian's absence until he could convince her to return. He supposed one could argue it wasn't strictly *necessary* they work on their newest album in America, but for some reason, Christof felt it was imperative they do so.

Perhaps it was because he'd never been across the Atlantic. Or because as an aspiring musician he'd cut his teeth on American bands like Ratt and Whitesnake. There was also a small chance he'd initially aimed for New York City because he and Gillian had stolen their first kiss while watching an old VHS of *Moonstruck* on the ugly green couch in Waldo's basement.

Maybe he'd thought a change of scenery would reinvigorate their desolate bedroom life.

Or maybe he'd wanted a young, attractive Cher to kiss, and of course he'd felt a bit guilty about that, but surely Gillian couldn't have known about his secret fantasies. He'd been nothing but the most devoted boyfriend for the entirety of their ten-year relationship, always complimenting her hair and picking up after her and buying her favorite candy bar when she was melancholy. Which, to be fair, *had* been more often than usual, but—

Ah, well. Gillian was most likely taking a moment to sort out her feelings about him, and she would come back on her own, and the band would be fine, and the album would come together brilliantly!

Probably.

Although he was not entirely certain.

The email had been rather . . . brusque.

He shook his head to clear it. "Very well, since I have all of your rousing support—"

"We should postpone the album," Sibylle intoned. The quiet sound of paper tearing indicated her pencil was now producing a layered masterpiece.

"—*rousing support*—" Christof tried again.

Waldo gasped. "I could learn to play keyboard!"

Scratch, tear, scratch. "You can barely play drums."

Christof cleared his throat. "As I was saying! Your! Rousing! Support!"

"Okay. I trust you, man."

"Thank you, Waldo." Christof then looked at Sergei.

It was easy to overlook Sergei, who rarely spoke unless it was related to his one and only interest: playing the guitar. He was the only member of Nachtmusik who hadn't grown up in their small hometown; they'd found him by posting an ad for a guitarist when they'd moved to Berlin. Sibylle continued to insist Sergei was secretly a vampire—which had been a selling point, in her estimation—but aside from Sergei being rather quiet and occasionally lurking in the shadows, Christof wasn't quite sure there was enough evidence for it.

"I will go," Sergei said.

"Ugh, fiiiiine." Sibylle threw down her sketch pad. "We'll go to stupid *Nevada*."

"*Haunted* Nevada," Christof corrected, wiggling his brows in what he hoped was an enticing way. "The website noted the Paris Opera House was founded by a real Frenchwoman who was murdered by a falling chandelier, purportedly sabotaged by a jealous lover."

Interest sparked in Sibylle's eyes before she could hide it from him. "Yeah, whatever." A pause, then a reluctant "Does said accused murderer have living descendants, possibly still in town?"

He had no idea. "You might ask that very question of the proprietress of the establishment—she is the dead Frenchwoman's great-great-granddaughter."

His sister's eyes widened, and she breathed, "A living connection to the spirit realm."

Waldo gaped at them, then clapped both hands to his cheeks. "Whoa. *Whoa*."

Sibylle raised a brow. "You okay there?"

Waldo managed to nod.

Christof's sister shrugged, then turned back to him with narrowed eyes. "Is she pretty?"

"Who?"

"The proprietress."

He thought of the picture he'd found while trying to dig for further ghost-related information and felt his ears heat. "Why? What relevance does it have?"

"Just curious why you're suddenly so . . . eager."

For a second, his heart stopped. Did Sibylle suspect? Had Gillian said something to her before leaving? *Ignore her. Simply ignore her, and she'll drop it—*

"Does she look like Cher?"

He was going to strangle her. Still, relief spurred his pulse back to life. "No, she does not, but I hardly care because I only have eyes for my true love, Gillian." Then he lowered his voice. "And I told you that in confidence, you miserable creature."

Sibylle's smile was, quite frankly, disturbing. "Whatever you say, Big Brother."

He desperately needed to regain control of this conversation.

"Okay, then. It's settled!" Christof clapped his hands for attention. "We leave tomorrow morning. Sibylle, go pack your bags. But not the crows. We are not taking the crows. Waldo, go lie down. And Sergei . . ."

Sergei stood. "I am ready."

"And Gillian? Are you going to tell her where we're going?" Sibylle asked.

Christof scoffed. "Of course. I am confident she will be joining us very, very soon."

He beamed at his band and crossed his fingers behind his back.

CHAPTER 4

When Erika peered out of the auditorium and into the foyer, the first thing she saw was a mountain of suitcases. Big ones. Some of which appeared to hold instruments.

With a sinking feeling, she took in the two *Labyrinth* movie rejects loitering under the chandelier. No way was the German rock band here already. Surely they couldn't have gotten their shit together that quickly. These guys were in a *rock band* . . . didn't they have drugs and sex to do? And if they were so organized, why hadn't Christof emailed back to confirm the travel dates?

And yet. Unless she'd missed the news that La Rose was hosting a vampire cosplay convention, Nachtmusik was standing in her entryway. And all she'd managed to accomplish over the weekend was laying down a sheet of plywood over the hole in the stage. If any reasonable band manager saw the inside of that auditorium, they'd laugh and walk right back out the door.

Leaving Erika with exactly zero dollars to pay down her debt due in twenty-eight days.

Okay. *Okay.* She was an actress; if anyone could sell this, she could.

Erika smoothed her side-parted hair, ensuring the locks in front covered most of the left side of her face, and stepped out into the entryway.

A woman who looked like a punk rock version of Elvira inspected the painting of her great-great-grandmother, Mistress Giry, at the bottom of the staircase. Her arms were crossed over a shiny black corset, with one of her six-inch-platform-goth-booted feet propped on the first step. She glanced up when Erika arrived, brow raised, then glanced back at the portrait of Erika's ancestor with a skeptical expression.

"You are the proprietress?" Her voice was flat and scratchy. Not a voice designed for singing.

"I am," Erika confirmed. "How may I help you?"

The other woman approached Erika, coming close enough to inspect the scars on her face. "Fascinating. Would you say the undead apparition who did this to you was more vengeful or more fearful?" Despite the heavy accent, her English was flawless.

Erika stepped back with a tight smile. "Vengeful, I imagine. And you must be from Nachtmusik."

"Mmm, yes, vengeful is ideal," the goth woman replied with a curt nod. Raising her voice, she announced, "Very well. This place will suffice."

Behind Elvira Lite was a light-brown-skinned man sitting on a large box suitcase, wearing a billowing white button-down tucked into torn black denim and incongruous robin's-egg-blue cowboy boots. A fall of curly fawn-brown hair cascaded over his shoulders and curtained his eyes, and when he looked up and saw her, brown eyes sparkled with delight. He lifted his chin and flashed her double rocker-horned hand signs . . . or whatever those things were called.

"'Allo, I am Waldo," he said, pronouncing it like *Valdo*. "Sie heißt Sibylle," he added, pointing at the woman (he said it like *Zee*-bill-*uh*), "und Sergei is there." Waldo pointed at the alcove next to Erika, and a dark-clad figure that she hadn't seen at first moved into the light, making her jump in surprise. Sergei was a dark-skinned Black man with vivid burgundy box braids tied back into a loose ponytail, piercing dark eyes, and his long nails manicured to sharp points and painted black.

"Nice claws. You must be the guitarist," Erika offered, trying to shake the unnerving sense that his whole "metrosexual Blade" vibe ran deeper than fashion.

Sergei gave an old-fashioned sort of bow, then asked, "A fellow musician?"

"Used to be." She gave a tight smile that did not invite follow-up questions.

Waldo continued in his heavy accent, "Und then we have—"

"Christof," a deep voice rumbled from above.

Now that's *a voice made for singing.*

Erika craned her neck to see the man who'd clearly ignored the No Entry Past This Point sign at the base of each stairwell and now stood on the second-floor landing, his bare forearms casually draped over the balcony rail as he surveyed the foyer like he owned the place.

And for the first time since the day in third grade when Erika had stepped into the spotlight and a hushed audience had stared back from the darkness, her stomach flipped.

Christof was . . . too much.

That was the only way to describe him.

He was egregiously tall, for one, and his skin was too fair to be wearing so much black. And it was way too early in the evening to have his shirt unbuttoned nearly to his navel, showcasing a fine dusting of chest hair that skimmed its way down a landscape of unnaturally defined muscle, tapering as it went, until it reached that single demure button he'd bothered to close before the blouse (and that was the only word for the too-silky garment he wore with the puff sleeves rolled up to his elbows) disappeared into the velvet (yes, really—*velvet*) pants he wore too low on his hips.

Was he auditioning for the cover of a pirate romance novel? For a pro wrestling persona? Was this a stage outfit or an everyday *look*?

And was that a guitar slung across his back, sans guitar case? What kind of serious musician walked around flaunting their guitar like it was some sort of accessory? How arrogantly, impractically absurd.

His hairstyle wasn't helping either. Bleached ice white save for dark roots, he kept his wild locks way longer than most men dared. The dark scarf circling his forehead screamed, *I'm a highwayman and I'm here to ravish you, but I shan't muss my hair whilst doing so,* and in theory, it should have looked tacky beyond salvation. It really, really should have.

But his *face*. None of the business above his shoulders should work. Each feature, on its own, was too big.

His sloping nose was too long.

His dark brow too heavy.

His jaw too square.

His lips too pouty—had he gotten fillers?

No, she decided. The bottom lip had a soft dip in its center, and you couldn't recreate that with an injection. She'd tried fillers once, and for weeks afterward, her lips had been so disconcertingly smooth that she hadn't been able to stop touching them in horrified wonder.

Natural, then. But still . . . too plush. No one needed lips like that. The term *obscene* seemed too dramatic a description, but perhaps . . . on the cusp? Yes, that was it. He was like a song performed entirely in fortississimo—every note expressed at top volume. A song like that would normally irritate her. But Christof's song . . . *compelled*.

She marveled at him posed up there on the balcony, her head tilted at an awkward angle to take in the view, unsure *how* he was pulling any of this off but certain, nevertheless, that he *was*. In spades. If *Pulling It Off* were a musical, he'd be its composer, writer, producer, director, and lead star.

"My brother does make an impression," said Sibylle. "But know this: he is spoken for. So don't be getting ideas."

Erika snapped her mouth shut, then scrambled frantically for her stage face, wondering why she'd dropped character at the mere sight of a man. A *fascinatingly beautiful* man, but Erika had once taken shots off Alexander Skarsgård's abs at an opening night party in the West Village and had also managed to power through an entire Tony Awards ceremony while seated two feet away from Daveed Diggs without fainting. She was difficult to impress.

Besides, Christof was taken, and Erika was a good person now. She didn't do forbidden fruit anymore—no matter how tempting.

Ignoring Sibylle, she stretched her lips into a welcoming smile solely for Christof. "You must be the band manager I've been emailing with. Sorry about the lack of welcome, but I didn't realize you'd be here . . ." She scrambled for a polite way to say *literally two fucking days later* and settled on, "So soon."

Christof frowned. "Did you not receive my confirmation email?"

Erika checked her phone again. "Nope. But it doesn't matter, because—"

"Ah, I believe I know what happened. I shouldn't have attached our hit single. These spam filters are very thorough." He pulled out his own phone and tapped on the screen, his brows drawn, as if it were really important she have access to this song, *right now*. "There. I have resent it as a link. Please confirm receipt."

Holy bejesus, was this guy a piece of work. "Yeah, got it!" she assured him. It would be a cold day in hell before she voluntarily listened to hair metal, but who cared? What was important was that his band didn't leave.

And that they paid up front. Specifically, that they paid up front before they got a good look at the place.

"Really can't wait to listen," she added. From the corner of her eye, she saw Sibylle peeking behind the curtain into the auditorium and thanked her lucky stars that the stage curtains were drawn, hiding the stage itself from view. Technically, the curtains were drawn because the mechanism to raise them was rusted stuck, but she'd run to the hardware store tonight and picked up some sort of metal . . . lube . . .

stuff. Erika had vague memories of stage techs with spray cans, and she prayed the internet would fill in the rest. "Anyway, I'm sure you're all jet lagged and want to crash, but if we sort out the payment situation now, I can have the theater ready to go for you to start using first thing tomorrow morning."

"We wish to begin our work immediately," Christof replied.

Erika wiped her sweaty palms on the skirt of her costume. But before she could come up with an excuse, Sibylle groaned. "Seriously?" This was followed by a stream of irritated German.

Christof cut her off with a pointed throat clearing. "English only, remember? We are fully immersing—"

"Oh, shut *up*. I'm going to my room and unpacking." She whirled and turned to Erika. "Do I have options? Because I prefer a room with good moonlight."

Sheer habit kept Erika's smile in place. "I'm sorry?" *They don't think they're staying* here, *do they?*

The Paris Opera House was not zoned for residence, and the brothel behind it—which was attached via a secret tunnel—was officially designated as a historical site, and that part was *definitely* not for rental. She'd already tried the Airbnb route and been shut down.

Waldo clarified, as if it was a translation error, "Our places for sleeping. Also, I would like a room that is good to entertaining guests."

"I'd also like my room to be the former site of a horrific tragedy, if possible," Sibylle added. "Also, what is the house policy on temporary chalk?"

"Actually—" Erika began, but Christof was already speaking.

"Sibylle, we have already spoken about conducting Satanic rituals upon rented property. And we are here to work, Waldo, not to socialize with the local prostitutes. This album will not write itself."

Sibylle rolled her eyes. "They're called . . . wie sagt man? *Spectral summonings*, and I need them to channel my ultimate creative energy. Don't be so uptight, Big Brother. Let Waldo have his sex parties."

"Stop calling me that."

"Why? You are my big brother."

"Yes, but that's not how you are saying it."

Sibylle's answering smile was fully demonic.

"And there will be no summonings and certainly no sex parties," Christof said through clenched teeth. He flashed Erika an apologetic glance. "Apologies."

Erika tried again. "There's a misunderstanding—"

"They are called *sex workers*," Waldo began, jumping up from the suitcase to glare up at Christof, "and it is a very hard job. Please show respect." He gestured to Erika.

Erika blinked, momentarily distracted. "I'm not a—this isn't a bordello anymore. It's a historical building. Which is why—"

"Because of the murder," Sibylle said in a knowing tone. She'd begun a slow strut around the foyer's perimeter, as if looking for something.

"In fact, no," Erika replied, reflexively slipping into tour guide mode. "The operation continued after Mistress Giry's death under the care of her daughter and subsequently her granddaughter until 1982, when the local government outlawed solicitation within Paris city limits. Afterward, it was used primarily as a burlesque theater." *Thus spurring the Paris Opera House's financial decline.*

"Ah," Waldo said, his face falling.

"Great, now Waldo will be pouting the entire time we are here," Sibylle scoffed, peeking behind a decorative curtain. "Tell me, has there been only one murder? Or have there been others since?"

Erika felt a sort of twitching in her left cheek and knew her scarred smile muscles were beginning to falter. "Just the one death, which was never officially ruled as a murder. But we should address—"

"Accidents, then? Unexplained disappearances? Sounds that could not be accounted for? Spectral balls of flame hovering menacingly over your place of rest?"

"None. The theater is *very* safe," Erika said in a reassuring tone worthy of another Tony nomination.

Sibylle shot Christof a scowl. "You promised a haunted bordello. This isn't haunted. And look at her! She's not even a real whore."

Debatable. Although to be fair, Erika hadn't had a good fuck in a long time. For all its charms, Paris had a real dearth of unavailable assholes. Which was probably for the best, because Erika was reformed now. She'd learned her lesson.

She tore her traitorous eyes away from Christof's bare chest.

"Enough!" Christof smacked his hands against the rail. "We are staying here, and that is the final word. We have promised the label an album in exactly three months. That is to be our only concern. You will accept whatever rooms our gracious host has available, and you will be awake and in the theater for our first session at noon tomorrow. Is this understood?"

Christof came off like a control freak with a giant ego. Against her will, a shimmer of *want* slithered down her spine and coiled in her abdomen. *God, I'm predictable.*

Good thing Christof was taken. She was *glad* he was off limits. Erika was completely uninterested in letting a man like that sexually disrespect her in the back of a costume closet before actually disrespecting her by never calling again, because she didn't miss making poor life choices.

Much.

Erika cleared her throat and girded her imagination. "We didn't discuss lodging in our email, and unfortunately, I'm not able to let you stay here. The brothel isn't zoned for residence, and I could get a huge fine if anyone catches on. However, La Rose, the spa resort outside of town, has lovely rooms. I hear the suites are equipped with waffle makers."

Waldo perked up.

Christof immediately shut him down. "We don't need waffles. We need to fully envelop ourselves in this album's creation. Immersion is key to success."

Sergei spoke up in a quiet voice that nevertheless hushed Sibylle's protests. "Perhaps we should inquire with Gillian as to whether she'd prefer to stay at La Rose. Should I reach out?"

For whatever reason, the mention of the name *Gillian* made Christof's expression go flat. Then, for the briefest instant, Erika glimpsed panic flash behind his eyes. When he blinked, it was gone—replaced by the same confident, implacable demeanor he'd had all along. "I have already cleared our choice of accommodations with Gillian. There is no need to bother her with our petty squabbles while she focuses on family. Therefore we will stay here, and that is my final decision." He nodded at Erika. "What is the fine if we are caught staying on premises?"

Before Erika could answer, Sibylle let out an affronted gasp, then accused Christof of something in German. This made Christof's glower turn positively frightening. This man did *not* like having his authority questioned.

Maybe someone should teach him a lesson, came the thought before she could squash it.

"We will double our payment," Christof announced.

"We'll absolutely *not*," sputtered Sibylle.

"We absolutely will," Christof repeated. "Four thousand US dollars a week. Will that suffice?"

Letting them rehearse in her theater before she'd gotten repairs done was already sort of bad, but letting them stay in the brothel on top of that would be *very* bad, and Erika wasn't a bad person anymore. Erika opened her mouth to issue another denial, then closed it. *Shit.* If they paid up front, she could pay the entire loan minimum. She wouldn't even need to keep doing tours.

No more cramming herself into layers of unbreathable satin to roast beneath the June sun, humiliating herself for a parade of holier-than-thou tourists day after day.

"I'll still need four weeks deposit up front," she heard herself say.

Christof withdrew a slim wallet from the waistband of his velvet pants and, with a magician's flourish, presented a black metal credit card to his audience. "We will charge it to the credit card that does not have a limit. This is what it's for, yes? Here, I will bring it to you."

As if compelled by sorcery, Erika ascended the steps to meet Christof—and the card in his extended hand—at the halfway point. As her hand reached out to take it, a last glimmer of indecision froze her in place.

Sibylle hissed in warning, as if Christof were giving away her favorite cat toy right before her eyes. "Remember when you told us that we were only using that card for *emergencies*? And when we flew across the Atlantic in *economy* because you said the extra-space seats were for spoiled Americans? And how you said that conservative financial choices were key to success?"

Waldo added a hesitant "Are you sure Gillian is okay with this price?"

A muscle in Christof's jaw twitched—a tell so slight that only Erika was close enough to see.

That confirmed it. Gillian must be the girlfriend. A girlfriend who was *not here* . . .

Erika's pulse thrummed. Oh yeah, having Christof sleeping under the same roof was a bad idea. Didn't she remember what had happened the last time she'd taken something that wasn't hers?

Bad things happen to bad people . . .

Except curses weren't real—and this limitless credit card *was*.

Before either of them could make wiser choices, Erika snatched the card from Christof's fingers. "I'll show you to your rooms."

CHAPTER 5

Christof followed the proprietress down a long, narrow hallway accessed through a discreet entrance on a far-left alcove of the theater's foyer, and he tried to think pure thoughts.

It wasn't easy.

This Erika had the kind of body that could only be described in the superlative terms of hair metal: she was a total babe. And in that outfit, with its laced bodice that thrust her breasts up to spill over the square neckline . . . well, he knew it was a costume, but had she been truly advertising her charms for sale, he could see her being extraordinarily successful.

Christof wasn't immune to her *other* charms, however, and since he was making an effort not to get caught looking at her ass, he inventoried those instead.

For instance, he liked the way her long brown hair fell down her back and curled to a little point at the end where it met the arch of her waist, and he'd also liked it from the front, where it swooped over the left side of her face, hiding most of her scars from view, which gave her the mysterious air of an old-fashioned film star. He wanted to tell her he'd always thought scars were badass, but after her icy reaction to Sibylle's prying, Christof imagined his opinion on the matter was equally unwelcome.

He also liked her enigmatic, bitter-chocolate eyes, and he thought it rather adorable how wary she'd seemed at first, then how visibly torn she'd been about the money—the way she'd nibbled that generous bottom lip compelled him to write lyrics.

But the thing that had really gotten under his skin—the thing that had set his pulse suddenly racing and his skin flash-heating with shame and desire—was how covetous her expression had been when she'd first seen him. She'd assessed him as if she wanted to devour his entire being—strip his flesh from his bones and consume him from head to toe. And he was a performer, was he not? There was no shame in wanting to be wanted. His ego *thrived* on that kind of desire. He'd once stroked himself off by recalling the pulsing rhythm of a crowd chanting his name.

Very well—it had been more than once. But he'd been—

And Gillian had rarely been—

Gah! He had to stop dwelling on Gillian. And what the band would do without her. And—

His lungs constricted, and he forced himself to stop thinking altogether.

Except when he stopped thinking, his gaze naturally fell on the most distracting subject: Erika's bottom.

He liked her bottom most of all, even hidden as it was beneath the layers of swishing skirts. It was less about the specific shape and more about the generous way her hips rounded. The hypnotic, side-to-side sway of her gait.

Thoroughly entrancing.

So entrancing that his forehead conked into a protruding wall sconce and dislodged the glass casing, which toppled off the wall and shattered all over the warped wooden floor at his feet.

"Scheiße!"

Erika whirled in alarm, and his bandmates came to a sudden halt behind him.

Christof rubbed his forehead and glared at what was left of the protruding light fixture. "It attacked me! You all saw this happen, yes?"

He turned to his brethren for confirmation, but Sibylle, who was a monstrous brat and clearly ungrateful for how he'd deftly managed the crow situation at the airport, proved she did not have his best interests at heart. "No," she said.

"Yes," he insisted. "It was sticking out. Like, in a very dangerous way. Did you not see?"

"No, I saw you walk into it like an Einzeller."

No, *she* was the single-celled organism. But he didn't say that, because he was supposed to be the reasonable, mature one. Instead, he gritted his teeth, vowed to murder Sibylle later, and flashed Erika an apologetic smile. "I will pay for the replacement, of course."

"Good. It's an original, so it'll be very expensive." Then she continued walking, as if that was the end of it.

Heat swept across his chest, and he wasn't yet clear if it was from irritation or lust. He'd said he'd replace the damn thing to be polite, and now she was taking advantage of his generosity? Was he not paying her $4,000 a week, which was objectively more than lodging at this crumbling antiquity was worth?

Gingerly avoiding the broken glass, he continued following Erika to wherever she was taking them. He hoped this would not take long; their suitcases and instruments were all in the entryway. Although he did have his precious guitar—it came with him, always. Right now, it was slung across his back, where it moved with him like an extra appendage. Other guitarists preferred to keep theirs in heavy protective cases while traveling, but not Christof. This guitar was his—*How do Americans call it? Ah, yes*—emotional-support pet. It was a one-of-a-kind Sky Galaxy Dragon guitar, designed by the Scorpions' guitarist for their fiftieth-anniversary concert, and it was the most valuable thing Christof owned—and not only in a monetary sense (although it did have a fist-size opal embedded in the base of the body). Though he could now afford to buy a dozen identical guitars if he so desired, it wouldn't be the *same* guitar. The guitar that had been with him the day they'd gotten to meet his heroes, when he'd gotten each and every one of their signatures on the back of the guitar's sleek body. The guitar that had rocked them out of obscurity and into European fame.

Soon to be *international* fame with this second album—if his band didn't self-destruct before recording a single song.

Erika gave them a history of the building as they came out of the tunnel and through a doorway that led to a dual stairwell. She continued up the stairwell to the left, but Christof paused on the landing. There was another set of stairs on the right, leading down into a shadowed alcove. "Where do these go?" he asked.

Erika paused before answering, "Basement."

"What's in the—"

"That area is off limits," Erika snapped. She resumed marching upward, her lush bottom bouncing in time with the squawking of each wooden step.

Waldo snickered. When Christof gave him a questioning look, Waldo explained, "Sex dungeon, you know?"

"Not a sex dungeon!" Erika called down.

Waldo looked as if the denial had only confirmed his suspicions.

They came up the stairs into a plushly appointed—if exceedingly faded—sitting room, and Erika resumed the tour. Christof was a rapt student. Primarily because of the throaty voice behind the lecture.

"The Paris Opera House was founded in 1908 by my great-great-grandmother, Mistress Antoinette Giry, a celebrated actress and opera singer who arrived here from the original Paris, France, on the arm of a wealthy gold-mining baron, Monsieur Leroux. He'd promised her fortune and fame at his newly constructed opera house, yet he abandoned her soon after arrival to seek even greater riches in Las Vegas, leaving her pregnant and penniless." Erika walked them around low-slung peach-hued settees and across emerald carpets that had probably once been very soft and lovely but were now worn away from a century of being underfoot. The air had the stale, perfumed smell of an elderly grandmother's home. "As a consolation prize, her rich benefactor left the opera house in her care, but she didn't have the funds to keep it running. Thus, this bordello was built behind the auditorium for her performers to both live . . . and work second jobs. This tunnel has a second entrance from backstage and was designed to allow theatergoers to discreetly meet their favorite dancers for more *private* performances."

"And the murder? When did that occur?" Sibylle prompted.

Erika replied, "Mistress Giry was crushed to death by the chandelier in the lobby twelve years after Leroux abandoned her. A brief investigation ruled it an unfortunate accident. But . . ." Her voice trailed off, coaxing Sibylle to lean in farther. "There were rumors, of course, that she'd been planning to sell the Paris Opera House and return to France with her lover, Gerard, who reportedly ran a gold-smuggling ring. Her lover was never seen again, and town legend has it that he arranged her death to cover his trail while he escaped with a full shipment stolen from Paris's sole remaining gold mine."

"A lover's quarrel," Sibylle determined, expression delighted.

"Perhaps." A small smile curled Erika's lips. "And perhaps not. Her daughter's diary reports smelling cigar smoke in the lobby minutes after the accident. The same cigars that Leroux smoked. And did I mention that the gold mine in question belonged to Leroux too?"

"Revenge," Sibylle breathed.

Erika shrugged, dropping all hint of the mysterious storyteller. "Or irresponsible theater maintenance. We'll never know, will we?" With that, she continued forward.

Her voice sounds nothing like Gillian's. Why was he comparing the two? It wasn't like he was looking to get over the breakup by immediately getting under another woman . . . even if Erika was like the tempting antithesis to Gillian's dazzling, near-angelic light.

Not a breakup, he reminded himself. Only a change in status from a romantic relationship to a friendly, professional one. Gillian would be back, because they couldn't record this album without her.

Which was why Christof had no business even considering an affair with Erika Greene. The album was top priority, and with the Gillian situation as precarious as it was now, he couldn't afford to risk complicating things for Nachtmusik to sate his own selfish needs.

The band always came first.

"Here's the kitchen, which was renovated in the late eighties with the newest appliances," Erika said, gesturing to an open doorway that led to a cramped kitchen. She flicked a fluorescent overhead light on, giving them a glimpse of an oven door caked in so much grime it was opaque, as well as *something* small and dark skittering across a laminate countertop before slipping into a crack next to the groaning refrigerator.

"Ooh, a microwave!" Waldo marveled.

Erika snapped the light switch off. "You'll need it. The oven is broken. I'll make space for you in the fridge, but I recommend ordering all your meals from the all-day diner in town, Le Dennis. It's a walkable distance at dawn and dusk."

"And during the day?" Sibylle asked.

"It's June in Nevada," Erika answered with a shrug. "I won't stop you, but try not to dress like pleather Catwoman if you want to avoid getting heatstroke. You won't like having to spend an afternoon discovering the merits of the American medical system."

Erika gave Sibylle a bland smile before starting up a nearby set of steps, apparently oblivious to Sibylle's expression of affront.

Christof nudged his sister. "Pleather Catwoman."

"Shut up."

"Oh, ja!" Waldo cocked his head. "You do kind of dress like Catwoman. You know, the one with the Michelle Pfeiffer—"

"Shut *up*."

The second story was laid out so that the stairs opened into a small sitting room with access to a tiny bathroom and four large bedrooms. Each room appeared to be decorated with a particular color theme, which Christof approved of since it seemed a rather practical way for one to keep track of multiple assignations. Practicality was key to success, after all.

"This was considered the VIP room, if you will." Erika walked them into a room with emerald-hued wallpaper and a set of hideous lime sofas bookending a mirrored table that Christof could only assume had once been used for the consumption of cocaine. "Almost all the more elaborate furniture pieces here were imported from France in the early twenties, when business was doing well."

"Expensive to replace," Christof translated. He tested the bed's mattress with a light push, and its rusty springs screeched in complaint.

Erika's lip curled ever so slightly. "Exactly."

Waldo surveyed the room with an approving nod. "Very large. Good light. Excellent table. Close to the kitchen. I will take it!"

Christof begrudgingly claimed a small red room on the third floor that had only one window overlooking the parking lot yet came with its own bathroom, and Sergei chose a purple room on the second floor with no window. Sibylle claimed the attic room on the fourth floor, which was sweltering thanks to two single-paned windows that seemed to suck in the sunshine and trap it within like a greenhouse. Eight unadorned wooden beds lined the walls, and Erika explained that these were where the dancers had slept when they weren't with customers, sometimes two to a bed.

"Perfect. Many dissatisfied spirits here," Sibylle said. She breathed deeply, presumably inhaling the scent of her own vivid imagination. "I hope they will allow me to commune with them."

"Good luck with that. If you speak to the ghost of Grandma Meg, tell her I'd like a word," Erika said in a dry tone.

"You don't believe in the supernatural?" Sibylle asked.

For some reason, this made Erika stiffen. "No, I don't. I don't believe in things like ghosts or vampires or . . . curses. I think people make that stuff up to explain unpleasant coincidences." Then Erika strode over to a wall cabinet and produced an oil lamp from within. "Oh, and there's no electricity on this floor, so you'll need this."

Christof fought a smug grin—and failed. Sibylle was going to regret being so demanding. The attic reminded him of the kind of tragic orphan home you might find in hell, and he'd have bet his favorite guitar strap that the windows didn't open. He *adored* the idea of Sibylle discovering that fact long after her pride allowed her to recant.

Sibylle scowled. "And how will I charge my phone?"

"Ectoplasm, I guess," Erika said. "If you change your mind, you can take any of the rooms on the second or third floor."

With that, Erika swept out of the room, effectively ending the tour without even so much as a final check-in to ensure they were content and settled.

Seeing his sister meet such a formidable match was a rare delight. He *liked* this woman.

When he turned around, Sibylle was eyeing him suspiciously.

"What?" he said gruffly, ignoring the heat prickling up the back of his neck. "I was merely looking at her"—*desirable body and fascinating attitude*—"scars."

Sibylle's eyes narrowed farther. "Is there something you want to tell me, Big Brother?"

"I have no idea what you're talking about."

"You're acting very strangely lately."

He crossed his arms. "If you are referring to the incredible pressure I am under from the responsibility of single-handedly coordinating the development of our album, which is due to the label in three months, while my infernal blood relation plots ways to sabotage our progress by smuggling live avian species through airport security in the name of casual necromancy, our drummer continues his quest to redefine the word *excess*, and our guitarist plots how to . . ." Christof threw up his hands, having run up against a logical wall too early in his rant but was as yet unwilling to back down. "Play guitar louder, I suppose?"

"You forgot to mention Gillian. You know, your *girlfriend*, who is worried sick over her ill relative."

He inwardly winced. "I was getting there, thank you," he bit out. "But as I was saying . . . if that is what you're referring to, then yes, I imagine that might have an effect on my demeanor."

Sibylle glared at him.

He glared back, daring her to push further—and hoping she wouldn't.

To his relief, she backed down first. Sibylle plopped down in the middle of the wooden floor and pawed through her shoulder satchel in a dejected manner. "Fine, whatever."

"And?" he prompted.

"*And* I'm sorry about the crows. I've never seen them go for the eyes like that before."

Christof only shook his head. He started down the steps, then stopped to glance over his shoulder. Sibylle looked so forlorn in that moment that, despite himself, another wash of guilt swept over him. Was he really so demanding? Maybe he should let up on the band a bit. "Sibylle, if you really want—"

"At least they didn't find the spiders!" Sibylle pulled a jar out of her bag and held it aloft. Her triumphant smile faded.

The jar was empty.

"Oops?"

CHAPTER 6

Erika ducked into one of the empty third-floor bedrooms, waiting until Christof's heavy boot steps had continued on to the lower floor and the sound of his bedroom door closing behind him echoed through the floorboards. She'd felt guilty about departing so abruptly and had returned to make sure Christof and the band had everything they needed, but look what that half-assed attempt at being a good person had gotten her: a disappointing earful.

I was looking at her scars.

She clenched her fists. It was for the best that he was as distracted by her face as everyone else was. What had she expected? For him to see past the deformities and the hooker costume and the stage makeup and the reflexive sarcasm because he sensed she had a heart of gold? Because she *didn't*. That was why she was here, after all—she was repenting for being a coldhearted bitch and doing a mediocre job of it.

No, it was good she'd overheard that conversation before her wretched loneliness could spin a forbidden-lust plotline out of the ether. Christof was seeing someone, and Erika's oddly urgent attraction to him wasn't conducive to saving the opera house.

At least now she knew that spark she'd felt was one sided, so she wouldn't have to work hard to resist temptation.

See? Problem solved.

Erika spent the rest of the day in her small office located off the theater's entryway, half listening for footsteps while she made frantic calls to contractors. But no one came out of the long hallway tunnel that lay adjacent to her office door. The band must have been sleeping off their jet lag. It gave her time to pay through the nose for a handyman to come in from one of the Vegas suburbs and actually nail the plywood board down to the stage so it was slightly less sketchy. The cost he quoted her for actually repairing the hole itself was astronomical.

"Wood's real expensive right now," he said with a shrug, making direct eye contact with her breasts. Erika would have been more offended if she didn't know how hard he was trying to not look at her face. By now, she was used to the way people's eyes slid away from her scars.

Mostly.

By nightfall, she told herself she wasn't disappointed that there hadn't been a peep from her new guests since their arrival. That she didn't *want* to see what outfit Christof might have changed into, and that she had zero interest in asking him about this Gillian thing he was acting so shifty about. She definitely didn't want a better look at the tattoo she'd caught a glimpse of along his rib cage. What was she, some sort of desperate fangirl?

The Old Erika would judge her so hard right now.

Especially if Old Erika caught her pausing her "Sad Broadway Songs" playlist and clicking on that music file attachment he'd sent. Merely out of curiosity, mind you. Hair metal was so . . . *cheesy*.

A wailing guitar and thundering beat burst out of Grandma Meg's ancient monitor speakers, and Erika recoiled. Alarmed, she fumbled for the volume button, her heart pounding for irrational reasons. It wasn't like Christof was going to choose *this* moment to walk into her office unannounced. And he'd sent her their hit single specifically so she'd listen to it, so there was nothing creepy about this at all.

And the pictures she'd pulled up on her browser, chronicling Nachtmusik's recent tour? That was research. For objective . . . research purposes.

But it definitely looked like some sort of snake tattoo—

There was a knock on her doorframe.

"Do you like it?" Christof asked, recognizing Nachtmusik's hit single, "Demon of Music," playing over Erika's computer speakers. He watched her fumble with the mouse, clicking rapidly on the screen until the song cut off right as Christof's own voice howled, "Verflucht, für immer zu rocken . . ."

Erika looked rather guilty, with her lush lips parted and her cheeks flushed, as if he'd caught her with her hand up her skirt. "I haven't finished listening yet, but from what I've heard so far, I can tell it's very . . . um. Exciting."

Christof hadn't been able to properly rest all day, though he should have been tired after nearly eighteen hours of travel. But instead of napping, he'd lain on his bed staring at the check mark on the text he'd sent Gillian begging her to return his calls, knowing she'd seen it and had either chosen not to respond or . . . well, his mind raced with catastrophic possibilities. It wasn't *like* Gillian to not respond. She was always so considerate and reliable.

Then again, it wasn't like Gillian to abandon their relationship and band without explanation beyond an email that said, I'm sorry, but I can't do this. I need some space to figure things out. Please don't call me.

He'd tried using one of his four meditation apps, but whenever he closed his eyes, he saw dark hair and scarlet lips and heard a dulcet voice with the slightest rasp luring him to her sex dungeon to do things to him that Gillian had certainly never been interested in doing. It was distracting and arousing. Not the best use of his time.

So here he was. Ostensibly on his way to set up the instruments so the band might make most efficient use of its rehearsal time tomorrow. Then he'd heard his own song filtering down the hallway and been compelled to stop.

He certainly hadn't been looking for an excuse to see Erika again so soon.

"Do you speak any German?" he asked. "I can send the translation of the lyrics, if you'd like."

"Not at all. I took French in high school." She paused. "And Latin. And a little Italian."

"Ah. That's too bad."

"Why?" She cocked her head. "You all seem to speak excellent English."

He felt his skin heat. Why *did* he care if Erika spoke German? It wasn't like he was planning on marrying the woman. Bringing her to meet his parents. His mother was Canadian, anyway. "Deutsch is a beautiful language," he said.

She raised her brow.

He cleared his throat and glanced around the stuffy, crowded office as if it would offer a smoother comeback. There was a window behind her desk, and the metal blinds were drawn to keep out the hot daylight. Nevertheless, a beam of sunlight snuck in through a patch where the metal bars were bent, and it highlighted her dark hair with bloodred fire. Old burlesque posters hung on the wall, their edges browned and colors faded, but their subjects' come-hither poses were still enticing enough to remind Christof that this had once been a den of iniquity. Erika certainly seemed at home in this context, but at the same time, the office provided him no clues about *her*, and that was disappointing. "Right, well. I came by to thank you again for letting us stay here."

"And here I'd assumed you'd come for your credit card." She held it out to him with a small, satisfied quirk of her lips. "I'm pleased to report that it works."

He stepped forward to claim it, mildly insulted. Did she think that because they were rock stars, they weren't fiscally responsible? He updated their budget *nightly*. In an Excel spreadsheet with color-coded conditional formatting. It had taken him forever to create, and it was badass as fuck, in his opinion.

"Of course it works," he scoffed.

There was a slight, split-second hesitation before she released the card. "I'll bet it does," she murmured.

"Sorry?" *Is she—*

Her eyes flicked up. Her expression went flat so quickly that he thought he'd imagined the glow of lust in her eyes. "Thank you for your payment," she said calmly.

He *had* imagined it . . . hadn't he? It had been so long since he'd flirted with anyone that Christof wasn't even sure he remembered how. Waldo had always been delighted to interact with Nachtmusik's more forward fans; Christof had been friendly, but he'd always made it clear he was in a relationship and wouldn't do anything that might disrespect Gillian.

But now . . . suddenly, he realized he was standing very close to where Erika sat, and he couldn't help but notice that she'd changed out of her costume into a black, thin-strapped top and a skirt that was rather short, and he had a brilliant view of her lush golden thighs squeezing together.

And now he couldn't breathe.

"It's a shame you're taken," Erika said. Her tone was light enough, but there was underlying sharpness to it. He snapped his gaze back up to her face. Her eyes were dark and narrowed.

Christ. Now she thought he was some sort of cheating scoundrel. "I'm not, actually," he blurted. Winced. "Technically. But that's not yet public knowledge."

"Of course it's not."

Oh no. That had not come out right. He tried to explain. "The rest of the band doesn't know yet because it's very complicated."

"Isn't it always," she said. "Good thing I didn't ask." With seemingly deliberate movements, she tucked her hair behind her ear, giving him a clearer glimpse of her scars, before turning back to her computer monitor. "Was there anything else you needed? I'm about to lock up for the night."

Her message could not be clearer: *Fuck extremely off.*

He tucked the card in his waistband and retreated to the doorway, silently cursing himself. "No. I was on my way to set up the equipment for tomorrow."

"Wouldn't you rather wait until morning? I'm sure you must be tired."

"Exhausted," he confirmed. He glanced at her over his shoulder and tried not to sound as dejected as he felt. "But the band's success always comes first."

Erika couldn't sleep that night. Again.

Groggily, she threw her long silk robe on over her nightgown and made her way toward the roof of the theater, where she had a plastic lounge chair set up for daytime sunbathing in the winter months. Sometimes, singing to the stars helped; they were a polite audience and didn't whine about how she sang the Patti LuPone version of "Don't Cry for Me Argentina" instead of the more popular Madonna version in a lower key.

Erika had come out of the tunnel through the backstage entrance when she noticed the lights were still on in the theater. Irritated that Christof had failed to turn them off when he was done with setup (did he have *any* idea how behind she was on electric payments?), she padded toward the lighting control panel.

A melancholy guitar chord rang out, and Erika froze. It was well after midnight—what was he still doing here?

She wore a wrinkled silk nightgown, and her hair and makeup weren't done. The wise thing to do would be to turn around and go back to her room.

Then again . . . as the theater's owner, was it not her solemn responsibility to observe late-night goings-on to ensure there were no hazardous activities being conducted on premises? Wouldn't it be important to know why the band's leader was lurking around, probably being all brooding and sexy and off limits, instead of soundly asleep in his bed, dreaming of this Gillian woman with whom he'd recently—*secretly (ha!)*—broken up?

Erika had heard that line before—a tried-and-true classic. Still, it pissed her off that Christof had the nerve to be so fucking *hot*.

Or maybe he wasn't. Maybe she was so horny and lonely that it was affecting her vision.

Best to double-check.

Erika quietly padded up the switchback stairs to the loft, where she could observe the man on the stage below. She crouched low on the catwalk, keeping to the shadows until she found a good vantage point, then squatted and rested her hands and chin on the lower rung of the handrail.

It appeared he'd already set up all the instruments and routed the cables, so what was there left to do, really? She watched for a few moments as he rotated between the keyboard and drum kit and amplifiers, adjusting minutiae. How industrious. It fascinated her, how intent he seemed to be on making everything perfect. He hadn't been kidding about getting to work right away on the album. *Not even a day to settle in and see the sights, huh?*

Good for him. She admired fellow artists with that kind of drive; it was a trait she shared. One didn't get to the top of the game without rigorous practice. Although Erika had her doubts about whether being in a Euro hair metal band was *really* that competitive. How much talent was required to screech purple prose into a microphone? Brief encounters with the genre had convinced Erika that every hair metal song was, in some thinly cloaked fashion, a metaphorical boast about the allegedly gargantuan size of the lead singer's penis.

That song he'd sent her was rather catchy, though, and disappointingly, it contained zero mentions of Christof's penis. From a purely objective standpoint, Erika could see why it was so popular. And from a technical perspective, Nachtmusik wasn't terrible. It was obvious none of them had any formal musical training, and some of the lyrics were downright comical, but the raw talent was there. And Christof's voice was a vital, beastly thing that drove the song under her skin and made her veins thrum.

The way he sang it, German *was* a beautiful language. But not in a dewdrops-and-flowers sort of way; in a velvet-and-sin, pinned-to-the-wall-and-fucked-hard sort of way.

Erika quietly fanned herself. Damn, it was hot up here. And yet she couldn't bring herself to leave.

Christof bent to fix a cord to the stage with gaffer tape, and the fabric of his black pants molded tight across his taut backside. *Not bad.* For a man that tall, he had a decent amount of lithe muscle, and he wasn't awkward or gawky like a lot of tall people she'd known. He moved across the stage gracefully, like a dancer or a . . . very long cat.

The thing about him she found most interesting was that he did everything with such purpose. Such serious intensity. He seemed like an organized, focused sort of person who had his shit together in life and was perfectly in control in all ways, but when he tested each instrument, it was always by playing the same mournful, unsettled chord. There was a lot of pent-up *something* in that man.

And it was none of her business.

She shouldn't have slipped earlier in her office and let on how attracted she was to him. Why was she playing with matches when she'd been burned so many times before?

But when she thought about unraveling whatever had Christof wound up so tight, her hands clamped hard around the railing.

The crux of the issue was that she really, *really* loved sex. Maybe too much, given the problems it had caused. And since her accident, she hadn't had any at all.

Two years was an offensively long time to go without, but could she really blame herself for having let it get this bad? For the first few months after her accident, she'd been recovering from the skin graft, and with her low pain tolerance and high penchant for self-pity, it had been an altogether *un*sexual experience. And then, for the next month or so, she'd been dealing with the psyche-crushing realization that the show had gone on without her and none of her purported friends cared enough to check in on her after the initial glamour of her tragedy had worn off.

This is rock bottom, she'd thought at the time, because how else to describe the utterly pride-eviscerating experience of glancing at one's phone screen on a Friday night and having not even a single notification? No texts, no social media invites to postshow karaoke nights, not one single fucking notice about inconvenient birthday parties at obscure dens in Red Hook . . . *nothing.* In the eyes of everyone who mattered on Broadway, Erika was the loathsome villain who'd gotten exactly what she'd deserved (what a poor, tormented Elphaba she'd been—so unfairly persecuted).

By the time the clouds had cleared enough for her to remember sex existed, Erika had already moved to Paris and begun the decades-long process of dying alone.

It would have been easier to ignore temptation if Christof were a good, loyal man who had politely but firmly explained he was seeing someone. But no—Christof was bad, like her. The way his pupils had dilated and his lips had parted like she was water and he was dying of thirst . . .

Guess her scars weren't a deal breaker, after all. That fact should have pleased Erika, as vain as she was. But it didn't. (Well, maybe a little.)

As she stood to leave, having told herself she was going to stop spying on him like a creep and get some goddamn self-respect, he froze in the middle of what he was doing, his shoulder blades drawing together as if he could feel her gaze on him. Erika darted back into the shadows a split second before he turned and looked up into the rafters.

Right at where she'd been standing.

Her heart hammered in her chest as she held her breath, waiting. When he turned back around, she crept silently down the steps and slunk back to her bedroom.

CHAPTER 7

Christof awoke with a sense of optimism that quickly devolved into disappointment and then, without warning, plummeted into dismay.

His phone alarm, which was programmed to play his band's hit single, woke him up. That was a point in the day's favor. It meant he hadn't been lying awake since the wee hours, worrying about expenses and responsibilities and the ever-present possibility of failure.

Plus, he loved "Demon of Music." It was an iconic hit—a sincere yet brilliantly self-aware tribute to the legends of rock, with a head-slamming riff, a bitching guitar solo, and an unforgettable refrain that would have one cranking the volume on the highway and singing along in the shower. How could anyone have a bad day that began with such a song?

He slipped out of bed and did his morning yoga routine. It was warm enough to conduct the practice entirely naked in the rather pleas-ant trapezoid laid out by the desert sun coming in through his bedroom window, which was another point in the day's favor. He wasn't sure he *liked* yoga, but he did it anyway, because healthy prevention was key to success. The fifty-year-old front man of one of the opening bands they'd toured with had turned him on to the practice—said he'd thrown out his back on tour once and that all the bending and stretching was good for undoing the damage that poor hotel beds and cramped tour buses wrought on one's body.

The only part of yoga Christof liked was the end bit, where he got to lie down, close his eyes, and "clear his mind," which he'd never been able to do anyway, so instead it gave him time to brainstorm song lyrics and melodies for the new album. The vast potential of ten to twelve unrecorded tracks lay before him, eagerly awaiting his creative expertise.

But instead of music, his brain strayed to Erika again.

Last night, he could have sworn he'd felt her watching him, yet he'd peered about backstage and felt foolish when he'd found nothing. At least it had spurred him to finally go to bed—he was so sleep deprived that he'd been fantasizing about having a stalker.

And if he'd caught a whiff of her subtle rose scent lingering in the air by the base of the steps to the loft? That had to have been his imagination too.

It was forecast to be quite warm today. Maybe she'd wear shorts. The kind that came up a bit past the demarcation between thigh and rear. He loved that little crease, and he suspected Erika's was really worth seeing. He wanted to smooth the flats of his palms up the backs of her soft thighs until they found that warm place, and then he could trace it with his fingers, lightly enough to make her shiver. The little hairs on her body would stand up, perhaps, and he loved that sort of teasing . . .

His abdomen tightened. *Well.*

It had been a while since he'd woken up with such a strong sexual urge, but he'd never been able to do anything about it before—not with Gillian usually still sleeping—besides sneak off to the shower for quick relief like some . . . cock-stroking bandit. But now, he was alone. *Free* felt like the wrong word, yet things were different without Gillian's presence. He could do whatever he wanted now.

Of its own volition, his hand snaked off the floor and over the swell of his bare thigh. He gripped his hardening cock. Perhaps he'd—

The timer on his phone went off. Yoga session complete.

For a brief, stubborn moment, he considered ignoring it. Would an extra fifteen minutes behind schedule *really* be so bad?

It would be. There was so much to do today. He'd agreed to conceive and record an entire album in three months! An ambitious goal, but doable if they set their minds to it. If they focused—

And just like that, his arousal deflated.

With a grimace of resignation, he pushed up to a seated position—and felt a sharp stab in the pad of his right hand. A splinter of wood, about two centimeters long, had lodged itself under the top layer of skin. *How?*

He tried to pull the wood out with his teeth, but the protruding end merely snapped off, leaving the rest of it buried. Cursing his own carelessness, he tried squeezing the flesh to push it out, but it was no use. Why this hand? It was the same one he'd been about to pleasure himself with. More important: it was the hand he used to *play guitar*.

The day lost a point.

Determined to get it back, Christof vowed to speak to Erika today. Clear things up about the Gillian situation and ensure she knew he was single. In case he *hadn't* imagined the flash of desire on her face. Despite the throbbing in his palm, a coil of lust made his cock twitch.

And what then? He sighed, because the question was rhetorical. He didn't have the bandwidth for a secret affair. It would be better not to say anything at all so he didn't have to add a battle with his suddenly out-of-control libido to his list of responsibilities.

But she was interested, wasn't she? At least he still had it: that sexual swagger. He'd be a shit rock and roll front man if he ever lost *that*.

Oh yes, that put him in a much better mood. Today, he'd wear his gold pants. Sibylle had once remarked the gold pants made him look like a vaguely homosexual pirate—an evaluation that pleased him immensely, as that was exactly the look he aspired to achieve. Needless to say, the pants were a fan favorite.

What was the joy in being a rock star if one couldn't dress like one?

Determined to start Nachtmusik's first rehearsal as perfectly as possible, Christof walked across town to Le Dennis to pick up breakfast for the whole band. It was then that his day truly began to lose points.

By the time he sauntered into the diner, he'd fully realized the error of his ways. By eleven in the morning, the temperature read a wildly shocking eighty-one degrees, and when he eventually remembered to convert to Celsius, it was too late, because he'd already convinced himself he was dying. His precious gold pants, made from an animal-friendly synthetic material, were now glued to his flesh with his own coagulated sweat.

Then, while waiting for his order to be prepared, he noticed a table of locals staring at him. Assuming they were admiring his trousers, he gave a polite wave.

A woman with enviably voluminous curly gray hair and a vivid floral shirt waved back. Then, before he knew what was happening, she got up from the table and sidled close. "I have to ask . . ." She lowered her voice to a conspiratorial tone. "Are you a Cirque du Soleil performer? We've heard rumors that Raoul was getting some big names in for Magnifique! I'm Dee, by the way. I used to run Le Meilleur Ouest here in town."

"Oh, no, but thank you very much! I dress like this because I am in a rock band. Have you heard of Nachtmusik?" He doubted many Americans had heard of them, especially in such a small town—but a part of him still hoped.

"Not Music?" She glanced at her three dining companions—two men in mesh-sided sports caps and a scowling woman in a Barry Manilow T-shirt—who all shook their heads.

"*Nacht*musik," he corrected. He smiled wider to hide his disappointment. Maybe someday. "We are visiting from Berlin while we create our second album here at the lovely Paris Opera House."

Dee's eyes widened, as if this was the most interesting piece of information thus far. "Is that so? I didn't know Erika was renting the space. And attracting international business, no less! How industrious."

One of the men snorted. "I'd watch out for that one if I were you."

"Bobby!" chided Dee.

"What? You said yourself she's a 'real piece of work.'" Bobby gave Christof a knowing look, and he realized they were referring to Erika. Christof's smile faded. He'd grown up in a town not much bigger than this one, and he knew all about how insidious such talk could be.

"She's been nothing but hospitable and professional to my band thus far." It came out sharper than he'd intended.

Dee hushed Bobby before he could say more, but the woman in the Barry Manilow shirt rushed to fill the conversational gap. "You watch out, young man. That girl acts like her little booty's too hot for this town, but we all know where she came from. Her great-great-granny was a hooker, her gram was a drunk and a two-bit con, and her daddy's a whackadoodle grifter. I heard he's in jail again, you know. Tried to steal astronaut secrets from Area 51 or something."

Dee bit out through her smile, "Not in front of this nice man, Bernadette."

"What? It's true. Besides, wasn't it you who told the whole bridge club that she used to be on Broadway but she got run out of New York after she got caught having *relations* with her understudy's husband? I don't know why we're defending that hussy. You feel sorry for her because of her messed-up face."

The fourth diner, a man who'd been silent until now, grunted. "You ever seen what's under there? I heard it's all gone. A mess of scars. Freakish." He gave an exaggerated shudder.

Hot anger swept through Christof, even though he hardly knew Erika. He knew enough to know she didn't deserve to be ridiculed behind her back with such malicious glee—*no one* deserved that.

The counter person handed him his bags of food, and he had a vivid fantasy of dumping the contents on these people's heads. If he hadn't known it would only come back to haunt her with even more spiteful rumors, he would have.

Christof left Le Dennis with a poor taste in his mouth—and a burning desire to ask Erika questions he had no right to be asking. Why did he want to know her with such strong urgency? It didn't matter who she had slept with—or hadn't—in her past.

But he did have other questions. Like whether she'd really been on Broadway. Why she'd left. Why she was here, running this theater and so obviously desperate for money. How she'd come by her scars. Why her eyes were so sad. What she'd look like when she came—

He stopped dead in the middle of the street. His brain was clearly scrambled from the hot sun baking him into the asphalt.

By the time he returned to the theater, he was drenched from head to toe in sweat. At that point, the day's tally plummeted into the red.

Sibylle, who was in the midst of undoing all his previous night's work and moving her equipment around on the theater's stage, burst out laughing when she saw him. Waldo and Sergei were there already, too—making Christof the late one.

The splinter in his palm throbbed anew.

"Look at your face! Did you not wear sunscreen?" Sibylle crowed.

Christof scrunched his burnt nose, but not a single witty comeback came to him. Why must his sister take so much delight in his misfortune? Sibylle could be a brat at times, but she'd been in ultrarare form these past few days. Gillian's calming presence had always tempered the band's stronger personalities, but now she was gone, leaving Christof to fend off the wolves alone.

Christof limped down the seating ramp to the base of the stage and plunked the bags at Sibylle's feet. "Breakfast is served," he said through gritted teeth. "You're welcome."

His bandmates attacked the bags without so much as a thankful glance in Christof's direction.

While they ate, he directed them to sit in the first row so he could address the day's plan. He withdrew his leather-bound planning book and uncapped a pen. "I am sure that over the past year, each of us has been developing many great ideas for songs. Therefore, before we begin, we will share our personal visions for what we'd like to see this album become. Who would like to start?"

Waldo raised his hand. "American cowboy!"

Christof waited for him to elaborate, pen poised over the page.

He didn't.

"Okay. Waldo, maybe you can give us some more detail?"

Waldo nodded eagerly. "The kind of songs about broken hearts and trucks that you can pick up cows in. Das . . . *Chevy*. Yeehaw!"

Christof took a deep breath and tried to smile. "This is not really our style of music—"

"But I thought we are updating our sound for the American audience," Waldo said. "I don't understand. Do you not want our ideas?"

Sibylle grumbled, "I bet he's already planned it all out himself."

"I have *not*." He absolutely had, although there were still some details to work out, and he'd always been terrible with lyrics. But that wasn't the point, was it? He was trying to be a good leader, and a good leader at least attempted to incorporate his band's creative tastes.

"Okay, then, Big Brother. What would you say if I proposed a track that was only a bass backing and no guitars? Something a little darker, more industrial."

Sergei looked up from what he'd been doing—dissecting his waffle, apparently—and narrowed his eyes. "No guitars?"

"We're simply discussing ideas," Christof assured them in what he hoped was a soothing tone. "Nothing is off limits. Look, see? I've written everything down. Waldo, broken hearts is a good theme. Our last album was very optimistic. Maybe this one we go a bit sadder, yes? Sibylle, perhaps you can compose a dark track about heartbreak."

Sergei repeated, "No guitars?"

A familiar tingling awareness settled over him, like it had the night before. Christof glanced up to see Erika watching them from where she stood, arms crossed, in one of the private boxes that ringed the theater. Her form was shadowed, so he couldn't make out her expression, but he sensed she was finding this entertaining.

Did she think their ideas were ridiculous, or was she intrigued by the process?

Was she wearing shorts? He couldn't tell from this angle, with the box's balcony rail coming up to her waist.

Christof wrenched his focus back to the group. "Of course, we'll have to have guitar on every track. But perhaps we can have a break for a bass-forward piece."

"We must have more guitar solos," Sergei insisted.

Christof clutched his pen in his fist, ignoring the stab of pain from his splinter. "We can always make room for more guitar solos."

His eyes strayed to Erika again. He couldn't help it. Now that he knew she was there, it was like some sort of compulsion.

Who was this woman?

Her brown hair was pulled forward again to cover half her face. Her dark, one-eyed stare swept across him like a hot stone and left cold skin in its wake. It was as if she could tell, even as he tried to project confidence, that he was barely holding his world together and that everything was dangerously close to crumbling down around him. In that moment, he was sure she'd stripped off his jacket, cracked open his bare rib cage, peered into the depths within, and said, *Mine.*

And Christof, who'd only ever been with one woman in his entire life and had been *thrilled* at his newfound freedom only this morning, was suddenly eager to surrender to her thrall.

He wanted to know her, and he wanted to *know* her. In precisely that order. And if she kept staring at him like that—

"Shouldn't Gillian be involved in this discussion?" Sibylle asked.

Ice-cold reality slapped him free of his trance.

"Right. Gillian." He cleared his throat. Gave a tight smile. Then fished his phone from the waistband of his pocketless pants, peeling the glass screen off his still-sticky hip bone. "Ah! Yes, I spoke to her last night to update her that we'd gotten settled in, and here's a message from her right now. She says she is wrapping up the visit with her family this week. Excellent news."

The lies were coming more easily now. That probably wasn't good. It certainly didn't please his stomach, which didn't seem to be taking his "Grand Chelem" breakfast well.

To lessen the severity of his untruth, he quickly issued Gillian a text that read: I need to speak with you urgently. It's about the band.

There. Now he was only 95 percent lying.

"Then we should wait for her," Waldo said. "Right?"

"Wrong," Christof countered. "We are paying quite a bit of money to stay here, and we'll make the most of it. When Gillian joins us, we will incorporate her feedback. Does anyone have any lyrics or song ideas they have been developing?"

Blank stares.

"We've been on tour! Go easy on us, boss," Waldo pleaded. "Can't we have a week to settle in?"

Sibylle hummed in agreement. "My creative reservoir is completely drained. I need to commune with the spirits. I sense they will guide my songwriting and replenish my arcane gift."

Christof looked to Sergei, hoping he'd be an unlikely ally in this battle with Waldo and Sibylle's poor work ethic, but the guitarist merely shrugged. As if to say, *I stopped caring about everything but the guitar a thousand years ago. Literally—I'm a vampire.* But, of course, Sergei didn't say anything and wasn't really a vampire, and Christof was once again the bad guy, carrying the responsibility alone.

He wanted to roar. Take his guitar—his precious child—and smash it into pieces on the stage.

After this meeting was over, he'd call Gillian and *beg* her to return, if only so this album wouldn't be doomed.

But . . . in her email, she'd told him not to contact her. He'd already called and texted, and she hadn't responded. If she wanted to speak to him, she'd reply to his text, and if she didn't . . .

No. He knew Gillian. She *would* reply, because no matter what was going on between them, she cared about the band. Her bleeding heart wouldn't allow her to stay away for long.

And perhaps he was overreacting with this sense of urgency. He had a tendency to do that. They had until September, didn't they? And how long could it take to record in studio once the songs were composed? These things could be done in weeks. *Days*, if copious amounts of drugs and excess musical genius were involved. Or in lieu of either of those things, a very prepared and organized band manager.

All he needed was his band's cooperation. And if it took a brief period of Christof letting everyone fuck around in order to get it, then he'd stomach the price. After choking down a $4,000-a-week price tag on their stay simply to distract from further questions about Gillian's absence, every other absurd accommodation seemed reasonable.

So instead of throwing a massive tantrum, he gave everyone a patient smile. "Very well. We will each spend the next week immersed in the creative process. Do whatever you must . . . commune with ghosts, absorb American culture, do your"—he considered Sergei—"er, guitar practice, perhaps?"

Sergei inclined his head.

Christof continued, "Whatever you require to unlock the doors of musical innovation. No restrictions. We meet again next Monday, and we will share our ideas. Agreed?"

The members of Nachtmusik had never come to a faster consensus. Within minutes, his bandmates had scattered, leaving Christof alone.

And when he looked up, Erika was gone too.

He glanced down at his notebook—*Heartbreak. Dark, more bass. Also more guitar. Call Gillian.*—and a sort of hollow, unsettled feeling swallowed several more points from the day's tally. The situation was well in the red now.

Without thinking about what he was doing, he snapped the notebook shut and went to find Erika.

CHAPTER 8

Erika plopped into her desk chair, stared at the multicolored spread of bills on her desk, and slowly let her forehead fall forward until it rested on the ocean of paper.

She had wandered to the auditorium on the pretense of making sure the band had settled into the space, but Erika knew the real reason she'd gone, and it wasn't because she'd wanted to escape her hell-in-a-box office and the insurmountably daunting task of determining which unpaid bills and urgent repairs she could afford to pay now that she had Nachtmusik's deposit and which ones she could weasel onto the back burner for a bit longer. She'd gone because she was still drawn to bad ideas and forbidden things, even though she'd told herself she'd changed.

Besides, an entire afternoon of phone calls and pleading with contractors awaited her. If there was anyone she should be feeling sorry for, it was herself—not the bare-chested man back there in a white denim jacket and gold pants.

Erika allowed herself a sigh of longing.

His outfit should have looked ridiculous, but nothing seemed to look ridiculous on Christof. He exuded a level of hypersexual glamour that seemed to have gone out of vogue decades ago with the likes of

Bowie and Bon Jovi—all the glorious *hair* and questionable codpieces and unapologetic eyeliner.

Above all, it was the confidence that came with the look. The kind that suggested Christof would be an absolutely world-class virtuoso in bed who wouldn't be satisfied until he'd fucked her so speechless she spoke a new language by the end of it.

By God, she'd love that man to teach her German . . .

As if he'd been summoned by her sinful thoughts, a knock on her doorframe—and the woodsy cologne he wore—announced his presence.

"I hope I'm not disturbing you, but I require your help with a small problem."

For the second time in a twenty-four-hour period, Erika lifted her head and saw Christof had propped an arm up to casually lean against the wooden frame. Was this going to be a pattern? Was she going to have to remain ever vigilant about the possibility of Christof appearing whenever she began thinking sublimely filthy thoughts about him?

Erika forced her libido into submission. *He has a girlfriend—probably.*

"What's up? Did something break in the theater? I should have warned you those chairs have been known to snap right off the rusted hinges if you lean back too far."

His brow furrowed. "That seems like a liability, yes?"

"I guess you haven't noticed the plywood-covered hole in the stage," she muttered.

"Sorry?"

"Just be careful on the stage, okay? I have someone coming in to replace the floorboards soon."

"And when will that be?"

Erika pretended to shuffle the top stack of bills, as if she were making complicated calculations in her head. "Soon."

Christof crossed his arms. "Is this venue up to code for performances? Because it was advertised as if it were, and I cannot afford to have any of my band members becoming injured. This album we are working on is key to our success."

Well, well, well . . . if it isn't my guilty conscience, back from outer space. I thought I quit you when I took that black credit card.

Erika used her pinkie finger to discreetly nudge the corner of the *Notice of Building Reinspection* letter farther underneath the unpaid electric bill. "Do you think I would have advertised the opera house as a performance venue if I didn't have permits stating it was up to code?"

"I suppose not."

So *trusting*. Now she felt even worse. But what was she supposed to do now? She'd already charged their credit card and paid the bank. Desperate times, et cetera. "So if nothing's broken, what's wrong?"

"I have a splinter I can't remove." He held out his hand to her so she could see the sharp line of brown bisecting the pad at the base of his palm.

Erika hissed in sympathy. "I have tweezers. Hold on." She pulled her makeup bag out of her purse and extracted the tool. She'd spent a lot of time working on old stages—splinters were a common job hazard. "Give me your hand."

He moved closer as she tugged on his wrist, bringing his palm near enough that she could see the injury site. The desk was still between them, but now he was pressed up against it, his crotch clearing the desktop surface. If she unzipped his pants—

Don't go there.

She was too horny for her own good. Focusing on the splinter, she tested the flesh by pressing lightly against it with the tweezer tips. His breath sucked in.

"Does it hurt?" she asked, probing for an entry point.

"Yes."

She glanced up in surprise. "Aren't you supposed to be all stoic and claim men can't feel pain?"

"But then how would I elicit the sympathy of a beautiful—*ow!*"

"Sorry. Thought I had it." She angled the tweezers and plucked at the end of the splinter. Maybe her unpleasant ministrations would shut him up before he tried flirting again.

"How is it that you owe so much money?"

Erika stilled. His snooping eyes had strayed to the papers on her desk. "Do you always let your bandmates prance all over your authority like they did back there?"

"That is not an answer to my question."

"It was. Maybe it got lost in translation. How do you say *that's none of your business* in German?"

"Ich mag deinen Arsch."

Something about his tone made her glance up at him again, but his expression was perfectly guileless.

Carefully, she returned to her work. Tried to ignore the warmth of his hand in hers and the pulse in his wrist beating strong and steady beneath her grip. And the way his breathing hitched when she moved the tweezers, which sent her thoughts spiraling to other things she could do to him to elicit that sound. This was more intimate than it should be. It felt wrong to be so close to him . . . which was why she liked it so much.

Erika knew her breath had gone shaky and hoped he didn't notice.

She'd caught the edge of the splinter again and begun to wiggle it free when he said in a low voice, "I wasn't lying about not being in a relationship any longer."

The splinter snapped in two, leaving the remaining half still buried. Biting back a curse, she doubled back to task.

"You don't believe me."

Erika pursed her lips. "You assume I care."

"Don't you?"

The rest of the splinter came free, and a bead of blood welled in its wake. "There. All better."

"Thank you."

The droplet of blood meandered down his palm and settled in the groove that ran parallel to his knuckles. She had the irrational impulse to follow its path with her tongue—which was a bit gross, if she thought about it. This man seemed to awaken strange things in her.

"Are you going to let go?"

She released his hand and tossed her tweezers aside. The office was sweltering. It was difficult to ignore how tall Christof was, standing over her like that. To ignore the seductive hint of that oak-cask scent he wore. The way his stare seemed to slide up and down her bare arm like a caress.

Erika looked away and stabbed the controls on her creaky desktop fan, even though it was already on the highest setting, using the opportunity to gulp down lukewarm air like she'd been starved of it. But even that wasn't enough to cleanse the impure urges Christof had awakened.

Bad things happen to bad people, she reminded herself.

"Allow me to buy you a beer at the bar across the street," Christof offered. When she jerked her gaze up in alarm, he added, "As a thank-you. For the medical assistance."

As if she needed her inhibitions loosened any more around him. "I'm not really a bar girl. Thanks, though."

"You don't drink?"

"It's best if I don't." She rarely drank anymore. Even though alcohol wasn't her problem, she had an endless list of *other* problems—questionable taste in men ranking highly among them—and booze had always made those problems worse.

"Ah." After a moment's hesitation when his square jaw worked as if he were wrestling with inner demons, he settled on one of the waist-high filing cabinets and said, "Gillian broke up with me last week. In an email. But I have not told the band yet."

Here we go. "How long were you dating for?" she asked, even as she internally cursed herself for taking the bait.

"Ten years."

Erika blinked. "You're joking."

"Perhaps eleven." He inspected his now splinter-free palm as if it were fascinating. Was he *blushing*? "Not entirely sure. We . . . all of us in Nachtmusik, except for Sergei . . . we all grew up in the same town. So Gillian and I were friends and bandmates for many years before we became romantic."

"And she broke up with you by *email*? After all that time?"

He finally looked up at her. His hazel, kohl-rimmed eyes were filled with what looked like genuine regret. "I don't even know where she's gone. I woke up in our flat the morning after our final show in Berlin, and all her suitcases were missing. She'd not bothered to unpack . . . left as if we were still on tour and she was checking out of a hotel."

Erika warred with the instinct to hate Gillian, despite never having met her. She tamped it down. He was clearly going for the pity angle. The classic "woe is me . . . won't you soothe my broken heart with a blowjob?" bit. Regret welled in her mouth and slipped off her tongue, sounding an awful lot like spite. "Did you cheat on her?"

"No!" he said, reeling back as if she'd slapped him. "I would never."

Erika shrugged. "It was a fair question."

"Never," he repeated, more quietly. He glowered at her in a way that made her skin heat. "And there was ample opportunity."

Erika searched his face, looking for hints of deception. She was an actress; she should be good at this sort of thing. But then again, the more he looked at her with that sooty-lidded, stern intensity, the harder it was to trust her instincts.

Ample opportunity . . . I'll bet there was. A tendril of arousal twisted, low and tight, in her abdomen.

She tried to focus on something that would dampen it. "You must be heartbroken. You had to have loved her a lot, to have dated for so long."

"Well." He cleared his throat. "That may have been the problem. I did love Gillian, very much. But perhaps not in . . . that way."

"Ohhhhh. I see." And suddenly, she did. Christof wasn't lying; he was *ashamed*. "You feel guilty because you're *not* heartbroken."

He grimaced. "Upon reflection, I realize I should have ended things years ago, but I hate to see my loved ones in pain—especially pain I have caused. In retrospect, perhaps we were both waiting for the other to make the decision."

Erika rubbed her forehead. Why did he have to look so *lost*?

"There, there," she offered, tentatively reaching forward to pat . . . some part of him. She'd already committed to the gesture when it became clear that the only parts in reaching distance were below the waist. After a second's hesitation, she settled on his left knee. "I'm sure it'll all work out."

"Thank you for listening. You are very kind."

Kind? Erika stifled a horrified laugh.

"You must not say anything about Gillian to the band, though. She was our keyboardist and second vocalist, so we will already struggle to record this album without her, but above all, I am worried the news will be extremely difficult for the others to hear. She and I shared the . . . leadership responsibility. We were like Mutti und Vater, because I am the tough, strict Vater, and she was the kind and forgiving Mutti. If they learn she's abandoned us, Waldo and Sibylle will feel our family is broken."

Erika didn't want to think about Christof in the "strict daddy" role. It was hard enough to resist Christof when she'd thought he was off limits—she didn't need to activate another forbidden kink. (Were she ever able to afford a therapist, they'd have a field day determining why *that* turned her on—or maybe it was something as simple as the fact that she'd never even met her real dad before he'd gone to prison the first time, for a smorgasbord of crimes so numerous that Grandma Meg looked like an angel in comparison.)

"They can't know that she's not coming back," he emphasized.

"What the hell did you tell them to explain her absence?"

"She is taking personal time to attend to an ill family member, and she will be joining us soon."

Erika raised a brow. "And how long do you intend to keep that little charade up?"

"Until I convince Gillian to return."

"And that will be . . ."

"Soon."

"Soon, like 'when I get the stage repaired' soon?"

His expression turned thunderous. She fought the urge to squirm in her wooden seat.

"You should repair that stage promptly. Preventative maintenance is key to success," he told her firmly. "And I will not see my band harmed."

She licked her lips. "Fine." If only it hadn't come out so breathy.

"I apologize. I didn't mean to come across so . . . controlling. It is your theater." He leaned forward, resting his elbows on his knees, and raked his hands through his riotous hair. In a coarse voice he muttered, "I need to get some proper sleep. I haven't been myself lately."

"Mmm," she murmured, still distracted by the way his voice had nearly *growled* in that low, commanding register.

He gave her a strange look. "Are you not bothered when I order you about like this?"

Yes, she wanted to tell him. *I'm an empowered, modern woman . . . how dare you order me around like the bad, bad girl I am?* Instead, she wisely demurred. "It depends. Are you planning to make a habit of it?"

He ran a thumb over his lower lip, like he was considering his answer. The press of that digit over the plush expanse, back and forth, was hypnotizing. "I've been told I'm too stern. Always telling everyone what to do. How to go about things."

"How awful," Erika murmured.

"I've been told that this is not an attractive trait."

"I guess it depends on the context."

He paused. "Elaborate."

Maybe he was toying with her, but based on the consternation in his expression, she doubted it. According to Nachtmusik's Wikipedia page—which she'd discovered was regrettably lacking on details about certain tattoos—Christof was only two years younger, which meant he *had* spent his entire twenties in a relationship. What if Gillian had been pure vanilla in the sack? And what if Christof was actually very adventurous, but he didn't *know* he was?

What if she could help him find out?

Keeping her tone as neutral as she could manage, she explained, "Some people like that kind of specific, exacting stage direction . . . in the bedroom."

"Ahh, like that movie with that woman with the very cute . . . how do you call it? Pony hair?" He gestured to his forehead. "You know this one? She's always biting her lip, like this?"

It dawned on her. "Are you talking about *Fifty Shades of Grey*?"

"Yes! Very popular film. I've seen clips. By accident, mind you."

"That movie isn't—" Erika shook her head. Just because she currently resided in what used to be a sex dungeon didn't mean she was qualified to give someone a rundown on BDSM culture. "Look, if you're looking to explore whips and chains, I can recommend some places in Vegas for you. The hard-core stuff isn't really my scene."

He fixed his bedroom eyes on hers. "What is?"

Her mouth was suddenly dry. She sat back in her chair and took a long sip from her water bottle, but water didn't quench a damn thing. A different sort of thirst grew dark and ravenous inside her.

Except Christof wasn't for drinking.

Well, he probably shouldn't be. Even though he was technically single. The idea they'd have to keep it a secret from his band felt a shade risqué.

(Even better.)

No, *not* even better. She was *reformed* now. Focused on saving her business, not indulging in delicious sin. Not embarking on a series of depraved, forbidden trysts with an outrageously handsome man who looked like he was about to entrap her in his magical labyrinth.

She was now a respectable woman looking for an equally respectable, aboveboard sexual relationship. At the very least, she wanted to sleep with a man with whom she could be seen in public the next day.

Erika swallowed. "I'd love nothing more than to introduce you to my scene, and any other scenes you're curious about . . ."

Every muscle in his body seemed to tense. Hoarsely, he replied, "Is that so?"

"As soon as you've sorted things out with Gillian and told your band what's going on," she finished.

He stood, eyes darkening, and closed the short distance between them with a single step. Hands came down on the arms of her desk chair, caging her in. Was he going to kiss her anyway?

Ignoring the thrill that coursed through her at the thought, she sucked in breath and tilted her chin up to meet his eyes. Her trembling voice came out only a shade above a whisper. "Does that seem like a fair deal?"

Footsteps sounded in the hall, giving them a split-second warning. Christof jerked back so quickly he rammed into the filing cabinet and sent the wheel of ticket stubs propped atop it careening onto the ground. It rolled toward the doorway, unraveling into a trail of little red rectangles as it went, only stopping when it hit the six-inch platform of Sibylle's left boot.

Sibylle looked back and forth between Erika and Christof, then down at the roll of tickets. Then back up at Christof. Then once again to Erika. Her brows rose.

"I required her assistance to remove a splinter," Christof said. He held up his palm with its dried smear of blood.

"Ah." Sibylle let the moment hang for long enough that even Erika's heart raced—and she *wanted* Sibylle to know what was going on. From a purely theatrical standpoint, Erika had to applaud Sibylle's flair for dramatic suspense. Finally, the bassist shrugged. "Anyway, I came to see if I can use the big pipe organ in the theater."

In unison, Erika and Christof replied, "No."

Sibylle's superior smirk was instantly replaced by a glower. "Why not?"

"Have you ever played a pipe organ before? It's very different from a piano," Erika asked.

Christof cut in, "She doesn't play piano either. She plays bass. And right now, she is playing with my patience." To his sister, he added, "Is this the best use of your time? I thought you were praying to the ghosts or some nonsense."

"Spirits. Don't be offensive," Sibylle snapped.

"The term *ghosts* is offensive?" Erika couldn't help but ask.

An aggrieved sigh. "It's like champagne and sparkling wine. Squares and rectangles. I don't have time to explain."

"But you have time to learn to play the pipe organ?" Christof growled. Despite herself, Erika felt that same thrill of arousal again.

Sibylle threw up her hands. "Fine! I was only asking. Stop acting like I *murdered* someone." As she stomped away, she muttered, "I can't wait for Gillian to come back."

They waited in silence until her footsteps could no longer be heard. By then, the residual lust had fully drained from the atmosphere, and Christof's face had once again returned to its former strained, exhausted state. "I can't tell them. Not yet."

She tried to hide her disappointment beneath a flippant tone. "Suit yourself."

Erika watched his fists clench by his sides and almost felt sorry for him. Maybe she was being unreasonable. Maybe her pride was getting in the way of what she needed. What they *both* clearly needed.

He left before her flimsy resolve could buckle under the pressure of another word.

Any word at all.

CHAPTER 9

Christof didn't know how to cope with his newfound obsession with Erika Greene. For the following few days, she was all he thought of whenever he closed his eyes. The more he tried *not* to think about her, the harder it was to wipe her from his imagination.

It would have been easy if he could have avoided her, but that was a challenge. Every time he exited the tunnel from the brothel to the theater, her office with its open door shone light into the hallway like a flame beckoning a moth. After the second day, he started leaving through the front door of the brothel, which let out into an empty dirt lot and required him to traverse the expanse of it to round a wire fence, then go all the way around the block to the front of the theater. Not exactly convenient, but he wasn't tempted to stop and visit Erika this way.

She fascinated him in a way that no one had ever captured his attention before. He wanted her, but he also wanted to know everything about her in ways that weren't sexual. Problem was, he suspected innocent conversation would lead to flirting, which would inevitably lead to him agreeing to do whatever she asked of him just to have the privilege of discovering whether her skin was as soft as it looked.

The hardest part of it all was that he usually distracted himself by working. But he'd been so proactive, so *prepared*, that he'd taken care of almost all the band's administrative tasks in advance in order to allow himself time to focus entirely on the album's development. And now here he was—sitting around with nothing to do while the rest of Nachtmusik relaxed and generated inspiration.

And for Christof, relaxing was out of the question.

Instead, he redrafted lyrics for new songs—then revised and revised again.

He played around with riffs, compositions, and chord progressions until his fingers ached and his brain was so oversaturated he couldn't tell what sounded good anymore.

He did yoga on the splintered floorboards.

He walked across town to the general store and bought tweezers, rubbing alcohol, and a large Eiffel Tower–printed beach towel to practice on.

By the final day of Nachtmusik's weeklong "break," Christof was beside himself. He'd barely slept more than a few hours each night, and when he went to the theater to find solace in performing for an empty house, he swore he could feel Erika's eyes on him. It had gotten so bad that he kept seeing her in the corner of his vision everywhere he looked—like a hallucination or one of Sibylle's restless phantoms.

I'll tell the band the truth about Gillian tomorrow morning at our first formal practice, he finally decided on Sunday morning. Gillian still hadn't called him back, and as hard as it was to accept, Christof was beginning to think she really wasn't coming back. Ever.

The decision should have been a relief, but instead it made a ball of cold nausea swell in his gut. Perhaps that was why he was so distracted that, as he parted the curtain to enter the auditorium from the foyer, he didn't notice Erika until he'd nearly collided with her lush body.

"Scheiße!" Christof jerked back to avoid barreling over her, but Erika caught his shoulders with her raised palms, steadying them both. Her touch sent electric heat sweeping through him, searing away the cold in his belly.

The heavy curtain fell shut behind him, cloistering them both in the dark entry alcove. The lights in the theater were off, and only a sliver of daylight from the entryway illuminated the space between their bodies.

"Very sorry," he managed. "I was distracted."

A tiny smile curled the edge of her scarlet lips as her hands fell away—slowly. "Nice shirt. Very . . . seasonally appropriate."

He glanced down at the sheer red top he'd left unbuttoned to midchest. "It's very hot."

"Yes."

"Outside," he added quickly.

She trailed the tip of her hair across her own collarbone. He couldn't tear his eyes away. "You've been busy this week, I've noticed."

"Very busy," he lied.

"Do you apply such intense focus to everything in your life?"

"I like to commit fully to things."

Her lips parted. "Admirable."

"Do you think so?" If he sounded surprised, it was only because Gillian had often told him such intensity was exhausting. But he'd let himself believe their differences were a form of balance in the relationship.

"I've always been the same way. Ambitious. Driven. Passionate." Her eyes flicked away. "Well, I used to be, anyway."

"What happened?" It had taken every shred of restraint within him not to search for answers on the internet. He'd already heard enough rumor spun by the locals; he wanted to hear Erika tell her own tale.

"Do you really want to know?"

He'd suddenly never wanted anything more. "I—"

His phone rang.

Specifically, it blared the song he'd written for Gillian on her twenty-second birthday, "Wish You Were Here."

Oh no. Why did Gillian have to call him now, at this specifically inconvenient time?

"Do you need to get that?" Erika asked.

He could let it go to voice mail and call her back later. He should. He really, really should.

But this was a matter that affected the band.

And the band *always* came first.

He slid the phone free of his waistband. Then he squeezed his eyes shut and braced himself for the metaphorical punch he was about to deliver to his own face. "Yes. I do. It's . . . band business."

He peeked at Erika through a slitted eye and saw her whole demeanor downshift. Oh, she'd guessed who was calling.

I'm sorry, he mouthed, swiping up before it was too late.

Christof took the call outside so that no one might overhear—a move that had guilt following him into the dreaded heat. He knew how suspicious he must look to Erika, furtively escaping with his cell phone, even though it was his bandmates he meant to avoid.

"What's wrong?" came Gillian's voice on the other end of the line. She sounded far away. Or perhaps she simply had him on speaker-phone. "Did Sergei quit?"

What? "Why would Sergei have quit?" Christof stopped at the base of the opera house steps and glanced back. His insides snarled up into a familiar knot. Should he be concerned about his guitarist quitting too? He shook his head, trying to focus. His thoughts were still jumbled after his encounter with Erika, every nerve ending still sparking under his skin. "Gilly, what's going on? I have been texting and calling you for the last week!"

Gillian sighed. "I'm sorry. I . . . needed some time to think."

And you couldn't send a single text while you did so? He gripped the phone hard and tried for patience. "Okay. So, you have had time to think, then. Do you . . . feel better?" He'd waited for this call for long enough that he didn't dare frighten her off with the force of his frustration.

There was a long pause. "I don't know."

He forced himself to keep walking. "What do you mean by this? Are you coming back? The band needs you. We are here in Paris—"

"France?"

"It's a town in Nevada, in the US. I emailed you the travel information and asked for your input."

"I've been detoxing from technology and only checked my messages today. Anyway, what's going on with the band, Tof? I'm surprised you went forward with the trip to America. I thought for sure you'd ask the label for more time."

Ask the label . . . He pinched the bridge of his nose. Sometimes, the weight of being the only band member to handle the business side of matters was impossible. Perhaps it was his own fault for not asking the band if they'd like to be involved. Then again, Gillian had told him she found meetings with the label too stressful, and the thought of letting Sibylle or Waldo interact with people who had the power to make or break their careers was terrifying. Waldo had once tried to bribe officers responding to a noise complaint by offering them tabs of acid, and since Christof and Gillian had been waylaid at the time with food poisoning, Sibylle had gone to pick up Waldo at the jail—and arrived at the station with a human skull whose origin she would not explain. Sergei would have been a fine business accomplice, but the guitarist had already expressed disinterest in the proceedings, as they detracted from time spent practicing guitar.

When he didn't answer, Gillian continued, "Did the band . . . how did they take the news about my sabbatical?"

Christof wanted to chuck the phone into the desert. "Sabbatical? Is that what this is?"

Another sigh. "Maybe?"

"Then no, I haven't told the band, because I don't know *what to tell them*." And because he was an enormous coward and the guilt about his part in Gillian's departure made him want to claw his own awesome hair out. "I don't even know for sure why you've gone in the first place!"

"I told you. I needed to figure some things out. When you proposed—"

"I wasn't proposing," he rushed to emphasize. "I tried to explain. There was a guitar pick on the ground—"

"But Tof, that's not the point! That moment . . . it made me realize that I needed space to think . . ." There was some shuffling in the background on her end of the line, then the echo of a loudspeaker announcement in a language he didn't recognize. "I'm sorry. I have to go. Can I call you later?"

"Can you at least tell me where you are?"

"I'm . . . traveling."

"Okay, when will you be back? You are coming back, right?"

"I can't tell you that."

"Why not?"

"Because I don't know!" Her voice broke. "I told you in my email I needed space, and it's only been eight days."

"Nine," he gritted out. "It's been nine days."

"Why can't you, for once in your life, be patient?"

For once in my . . . is she serious? "Do you have any concept of what I'm dealing with? You know how difficult it is to manage this band, yes? And now we're in a foreign country, writing an album in a different language, and our keyboardist won't even commit to a firm date on when she'll be returning. We made a commitment to the label—"

"No, *we* didn't do anything!" she snarled in a tone he'd never heard from her before. "*You* made that decision. You made it before speaking to me, and you assumed I'd go along with it because it's what *you* wanted."

Well. That was true. But hadn't it been what Gillian wanted too? She'd never said anything to the contrary.

Or . . . perhaps he'd never bothered to ask.

Fuck.

Wiping sweat from his brow and cursing himself for not having worn his silk headband, he begrudgingly said, "You are correct. I apologize. That was very . . . poor form. And you have every right to be upset with me. I simply ask you think of Waldo, Sibylle, and Sergei. You know they worry about you." *Or they would, if they knew the truth.* "Until I can update them on your return, they cannot properly focus on composing new songs."

He stopped at an intersection and waited for the stretch limousine barreling down the road to pass. As it approached, the heat-blurred air revealed a passenger jutting up from the sunroof with their arms raised, and when the vehicle whooshed past, a *"Yeehaw!"* echoed in its wake. Christof shook his head at the irresponsibility of it all. The risk of injury, the insects, the badly tangled hair . . . why were Americans so foolish and self-indulgent?

Gillian finally answered, "Give me two weeks."

He squinted at the receding limo. Something wasn't right. Why did that "Yeehaw!" sound familiar? "Two weeks," he repeated, but his focus was on the sudden notion that the passenger's long hair and shirtless silhouette were strikingly identical to Waldo's.

Where would Waldo have acquired a limousine? And with what money? Waldo was constantly losing his own credit card and had already done so this week. He'd also purportedly gambled away his American dollars at the slot machine in the gas station, leaving himself essentially penniless until his new card arrived in the mail.

". . . and he's been helping me with that. So by then, I'll have a clearer answer for you," Gillian was saying.

Suddenly, Christof had a flashback to earlier that morning, when Waldo had popped into the room during Christof's yoga practice and demanded the band's credit card to buy Trolli worms from . . . *the gas station.*

He was going to kill his drummer.

"Are you listening to me?"

"Ja, ja," he muttered, shielding his forehead with a hand and squinting down the two-lane road. It was no use—the limo was too far away to make out details now. But it did seem to be heading in the direction of the glowing **La Rose Resort & Spa: 15 miles** sign, and that narrowed things quite a bit.

"I'm so glad you understand. Thank you, Tof, this means the world to me. Anyway, I should go . . ."

Still distracted, he said his goodbyes and hung up.

Two weeks wasn't so terrible. If he told the band the truth now . . .

No, if Gillian was coming back, it made no sense. It would only impede their productivity on the album.

As for Erika, Christof could keep putting Nachtmusik's success before his own needs and desires for a little longer. When Gillian returned, everything would return to normal, and he'd finally be able to devote proper attention to romancing Erika.

Yes, that was the most efficient way to do things. In the meantime, he merely needed to keep his band out of trouble for two weeks. How hard could it be?

CHAPTER 10

Erika stared at the dim blue glow her phone screen cast on the ceiling over her bed and tried to resist the urge to succumb to her wicked impulses.

Like going to the theater to spy on Christof. *Again.*

Erika had expected to spend the week dodging Christof so that she didn't have to rely on her nonexistent self-control to make good choices, but apparently she needn't have bothered—he'd avoided her right back. At most, she'd caught secondhand evidence of his existence: a light under his door, a snippet of passing complaint about something he'd done from Waldo or Sibylle, or the lingering whiff of his cedar-forest scent in a hallway.

Which was a good thing.

Yet despite having had zero contact with Christof until this morning, she hadn't been able to stop thinking about him. It definitely hadn't helped that she'd been compelled to keep stalking his late-night solo concerts. She'd found a place in the back of Box Five where he couldn't see her from the stage but she could see him perfectly. A bag of chocolate-covered pretzels and a plush pillow to rest against, and Erika had herself a private, VIP concert experience.

He was good, she'd decided. *Very good.* His voice was a lush, layered natural tenor with an impressively expansive range. With proper training, he could rival some of the best Broadway singers she knew. Except as it was right now, he abused the hell out of his voice and was on a fast track to vocal surgery by forty. And some of the songs that he was working on for the album were painfully close to being ready. She'd been unable to stop herself from humming some of the protomelodies under her breath, making tiny tweaks and corrections as she went. If she could give him a few notes . . . a pointer here and there . . .

No, what she *should* be focusing her time on was the fact that Raoul Decomte's assistant had sent her two emails—and left a voice mail—requesting a meeting. The Paris Opera House was in the casino emperor's crosshairs, and all Erika had managed to do with Nachtmusik's money was temporarily stave off early slaughter by the bank. At least she had a plan for getting the business permit she needed to make Nachtmusik's venue rental actually, well, *legal*. The theater needed to pass its fire inspection to get that permit, but according to Grandma Meg's records, Hank, the county's fire marshal, apparently loved being gifted tickets to the hometown Aces WNBA games. So much so that he'd given this godforsaken tinderbox a perfect score on its annual inspection, year after year. And once Erika had that permit and didn't have to worry about having her whole operation shut down, she'd be able to focus on finding some way to keep Raoul's bulldozers from pawing at the front doors.

For the first time since she'd arrived in Paris and discovered that her so-called fresh start was a stinking mire of debt, she'd finished a Friday afternoon with a sense that she was swimming toward the surface.

Thanks to Christof. Her knight in shining . . . gold pants.

Ugh, you're pathetic. Erika shoved her covers back and snatched her phone off the cracked-leather whipping post she used as a nightstand—2:16 a.m. Great. Sleep clearly wasn't in her near future. At least Christof usually wrapped up his private rehearsals by now, so Erika could have the theater to herself. There was no grand piano there, like the one she'd played growing up, but the old-fashioned pipe organ made for a reasonable substitute. Besides, pouring her misery out through something so opulent yet melancholic soothed her thespian's soul.

She shrugged on her floor-length black silk robe. This time of year, the temperature rarely dipped below sixty degrees at night, but she'd rather not waltz around the opera house in only the strappy nightgown she wore to bed. The matching ensemble was one of the few nice things she'd kept from her former life—an apology gift from one of Tom Ford's designers, who'd stood her up on a date after receiving a last-minute invite to Julianne Moore's pool party in Montauk. The silk pulled tight around her hips now that she was no longer a size nothing, but the fabric was decadently cool against her skin, and the robe rippled like a midnight waterfall when she walked, so she adored it. Plus, wearing it made her feel like a glamorously tragic stage actress—not the pathetic, self-pitying has-been she saw every morning in the mirror.

She glanced at her rat cage, where Jean and Javert were busy doing their favorite activities—eating and gnawing at the cage bars, respectively.

"Don't get into any trouble while I'm gone," she instructed. Using her phone as a flashlight, she made her way up through the brothel's main floor and through the tunnel toward the backstage entrance.

Christof had turned off the lights when he'd finished, leaving the theater dimly lit. Only the glowing exit signs and a single row of wall-mounted wash lights illuminated her path to the organ. Erika wove her way through the rows of seating, letting her fingertips trail along the time-smoothed wood at the top of each chair.

She would play the Bach piece. Sure, it was cliché, but it was the one she was most familiar with on the organ, and she didn't feel like reading sheet music on her tiny phone screen tonight. She needed to lose herself in the act of expressing something beautiful.

Untying the sash on her robe so she could sweep it behind her, she settled herself in the curve of the organ's bench and lit the rose-scented jar candle atop the console that she reserved for this purpose. Then she ran her splayed fingers across the keys. They felt both familiar and strange under her touch—like a piano, yet not. It had been quite the transition, going from the percussive piano to what was essentially a wind instrument, but this was far from her first sleepless night here at the Paris Opera House.

"Hello, handsome," she murmured.

In her mind, she was greeting a lover. Teasing him with a caress before she began to stroke him in earnest. The instrument wasn't Christof—or any other man who might sate her longing for human touch. For connection. But her relationship with music had never let her down the way humans had either. This was the safest way to find release.

Breath filled her lungs. Her eyes closed. And she began to play.

She's bewitching me.

Christof watched Erika play from the shadows of the balcony's first row and fought the all-consuming urge to rush downstairs, prostrate himself at her feet, and pray to his new muse.

Her haunting song burst free of the organ's pipes, air rushing from each chamber in plaintive wails. It was a song he recognized—though not by name—yet Erika seemed to *do* something to it. Something different. It sounded as if she were pouring her secrets out onto the ivory keys—and if it was a confession, it was not a pious one.

And the way she moved over the manuals, her spine curved forward, her silk robe trailing behind her . . . she was a seductive spider, spinning an invisible web for his ears alone.

He'd never wanted anything so badly as to be her prey.

He should have let her know he was there before she'd started playing. But he'd been a coward. Afraid that he'd have to explain why he was still awake. Why he was hiding in the shadowed first row of one of the private boxes, still staring at the same empty page he'd meant to write lyrics on when he'd come up here five hours earlier. He should have gone back to his room, but he'd been wandering about the second-level seating in restless exploration and found a pillow in this intimate space that smelled like roses, along with a half-eaten bag of bitter-chocolate pretzel sweets. And he'd wondered.

He'd spent all afternoon convincing himself he was *glad* Gillian had called when she had, because in the span of the single week since he'd met Erika, he'd managed to forget that the band always came first. That focus was key to success.

So here he was. Secretly watching his obsession play the pipe organ while he pretended he wasn't thinking about bending her forward over those four rows of black and white, fisting her silk nightgown until it bunched at the tops of her generous thighs, and impaling her from behind with his hard cock.

He'd demand she keep playing while he fucked her, wouldn't he?

As soon as he thought it, his skin felt too hot and tight. Shame. What was wrong with him? He'd *never* have thought to do something so controlling with Gillian. She'd have defenestrated him for even suggesting it.

But Erika . . . she'd implied that she'd like that sort of thing.

He'd insist she keep the rhythm and make no mistakes. And should she err, he'd punish her by withdrawing the fingers over her clit and stilling his thrusts, until she began again from the beginning. He'd let her come only when she played the piece flawlessly.

He sucked in air through his teeth and tried to ignore the fact that his cock was so hard it strained against the stiff material of his coated denim pants, and he could feel his pulse throbbing and his muscles tensing in anticipation of overdue release that he could not have. Not here. Not now.

It would be best if he returned to his room and took care of himself. Maybe once he'd taken his cock in hand and finished the job his imagination had started, he could finally sleep.

He tried to slowly lift himself out of his seat, moving as quietly as possible—but he'd forgotten about the leather journal in his lap.

Thunk.

He prayed she wouldn't hear it over the organ's bellowing, but the sound echoed loudly in the empty auditorium. He froze in place, but it was too late.

The music stopped. Erika spun, her gaze flying up to pinpoint his exact location with what seemed like preternatural dark vision until he realized that half standing as he was, the top of his head was perfectly backlit by the sole light illuminating the hallway behind him.

He saw her lips part in surprise, but no sound came out. He imagined her quiet gasp anyway and somehow felt the shimmer of her exhalation on his skin, because his flesh tightened like she'd done something terribly intimate to him, and his cock throbbed with new urgency. He registered the warm drip of precum against his thigh and fought the urge to press his hand over it—to hide his shame—even though the waist-high balcony wall shielded his lower half from view.

Her gaze trapped him. Held him in limbo, unable to move. Dimly, he knew he should apologize for not letting her know he was there. He *should*.

Another second passed. Then another.

She seemed to consider him, even though it was hard to read her expression. The flickering candle atop the organ cast the right half of her face in golden light; the left remained in shadow. She was probably wondering why he was poised there like a blushing boy caught fondling himself in the back of math class.

Inwardly cursing his own cowardice, he finally drew all the way up. If he was going to lurk like a creeping sex fiend, he might as well have the spine to own it.

He opened his mouth, about to sputter some excuse he hadn't concocted yet, but Erika stopped him with a finger to her lips.

What's this?

Then, slowly, her hands lowered to untie the sash at her waist. Fingertips trailed up her torso and lingered over the swells of her breasts before continuing upward. Then the robe came slipping down over the golden curves of her shoulders, revealing the graceful expanse of her collarbones, and from above, he had a premium view of her generous, braless chest dipping into the low neckline of her thin-strapped sheath.

His mouth was suddenly parched. His head felt too light. His hands closed over the banister in front of him, and he wasn't sure if it was to help himself stay upright or to prevent his hands from straying. *She can't see below my waist from where she sits . . .*

He gripped even harder—until the wood groaned under duress.

Christof had never been with a woman with such a bounty of cleavage. Even though Erika's posture screamed, *Look at me, mortal, and bow before my magnificent bosom,* Christof fought the urge to politely look away. Because, well, it was *wrong* and a bit shallow and possibly even a shade misogynistic to drool over large breasts . . . wasn't it?

Look at those poor girls . . . aren't they cold with their chests hanging out like that? Gillian would often remark as they pushed through throngs of lingering fans, and Christof would dutifully agree that, yes, he felt only sorrow for the plight of breasts too abundant to be carefully stowed away behind the protective warmth of a modest neckline. And once safe on the tour bus and shielded from the dangerous onslaught of chilled nipples pressing against too-tight spandex, he'd assure Gillian that he loved her petite, sprite-like physique—and he hadn't been lying, because he *had* appreciated Gillian exactly as she was. But late at night, while she slept peacefully beside him and he stared at yet another hotel room ceiling, wrestling with the odd feeling that all the fame and fortune and success they'd built were about to catastrophically collapse around them and this dire fate could only be averted with enough careful planning, he'd soothe himself to sleep by imagining how his hands would warm those overlarge breasts he'd seen to nobly drive away the specter of hypothermia.

Erika was still staring at him with that dark, unreadable gaze, as if waiting for him to do something.

Should he applaud? Compliment her beauty? But as soon as he thought it, her hands moved again, sliding back down to cup her own breasts. And then her thumbs came up to press against the silk where her nipples peaked the fabric, and she bit her lip as if to stifle a whimper.

And the whole time, she watched him. Made sure he saw.

Spots danced in front of his eyes, reminding him to breathe. He sucked in a shallow breath, then another, but she was still watching him, and he suddenly sensed she was still performing. That he was her audience now, and he shouldn't make any sound at all.

Did she want him to—

No, of course she didn't want him to do *that*.

He could watch without unbuttoning his fly to relieve the pressure on his erection. He would stay still as she shifted, swinging one leg, then the other, over the bench to face him with her back to the organ. He must continue to remain in control of himself, even when a languid hand strayed lower and dragged that silk skirt up her thighs, bunching it shy of the shadowy apex between them.

Her head tilted back, cascading her midnight locks all over the rows of keys behind her.

Much, much later that night, he'd realize that if she hadn't been positioned with the candle above and to the right of the console, casting her features in shadow, he'd have seen all of the face she'd kept half-hidden during the day. But during that exact span of moments, he wasn't looking at her face, and he most certainly wasn't *thinking* about her face. At all. What a disrespectful, deviant man he was, to be fixated so entirely on the path of her hand as it trailed—

Oh, sweet fuck . . . she's really doing it.

One hand still cupped her breast, teasing the silk-clothed tip between thumb and forefinger. The other came between her legs. He couldn't see what she was doing beneath the shadow of her gown, but he *knew*. He knew when she touched herself, because her gloriously bare thighs, spread just wide enough to allow access, tensed. And in the twilight stillness of the theater, her muted gasp echoed like a thunderclap. Her hand moved, slowly exploring. Then faster, with more precision. The curve of her belly jumped, tensing as she quickened her rhythm, then relaxed as she seemed to force herself to slow.

A minute passed—two minutes? Three? Maybe more, but he couldn't tell, because time had lost all meaning. Fire coursed up his spine. His abdomen was tightening with near-painful intensity, twisting with that hot, familiar tension that in normal circumstances would be shortly followed by cum exploding from his cock. But that wasn't happening now. Obviously. He wasn't stroking himself; he hadn't even moved. He was being so responsible. So courteous. It wasn't like he'd never seen a woman touch herself before.

In an empty, silent theater. For his eyes only.

Wait—was she thinking about *him*?

He couldn't stifle the groan—not entirely. He tried, pressing his lips tight, but it came up through his throat and vibrated through his clenched teeth and jaw.

She must have heard him, because even though he couldn't see her expression, he sensed she'd turned to look at him. Saw a brief glint of light reflecting off her eyes.

Her hips lifted off the bench, bucking toward him, and then suddenly she was sitting forward. For a brief, stricken moment, he was sure he'd offended her. Made her stop. But then she threw her head back again, and he saw she was trembling uncontrollably, the fingers at her nipple clenched in feverish strain and her bare toes curled in ecstasy.

And somehow, he held on to a single thread of control.

Until she let out a single hushed moan.

97

He tore his eyes away, but it was too late. Frantic, he scrabbled for the snap of his jeans, thrust his hand inside, and gripped his cock. It took a single stroke.

He held his breath, every muscle in his body seizing as the orgasm slammed into him so hard that he would have doubled over if his left hand hadn't still been gripping the banister for dear life. An airless curse ripped out of his chest. Hot cum filled his other palm.

On and on it went, wringing him dry with the pent-up force of every pleasure he'd denied himself since he'd gotten here. Hell, longer than that. Months of stifled needs. *Years* of repressed desires.

When he finally finished, his body hot and his mind numb and every last muscle thoroughly worn out, he dared to look at Erika. He expected scorn. Or disappointment, even. What kind of man came in his pants? That sort of thing wasn't done.

But she wasn't looking at him at all.

She primly smoothed her skirt down and gathered her robe, slipping it on with so much grace that he thought he might have imagined her spasming in the throes of ecstasy only moments earlier. Then she stood, blew out the candle, neatly tucked the bench into place, and walked away from him. All without a single backward glance in his direction.

He should say something, shouldn't he? Thank her for the most unbelievably erotic experience of his whole damn life?

Cool air caressed his heated skin, reminding him he was still standing there with his dick in his hand, slicked with evidence of his own illicit orgasm. A feeling swept over him that wasn't *shame*, precisely, because even though he told himself he should feel guilty for what he'd done, he couldn't seem to summon the appropriately puritanical energy.

Still, when he opened his mouth to call to her, nothing came out, and a nervous tingling seemed to have taken up residence in his chest.

For the first time in his life, Christof experienced what it was like to be shy.

Only after she'd disappeared into the recesses of the stage—presumably returning to wherever she slept via the tunnel—did he notice the misshapen shadow of something small and delicate draped over the bottom row of organ keys. He leaned over the railing, squinting in the dim light. And then he realized.

She'd left him her lace thong.

CHAPTER 11

Erika couldn't concentrate on her Monday-morning emails.

Which was a problem, because she still had a lot of theater-related things to be concerned about. The fact that Hank hadn't called her back yet about that fire inspection, for one. Or that the few urgent repairs she'd made last week had already blown through what was left of Nachtmusik's deposit after covering the loan minimum, yet she was still at least one missed payment behind on nearly every utility bill.

Except she wasn't thinking about bills and responsibilities at all. Instead, she spun in her creaky chair and reveled in the thrill of what she'd done last night, biting her lip to stifle the smug grin that threatened to steal over her face.

She imagined Christof discovering the gift she'd left for him, and bubbles of glee danced in her veins. She crossed her legs to soothe the residual flare of heat that came when she recalled the tortured expression on his face. When her memory replayed his rough groan, Erika fanned herself with an overdue invoice.

Erika had always wanted to do something like that, but she never had. Though she wouldn't technically call herself an exhibitionist, her years in theater had spurred more than a few performance-centered fantasies. Christof had given her the perfect opportunity to fulfill one of them.

And she would bet all the money she didn't have that *he* sure as hell hadn't had a woman masturbate for him in an empty theater before. She was his first. And because she was a Leo by birth and a diva by training, that fact made her ego purr.

Somewhere beneath all that gloating was her beleaguered conscience, whining, *Stop being proud of yourself. You know what you did was a bad idea.* What if Christof thought her private show was a green light to get down and freaky on a nightly basis?

Erika shivered, despite the heat, and sucked in a breath to recenter herself in the present.

Just in time for reality to come barreling into her office in platform goth boots.

"Hallo, have you seen Waldo? Also, do you have a bar for prying?"

Erika jumped, clicking her email window closed on instinct, even though the X-rated material was all in her head.

"Good morning, Sibylle," Erika said, pouring on the syrup to distract from her flushed cheeks. "No, I don't know where Waldo is. How have you been settling in this past week? It's not too hot in the attic, is it?"

Sibylle rolled her eyes. "Ja, good morning. To me, it's very hot. And that is why I need a—"

"I can't let you pry the windows open with a crowbar."

"Crowbar," Sibylle repeated slowly, rolling the word around on her tongue. Likely memorizing it so she could ask someone else for one. "And why not?"

"I believe the windows are originals, so there's lead in them. And the paint too. Wouldn't want you to get lead poisoning."

"I am not afraid of poison."

"Of course not. It's simply that the opera house can't afford any more gruesome deaths. Just in case, could you provide me a quick bio for your ghost dossier?" Erika picked up her pen and waited.

Sibylle scowled. "Very well. I will not make the windows open."

"Is there anything else—"

Sibylle stomped off.

Erika shook her head and reopened her email. Now, she would focus.

A prickling down her spine warned that someone was watching her. Her L-shaped desk had a side facing the door, but Grandma Meg's ancient computer monitor only fit in the corner, which required Erika to angle herself so the door was a hair out of her peripheral vision. She cautiously swiveled in the chair and found the vamp—er, Sergei—lurking in the hallway, outside the office's threshold.

"You can come in," she offered, in case he was waiting for an invitation.

He tilted his head to decline. "Waldo is not here?"

Erika made a show of looking around her office, which was small enough that if a tall person with long, elegant limbs—like, say, Christof—were to stand in the middle, he'd be able to touch both walls.

"Apologies for the disturbance," Sergei said, silently receding into the hallway.

Shaking her head, she whispered, "Creeeeepy."

She opened the next email. Ooh, look at that, a sale at Victoria's Secret—those *never* happened. She started to drag the email to her trash bin, then hesitated.

It wasn't like she was planning on giving away more of her underthings. And she didn't really have the budget for silk and lace right now. But she was rather low on underthings in general, wasn't she?

Is Christof more of a demure-bows-and-lace man or a fire-engine-red-and-crotchless sort of man? Erika snorted. Definitely the latter, though he'd probably get all flushed and bothered at the word *crotchless.* What a contradiction he was. A rock star who dressed like an überconfident sex god, and yet he'd blushed at the idea of ordering her around in the bedroom.

She wondered if it had been hard for him to be so faithful to Gillian, with the fans and the touring lifestyle. So many temptations to resist. And if his bedroom life with his ex had fizzled years ago, that kind of self-denial would wind anyone up tight.

What a good boy Christof had pretended to be . . . before he'd met Erika. Last night had revealed that he was actually quite bad, indeed, and it would take oh so little to coax that badness out.

Good thing she was such a good person now that she wouldn't even *think* of doing that.

Wiggling in her chair, she carefully restored the email to her inbox. For browsing only. When she was done with her work.

She clicked on the next email down.

Stomp, stomp, stomp. Sibylle announced without preamble, "I require use of an extension cord."

Erika blinked at her inbox in surprise. It was a personal message from Raoul. Ms. Greene, it read. My assistant, Maurice, informs you are rather challenging to reach, but I assume this is because you are well occupied running your business. As an ardent disciple of profit myself, I admire your devotion to the cause. Nevertheless, should you find a moment to step away this weekend, it would be my pleasure to host you as an honored guest at my premier property in Las Vegas, Carte Blanche Hotel and Casino. Every expense will be with my compliments, of course. All I ask for is a few moments of your time to discuss a mutually beneficial proposition. Bien cordialement, Raoul.

"Are you not hearing me?"

Erika blinked and gave Sibylle her full attention. "What do you need an extension cord for?"

The bassist's chin rose. "Required changes to my amplifier connection."

"Yeah? What kind of changes?"

"Changes."

Erika smiled, and this time she showed her teeth. "I already told Sergei earlier this morning that the stage circuits can't handle any more than ten connections."

Sibylle narrowed her eyes. "It will go to eleven."

"It does *not* go to elev—"

With an ominous pop and her computer's whirring exhalation of death, the power went out.

Erika stormed toward the auditorium, Sibylle at her heels. Even from the hallway, she could smell the acrid afterburn of a blown electrical circuit, and there were faint wisps of white smoke illuminated in the morning light streaming in through the foyer's stained glass windows. Her temple began to throb at the thought of what it would cost to get an electrician to come out today—if she could even *find* one on such short notice.

At that moment, Christof pushed through the entry doors with a take-out bag in hand, his expression cheerful despite the sheen of sweat on his forehead. Even his long fluffy hair drooped from the morning's already oppressive heat. At least his smoky eyeliner was pristine. Today, he wore snow-leopard-patterned pants and an oxblood velvet bomber jacket—once again, no shirt. Only a length of black silk looped once around his neck.

The minute he registered the scene, the smile melted off his gorgeous face.

"What happened?" he demanded, dropping the bag. For a brief moment, his gaze caught on her, and the tail of his snake tattoo twitched with his sharp inhalation of breath.

She knew, without a shadow of a doubt, he was thinking about last night. And despite the fury coursing through her, her yearning lady parts clenched in want. Did he have the thong with him? Had he woken up this morning thinking of her and gripped his morning hard-on with her lace wrapped around his fist? Had he been deliciously perverted and held it up to his face to inhale her scent—

"Do not be upset, Big Brother. It was an accident."

He looked past Erika to fix his glare on Sibylle, and his jaw hardened. "What have you done?"

Sergei materialized from the darkness of the auditorium. "It was my error. I wished to increase the volume of my amplifier."

"We've talked about this," Christof said.

"We have. And I informed you I cannot play guitar under these conditions. I need more power."

"Well! Now you have none, so there will certainly be no playing now. If you had *listened* to me . . ." Christof threw up both his hands. He was the eternally aggrieved band manager, agent, and front man, and he was rolled up so tight Erika half expected his insides to start pouring out his ears. "And where is Waldo?"

No one answered.

Sibylle muttered under her breath, "This would not have happened if Gillian were here."

Erika was torn between pity for Christof and annoyance, since he *was* responsible for these clowns. But when it came to preserving the one thing she had left that mattered, Erika couldn't let her lust turn into accident forgiveness.

Time to take charge.

She cleared her throat. "I'm going to get a flashlight and take a look at the circuit breaker backstage. I'll assess the damage and go from there. I assume you all have cell service, so when I return, I expect to see a list of available electricians." Before anyone could whine about it, she added in a sugary-sweet tone, "After all, the sooner we repair *and upgrade* the unit . . . at your band's expense, of course . . . the sooner Sergei can play guitar at whatever obnoxious volume his little heart desires."

She took exactly two steps toward her office—and saw the woman standing outside, her hand cupped to peer through the glass door into the lightless entryway.

Erika's stomach plummeted.

The visitor wore the same red polo shirt with the fire department logo that Hank used to wear. But this wasn't Hank, the bushy-bearded Santa look-alike who took bribes and cheerfully signed flawless inspection reports. This was a stocky Asian woman with cropped salt-and-pepper hair, an unamused expression on her face and a no-nonsense clipboard tucked under her arm.

"Shit," Erika whispered. She turned to the band. "You all need to scram. The fire marshal is here."

Sibylle asked, "Why? Sergei did not set a fire."

A pause. "The stage is not currently on fire," Sergei said.

"I don't know. But you all need to hide your bags and shit. Make it look like you're not staying in the brothel in case they're here to do an inspection." Erika shooed them away, and Sergei and Sibylle scurried off.

The woman rapped on the glass. Her muffled voice came through and said, "Can you open up, please? I'm Jocelyn Song with the Paris County Fire Department."

Christof lingered. His beautiful mouth was pressed flat with concern. "Can I assist you with this? Perhaps I can speak to her. Women find me very charming."

Erika bit her lip. Back in New York, she'd always had other people offering to fix her problems for her. Simpering "friends" who wanted to buy social currency, stagehands who were too terrified of her to say no, or privileged men who thought if they threw enough money and influence her way, they'd get a clandestine blowjob out of it.

God, she missed being pretty and popular. Being an independent, empowered, adult woman was absolute bullshit sometimes.

Bless Christof for offering, though. Maybe he'd get a clandestine blowjob out of it anyway.

She shook her head and asked him to double-check whatever Sergei and Sibylle had gotten up to in the auditorium to make sure there were no further electrical hazards they needed to hide. He didn't argue.

Erika took a breath to settle into character, then let Jocelyn inside.

"Sorry it's so dark in here!" she trilled, as breezily as if it were a minor, everyday thing. "I was vacuuming, and I think it tripped the breaker. You know how these old buildings are."

Jocelyn's hawkish gaze swept the entry before landing on Erika. A tight, obligatory smile flashed across her face, then quickly disappeared. Jocelyn didn't even do a double take at Erika's scars. "You're the owner?"

"Erika Greene. How can I help you?" Erika pretended to notice the logo on Jocelyn's shirt. "Oh! You're with the fire department. How's Hank? My grandma Meg and I used to love getting visits from him." Okay, that was a fib—Erika had never been to visit Paris while Grandma Meg was alive. Her socialite mother had warned that Erika would be better off having nothing to do with her no-good daddy's side of the family. If only she'd listened.

"Couldn't say. Heard he retired. Moved to Florida."

"Oh."

"I transferred out here from Clark County at the beginning of the month to take over his role as fire marshal." *Shit.* "Just getting around to introducing myself to all the businesses in town. Figured you should get used to seeing my face, since you'll be seeing a lot of me this summer. Looks like we're due for another dry one, and I pride myself on fire control through prevention." *Double shit.* "Oh, and I received an anonymous tip suggesting that you might be renting this theater out as a performance venue, and I can't seem to find your current inspection report on file. You know anything about that?" *Shiiiiiiiiiittttt.*

"That's odd," Erika forced out through her tight throat. "I feel like Hank was *just* here."

She'd thought Hank was in the bag—a done deal.

But Hank was in Florida.

Which meant Erika was so, so very fucked.

Jocelyn unhooked a small flashlight from her belt and smacked it against her palm in a way that looked vaguely threatening. "Why don't we start by taking a look at that breaker box?"

An hour later, Erika closed the door behind Jocelyn, strode to the foyer's western staircase, and let herself collapse on the bottom step like a deflating balloon. She threw the stack of fire-code violations up in the air so they fluttered around her in clumps.

Boots sounded on the steps above her, and she tilted her head back to treat herself to an upside-down view of Christof's gorgeous, towering form. His green-gold eyes scanned her sprawled body, full of concern, and despite her dour mood, warmth suffused her whole being. His gaze had felt the same way on her skin last night too. Erika bit her lip at the memory, and his eyes locked on her mouth—and then tore away.

He cleared his throat, but his voice was still rough when he spoke. "The inspection did not go well?"

Erika groaned in answer.

Hug me, she wished she could tell him. *Tell me everything's going to be okay.* But that was ridiculous, because she barely knew him. Besides, two other sets of footsteps in the entryway warned her that Sibylle and Sergei were back, and they thought Christof was still with Gillian. Not a smart idea to let on that there was anything romantic going on.

And there wasn't . . . yet.

Sibylle's head popped into view, her thin brows raised in amusement. "And I thought *I* was dramatic."

"I was in *theater*, okay?" Erika snapped, but she pushed up to her elbows anyway so she looked less pathetic. "At least there's an electrician on the way, thanks to Jocelyn's pull with some company in Vegas." Erika didn't even want to think about the cost, but that was the least of her concerns. The "problem areas" Jocelyn had identified were so numerous that Erika was surprised the Paris Opera House wasn't already a pile of ash.

Now Erika had forty-five days to get the opera house up to code, or Jocelyn would shut the whole place down and Erika could be fined $1,000 a day until repairs were made—or worse. *A few months in the slammer.*

Erika was absolutely fucking *not* going to give everyone in Paris the satisfaction of gloating that she was off to spend quality jail time with her daddy.

Christof picked up one of the pages of the report and wordlessly inspected it. After a moment's consideration, he descended the steps and began collecting the rest of the papers. "There appear to be many safety hazards here. This may not be the safest place to rehearse."

Sweat broke out on Erika's palms. He wasn't thinking about leaving, was he? Without Nachtmusik's rent for the next two months, Erika wouldn't even be able to buy a hammer, much less an entire contractor. "Don't be silly! These are tiny, simple little fixes I can have done right away."

He held up the top sheet. "Installing a fire-suppressant system in the auditorium? This could be weeks of disruption."

"I can have it done at night." Her heart raced. *I'll do anything,* she silently added . . . as if there were anything Christof could ask of her that she hadn't wanted to do with him already.

"I'm responsible for Nachtmusik's safety. The band always comes first." Christof placed the last paper atop the stack and handed it to her, his full lips pressed into a firm line. "I'll call La Rose and see if they have available space."

He still wouldn't look at her. And suddenly, Erika knew what this was really about: he'd liked watching her last night, and it terrified him. He felt it, too—the obsession. The sense that if they gave in to whatever inexorable flame drew them together, it would incinerate them both, and neither of them would care. Not when it felt so good.

Coward.

"We have a contract that says you'll stay for two months," Erika bit out.

"We have an email exchange," he countered, his voice equally terse. His gaze was fixed on a point over her left shoulder. "I advise you not to press this matter when you've been operating without proper permitting."

Somewhere in Erika's chest, a trapdoor opened and her last shred of hope fell through. Christof's hair was fluffy, but his mind was slick as hell. If he weren't about to abandon her to this new, even-lower-than-before rock bottom, she'd be turned on by it.

Sibylle scoffed, "Good luck getting compromise from Herr Stinkstiefel."

"I am not the stinky boot," Christof bit out. "Do you think I *want* to be the bad guy, always?"

"Why not? You are so good at it. Come on, Sergei. We pack our bags."

Sergei nodded.

When his sister and guitarist were gone, Christof finally looked at her again, his hazel eyes full of regret. "I'm sorry. It's for the best."

Erika stood on the second step so that she could meet him at eye level. Then she dusted off the backs of her thighs, smoothed her hair over her shoulder, looked him square in his angelically fuckable face, and summoned her diva within. "I'm keeping the four-week deposit," she told him.

"Erika—"

"And charging for an additional week. For the inconvenience."

He reached for her hand, and for some reason, she let him take it, even though it undermined the imperious aura she was going for.

His fingers were callused and hot; his grip was firm. His thumb brushed along the sensitive flesh between her pinkie and wrist. Unnerving static spread from that single graze. It swept up her arm, coiled down past her budded nipples, and lit up every nerve ending along the way.

In a low voice, he said, "It would be a bad idea to stay." They both knew he wasn't talking about the renovations.

"Is it?" Then she shifted her hand in his grip, coiling her fingers out from under his to take control as she wrapped them around his wrist.

Desperate times . . .

She tugged.

He stumbled forward, boots running into the lowest stair, before he stepped up so he was directly in front of her. His breathing went uneven. Raspy.

Last night hadn't taken the edge off. Not at all. It had only soaked the edge in napalm, and now she'd tossed a match between them and started an inferno.

He swallowed. "We shouldn't."

She pretended he was still talking about the venue. "Stay and find out. Take a risk, for once. You might like it."

"Anyone could see us."

That wasn't entirely true. The stairwell was mostly out of range of the daylight streaming in through the front doors, and without the lights on, anyone peering in from outside wouldn't be able to see a thing. And what were the odds that Sibylle and Sergei would come back so soon? Erika took bigger risks in her sleep.

But Christof didn't, did he? He probably found this tiny whiff of danger excruciating.

"So?" She looked at him through her lashes, knowing the darkness and the fall of her hair hid the way her lips quirked in wicked satisfaction at his torment. "We're not doing anything wrong." *Yet.*

"We are standing very close."

"Is that a crime?"

"If I leaned forward . . ."

She raised a brow. "So don't, then. You're in control."

He swayed closer, then stopped. Seemed to catch himself. Drew back. His forest-floor eyes squeezed shut. "I'm in control," he repeated, but it came out strained.

She almost pitied him. Except her own control wasn't much more than a facade. His proximity lit her up like a thousand spotlights. Heat coursed through her and made its way down to melt the tight core between her legs. And she hadn't even kissed him yet.

I need this, bad. The temptation to make up his mind for him—to take the kiss he so clearly wanted—was a powerful drug. She fought it anyway.

It wouldn't be right, her conscience reminded her.

Yes, that was why.

Not because she was a greedy, wicked woman who wanted to taste his capitulation on her tongue.

"Live a little. No one will know."

He opened his eyes. "Only once," he warned.

Yessss. The jolt of pure elation that went through her kicked her pulse into overdrive.

"Only once," she lied.

His fingers twined with hers and tugged her until she skidded to the edge of the stair, teetering. He steadied her by clamping his free hand on her waist, as if they were about to begin waltzing, but he wasn't gentlemanly about it. His grip was strong, his movements rough and jerky.

Breath stuck in her throat, and she must have made a noise, because his brow creased as he searched her expression—and then he seemed to realize. This was what she wanted. *Needed.* His pupils expanded.

His lashes lowered to half mast, and he leaned in—

Someone pounded on the front door.

CHAPTER 12

The pounding snapped Erika back to earth.

Christof jerked back so quickly he lost his balance, and he would have dragged her down with him if he hadn't let go to latch on to the railing. "Scheiße!"

For an interminable second, Erika stood there in a haze of lust, blinking, her body unwilling to recognize that the prize she'd fought so hard to win had been ripped away.

The pounding came again, and the thought of the glass door shattering set her in motion. Through the glass, she could see the culprit was a tall Paiute woman with an impressively muscled silhouette and a familiar glare. It was Lucy Crane, La Rose's head of security, and she was accompanied by a man who looked disturbingly similar to Waldo, except this version was pantsless, soaking wet, and clearly unable to stand without assistance.

Lucy's voice came through the door, muffled. "If you don't open up, I'm leaving him here!"

And she would do it, too, out of spite. Lucy was not a fan of the Greenes, and fairly so—Grandma Meg had gotten banned from La Rose for failing to pay her bar tab, and Erika's dad had gotten arrested breaking into the spa and stealing all the salt lamps from the treatment rooms.

Lucy probably wouldn't have held any of that against Erika if Erika hadn't accidentally backed into Lucy's brand-new Tesla a few days after arriving in Paris. (Was it really Erika's fault that her driving was abysmal? It wasn't like she'd needed a driver's license in Manhattan!)

Erika darted around Christof and shoved the door open.

"Lucy! Wow, so good to see you." Erika beamed as hard as Lucy was scowling.

Lucy grunted and nodded to Waldo. "This yours?"

"Whasssuuuuuppppp!" Waldo waggled his eyebrows and lurched forward—and tumbled into a heap in the doorway. Undeterred, he flopped onto his back and stared up at Erika and Lucy with a sloppy grin. "America, so beautiful! *Amerrrrrrica, Amerrrrricca, daaa naaa naaa* . . ." What followed was a four-bar musical interlude vaguely recognizable as "America the Beautiful."

"We found him eating chicken wings in the lobby fountain. He told us he was staying here, which is interesting, considering I was unaware that the Paris Opera House and Brothel was coded for residence of any kind," Lucy said.

Erika gasped with concern. "Poor thing. He must be very confused."

"Mmm-hmm."

Waldo's singing cut off as he chuckled. "Ja, ja . . . ich bin ein land shark."

"Yes, he kept pulling guests aside to inform them of this." Lucy took a deep breath, as if mustering reserves of patience. "There were . . . *complaints.*"

"I'm surprised you didn't call the cops."

Lucy's eyes narrowed. "That's not how we do things at La Rose. But this one is permanently barred from the premises."

Christof appeared at Erika's side, rage radiating off him like a furnace. "Waldo has been barred from the premises since the very first day. By *me.*"

"Feiern wir jetzt?"

"No, we are not partying right now!" Christof growled.

Erika fought the urge to hug Lucy. Now Nachtmusik couldn't stay at La Rose after all, and with Le Meilleur Ouest out of business . . .

When Lucy departed, Christof turned back to Waldo and continued, "There will be no more parties. No more fun. No more *indiscretions*."

That last part sounded awfully personal.

"From here on out, the album is our sole priority. No one leaves this place until we have at least one . . . no, three! Three songs ready for the album."

Erika gave Christof a sideways glance. "This does mean you're staying, right?"

"We're staying?" Sibylle said, suddenly reappearing in the lobby. With both hands, she dragged a long nylon duffel bag that had a striking resemblance to a human body stuffed into an anaconda's belly. When she saw their drummer sprawled on the floor in his smiley face briefs, her face lit up. "You found Waldo!"

"They have drugs in the shrimp," Waldo told her in a conspiratorial tone, producing a plastic baggie of what looked like chubby paper cocoons from *somewhere* and holding it aloft with pride.

"Where did you get the money for this? Tell me you didn't put it on the band's card," Christof demanded, snatching the contraband.

"Told them to put it on my tab."

"Your *tab*."

"Ja. Said you'd take care of it. You always take care of it."

"Then where is the card?" Christof asked.

Waldo blinked. "What card?"

Christof took a deep breath. Then he said tersely, "Your deepest wish is granted, Sibylle. You are about to personally witness a man's soul departing his body."

Sibylle sighed. "Calm down. I have it." She made the card in question materialize from the bosom of her shiny black corset and handed it over. "I needed to order some specialty items for the séance. Are we staying? Because if not, I need to make sure that package goes to the correct address."

Christof's jaw worked. "Yes. We stay for now."

"Wahoo!" Waldo cheered. Erika stifled the same reaction. Relief made her dizzy.

"For the sake of the album," Christof added.

Before anyone could reply, Waldo announced that he was definitely, *absolutely* going to vomit, and Christof whisked his drummer into the restroom.

Sibylle shrugged and shuffled off with her body bag, leaving Erika alone in the theater's dark lobby, reeling with whiplash from hopes being crushed and then rescued in such a short period of time. The Paris Opera House was being given one last lifeline, and she couldn't afford to screw this up.

Her gaze landed at the spot on the steps where she'd been mere seconds away from kissing Christof. Breath snagged in her throat. Yet the code violations clutched to her chest reminded her this was no time for fantasizing about what might have been. Better to leave Christof alone from now on; if he spooked again and moved Nachtmusik to another venue, this show was over. Curtain down, house lights on—and this grand staircase replaced by an Édith Piaf–themed waterslide.

Erika retreated to her office. Before she could second-guess herself, she replied to Raoul's offer—accepting it. She'd go to Las Vegas next weekend, hear him out, and . . . weigh her options. The gift of a mini vacation didn't mean she was obligated to accept a damn thing. Men had once lavished expensive presents on her with all sorts of expectations, and Erika had disappointed the vast majority of them.

CHAPTER 13

"You're only going to watch," she reminded her reflection. No letting Christof know she was in the back of Box Five, and *certainly* no more illicit performances. Look where *that* indiscretion had almost gotten her.

But the woman staring back at her didn't look the least bit guilty for planning another postmidnight theater sortie. In fact, her lips shone as if she'd reapplied stain, and her bare toes gleamed with a fresh coat of berry-hued polish.

It wasn't Old Erika in the mirror, but for the first time in two years, there were hints of familiarity. Skin flushed, eyes sparkling, insides tingling with anticipation . . . Erika felt more like herself than she had in a long time. The Old Erika hadn't been a good person, but she'd loved being alive, and above all, she'd *wanted* things and pursued them with vigor.

She'd forgotten what it was like to crave something so badly that her skin hummed with anticipation.

Not that I don't want *the opera house to succeed,* she mused as she ascended the stairs to the ground-floor sitting room. But that felt more like familial duty.

Wanting Christof was something akin to hunger.

Strains of song—an unplugged guitar overlaid with Christof's singing voice—filtered through the backstage door when she came out of the tunnel. This was where she usually kept walking and crept up the backstage stairs to the private seating level.

She peered around the curtain, pressing a hand to her stomach to quell the fluttering within. It was risky to spy on him from so close, which was exactly why she couldn't resist. Danger tasted good. Better than the dark-chocolate-covered pretzels she'd brought to snack on while she slunk around in the shadows, stalking her object of lust and playing at being the phantom of the opera house.

Christof was barefoot, standing in the middle of the stage wearing torn blue jeans and a black T-shirt with cut-off sleeves. If it weren't for his obnoxiously flashy guitar and his glorious silvery mane, he'd blend right in with the locals.

"Yeah, baby, not running from this fight, going all out tonight, we're rockin' you so right . . ." He screeched the last word, phasing it into a gravelly howl before launching into a bland chorus about further rocking and how unbelievably hard that rocking would be when commenced. Halfway through the second refrain (which was a reminder that once he entered the arena, he would not, in fact, cease rocking, even if a tornado of fire were to come and demand he do so), his voice cracked on a high note.

He broke off with a string of German cursing, which was thrilling because German swear words sounded more viscerally threatening than American ones. Then he kicked his journal off the stage and paced to and fro, brow furrowed, the corded muscles in his arms twitching with tension.

When he was done with his tantrum, he retrieved the journal and started over from the beginning.

Don't do it, Erika. You are not his voice coach, he didn't ask for your input on his songwriting, and one thing will lead to another . . . next thing you know, you've scared him off, and you'll be selling feet pictures for ten bucks a pop to keep the theater afloat. Then you'll be sorry, won't you?

She squared her shoulders and started up the steps.

"*. . . rockin' you like a fi-i-re tornado*—argh!"

Erika halted midstep and marched back down the stairs. This was beyond the pale. Christof was going to murder his vocal cords if he kept abusing them like he was, and what kind of integrity did a classically trained vocalist have if she let him do that on her watch? It would be like witnessing someone intentionally slathering sriracha over a bespoke Elie Saab evening gown and doing *nothing* to stop it.

"Have you tried gripping the guitar harder?" she called out as she strolled onstage and into the light. "Because I've heard you're not really rock and roll until you've decapitated your instrument onstage at least once."

Was that a flush spreading across those model-perfect cheekbones? She drew closer. It *was*.

"Erika." His voice came out like a rasp. "I'm sorry you have witnessed this. I am not at my best."

"I can tell. Your voice is naturally stunning, but that last go-around was offensive enough to wake the dead." There was a stool behind the drum kit, and she detoured to pick it up. "That'll make your sister happy, at least."

"Sibylle is never happy, no matter what I do," he said, but the last syllable ended on a cough. Apologizing again, he unscrewed a metal water bottle and tipped it back.

"My understanding is that bassists rarely are. It's part of their charm. Don't take it personally." She set the stool down a respectable six feet away from Christof and perched atop it. Close enough to chat but not close enough to touch: a distance that communicated, *Business, not pleasure.*

Although if Christof kept chugging water like that, with sweat glistening on collarbone and his sinewed throat bobbing with each swallow, a measly six feet wasn't going to protect either of them.

When he finished hydrating both himself and her silk underpants, he capped the water bottle with a sigh. "The development process for this song is at a rather . . . early . . . stage."

"I've heard worse. Did you know that Elton John composed music for an *Interview with the Vampire*–themed musical? I was at Juilliard at the time, and some classmates thought it would be fun and ironic to get wine drunk and sit through a showing."

"Oh! That sounds very cool."

"It wasn't." Erika's lip curled at the memory—and not only of the mincingly morbid musical numbers. Her roommate, Trina, had fallen asleep at intermission, and Trina's dirtbag, discount–Ryan Seacrest boyfriend, Jeff, had spent the second half of the show trying to slide a hand up Erika's skirt—and she'd let him do it, because it had made her feel powerful and desirable. She'd puked in the taxi ride back to her apartment.

The musical had shuttered the following day.

A part of her was tempted to tell all this to Christof, though she didn't know why. Maybe to scare him off. Or maybe because she secretly hoped it wouldn't—that he'd accept her flawed, trash-human soul just as it was. But the thought of him turning away in disgust made her palms sweat, so instead she said carefully, "Where did you learn to sing like that?"

"Waldo's garage." He looked down at his guitar and busied himself toying with the strings. "We were Scorpions superfans, so that's how it came about at first."

"You taught yourself?" Unsurprising. And yet—she hated to admit it—impressive.

"We practiced until we could play all their songs, but we hadn't thought about starting a proper band until Sibylle came along."

"So she was into hair metal too?"

Christof laughed. "No! I think she despised it. But I was the oldest, and she was the youngest of four. There is a six-year gap between us. Sibylle was this annoying, angry little stranger who used to follow me everywhere. I think she demanded to be included because it made her mad to be left out of something cool. Waldo and I only hoped she wouldn't tell our parents that we'd been sneaking cigarettes from Waldo's father's toolbox. But we needed a bassist, and she's quite clever when she wants to be. She'd gone off on her own and already learned all the Scorpions songs, so how could we say no?"

"The Scorpions . . . are they the ones who did 'Wind of Change'?"

"That's their most popular song, yes. But it is not their best. In my opinion. And my opinion is very informed on this matter." He began to pace again, but now his eyes were sparkling, and his shoulders weren't up by his ears anymore. "I wrote them so many letters they eventually invited me to come backstage during their fifty-year reunion tour. I am sure I was one of their youngest fans." His lips curved wryly as he flipped the guitar over to show her a cluster of sprawling signatures on the body. "I have every autograph from the members of the band. Both drummers, as well."

"That's very sweet," she said politely.

His hand swept over the electric-blue lacquer. "This is my most precious possession."

"But you use it as your primary guitar and take it everywhere with you. Aren't you worried about it getting damaged and depreciating in value?"

"Every time I play it, it *increases* in value. I am Christof Daae of Nachtmusik." He managed to look affronted. "And, of course, I can watch it at all times this way."

She fought a smile. "What is your favorite song, then?" Not that she cared about this music. At all. But the fact *he* cared so much fascinated her.

"My number one song is 'No One Like You.' It is a romantic power ballad, but it is also hard core! There is also 'Rock You Like a Hurricane,' of course. A crowd favorite. One of mine, as well, and if you know the song, you'll see the inspiration for this one I am working on, 'Coming Like a Fire Tornado.'"

A horrified laugh tried to escape her mouth and nose, but she stifled it in time. She pressed her lips together and nodded as solemnly as she could muster. "Mmm-hmm. Yeah. Are you open to input on the song title?"

He waved a dismissive hand. "It is in progress."

"Right, but . . ." She bit her lip.

"What? It refers to this part, here . . ." He strummed the first bars of the chorus. *"Dun dun da . . . I'm coming in, I'm coming to rock, I cannot be stopped, I'm coming like a fire tornado! Rocking like a fi-i-ire tornado . . ."*

"Coming *in* like a fire tornado," she corrected.

He frowned. "That has too many syllables."

"But you know *coming* has a different meaning in English, right?"

"Yes, I know." He strummed a petulant note, and then his hand froze. He looked up at her, brow unknitting. "Ah, now I see."

"Because *coming* like a fire tornado would imply—"

"No. No need. It's quite clear now."

"—that you're—"

He groaned. "Must you?"

She couldn't get the rest out through the laughter that had broken free of its restraints.

Christof buried his face in his palms and groaned louder, but she could tell he was trying not to laugh too. When this made her laugh even harder, he fell to his knees in front of her and clasped his hands like he was praying. "Promise you'll tell no one, Erika! Fire semen is very not metal!"

Through snorts, she managed to argue, "What are you talking about? That's the most metal thing I've ever heard!"

When she'd fully recovered, she sat back and grinned. "Thanks for that. It's been way too long since I had a good laugh."

That seemed to sober him. "The same for me."

"But that's reasonable. You're focused on this album. Plus, you're still burned out from tour. You're doing the work of three people. And you were dumped by your long-term girlfriend."

His expression turned despondent, and suddenly she felt like she'd shoved a puppy off her lap right when he'd gotten comfortable.

"Besides, you're German. So . . . you know."

"Sorry?"

"It's a joke! I'm joking. Because the stereotype is that Germans are really stern." She raised her hands in surrender. "I was trying to lighten the mood."

His response was to narrow his eyes and stalk closer until he could tuck a finger under her chin. The result was vaguely intimidating and downright hot as shit. "Stern? How do you mean . . . stern?"

"Um . . ." She licked her lips.

His hazel eyes went inky.

And then he seemed to snap out of some trance. His finger fell away, and he nabbed the bag of chocolate pretzels from her loose grip, grinning brightly enough that Erika wasn't sure if she'd imagined the tension between them a second ago. "Only having a bit of fun with you," he said in a light tone. "I had a secret motive."

He popped a pretzel in his mouth and handed the bag back to her. A hum of pleasure escaped him as he devoured her treat, and it killed her that he wasn't between her legs, making the same noise.

"I knew that." She shifted in her seat and tried to breathe normally.

He stepped back to the center of the stage and adjusted his guitar position as if he was going to start singing again. As if nothing had happened.

She mentally shook herself. *Focus on the music.*

"You don't mind me being here while you work?" In explanation, she added, "I can't sleep."

"I have never been shy about performing," he said, but he was still blushing when he eased into the song where he'd left off. "*Fi-i-re tornado*—what's wrong?"

He'd caught her cringing.

"It's just . . ." She bit her lip and tried to say it nicely. "If you keep singing like that, you'll be retired by forty, if not sooner."

"This is how metal is sung!"

"And where are those hair metal bands of the eighties now, hmm? I'd hate to see you end up on one of those 'Whatever Happened to These Twenty-Eight Hottest Singers?' BuzzFeed compilations."

His brows drew together. "Is it ranked in order?"

"Of what? Hotness?"

"Yes. I think I should know what my rank would be before I determine whether I'd like to be included."

Erika raised a brow. There was absolutely no way to answer that and still pretend she wasn't flirting. She demurred, "Is your vanity so fragile it needs a boost from an imaginary list?"

Christof scoffed. "My vanity is invincible. Now, tell me why you think I should change the way I sing."

"For one, you're tightening your throat to hit the high notes, and it's causing undue strain on your vocal cords. It's clear you have natural talent, but you're completely untrained. And one of the things you learn from formal coaching is how to strengthen your diaphragm and muscles in your throat so you don't blow out your voice box."

"Ah." He sighed—a frustrated puff of air. "Proper training is key to success."

"Exactly."

He nodded. "Very well. You will give me lessons."

"What? No!" She clutched her bag of pretzels to her chest like a shield, if only to protect herself from how much she really wanted to say yes. Alone in the theater with Christof every night, doing the one thing she loved that *wasn't* sex? Except that was a horrible idea, because with

Christof, the line between music and sex was awfully blurry. "I don't have time for that. I was suggesting you hire someone. These days, you can even do lessons remotely, over the internet."

He raised a brow. "Were you not a famous Broadway singer? Classically trained, yes?"

A spotlight's warmth on her cheeks. The scratchy seam of her costume dress against her rib cage. Audience faces like fuzzy ovals, watching from the shadows. The sudden screech of metal—

"I don't perform anymore," she blurted. Then, because his raised brow made her aware of how suspiciously melodramatic that response sounded, she narrowed her eyes and went on the attack. "And exactly how do you know that? Did you google me?" Oh God. She hoped he hadn't found gossip about her accident. The lurid speculation. The cloying, faux-sympathetic, double-edged quotes from her costars calling her "an enormously talented diva" and "a tragic star plucked from the sky before her time." The thinly veiled insinuations that it had been staged for attention . . .

"I hadn't considered it," he said to her enormous relief. Then a devilish gleam winked in his hazel eyes. "Are there nude photos?"

Topic change. The fist in her stomach unclenched in gratitude. "Sadly, no. Though it's too bad . . . I looked amazing back then. I mean, I look amazing *now*, but back then I made all of Broadway weep with envy at how effortlessly I resembled a woman dying of tuberculosis."

"And that's . . . desirable?"

She shrugged. "Depends on who you ask. The shallow hordes of so-called friends, socialite bloggers, and theater critics I used to hold court over seemed to think so."

"Well." He cleared his throat, then proceeded to give her the kind of thorough, unapologetic eye fuck that made her knees precariously mushy. In a low voice he said, "I adore your current physique, very much."

He shouldn't be encouraging this boldness she felt by feeding her admiration—her favorite food group. Didn't he know how ravenous she was tonight? And what with him standing there in low-slung jeans with an unapologetic bulge at the front, like some slutty *Rolling Stone* cover from the eighties . . . Erika was ready to feast.

Smoothing the silk over her thighs, she looked up at him through her veil of hair and, despite the howling protests of her conscience, heard herself say, "I'm glad you enjoy the view. Maybe I should take some nudes for you to find in a . . . personal search. Wouldn't you rather have that from me than voice coaching?"

"I will accept both. Thank you."

She tsked. "So greedy. You can't always get everything you want."

"Yes, I can." Christof raised a finger. "It simply requires careful planning, hard work, and determination."

"You're wrong about that. The world is an unjust place. No matter how hard you try, all it takes is one little mistake, and you could lose everything."

The playful spark between them sputtered.

She'd tried to say it lightly. But some of her bitterness must have bled through, because he looked at her quietly for a long moment before answering.

"Is this about the accident?" he asked quietly.

She squeezed the bag of pretzels tight until she could feel them crunching to pieces in the bag. "So you *have* looked me up."

"Overheard at the Le Dennis."

Self-consciousness spiked through her and left a puncture wound that only bravado could fill. "Well, at least they're talking about me at all. If you can't get the audience to love you, at least get them to loathe you. Either way, they're watching."

He dismissed this with a wave of his hand. "Ignore your detractors. Those who cannot do, criticize. You are perfect as you are."

"You wouldn't call me *perfect* if you saw my scars up close."

He strode toward her and gestured for her to pull her hair back. "Let's see, then, shall we?" A challenge.

Her hand rose, but she hesitated. They had a good thing going here—whatever this *thing* was. Why ruin it with the chance that what he saw would kill his attraction to her? People liked to pretend to be all deep and enlightened, but deep down, a base animal instinct spurred them to shy away from things that didn't look *right*. The scars weren't so disgusting he'd puke at the sight of them—not anymore, anyway—but they sure weren't most people's idea of cute, and she already knew he'd been unable to keep himself from staring when they'd first met.

As if sensing her thoughts, he tilted up her chin with a finger and gave her a half quirk of a smile. "I promise I won't scream. As you said, I can't afford to stress my vocal cords."

"Fine." Erika yanked back her hair before she lost the courage. Tilting her cheek to better catch the overhead lights, she asked, "Happy now?"

Christof stared at the burn scar on Erika's face and felt anger and sorrow ballooning in his chest. He wanted to go back to when this had first happened and hold her close. Stop it from happening somehow. Protect her.

The makeup she wore hid most of the discoloration, but light reflected off the tight skin, highlighting the ridged edges like a mountain range on a topographical map. The textured markings hugged her cheekbone to the edge of her hairline, swept under her eye, and bisected her brow. She'd colored in the missing half of her eyebrow so expertly that from a distance he wouldn't have noticed it missing. Her eye was nearly untouched, save for a slight downward pull where the skin went taut at the bottom left corner.

It looked like it had been painful.

The defiant tilt to her chin said the pain hadn't been solely physical. "Gruesome enough for you?" she prodded.

He wordlessly shook his head.

It didn't make her less beautiful. Not in the slightest. Then again, he'd already decided she was a witch—she'd cast a spell that made him so obsessed—because he was hard pressed to think of a damn thing that *would* make her less attractive to him.

Maybe a face tattoo. Something ill advised.

He tried to envision her straddling him with inked zebra stripes across her face, and it still turned him on. With a little lock of hair curling over her forehead, like a little pony—

Best to cut that vision short before it aroused him more than he cared to consider.

Something worse, then. Something vaguely offensive and mildly repulsive: the word *POOP* splayed across her face in block letters. Yes, that did it. Perhaps that did it *too* well.

He bit his lower lip, but it was of no use.

"Are you *laughing* at me?"

"It's not what you think."

She pulled away, and her hair fell back over her face. "This has been fun, but I'm going to bed."

She stood, and it brought her nearly flush against him. If only his guitar weren't in the way, he could reach out and pull her close. Feel her soft, generous curves melt against his lean hardness.

He stepped back, conscious of not wanting to crowd her, even though Erika was the last person he'd ever imagine shrinking away from him.

If he could explain that he hadn't been laughing *at* her . . . "I tried imagining you with a tattoo."

"A tattoo," she repeated flatly.

"Yes. To make you ugly. Imagine it . . . *P-O-O-P*. Right across your forehead. Big, round letters."

She blinked at him. "Are you comparing my career-ending disfigurement to a *poop tattoo*?"

"Yes?"

She shook her head slowly. *"Christof."*

He scrubbed a hand through his hair, fluffing the locks at the back of his head to restore its volume, and tried to look contrite. "I now see this was wrong."

"Heinously so." She tapped her foot—a teacher awaiting her student's slow-moving attempt at deductive reasoning.

Racking his brain for a suitable alternative, he settled on the obvious. "I should have said something to praise your beauty."

"Do I look gullible enough to fall for flattery?"

Is this a trick question? He hesitated—a fraction of a second too long, based on the scalding strength of her glare. "Absolutely not," he declared.

"Exactly!" She began to pace with her hands balled on her hips like a silk-clad dust devil. The intimidation factor was mitigated by the bag of pretzels jutting out sideways from her fist. "I used to be a *star*, Christof. I've been seduced by everything from impoverished foreign royalty to nouveau riche influencers—I can smell back-row bullshit all the way from center stage. *Try again.*"

If not praise, then what did she want? A better idea clicked. "I should have recoiled in fear."

"Fear," she repeated flatly.

"Yes. Like in *Frankenstein*. Or that Batman movie." He threw up his hands, demonstrating a properly dramatic cower. *"Ahhh! What is this pitiful creature of darkness before me? Begone, abomination!"*

A gasp of outrage. "Abomination?"

"Too far?"

"What's wrong with you? I've bared my deepest, darkest insecurity to you. The least you could do was tell me I'm pretty!"

"But you said—"

"I didn't want *false* flattery. I didn't say I wanted to be insulted."

He dabbed his brow with the back of his hand. "This is very confusing," he admitted. This was the price he paid for being out of the dating game for a decade—he had the wooing skills of one of Waldo's Trolli worms.

The irony of it all was that he'd always considered himself a generous compliment giver. Had he not regularly praised Gillian on the superlative volume of her hair and the badass quality of her keyboarding? While on tour, had he not taken the time to praise fans during song breaks for excellent penmanship on their **WISH YOU WERE HERE . . . IN MY PANTIES** signs? And there was even one time when he'd told Sibylle that she played bass with skill reminiscent of Rudy Sarzo—although, in retrospect, he should have recalled Sarzo's pre-Whitesnake stint with Ozzy, because Sibylle held a rather unreasonably vitriolic disdain for Mr. Osbourne, and she'd subsequently suggested that Christof should insert his guitar headstock first into a small orifice.

It slowly dawned on him that perhaps the issue wasn't the frequency of his compliments but the composition thereof.

Carefully, he intoned, "You are very pretty. I mean this sincerely." Even though *pretty* didn't begin to do her justice. That was like saying David Hasselhoff was popular back home—a grievous understatement.

Erika crossed her arms, dissatisfaction written plainly on her face.

A brilliant idea came to him. "I will write a song about you instead. That is where my skill lies, really."

"Oh God. Not a cheesy power ballad." Was that a spark of interest peeking through her pout? It had to be. Who on earth wouldn't want to be serenaded in such an extremely cool way?

"For you, I will create the mightiest, most earnest power ballad you've ever heard," he vowed. Inspiration was already sizzling through him.

"On second thought, I prefer the recoiling in horror."

He strummed the chord he already had in mind, and it pealed through the hushed theater like a musical prayer at the altar of schmalzig glamour. *Yes, this is perfect.*

"Christof? I'm serious! The only thing I hate more than power ballads are trite acoustic covers." She appeared vaguely panicked—no doubt worried he'd insult her by recording fewer than seven solid minutes of high-impact crooning followed by a two-minute solo guitar outro. Did she not know he was Christof Daae of Nachtmusik, a man whose sole purpose in life was to create music so epic it brought forth tears of glittering awe?

Undaunted, he toyed with lyrics. *"Girl, you look so right . . ."*

"I deeply regret everything about this," she groaned.

". . . hot body unfurling in splendor . . ."

"That doesn't even make sense!"

". . . you're my lady of the niiiiiight!"

"Once again, the *phrasing.*"

Before he could launch into yet another brilliant lyrical platitude, she rose on her toes and pressed a soft kiss to his cheek. A hand briefly touched his left shoulder for balance, and then she murmured, "If you shut up right now, I'll give you those voice lessons."

His mouth snapped closed. When she pulled away, both his cheek and the spot on his shoulder glowed with heat.

"Tomorrow night at midnight, right here. Don't be late."

"I am never late," he vowed.

CHAPTER 14

At precisely 11:55 p.m. the following night, Christof walked onstage with the intention of prudently bowing out of voice lessons altogether—and froze in his tracks.

Erika was waiting for him, and she looked fucking incredible.

She arched a brow when she saw him. "Five minutes early. Very good. I like a student who respects my time."

"I . . ." The excuse he'd prepared vaporized on his tongue.

Skintight skirt. Oversize button-down shirt tied at the waist and left to splay open. Underneath: a lacy, rib-cage-hugging, breast-overflowing, mind-boggling bra-top . . . contraption. Scarlet lipstick and a—was that a *riding crop* she was gently patting against her opposing palm?

No, not a riding crop. Some sort of short, tapered stick that Waldo would have claimed came from the secret sex dungeon. Whatever it was, it looked authoritative and sexy and vaguely intimidating.

Suddenly, Christof was no longer tired from a sleepless night and a long day of contentious rehearsal. Though he was a bit light headed from the speed his blood had rushed to his dick. He fumbled for something to lean on and came away with a handful of dusty curtain.

Was Erika trying to seduce him? The thought made his blood pulse with a thrilling intensity, which was exactly why he'd intended to cancel.

Being alone in a dark theater with Erika Greene did not beget responsible decision-making.

"Actually, I feel a bit tired. Perhaps we might—"

"Center stage, please," she instructed.

He obeyed without thinking. This was very concerning. What if she instructed him to undress? Or shove up her skirt and bury his tongue in her hot, wet—

He blurted, "I'm feeling unwell. I think it would be best if I"—*go back to my room and masturbate*—"rest."

"You're sick? What's wrong?" Her genuine concern was enough to make him ill in truth.

"Only tired," he corrected quickly. "I will still pay you for your time, of course, since you've gone through the trouble of . . . preparing."

This made her pause. "You're paying me?"

"Of course. Was that not clear?"

Erika blinked. Then her chin rose, all traces of vulnerability gone. "You know, I had a voice coach when I was growing up. A former opera singer. One of the best in the world." Erika strolled toward him as she spoke, her hips rolling seductively. The way the dark material strained, drawing tight across her pelvis where her hips flared . . . he wasn't sure he remembered his name anymore, much less the reasons he'd planned to cancel. Erika continued, "My mother paid her three hundred bucks a session. I could probably charge the same, since you can obviously afford it. But for some reason, I'm not. These lessons won't cost you any money at all. It's probably because I'm such a good person."

At that last bit, she smirked, as if it was an amusing joke. Then Erika's gaze swept over him like she was measuring him for slaughter, and it didn't seem as if her intentions were very altruistic at all. Nevertheless, he managed to reply, "I insist on compensating you."

"You'll find a way to demonstrate your gratitude, I'm sure." She stopped in front of him. She was so close he could see right down the forbidden valley between her breasts if he glanced downward. Which he did.

His responsible nature only went so far. A man had his limits.

The smooth glide of her pointer stick down his front broke the spell. He instinctively jerked away, his stomach clenching hard at the instant bolt of arousal. "Let's begin."

"But—"

"We'll start with your posture." She trailed the stick down his thigh, leaving a trail of scorched flesh in its wake, and lightly tapped the inside of each calf. "Feet hip distance apart. Firmly planted, weight evenly distributed. Engage all those delicious abs of yours so there's space for your diaphragm to fill all the way up with air. All of this slinky, codpiece-thrusting, rock-star-esque slouching does wonders for your onstage sex appeal, but it's stifling your vocal capabilities. Is that what you want?"

"No," he croaked. This was a bad idea. He clearly wasn't himself tonight.

"Then what *do* you want, Christof Daae?"

He closed his eyes, summoning a calming breath that only danced further out of reach.

When he looked again, her haughty expression was gone. "Your hands are shaking. Are you okay?"

He clasped his hands behind his back. "The stick thing is a bit distracting."

"Stick?" She glanced down. "Oh, this. It's a bit much, isn't it? I guess I have a habit of leaning too hard into a role, especially when it involves theme dressing."

"Is it some sort of . . . classical teaching implement?"

"It fell off the window blinds in my office a couple days ago. I thought it would make an appropriate pointer stick. Give me an air of authority. Make you a bit nervous so you'll be more likely to give in when I try to lure you into the costume closet for a hands-on tutorial."

She could have been joking, but he wasn't sure. Wasn't sure he *wanted* her to be joking.

He groaned. "Christ, you're going to kill me."

For a second, it seemed she was going to draw close enough to shred his last fiber of resistance. Then she sighed, tossed the stick into the audience where it clattered somewhere in the shadows between rows, and walked over to Gillian's keyboard. She sat primly on the stool. "You're right. I'm here to help you sing, and this is distracting us from our purpose. The music is the most important thing, after all."

"Yes, always," he agreed with a fervor that he hoped disguised the way his mind was currently concocting a vision of *composing music* all over her breasts.

He ran a hand down his face to clear the image and reminded himself that focus was key to success.

She flicked the synth pad's power switch and pressed a key, making the instrument peal in harmonic ecstasy. The tone cut short when her hand recoiled in apparent disgust. "Synths? Does this thing have a normal piano function?"

"No," he lied, knowing she couldn't read the German instructions printed above the keys. "It only plays badass sounds. Custom edition."

She wrinkled her nose, then gingerly pressed the same key. "All right, it'll have to do. We're going to warm up by running through scales." She demonstrated with an open-mouthed "ah" tone in the same note she'd pressed. Half a stage away, her voice slipped under his top layer of skin and made his flesh tingle. Or maybe he was imagining it because he was so on edge. "Remember to breathe low in your stomach, not your chest."

He dutifully played along with the warm-up for as long as he could manage, which was about ten minutes. At least focusing on the sounds coming out of his own mouth distracted his brain long enough for his system to reset, and before long, his heartbeat had slowed to something reasonable. He no longer felt like he was going to combust if she touched him again. Nevertheless, the warm-up was boring and repetitive, and impatience made him want to pace. His back was already aching from maintaining such a stiff posture.

When she started having him do neck exercises, he hit his limit. "Is this really necessary? I've sung to full stadiums. I believe I am promoted past these games for choir children."

Bloodred lips curled into a smirk. "Even Patti LuPone warms up before a performance."

Who the fuck is she? "Clearly, I am more skilled than Patsy."

"Oh? Even as conceited as I am, I wouldn't dare challenge Ms. LuPone's vocal expertise. So does that make you a better singer than me?"

There was only one right answer—and he was too proud to give it. He grunted, "Possibly."

"Is that so? Then sing for me. All I need is a few bars. Lay your most *badass* singing on me, hot stuff." She raised a brow when he hesitated. "Go on . . . *sing*."

He shrugged. There had never been any question about his talent, in his mind or in the minds of his hundreds of thousands of devoted fans. Perhaps it was time to show Erika what he could really do. Earn a little respect on Nachtmusik's name while also showing her that hair metal wasn't just caterwauling.

He reached for his guitar, but she stopped him. "You don't need that."

"I never said I did."

"Great."

He flexed his empty hands and tried not to feel naked without something between himself and the audience. *This is fine.* There were plenty of songs he knew could work a cappella. But he didn't want to merely sound good—he wanted to blow her away.

"Whenever you're ready," she prompted.

"I'm *preparing*."

She raised her hands in innocence.

Before he could second-guess himself further, he launched into the chorus of one of Nachtmusik's more technically demanding songs, "Schlüssel zum Erfolg," which not only rocked extremely hard but also flexed his melodic range with drawn-out high notes belted at maximum effort.

When he finished, Erika clapped politely. "Impressive."

"See? Hair metal is not so much easier than Broadway."

She stood. Took a sip of water. Took a deep breath. And copied the song he'd sung in German, note for note, with such precise accuracy—if not pronunciation—that it dawned on him she must have listened to this song several times before.

Except Erika sang it a full octave higher.

Every single note rang out clearly, backed by lungs that wielded air like a weapon. And when she hit the high note, she held it.

Then she jumped up a full octave—and kept holding it.

Her voice pierced the fabric of the air in the auditorium and left it vibrating. The wood beneath his feet trembled. He half expected the bulbs in the lighting fixtures to shatter.

She was incredible. Majestic. Possibly inhuman.

As the last note quavered in the rafters, he stood stock still, too blown away to move. Erika calmly crossed the stage until she reached him. She slipped behind him, and a fingernail drew a whisper-light line across his shoulder blades, sending live electricity down his spine. "I'll be here at midnight tomorrow. But bring your humility along to the lesson next time, will you?"

With that, she disappeared into the backstage shadows before he'd recovered the ability to speak.

CHAPTER 15

He came back the next night, thank God, because Erika had spent the entire day replaying the previous night's lesson on repeat in her head. Second-guessing why she was doing any of this in the first place, given that she hardly had time to be playing music tutor—and flirting with her student. Besides, she was supposedly *reformed*, and her tenuous live-work-own situation at the Paris Opera House was exactly seven seconds from collapsing around her at all times.

And that's exactly why I deserve this, she'd justified to herself as she'd checked her lipstick application. A little treat, just for herself. An amuse-bouche to distract the hungry monster inside her. As much as it pained her to admit it, helping Christof improve—without expecting any direct return for herself—made her feel . . . nice. Altruistic, even! Maybe this whole "being good" thing wasn't so excruciating, after all; she was already getting high off fantasies of breezing past the doorman at the pearly gates, explaining with a serene smile, *I'm on the list, darling. I rounded up at the grocery store checkout.*

Christof was still far too cocky throughout the night's lesson, but at least he didn't complain during warm-ups, and his posture had already improved. She walked away that night with a sense of accomplishment she hadn't felt in a long time.

By the following evening's lesson, he was ready to start working through some of his older songs.

"We're going to fine-tune your delivery," she told him. "Sing them for me how you normally do, and then we'll work on the places you're stressing your voice."

He improved with each lesson. So much so that a part of her wondered how much he'd really need her after another week or two. And that thought made her melancholy, even though she'd initially railed against giving him lessons at all.

Erika liked listening to Christof sing. Especially when he sang to her, his moss-brown eyes locked on her own. He performed like he'd been spat out from the depths of hell—the eternal wellspring of rock—and treated the stage as if it were his demonic birthright. While he sang, he strutted. He rolled his hips. He performed immoral acts with the mic stand.

It was all very excessive and lurid. And—out of context—highly ridiculous.

But *in* context, with the backing track playing under his vocals . . . well, no red-blooded human was going to sit through that and *not* be assaulted with the urge to rip their undergarments off and fling them onstage. And when he belted and growled those nonsensically sappy lyrics of his, it was hard not to squirm in her seat and question her devotion to maintaining her pride. Because if Christof didn't voluntarily fuck her by the end of the week, she would throw herself into the Bellagio fountains and let her bones be found by vultures when the desert ran dry.

Or worse—she'd have to ask him nicely. Shudder. What was she, an impoverished orphan of the casual-sex realm? *Please, sir, might you spare an orgasm?* No. She'd sunk to low places in her life, but never to these depths of desperation.

Even if he was the only person who'd seen her face and hadn't flinched.

Even if he made her laugh for the first time in two years.

Even if thoughts of him kept her awake at night and—

Oh, this was bad.

Sappy, spiraling-into-emotional-turmoil bad. *Power ballad* bad. And they hadn't even kissed yet.

"Is this song so bad you've fallen into a trance, or are you as exhausted as I am?" Christof interrupted her musing.

She blinked at him. It was the following Friday night and their eleventh lesson. She'd offered to play keyboard accompaniment to a new duet he was working on—ostensibly meant to be sung with Gillian— and he'd taken all her suggestions about the composition seriously.

"No, sorry. Thinking about my drive to Vegas tomorrow morning," she demurred. "Ready to take it from the top?"

"You're leaving for the weekend?"

He seemed surprised by the news, and Erika realized she hadn't mentioned it. "I have a meeting with some hotshot casino magnate who probably wants to buy the theater, which I have no intention of selling. But I get a free night's hotel stay out of it, and I have some errands to run that require more civilization than Paris has to offer."

Christof was suddenly fascinated by his guitar pick. "Ah. And when will you be back?"

"I'll be back Sunday night in time for our lesson."

He gave a noncommittal grunt.

She rushed to add, "Unless you're done with missing out on sleep for these midnight meetings. I think you've gotten the gist of things, technique-wise, and you'll probably have Gillian back by then. So you won't need me to fill in anymore on keys."

"Right . . . Gillian." Christof busied himself unplugging his guitar from the amp and neatly coiling the cable.

Christof hadn't said a peep to the band about it all week, beyond a curt note that her "sick Tante Helene" had suffered a minor relapse that delayed Gillian's return. Erika had desperately wanted to ask what the truth was, but she'd held off for fear of appearing too invested in his ex-girlfriend's whereabouts. Now, she couldn't bite back her curiosity any longer. "You *have* heard from her, right?" Erika prompted.

Instead of answering, he finished settling his guitar into its stand—one of the few times she'd seen him set it down—and came over to where she sat at the keyboard. He loomed over her, his expression unreadable, and Erika tilted her head back, fighting a giddy rush of anticipation.

Then, to her catastrophic disappointment, he reached over her to examine the notes she'd scribbled in the margins of his lyrics. "Hmm. These are very good," he murmured. When he set the pages back down, the shadows under his eyes looked even more prominent than usual. "It's been nearly two weeks since I've heard from her. I've called. I've messaged. Nothing."

"Well . . . shit," Erika said. Because as much as she might try to deny it, she *was* invested. Far more than she should be.

"I can't help but worry. Is she quitting the band? Is she sick or injured somewhere? Is she doing it to punish me?"

Angst twisted his beautiful face, and Erika suppressed a surge of indignation on his behalf—as if she'd never been guilty of ghosting a lover for her own selfish reasons. Glass houses and so forth. Better to give Gillian the benefit of the doubt. "Has she done something like this before? Is there a chance she's on an epic bender in Ibiza?"

"Never." He paced back and forth in front of the keyboard. "Gillian was never a big party girl. She was always the first to bed. She brought her knitting on the tour bus and would knit outfits for the appliances. She had this pink, fluffy robe thing she wore all the time, because she likes to be cozy. If she went out to the shop, she would text us pictures of the local cats she saw on the walk there. She always seemed so . . ." He searched for the word.

"Insufferably twee?" Erika muttered.

Christof's brows shot up. "I was going to say *content*."

Erika pressed her lips into a facsimile of a smile. "She sounds lovely. Good for her." *Don't mind me—I'm a bitter hag who's envious of anyone managing to cling to a scrap of joy in this miserable world.*

"But if she was happy, why would she leave us like this?"

"Sometimes unhappy people don't know they're unhappy." She didn't intend to say more, but somehow, she did. "You know, I remember getting the call from my agent about my Tony nomination and thinking, *This is the happiest moment of my life.*"

"You were nominated for a Tony? That is incredible!"

"It was. I mean, it *is*. And don't get me wrong: I made all the appropriate squealing sounds and acted outrageously delighted, because that's what was expected of me, and all the while I remember feeling . . . absolutely nothing at all. At the time, I remember recognizing how strange that was, but I chalked it up to stress and a bad hangover."

Christof's brows drew together. "Stress can be very detrimental to happiness."

"That's true," Erika said carefully. "I wonder, though, if it's like that for a lot of people. Going through their whole lives oblivious to how miserable they are. Until one day something happens, and it's like they wake up from this . . . trance. And suddenly, everything about their carefully constructed life feels unbearable. In that moment, running away might feel like the only way to make that feeling stop."

He'd stopped pacing. The way he looked at her, with such *pity* . . .

She rushed to clarify. "Anyway, that might have been what happened to Gillian."

"Is that why you're here?"

Erika crossed her arms. "We're not talking about me. We're talking about why you don't have a keyboardist right now and are lying to your band about it."

He scraped a hand through his hair. "Fuck." He let out a long groan. "Fuuuuuck."

"Tell your band. Rip the Band-Aid off. Because this whole 'crossing your fingers and hoping Gillian magically returns' thing doesn't seem to be working for you."

"You don't think I know that? It's too late. If they find out I've been lying to them for *three weeks*, everything will fall apart! And with this ambitious schedule for the album . . . I can't."

"But—"

"I have devoted the last decade of my life to Nachtmusik. Sacrificed so much." His eyes were pleading, like he needed her to understand or else the world would end. "This album . . . this *band* . . . it is everything to me. I can't let it fall apart when we're so close to becoming international badass rock stars. I've been dreaming of this moment since the very first day I picked up a guitar."

Before she could think about what she was doing, she found herself getting up from her stool and moving toward him. What a sucker she was, falling for his sad eyes and lush pout. Misplaced pity was always how a woman's downfall began. That and tequila shots.

And yet here she was, standing in front of Christof with a gooey sort of feeling in her stomach that was entirely unrelated to sex. Well, mostly unrelated.

Everything was related to sex when it came to Christof.

Her hands found their way to lie flat against his chest. He wore his black silk blouse tonight—the same one he'd been wearing when Nachtmusik had arrived—and he'd left it unbuttoned to the waist again. Had he cycled through all three suitcases' worth of outfits already, or did he somehow know that she loved the way he looked in black? Her thumbs grazed bare flesh, and answering heat spread up her forearms.

"You can't control everything in the world around you. You can't control Gillian. You can't control the other band members. And as your vocal coach, it's my duty to inform you that all this tension you're holding here . . ." She patted the firm pectorals guarding his chest. "It's holding your voice back. You have to let go of this tension."

Her hands lingered. She was close enough to see goose bumps dapple his pale skin in response to her touch. Feel his small nipples harden under her hands. What a flimsy barrier this silk shirt was, but it still pained her to have it in the way. She wanted to slip her hands beneath the fabric and scrape her nails over his flesh. Mark him: *Mine.*

He stood stock still, as if he sensed the danger he was in. In a low voice he asked, "And how do I do that?"

She opened her mouth to reply—and heard voices from the back hallway that let out into the far-left wing of the stage.

Christof reared back. "We can't be seen."

Shit. He was right: this would look bad. Her dressed like a professor in a porno; Christof all flushed and bothered like he was, standing intimately close to a woman who wasn't his supposed girlfriend. Even Erika had to admit this was the wrong way for the band to find out about Gillian's departure.

She grabbed Christof's wrist and bolted toward the right stage wing, snatching the note pages off the keyboard with her free hand. The only place she could think to hide was the costume closet. They didn't have time to make it anywhere else, and hiding backstage was too risky.

The door creaked loudly as she opened it and shoved Christof in before her, but it was too late to back out. She spun and reversed into the closet, catching a glimpse of Sibylle and Waldo walking onto the stage as she jerked the door closed. It stuck, and she threw her muscle into it, forcing the door into the warped frame.

Safe.

Erika leaned her forehead against the door, breathing hard.

Waldo's voice filtered through the wood, muffled but still audible. "Did you hear that?"

Silence. Erika's pulse beat hard at the base of her neck. Then she heard Sibylle answering, "The phantoms must be restless tonight. This is a good omen for our séance."

"Sergei must have left the lights on. Look, he left the keyboard on too. Major bummy."

Sibylle made a sound of disgust. "Stop trying to do slang. No one thinks it's cool."

"Nein, American babes think it is übergeil."

In a terrible American accent, Sibylle intoned, "Whatever, man."

"Wow! You are a natural!"

Sibylle said something in German that sounded derisive and shuffled around for a bit. Then: "It's good we're here. Christof will bury us if he finds the instruments like this." A pause. "Come. Help me to set up the candles."

Erika gritted her teeth. Hadn't she specifically told Sibylle no candles in the theater this afternoon? The candle she kept on the pipe organ was an *exception*. One she was allowed to make because she owned the damn place, and it was her ass on the line if it went up in flames.

She felt Christof shift behind her, something steely and warm brushing against her backside—his upper thigh, probably—and her entire being came alive with a violent jolt of arousal. Air rushed out of her lungs. Thank God he was too tall to line up his pelvis with hers, because she suddenly didn't care if the theater burned down with them inside.

The costume closet was barely larger than her walk-in closet in Manhattan—insomuch as the term *walk-in* was more aspirational than descriptive. They'd been able to walk *into* the closet, but after that, there wasn't anywhere else to go. Headless felt mannequins and fraying rolls of upholstery fabric hogged most of the floor space, and along the walls, overstuffed racks bowed under the weight of decades' worth of dresses and capes, with hangers crammed so tightly that several costumes might have actually fused together—Erika wouldn't know, since there had never been a proper theater show here during her tenure. The air had a distinct papery bookstore scent, which seemed like the wrong smell for fabric to give off.

There was no window in here. Not even an overhead light. Just pitch-black air, hot and still.

And Christof. Six feet infinity of rangy muscle and barely leashed sexual repression, crammed up hard against her ass. His complex woodsy cologne and the lightest hint of whatever hair spray he used. The creak of his coated denim pants; the silky slide of his breath coming deep and steady—not fast and shaky like hers.

Rustling fabric sounded by her left ear, and he shifted, as if he was searching for something to balance himself against. His lips brushed the sensitive shell of her ear, and she reflexively seized up, her nipples tightening into hard tips rubbing against the stiff fabric of her demi bra.

"Sorry," he whispered, the contact disappearing. "Are they still there? Can you hear anything?"

Her hot breath puffed against the door and fanned her cheeks with humidity. She was a fool to have come here tonight without getting herself off first. She'd abstained all week, for some fucking reason. As if she were *saving* her orgasms for him. She'd thought it would make it all so much more titillating—to deny herself until he was ready. It wasn't like she couldn't control herself around him.

Now it seemed like a horrifically naive idea.

She swallowed. Managed to whisper steadily enough, "Seems Sibylle is hosting a séance."

He bit off a soft curse. "This could take hours." He moved against her again, and the door gave a tiny groan. Heat enveloped her back. It took a second to realize he'd propped at least one hand above hers on the door for purchase. "Ah, that's better."

No, it's fucking not. Hours? She had maybe five seconds left, if he kept pressing against her like that. She throbbed, head to toe, in need; she was already so soaking wet she could feel moisture seeping through her silk underwear and slicking the tight valley where inner thighs squeezed together.

Raw, filthy wants poured through her imagination. No finesse; this fantasy was about unadulterated mauling.

She imagined Christof shoving her skirt up and kicking her legs wide, tearing the hem. His hands rudely jerking her breasts free of her bra. His unforgiving cock ripping through damp silk to bury himself hilt deep in her on the first thrust. Slam into her so hard her toes left the ground and he pinned her against the door with the penetrating force of his—

A whimper escaped. Tiny. Breathless. But in the impossibly intimate darkness, it was as loud as a banshee howl.

"Erika?"

She'd never been a sucker for accents before, but she loved the way Christof said her name. Adored the rich complexity of his voice: his hard consonants, his long vowels, the growly texture underlying it all. Her own name rumbled over her skin like she was standing over subway tracks as a train barreled through, and she trembled, her bones vibrating solely for him.

Her eyes squeezed shut. *Get it together.* "We need to get out of here."

"Are you fearful of small spaces?"

She shook her head, then realized he couldn't see her. Through clenched teeth she replied, "No."

How could he be so oblivious?

And frankly, it was a little insulting that he wasn't as frantic as she was to escape, given that he clearly wasn't about to give her aching body the sexual reckoning it demanded. What *exactly* was his fucking problem? He'd signaled he wanted her from day one, so she wasn't hopelessly panting after a man who preferred other things; plus, he'd even seen her scars and claimed she was as smoking hot as ever. Could it really be that he was so loyal to his musical aspirations that he wasn't willing to stray from the righteous path the tiniest bit?

No. No fucking way was anyone that much of an angel. Even angels succumbed to temptation eventually. There were entire books devoted to the topic.

"It is rather close in here. Are you comfortable?" His whisper was rougher now, like maybe he wasn't as unaffected as he'd first seemed.

"No, I'm not fucking comfortable, Christof," she hissed.

His weight against her lessened, as if he was somehow finding the space to back away. "There isn't much room to—"

Enough. She flipped herself around and clawed for the edges of his shirt where it parted along his chest. When she found them, she fisted the material and jerked him against her.

He came willingly. Too willingly. He slammed against her, and the door behind them shuddered.

Distantly, she heard Sibylle say, "Did you hear that?"

But Erika didn't care. "Either kiss me right now, or get the fuck out of this closet and make up some excuse for why you were in here. I don't care which one you choose, but you'd better do it goddamn quick."

CHAPTER 16

Christof didn't move—didn't even speak—and Erika's heart did a dizzying nosedive. The tight space that had seemed so intimate a second ago suddenly felt smothering.

"I want to kiss you," he said in a guttural whisper. Something lightly brushed across her cheek. His thumb.

She stilled. Afraid to breathe, in case she ruined the moment.

His thumb trailed a path down her cheek and slid over her lower lip, feather light and reverent. "But it has been so long since . . . since I've done this."

"Kissing?" She released the balled fabric in her hands and slid her palms up to his shoulders.

"For the first time."

"First kiss, hundredth kiss . . . it's all the same." She nipped at his thumb. Tasted the salt on his skin.

"Not with you. Not to me."

Then the pressure of his thumb disappeared, and his mouth lowered to hers. His lips were velvet, his breath warm and sweet. Tingles of static pleasure spread across her skin, and her nails curled into his shoulders. He angled his head, searching for more, and she parted her lips for him, deepening the kiss until it turned from sweet to decadent.

It was all so very . . . lovely. Reminiscent of rose petals and drizzled chocolate. Soft.

I don't like soft, her brain protested, but her body reacted like it most certainly *did* like soft. She melted into his body, her clawed grip easing so she could smooth the fabric of his shirt, petting him like one of her rats.

On and on it went.

She kept waiting for him to ease back. But he kissed like he had all night and no place to be; no plans to go further but no plans to do anything else but kiss her either. It was torture. Pure, brilliant torture.

It had been either five minutes or five thousand years, and her lips were swollen now, and the ache between her thighs was spreading to every square inch of her flesh. Making her skin so sensitive that every light touch of his body against hers, every rasp of his tongue, every chaste caress of his fingers against her cheek and along the side of her neck, was magnified. Overwhelming her nerve endings.

She broke away. "More," she moaned. It came out louder than she'd wanted, and her breath caught. He stilled, his mouth still on hers. Both of them listening.

Through the door, Erika heard the chanting stop, then Waldo's excited cry: "I think I hear a ghost!"

"*Shhh!* We are almost finished," Sibylle chastised. After a breathless series of seconds, the chanting continued.

Erika slowly released her breath through her nose. She had to remember to be quiet, or all this would come to an end. And it couldn't end yet—not until she'd gotten off. She was so close . . . yet so far.

But the idea they *could* be caught . . .

It stoked the need in her core so intensely she could melt glass.

Christof's lips hovered over hers, unsure. But by the way he'd gone tense, his grip on her cheek reflexively tightening, he felt the illicit thrum of danger, too—and didn't know what to do with it.

But Erika did.

"They could catch us," Erika rasped against his mouth, infusing her voice with enough wavering uncertainty. As he began to pull back, she hooked a leg around his thigh and urged him closer. "But don't stop."

A quiet, tortured *"Nnngh"* spilled out of his chest, like someone had punched him in the solar plexus. His mouth slammed down over hers. This time, it wasn't gentle.

He kissed her so hard her shoulder blades dug into the wooden door at her back. His thigh ground against her wet core. She arched against him, wanting more of the rough friction from the material of his pants, but her skirt held her trapped, stretchless rayon pulled tight across her thighs.

She freed a hand from around his neck to reach down and jerk the hem of her skirt up, baring skin up to her thong-clad ass. Whorls of dark, steamy air caressed her inner thighs.

Christof must have sensed what she'd done, because he released his protective grip on her jaw, his hand gliding over her shoulder and down her rib cage as if he were reverently stroking a religious statue. Then he found her bare ass, and he palmed her bountiful flesh, greedily massaging in a way that was as far from religious virtue as a man could get.

He broke the kiss to trail lips and teeth along her jaw. "Ich liebe deinen Arsch," he breathed like a prayer against the place below her earlobe. The phrase rang some vague memory, but Erika couldn't place it. Her thoughts moved in slow motion, ages behind the quicksilver urgency of her body's movements. Any stray multisyllabic thoughts were drowned out by a steady refrain: *Need. Want. More.*

Her hips bucked forward and back along the length of his thigh, and her reward was doled out in climbing jolts of pleasure, each pulse stacking on top of the last one, increasing the intensity until her pants came out painfully short, and prickling heat spread out across her chest and neck. She was so fucking close already. Moisture already soaked the patch of denim she rubbed against—he had to feel it wetting his thigh. He didn't even need to do anything more; another minute of grinding against him while he whispered unintelligible nothings against her neck, and she'd unlock the mind-blowing orgasm now within reach.

His thigh withdrew.

A whimper of protest escaped her lips. Like an addict, she tried wiggling closer, but his grip on her ass tightened. Shifted higher. Grip firm and sure, he locked her hips in place, forcing her backside flush against the door.

"Christof," she hissed in warning, nails digging into the flesh of his back. "Let me—"

He nipped her earlobe. "I have you," he murmured into her ear.

His other hand—the one that had still been cradling her face—disappeared. Fabric rustled. And then she heard the gorgeous, halcyon sound of a zipper opening.

Elation bubbled up. This was even better than she'd hoped. Her entire being was fizzy with the ecstasy of it. Already, she could *feel* the overwhelming, incomparable moment when he would stretch her slick opening wide, filling up the emptiness inside her and making her pussy gloriously whole. Heaven.

She allowed herself to indulge in that spark of joy for a second longer before miserable reality kicked in and she forced herself to whisper: "Condom?"

"I didn't . . ." A pause. "Forgive me."

Erika's long sigh filled the closet with the sound of her despair. Of course not. Of fucking *course* not. Christof had no experience with casual hookups, so he hadn't come to his voice lesson with a condom in his back pocket, because why would he? She was the one who'd fantasized about luring her hapless student to the dark side. This should have been her responsibility.

But she'd never been the one to take the lead before either.

"Hey," he rasped. "I still have you."

His hands closed around her waist, and suddenly her feet were off the floor, and he stepped in, pinning her to the door with his weight. With his cheek pressed to hers, he instructed, "Bring your legs up."

What was he thinking? They couldn't—

He pressed his pelvis against her core, and when her inner thighs rubbed against cotton, she realized his briefs were still on. Through the soaked-through silk of her thong, the length of his cock jutted against her clit, a gently bowed, cloth-covered rod of hard, steely heat. Her legs snapped up to lock behind him, and he gave a satisfied grunt, locking teeth on her neck and hands under her ass.

"Yes," she breathed. And at the sound of it, his hips rolled forward. Slow. Testing. Pleasure spiked deep and hard, and it was so, *so* fucking good she couldn't help but echo another thankful *"Yesssss."*

He thrust against her again, longer and deeper, and her calves squeezed tight against his clenched ass, urging him on. Soothing the ache in her clit even as it spiraled outward into something sharper and bigger and more intense. The impact shuddered the door behind her in its frame, probably loud enough to be heard, and she didn't even care.

She dug her heels in and did it again. And again. Setting the rhythm and demanding he meet it. And he did.

Holy shit, did he ever.

Christof's movements were a sexual symphony. Every thrust, every glide of his hips, every harmonizing caress of his mouth on the sensitive skin along her neck—*flawless*. Precise. Poetic. He played her body like it was the only instrument that had ever mattered to him.

There was nothing for Erika to do but allow her head to fall back against the wood and let go of the reins, and so she did, reveling in the rough glide of contrasting fabric against her swollen folds. Her clit was already so sensitive that with the darkness amplifying sensation, her senses lasered in on the point of contact, making her hyperaware of every ridge and vein on his cock, the tiny rows of cotton weave wrapped around it, every stitch along the edges of her thong . . .

And it wasn't just there. She felt everything. The guitar-string calluses on his fingers where they sank into her skin. The rasp of beard hairs below the top layer of skin on his cheek against hers. The soft scratch of hair on the tops of his thighs slipping against her freshly shaved legs. The dewy heat of their mingled breaths. The itch of sweat dappling her skin.

She felt it all. The darkness was vibrant and three dimensional, and she was a monochrome cutout suddenly being showered with an explosion of sensation. It made her giddy. Even as the muscles in her abdomen spasmed in anticipation, the orgasm coalescing like an unstoppable colossus, she had to bite her lower lip to stop a wild giggle from escaping.

Writhing against Christof's cock as his muffled grunts vibrated against her neck was like salvation. It was gulping cool water after two years of thirst. Her entire being was sparkling and alive. So goddamn *alive*.

And then, before she'd even had time to prepare herself for it, her body seized at the sudden, surprising force of her orgasm breaking over her. The back of her skull slammed into wood and breath ripped free of her lungs, and with that breath came a raw, desperate moan in a key she'd never uttered before.

Christof's hand clamped over her mouth to stifle her cry. Her teeth scraped flesh. She tasted salt.

And dimly, she heard his velvet voice whispering against her jaw, "Good . . . come for me . . . meine Hexchen."

When it was over, she floated down to the floor—or he lowered her, more likely. Her knees wobbled, but his hands on her waist steadied her. Slowly, she released her death grip on his shoulders, letting blood rush back into her fingertips.

She couldn't remember the last time she'd come so hard—and certainly not from someone else's touch. God, did he deserve an award for that performance. A standing ovation.

"Amazing," she breathed through numb lips. An understatement. His exhale was strained. "Yes."

She let her hands fall down his front, smoothing fingers under the sweat-dappled fabric against his breastbone, and he shuddered under her light touch. Her index fingers brushed a meandering path around his small, pebbled nipples, and the pectorals beneath hardened to stone with tension. This was a man who hadn't come yet, and yet he held himself stock still as she teased him. The perfect gentleman.

He deserves a reward.

She sank to her knees.

In the second it took him to register what was happening—his hands fumbling in the dark, finding her hair, and burying his shaking fingers deep in her locks—she'd already rolled his briefs down and had his cock in her half-circled grip. Her touch explored the velvet length of him—smooth and slick with mingled precum and the smell of her own sex. At the top of his cock, his sheathed skin pulled back as her palm passed over it, the blunted head slicking her hand even more. He was uncircumcised, and that was enough of a rarity in her experience that she delighted in it. Took extra seconds to explore it, even after he hissed and his thighs began to tremble.

"Erika," he warned in a choked whisper.

Her tongue flicked out to taste his wet tip—bittersweet and savory all at once—and his hips jerked forward the tiniest bit. Enough to know he was holding himself leashed and it still wasn't enough.

"Don't come on my face," she murmured, and not because she meant it.

A strained exhale. His hands clawed in her hair, tugging briefly at the locks—not enough to seriously hurt but enough to send zings of electricity back through nerve pathways that should have already sizzled out with her orgasm.

And then she took him in her mouth, one hand clutching a taut buttock for control, the other wrapped around the base to deepen the stroke, and as she began to suck him into her throat, he lost his ever-loving shit. Obscene noises wrenched out of his throat—choked grunts and broken whimpers. Like some frenzied animal.

Erika loved it beyond reason, and she hummed in pleasure at the way he shuddered so helplessly in her thrall. God help them both if someone was still out there, because there was no discretion in what they were doing anymore. As hard as Christof tried to tamp down his response, his frantic vocalizations broke free anyway, and the wet slick of her mouth over his cock sounded so loud in the confines of this tiny, pocket fuck universe they'd created that they might as well have blasted them through an amp. And it didn't matter; if someone were to fling the door open right now, Erika doubted she'd be bothered enough to stop. Not until she had his cum filling her mouth and the rest of his soul wrapped around her little finger.

Because *this* . . . ruining Christof with her mouth . . . this was her new favorite thing in the world. Better than the thunderous praise of a packed house. Better than seeing her name on the marquee. Better than chocolate-covered pretzels.

Even though her knees and jaw ached and heat made rivulets of sweat tickle the back of her neck, she never wanted it to end. But she barely had time to luxuriate in the moment when his muscles tensed all at once and hands released their clutch on her hair. He writhed in her grip, attempting to break free. In a voice like broken gravel, he gritted out, "Enough."

She held on. Took him deeper, slowing so she could feel his rounded head sliding against the back of her throat. It had to be torturous for him.

"Can't—" His voice broke. *Too late.*

Then he shattered all around her with his buttocks spasming and the smack of his hands slamming against the door for purchase.

And his cock twitching helplessly against her tongue, filling her throat with hot spurts of cum.

When he was done, he seemed to lose the ability to stand. He lowered himself to the ground in front of her, scooped an arm around her shoulders, and settled them both so he spooned her between his legs with his own back against the door.

She was glad for the respite. Her own pulse hammered in her throat, her satiated muscles finally able to relax but now too exhausted to properly hold her upright, and his chest still rose and fell heavily against her—his newly trained diaphragm at work.

Since it was so dark and no one could see, Erika allowed a giddy, love-drunk smile to steal over her face. "Now *that's* a first kiss."

By the time Erika and Christof emerged from the closet, Sibylle and Waldo were gone, and the auditorium was dark and quiet. With a single knowing look, they snuck back to their rooms like professional thieves parting ways after a heist—silently and separately.

This was a familiar experience for Erika, this reshuffling of clothes and smoothing of hair and composing of features, followed by a surreptitious exit. Except this time, there was a moment that felt different.

A moment when they both hesitated before parting at the door to the backstage passage, unsure. A strange urge compelling Erika to ask Christof to come back to her room. A welling of desire to feel his skin against hers and fall asleep in his arms.

Terrifying.

She forced herself to keep walking. In her room, Erika collapsed on her bed with Jean cradled to her breast. She didn't need Christof to feel less alone—she had her rats.

If she let her guard down, she might fall headlong into feeling things that posed a serious danger to her heart. Christof could only be a temporary diversion; in six more weeks he'd return to Berlin and his furious drive toward international fame, and Erika would devote her full energies to rescuing the Paris Opera House, and they could both look back on this time they'd spent together and reminisce on how *deliciously* wicked it was.

Erika bit her lip and allowed herself one deep sigh of satisfaction. Six more weeks of what had happened back there in the costume closet? Sign her up for a season pass. It almost made her want to skip the Vegas trip.

Almost.

Even with her skin still flushed and her body pulsing with residual pleasure, Erika had the wherewithal to know that leaving town was the best possible idea right now. Distance would give her time to gather these loose tendrils of longing and lock them up tight inside her chest. And the meeting with Raoul would doubtless be an ice-cold reminder that the theater's fate should be her priority.

CHAPTER 17

Christof slid naked into the sheets and stretched, absently humming a riff that had wormed itself into his head despite Erika's explicit warning not to compose a song about her. Erika—his little pet witch. So impossibly sexy. So talented. So perfect.

If he had the energy, he'd worry more about the dangers of conducting a secret affair or question—with ever-mounting dread—how easy it was to fantasize about settling down with a woman who looked and acted exactly like Erika. But instead, he drifted off to sleep within seconds. His brain was wrung out. Too spent to whip itself into a maelstrom of what-ifs.

The magic even carried over to the following morning. He sauntered downstairs to Saturday rehearsal with extra volume in his hair and last night's tune on his lips.

Today was going to be different, because *he* was different, thanks to Erika. This was the dawn of a new Christof. New Christof was a laid-back, easygoing, cool guy!

He'd start by being patient with Sibylle. Her new song, "Crowbar," wasn't completely hopeless—what if they picked up the beat and threw a harder guitar line over it? Crowbars could be badass; criminals used them. And Waldo's hoofbeats had potential. Perhaps they could transform that track into an homage to American country music, like Bon Jovi's "Wanted Dead or Alive"?

Except when he came into the theater, no one was there.

He looked over the empty auditorium, searching for Waldo's prone body or a stray spike of Sibylle's hair poking up over one of the chair backs. Even the shadows where Sergei often lurked were empty. All the instruments onstage were exactly as they'd been left the night before.

"They've gone to Vegas," came Sergei's deep voice from behind Christof.

He spun to find the guitarist standing in the entry alcove Christof had come through. Christof hadn't seen anyone on the way in, which meant either Sergei had materialized from the ether, or Christof had been so lost in his self-congratulatory reverie that he'd walked right past him.

"Vegas?" Christof prayed he'd misheard. Surely his band wouldn't *depart town* during such a critical juncture in their album's development.

Surely they wouldn't have done so without telling him. Their lead singer and guitarist—and band manager. And older brother. And, apparently, the only member of this band who cared about Nachtmusik's future.

Despite the early-morning heat, his fingers went ice cold. Ah, there it was: worry. His entire miserly personality, back in black.

What were they thinking? First Gillian, and now Sibylle and Waldo? They couldn't simply . . . leave without notice.

They had *rehearsal*. Regular rehearsals were key to—

"Vegas," Sergei repeated stoically.

Christof made his face relax. He had to. Sergei was the only Nachtmusik member responsible enough to stay. Best not to scare him off too. "This won't be a problem," he heard himself say, as if from the back row in his head. "In fact, this is a wonderful opportunity. You and I will spend the weekend really hammering the guitar portions. Work out a couple of mega solos. It will be very epic, yes?"

Sergei cleared his throat. "Er."

No. *No.* "You're going with them? What could you want to do in Vegas?"

"Visiting an old friend."

"This is absurd," he snapped. He swept past Sergei into the entryway and spotted his demonic little sister clambering into the passenger side of one of those trucks one saw in nostalgic American films about growing up poor on a farm. The entire back of the truck was open to the air with only a few feet of metal barrier preventing the contents inside from tumbling to certain death, and surely Waldo wasn't planning on riding in that thing. Christof knew American safety laws were lax, but this was unbelievable.

He stormed out of the building and toward the truck.

He knew the moment they'd spotted him, because Sibylle's smug smile wilted and Waldo turned into a goggle-eyed bug, scrambling to get out of the back of the vehicle.

But Sibylle stayed put. She rolled down the window. "Guten Morgen, Big Brother. Did Sergei tell you our plans?"

"Get out."

"It's only a weekend trip. The phantasmal energies guided me to purchase tickets to sorcerer Criss Angel's show—"

Christof kicked the side of the truck. "Get. Out."

"Hey! Stop kicking my truck." Erika's voice broke through his single-minded focus on murdering his sister. The driver's side door squealed open, and she levered herself up to prop her arms on the roof of the cabin, and his breath died in his throat at the sight of her. "This was my dear, dear grandma Meg's truck, and it's in mint vintage condition"—Christof highly doubted *that*—"so it'll be very expensive to replace parts if you break them."

She'd tied the back of her hair up, and it streamed over her bare shoulder like an inky serpent. He shouldn't be able to smell her rose-scented shampoo from where he stood, but the memory of the scent filled his airways anyway. A black sundress hugged her breasts tight but hardly covered much else, and all her skin was golden in the light. With a bolt of unexpected lust, he remembered that he knew how that skin tasted like salt and honey on his tongue.

Suddenly, his mouth was dry with want, and nothing else mattered.

Waldo clapped him on the shoulder, breaking his trance. "Come with us! We can work on the album on the drive. Very old school, ja?"

Christof ignored his drummer, which was for everyone's benefit. Staring at Erika was the only thing keeping him from tossing Waldo into traffic. Although given Erika's uniquely hypnotizing effect on him, staring much longer risked dire consequences. Consequences like Christof forgetting that he gave a damn about anything else except rounding the vehicle, snapping her dress straps with his bare hands, and mauling her magnificent breasts right here in broad daylight, where his band and all of Paris could watch.

Erika raised her brow, and he wrenched his thoughts away from what her tongue-slicked nipples would look like as they gleamed under the sun.

"May I ask why you are taking my band to Las Vegas when we have an important album to work on?" he asked, as evenly as he could manage.

Guilt flashed across her face, and then it was gone. "You're paying to rent my opera house, not for me to babysit three grown adults. If your sister wants to offer me fifty bucks for gas money in exchange for a ride to someplace I'm already going, who am I to argue?"

Very well, she had a point. Just because they'd spent the week singing together didn't mean they were friends, and although last night they'd shared the hottest sexual experience of his entire life, that didn't mean she owed him her undying loyalty. In fact, Erika had no reason at all to care about his personal career ambitions—just like he had no reason to feel irrationally hurt that she didn't.

It was his own fault if he'd fallen asleep to fantasies about being half a musical power couple—Christof Daae and Erika Greene combining their powers to achieve legendary things. This was simply a far harsher awakening than he cared to admit.

His glare locked on Sibylle. "This is your doing, then?" He marched over to the passenger door and attempted to open it, but Sibylle smashed a hand over the protruding door-lock pin. "Open this door right now," he demanded.

"No."

He reached through the open window and fumbled for the lock.

Sibylle squeaked a protest and dived for the old-fashioned window crank, driving the window slowly up and into the underside of Christof's arm.

"Stop that," he snapped.

The window kept rolling. "No, *you* stop!"

Erika slammed her fist on the hood. "Everyone stop!"

Christof yanked his arm back but continued glaring at his sister, who made a pig face at him.

Erika swept a disgusted glare over them all. "I didn't ask to be involved in your little band drama. If gas weren't over four bucks a gallon right now, I'd ditch all of you and enjoy a peaceful drive filled with an hour of solo karaoke." She then withdrew a crumpled fifty-dollar bill from somewhere within the vicinity of her left breast—had she been storing that in her brassiere?—and waved it around. "Good news is, Miss Priestess of the Underworld over here paid cash up front. So everyone better untwist their fucking panties real fast, because I'm leaving in exactly sixty seconds, and anyone not in this truck gets left behind."

Sergei silently climbed into the truck bed, settling into a cross-legged position with his guitar case in his lap.

Christof clenched his jaw. "There are no seat belts. This is extremely dangerous. Why would you both risk your lives—"

"Thirty seconds!" Erika warned before slamming her door shut and settling behind the wheel.

With a sheepish glance, Waldo explained, "They have a Margaritaville."

Then Waldo climbed back into the truck, and a second later, the engine revved. Sibylle's gleeful cackle filtered through the cracked passenger window.

They were really leaving. No warning. No remorse for how it would affect his—*Nachtmusik's*—future.

Just like Gillian had done.

The floor of his stomach fell away, and before he could process what he was doing, he was moving toward the back of the truck and hauling himself up onto the back bumper.

"I will not let this band escape rehearsal," he announced, just as the truck lurched forward. Alarm made him yelp as the acceleration threw him off balance. His back boot slipped off the bumper, and his guitar slipped forward from where it was slung across his back, forcing him to choose between protecting his instrument and protecting his knees from slamming into the metal siding.

The impact sent shards of ice-white pain up his thighs. With one hand, he clutched the metal siding with all his strength. With the other, he held his guitar aloft so it wouldn't smash into anything. This was far too precarious a position to stay in much longer—Christof was in danger of toppling backward onto the shimmering asphalt. "Wait!" he called over the noise of the engine.

Waldo whooped in joy, oblivious to the life-or-death struggle before him. "Christof is coming! Now we party for real!"

"Help me up," he bit out. The truck was picking up speed as Erika merged into the light traffic on the town's main thruway. If she saw him dangling from the back, her driving didn't reflect it. Thankfully, Sergei had the sense to rescue his bandmate from the clutches of death. He hauled Christof up just in time for Erika to make a hard right turn, sending all three of the men in the truck bed sprawling.

Christof rolled onto his back, clutched his guitar against his stomach, and blinked up at the cloudless blue sky.

The window panel behind the front cabin squeaked open. "Sorry, forgot you guys were back there!" came Erika's voice. She did not sound particularly sorry. "The brakes on this bad boy are a little loose, so I recommend holding on to the ropes."

Christof stretched out an arm, feeling along the corrugated floor of the truck bed until he found the aforementioned nylon rope. He tugged, testing its strength.

It came free with zero resistance. He held the frayed end up to the sky.

"This rope?"

"Oops!"

He flung the length over the side of the truck. "This cannot be legal," he shouted.

"Don't worry, I have a valid license!"

This is how my life ends, he thought darkly. *En route to Las Vegas in a dilapidated American-made wagon.*

On the heels of glum acceptance came a slow-burning fury.

If he died now, he'd never play to a screaming crowd in Madison Square Garden. Never be inducted into the Rock and Roll Hall of Fame. Never grace the cover of *Rolling Stone* in the ultraviolet spandex leggings he'd purchased solely for the purpose while at a tour stop in Antwerp, on a day when he'd been feeling particularly ambitious.

Worse yet, he realized with dawning horror, he'd go to his grave never having had proper sex with anyone except Gillian. He'd never even had a clandestine encounter in a semipublic place before last night—what other wicked sexual exploits would he be forgoing if his corpse went careening off into the desert at the speed of a hundred kilometers an hour?

Waldo's giant head moved into his frame of view. "Are you solid, mein brother? You look mega sick."

"Never been better," he said through clenched teeth. If he survived this ride, there would be a reckoning. The *minute* they arrived in Vegas, he was calling them a car and physically dragging his band back to Paris for rehearsal.

And Erika . . .

"Do you know that you are making dog noises? *Grr, grr*," Waldo mimicked. "Are you sure you don't need to vomit? It often helps for me."

He snarled.

Waldo's head disappeared from view. "I think he is mad at us!"

"You think so?" came Sibylle's voice from the cabin. "Awww, I think he's cute like this. Like a schnauzer."

Christof ignored them. He locked eyes with Erika in the rearview mirror, and heat flared up inside him, incinerated the coil of anxious fury in his belly, and transformed it into something new.

If he'd spun up fantasies of friendship and romance, that was his own mistake. But sexual attraction between them? That was real. Necessary, even. Because when he'd been with her in that closet last night, it was the only time in recent memory he'd felt free.

And as her gaze seared through him, he knew that unless he distanced himself from her before tonight, it would happen again.

CHAPTER 18

"What is this music? Are we at the widowed-grandmother night at the pub?"

Was Sibylle serious? The desert highway in front of her was empty far off into the distance, so Erika took the opportunity to fix her driving companion with a look of disbelief. "Excuse you? This is *West Side Story*. You're talking shit about the soundtrack to *West* fucking *Side Story*?"

"West side, east side, inside, outside . . . I don't care; it's garbage," Sibylle replied with all the artistic certainty of a woman who'd spent the past hour of the drive scrawling what appeared to be zombie erotica poetry in her sketch pad.

When Sibylle had found Erika loading her suitcase into the truck and had offered her fifty bucks for a ride, Erika had impulsively said yes. The decision had been driven by a painfully trite longing for female companionship.

One Erika now deeply regretted. Trying to befriend Sibylle was like hoping a feral grizzly bear might like to come inside to watch *Moulin Rouge!* and do pedicures. And seeing the hurt on Christof's face had been an unpleasant reminder that she cared way too much about him and his band.

So much for using the weekend to smother her kindling feelings for Christof Daae.

Erika patiently explained to Sibylle, "This soundtrack has won dozens of awards."

"Awards are for unloved children." Sibylle poked at the cassette deck. "How do I connect to the Bluetooth here? I will show you Type O Negative. That is good music."

Shudder. "Stick your phone directly in the slot." The truck was a 1982 Chevy, and as far as Erika could tell from the haphazardly mounted console, the only reason this thing had a cassette player at all was that the original console had been either sold or stolen, and someone had replaced it with a cassette deck that was too small for the slot and duct-taped it until it stayed in place. It was on brand for Grandma Meg, who hadn't had the truck listed as an asset when the bank had come calling for blood, yet when Erika had gone through the drawers at the opera house, she'd found the keys and a (questionable) title of ownership that matched the rust-brown truck parked behind the dilapidated garden shed in the brothel's gravel lot. Who knew why Grandma Meg had needed a pickup truck in the first place. Nor did Erika have any idea why that garden shed housed what appeared to be a hatch to a cellar—Erika had taken one look at the spiderweb-encrusted hole in the ground and noped right out of that death trap.

"It doesn't fit."

"Oh, that's too bad." Erika tsked. "Guess we'll have to listen to my music." She spun the volume wheel up and began to sing along to "Tonight." After a few bars, she shouted over the din, "Feel free to jump in and sing Tony's part! It's in your range!"

Sibylle made gagging sounds.

Point made, Erika lowered the volume before her own eardrums suffered. "You can always go sit in the back with the boys."

In unison, she and Sibylle looked over their shoulders to see Christof glowering at them from his position at the back, his long arms stretched out to capture both sides of the truck in a white-knuckled grip. His icy mane whipped around his face and his half-unbuttoned shirt billowed like he was some dashing pirate on the cover of a romance novel.

Waldo was curled up in an apparently blissful nap, and Sergei was strumming something inaudible on his guitar.

"I would rather die," Sibylle muttered.

Christof's mouth moved. It looked an awful lot like he was yelling at Erika to "turn around and pay attention to the road."

Erika gave him a serene smile and obeyed—very slowly. From the corner of her eye, she spied Sibylle fixing her with a narrow-eyed glare.

"He's seeing someone, I will remind you." Sibylle's tone was unreadable.

"Is that so?" Erika replied coolly, even as embarrassment prickled under her skin. Had she really been so obvious? She'd always prided herself on her ability to play it cool when encountering her hookups in public. A childish instinct made her say, "Although that's never stopped anyone before, has it?"

"It's stopped my brother. In ten years, he has never looked at another woman."

"Ooooh, a real saint."

"He is. He's an annoying, bossy know-everything, but he's very loyal. He would never hurt Gillian."

If only Gillian had felt the same way, huh? Then your brokenhearted brother wouldn't be twisting himself into a distressed pretzel trying to cover for her. "Lucky her." Erika stared straight ahead at the highway, not trusting herself to glance at Sibylle.

The bassist said, "He has been acting oddly, though. And it's weird that Gillian hasn't responded to any of my texts. Waldo thinks something happened between them before our final concert, but I don't know why he wouldn't tell us."

It wasn't her secret to tell, though the thinly veiled hurt in Sibylle's voice made Erika want to do so. Was telling Sibylle the right thing or the wrong thing to do? Trying to be *good* was fucking complicated.

"Could be he's focused on this album you're trying to record and doesn't want Gillian's absence to be a distraction."

"Ugh. Stupid album." The sound of pencil furiously scratching on paper filled the small cabin. "My brother loves talking about how we're a family, but all of the decisions, *he* makes. It's like he doesn't have trust for us!"

Erika took her eyes off the road long enough to fix Sibylle with a skeptical look. "And why might that be, do you think?"

Sibylle shrugged. "Oh, like you never have made mistakes. At least you don't have a big brother reminding you every day of every small thing you have done wrong for the last twenty-four years."

Erika laughed darkly. "I don't need one. I only have to look in the mirror."

The scribbling stopped. "Oh no. Don't steal my thing."

"Your *thing*?"

"Yes. In this band, I am the melodramatic one. You can't be that one."

"I'm not in your band," Erika reminded her. "And for the record, I'm a Tony-nominated Broadway star. If I *wanted* to be melodramatic, you'd be hopelessly outclassed."

"Ha! You? Please. I once hatched two crows from eggs and named them Death and Despair."

Were Erika's ears deceiving her? Because it almost seemed like, in her strange, misanthropic little way, Sibylle was attempting to . . . *bond* with her. And for some inexplicable reason, this made Erika vaguely, triumphantly giddy.

"I live in a basement sex dungeon with my pet rats," Erika countered. "By *choice*."

"See the vial on this choker?" Sibylle pointed to her spiked collar. "This is my ex-lover's blood."

Gross. But Erika would rather die than be upstaged. "And *I'm* horrifically scarred." She pulled back her curtain of hair and tilted her head toward Sibylle to flaunt her skin graft.

"Mega geil," Sibylle breathed.

"And!" Erika gloated. "I slept with my understudy's boyfriend, and when she found out, she cursed me in dramatic fashion, which resulted in a freak accident that caused this scarring. An affliction which then exiled me from Manhattan high society and my theater career in one fell swoop, leaving me no choice but to retreat to this hellish shithole to wither away in solitary misery whilst ostensibly repenting for my many, many sins. Which I will continue to do until the opera house inevitably fails or I, presumably, die. Whichever comes first, I suppose." Saying it aloud made it sound even more ludicrous, but Sibylle only sucked in her breath in a way that was openly envious.

"Yes? Well, I . . ." Sibylle tapped her pencil against her lips, thinking. "I lost my virginity in a cemetery. On my *mother's grave.*"

Erika smirked. "No, you didn't."

"Fine, that was Mary Shelley," Sibylle grumbled, slouching impossibly farther into her seat. At this point, her knees were up to her chin, her platform boots propped on the dashboard. "But you still have to pick a different thing if you want to be in our band."

"I don't want to be in your band, Sibylle. I don't even like hair metal."

"You don't?" Sibylle sounded confused. "Then how come you and my brother keep sneaking down to the theater to practice late at night?"

Her blood froze. Erika clutched the steering wheel in a death grip. Had they been caught last night, after all? Had Sibylle been toying with her—playing the long game?

Nausea kicked in: an old, guilty reflex. *Don't let the audience see you sweat.* "He's paying me to help with the album." Paying in sexual gratification, maybe, but it wasn't entirely a lie.

"Oh." Did Sibylle sound disappointed? Surely Erika was imagining it. "I thought maybe he wanted to replace Gillian on keys. Like maybe she was leaving the band so they could start a family or something. I always wanted to be one of those cool aunties who took the kids to haunted castles and bought them illegal pets."

Erika was getting whiplash from the directions this conversation was taking. "Does Christof *want* kids?" she blurted. The answer didn't matter. It *didn't*. Except Erika's own career dreams had never involved children; she'd imagined finding a partner someday who was equally ambitious. Someone who would understand why she could never be the nurturing type, because the music she created *was* her progeny. For a brief, silly moment, Erika had imagined Christof could be that person.

"I don't think so, but I know Gillian does." Sibylle sighed, and Erika fought the most ridiculous wave of relief. "Guess I'd hoped you really were joining the band for that reason. And you are pretty good. Maybe even better than Gillian."

"Well, I'm not joining the band," Erika repeated, but less firmly this time.

Sibylle made a chuffing sound but didn't reply. The minutes stretched, and the bland brown-and-beige desert zipped past the window.

Like an addictive habit, Erika glanced in the rearview mirror again, and her heart stuttered when she found narrowed hazel eyes already locked on hers. There was intention in that look, and it was not chaste and gentle.

She wrested her attention back to the road, but it was too late. Anticipation hit her hard and fast. Dizzying heat already spun its way through her belly and down to the apex of her thighs.

Her shaking hand fumbled for the air-conditioning wheel. A futile endeavor: the AC was already on full, and it still blasted out of the vents at ambient air temperature.

"So . . ." Sibylle's voice broke through the delirium. "I did a séance last night . . ."

"Is that so?"

"Yeah, I asked for your grandma Meg like you told me to, but she didn't answer."

"When did I—" Erika shook her head, trying to focus on the fact that Sibylle wasn't, in fact, calling her out for hooking up with her brother. "Never mind. I'm not surprised Grandma Meg isn't taking calls. She probably thinks you're a bill collector."

Sibylle's expression lit up. "However, I did speak to your great-great-grandmother, Mistress Giry! She wouldn't tell me about the murder, but she said to let you know that . . . what was it, again? Right. 'To find what you seek, you need only look beyond the mirror.'"

"I highly doubt I'm going to find a Tony Award in the mirror."

"You want to return to performing again? I thought you were retired and doing this theater business."

"Right. That's what I meant." Erika scrunched her nose. After two years, she should have gotten used to her new life, but it seemed a part of her was still living in the past.

"Help me to understand, yes?" Sibylle said slowly. "You don't want to be in our band, but you're not going back to singing. I don't think your scars are so hideous at all. So are you sure you can't go back to Broadway?"

"You don't understand how shallow the theater world is." The truth was, she hadn't even bothered to try after the accident. She'd stopped taking her agent's calls. Even stopped checking Broadway news, for fear she might read that Carla had been chosen to permanently replace her in *Les Misérables*. She hadn't wanted to deal with the specter of rejection from auditioning for new roles; better to run away before she could find out.

"Ja, okay. If you say so. Maybe Tony nominations are not a very big deal."

Erika sighed. How to explain in a way Sibylle would understand? "After my skin graft, I was recovering for weeks, and *none* of my friends or costars came to visit after the first few days. They only came once, to gawk at my hideousness and then gossip about my downfall."

"This sounds like a problem you have caused for yourself, so I have only small pity for you."

"So it's somehow *my* fault all my friends were shitty?"

"Yes," Sibylle answered, matter-of-factly. "You should pick better friends. For example, I would have visited you, if you were my friend. Of course, you are stealing my thing. So we're not friends."

"Thank Streisand for *that* mercy."

Sibylle hissed.

Erika hissed back.

Someone banged on the back window. Erika glanced over her shoulder to see Christof angrily pointing at the road.

She fluttered her eyelashes at him and turned around.

"What is his fucking problem?" Sibylle grumbled.

"Probably wanted to point out I'd drifted into the wrong lane," Erika said. Since there were no cars currently coming in the other direction, she took her time veering back to the right side of the road.

"Ugh. He is so verklemmt."

"Does that mean 'ass clenched so tight he shits into another dimension'?"

A tiny smile slid across Sibylle's face. "Yes."

"So I shouldn't tell him I never actually passed a driving test."

"Oh no, tell him. And make sure I am there to witness." Sibylle leaned forward and ran a desultory inventory of the cardboard box of cassette tapes wedged between the gearshift and the dash. "These are all musicals?"

"Sorry to disappoint you, but yes. Grandma Meg had singular taste. Except for her collection of Sting singles. I burned those."

"Good."

Inspiration struck, and Erika plucked a tape out of the box. "Here. Maybe you'll like this. It's a horror musical."

"*Sweeney Todd*?" Sibylle flipped the case over and inspected the track list. "They sing about pie?"

"Not just *any* pie." Erika waggled her eyebrows.

"Ahh." A feral grin spread over Sibylle's face. "Evil pie."

Erika found herself matching the expression. "Exactly."

By the time Erika pulled into the valet pavilion at Carte Blanche Casino and Hotel, Christof was thoroughly wrecked. His bum ached from the metal vibrating against his tailbone, his hands ached from gripping the sides of the truck, and his skull hosted a colossal headache from the strain of . . . *everything*.

To make matters worse, he was 99 percent certain Sibylle and Erika were now conspiring against him. The way they'd gone from barely sheathing their claws to becoming bosom duet partners in the space of an hour? Well, it was highly concerning. Sibylle was enough of a menace when left to her own devices, but Erika was far more intelligent, experienced, and unapologetically wicked than his sister, and the last thing Christof needed was for those two to team up and concoct all manner of chaotic feminine plots.

The fate of Nachtmusik was already hanging in precarious balance. He needed to wrest things back under control.

Christof carefully disembarked from the truck bed and joined Sibylle, Waldo, and Sergei at the foot of the casino's opulent steps. Eyeing their surroundings, Christof said darkly, "This place looks expensive."

"More expensive than four thousand dollars a week?" Sibylle gave him a pointed look. From the corner of his vision, Christof saw Sergei disappear into the casino.

"Sergei!" Christof called, but it was too late.

"I will find him!" Waldo volunteered, dashing up the steps.

"No, Waldo—"

Then his drummer was gone too. Christof scowled and turned back to his sister. "We won't be staying here. I'm calling us a car, and all Nachtmusik members will be returning to Paris."

"I don't think so, Big Brother. Erika said she can get us free rooms to stay overnight. Right, Erika, my new friend?"

"We're not friends," Erika mumbled in an unconvincing tone, and he read guilt in her expression. "But yes, I'll ask at the front desk to have rooms reserved under each of your names. Sibylle made some very good points about the band needing a break. Sometimes, creativity needs air to breathe—"

"May I speak to you privately?" Christof growled in a low tone. Sibylle was watching their interaction with rapt attention, so he shooed her inside. "You, go find Waldo and Sergei and bring them back here."

Sibylle rolled her eyes, but she complied.

"Relax," Erika said when Sibylle was out of earshot. "It's just a weekend."

Relax? Was she speaking to someone else? "You know how much this album means to me. I thought we had an understanding."

"Do we?" Her scarlet lips flattened. "I *understand* I'm giving you voice lessons out of the goodness of my heart. I *understand* that what happened last night in the closet is something I very much enjoyed and would like to do again."

His abdomen tightened. "As would I."

"But I've also decided that I like your sister, and I think you're being unfair to your band by not telling them the truth. And it's also unfair to *me* that I'm burdened with keeping your secret and have to sneak around in the dark of night just to get laid. So why don't you tell your band the truth, and in exchange, I'll convince Sibylle to round up the others."

He gritted his teeth. She made it seem so easy. How could he explain that he lay awake at night worrying about all the ways Nachtmusik's future could catastrophically implode? Every single thing he did, he did with the goal of *avoiding* that fate. "I can't do that," he bit out. This wouldn't be forever. Gillian would come back soon.

She *would* come back.

And then everything would be fine. He only had to hold it together a little longer.

"Then enjoy your weekend in Las Vegas. Maybe it'll be good for you to let loose a little. Because, after all, *you*"—she poked him in the chest with a crimson-tipped nail—"are Christof Daae, front man for a wildly popular European rock band."

"Yes, I know." He cocked his head in confusion.

"The problem is, you're not *acting* like it, Christof. Stomping around and glaring at everyone and everything, scolding your band-mates in public . . . if you didn't have your guitar strapped to your back like a traveling court jester, I'd think you were someone's parole officer. At least the rest of your band is playing the part. But you . . . if they filmed your *Behind the Music* special right now, I'd fall asleep ten minutes in. You'd probably spend half your interview time showing off your daily planner."

What was wrong with his daily planner? And how was it that *she* was lecturing *him*? He was the one who was angry! And he had every right to be.

Didn't he?

He forcibly made himself ignore the twinge of doubt. It was the same one that seemed to occur whenever he was in Erika's presence, and therefore, he decided, she must be in some way responsible for his current angst. All of it, perhaps?

Not *all* of it. But certainly a great portion thereof. And if he could bury his cock in her and demand that she ride him until his brain went numb, he'd finally purge this inner restlessness and become refreshed, calm, and entirely capable of solving Nachtmusik's problems.

Erika held something out for him to take, and without thinking, he accepted her car keys. Then she breezed past Christof toward the lobby's rotating doors.

Tension roiling in his gut, he hurried after her into the lobby, only to be stopped by the valet. "Sir, is this your truck?"

"Er . . ."

The valet looked pointedly at the keys in Christof's hand, and he realized Erika expected him to sort out the parking situation. The gold-plated sign next to the valet stand advertised valet service for twenty-five dollars a day. What an unreasonable expense! "Please direct me to a free parking area."

Fifteen minutes later, Christof blinked as his eyes adjusted to the dark, windowless lobby of Carte Blanche—and decided he hated this Gilded Age, banking-themed den of iniquity on principle. A misguided soul could easily fall to temptation here, surrounded by soft forest-green carpets, gale-force air-conditioning, and a thousand rows of slyly chiming slot machines and game tables beckoning from every side.

Erika was nowhere to be found, but to his enormous relief, he saw his bandmates hadn't gone far. The three of them crowded around a slot machine in the casino's lobby. A glittering marquee above it declared, **WIN A ROLLS-ROYCE PHANTOM.** The car in question lurked behind the display on a slowly rotating platform, its pearlescent slate coat glistening under moving lights.

Christof wove through the crowd toward them, trying to ignore the siren calls coming from all sides.

Take a chance, whispered the softly glowing slot machine on his left. *What harm could it do?* cajoled the rhythmic thwap of cards being shuffled atop dense felt. The clattering of a roulette wheel urged, *Come on, Christof. Have a little fun, for once . . .*

He fought a tug of longing. He couldn't relax here, no matter how much he wished to. People acted irresponsibly in places like this, and responsibility was key to success.

"One hundred dollars a pull? No fucking way!" Sibylle was saying when Christof stormed up to the machine.

Waldo's expression brightened when he noticed Christof's arrival. "Tof, can I borrow—"

"No."

Erika reappeared at Christof's side, balancing an overflowing gift basket against her hip. "Here," she told Waldo, handing him a large golden coin of some sort. Then she offered one each to Sergei and Sibylle too. "Compliments of the house."

"Fuck *me*!" Sibylle held up the coin to the light. "A hundred each? The casino owner gave you these for free?"

Erika gave her a pointed look. "Nothing's ever really free, is it?"

Sibylle smirked, then spun around to join Waldo and Sergei at the slot machine, where they'd surely waste their newfound fortune in record time.

Christof silently counted down in his head. *Three . . . two . . . one . . .*

"Noooo!" Waldo cried. "It stole my coin and gave me nothing!"

Sibylle looked at the screen. "You lost, Dummkopf. You shouldn't gamble. You are bad at these things."

"What have I done wrong?" Waldo entreated.

"Your energy is bad. Step aside; I'll show you." Sibylle shouldered Waldo out of the way. With a deep breath, she closed her eyes and raised her hands to her face, palms inward. "Yessss . . . yes, I sense there are many haunted souls here. Undead spirits, hear me. Find me worthy of these riches."

Christof gave a derisive snort, though no one paid him any notice.

Except Erika. "Oh, don't be such a party pooper. You get one too," she told him and held up another token between two fingers.

He snatched it without thinking. Not that he intended to *use* it. He'd sensibly cash it out later.

Erika cleared her throat and announced, "Anyway, I'm going to check out my room. Have a lovely weekend, everyone."

"Thank you, Erika!" Waldo said.

Erika brushed past Christof, and as she did so, her bare forearm grazed his sleeve. His body seized at the contact as if she'd scalded him with a hot pan. In a voice barely loud enough to hear, she said, "If you change your mind . . ."

Something hard and flat pressed into his palm. He instinctively closed around it before he'd even registered that it was her room key.

Before he could think better of it, he followed her around a corner to the elevators. When she reached out to press the call button, he grabbed her wrist. "You are a poor influence on my band."

"Is that so?" She gazed up at him through her curtain of hair. "It sounds like you have some feelings to share."

"I have more than *feelings* to share with you, Erika."

"Good. You know where to find me tonight."

She began to step away.

He tugged her close, bringing her flush with his body, her forehead inches from his chin. "What about now?" He didn't even care that they might be seen; nothing mattered except his fury and desire.

"Right *now*, I'm busy." She slipped free of his hold and gave him a placid smile. "I have errands to run, and then our host extended a generous credit on my tab, so I'm going to see how fast I can spend his money before my meeting with him tomorrow. I should be back in my room around, say . . . midnight?"

The elevator dinged open.

As if bespelled, Christof stepped forward to follow, when Sibylle's voice echoed through the lobby: *"Fuck!"*

He couldn't see the slot machine from this angle, but he recognized the sound of Sibylle's thick-soled boots slamming into metal, and his brain reflexively clicked back into Responsibility Mode. He should intervene before Sibylle got Nachtmusik banned from yet another establishment.

Erika glided into the elevator, the skirt of her long black sundress rippling around her legs like a serpent's tail. "I guess you should take care of that, shouldn't you?"

He almost didn't. For a split second, he paused, tempted to ignore his sister's plight and do something wholly irresponsible and selfish.

It was his hesitation that cost him as the elevator doors slid shut in front of his nose, leaving Christof staring at his own miserable reflection in the elevator door.

Erika pressed her palms onto the elevator doors for support, thankful she was alone in the small space. Her eyes squeezed shut to block out the reflection of her flushed, need-drugged expression. Her breath came in hot, ragged puffs.

It was good he hadn't followed her. It *was*.

The elevator buzzed at her to pick a floor, and she reluctantly pressed a button.

For the sake of the opera house and her pride and her shaky attempts at being a good person, she prayed he wouldn't end up staying the weekend. That he wouldn't come to her room tonight and do the unspeakable things the fury in his dark gaze had promised.

And she also prayed he would.

When he returned to the lobby, his bandmates were gone.

No. No, no, no . . .

Desire evaporated, leaving him chilled.

It had just been a small slip. A few minutes of selfish distraction. But now his band had gone rogue, and his plans for Nachtmusik to practice all weekend were slipping even further out of reach.

This is what happens when I let my guard down. He could never do that again. Never.

As Christof searched for his bandmates in the maze of the casino, the crowd seemed to close in around him. The chiming machines became louder. The lights flashed more brightly. Bodies flowed in and out of the lobby like a tide, and where he stood in the middle of the pavilion was the worst place to be. There were no straight lines in this casino—everything was curved and zigzagged, and way signs were printed on dark mahogany and hard to find. It was a labyrinth, designed to suck its victims into its chaos and drain them of all reason and agency.

Maybe some people wanted chaos. That was why they came to Las Vegas, wasn't it? People came here to lose themselves and forget who they were—and what really mattered.

Someone bumped into him and didn't bother to apologize. Fearing for the safety of his guitar, Christof lurched away from the flow of traffic and managed to find the front desk. As promised, a room had been reserved for him. He only needed it for a brief respite—a half hour, at most. A place to catch his breath and recoup before he redoubled his efforts to gather the band.

By the time he made his way upstairs and slid his room key into the slot, his pulse was racing so fast that he felt vaguely ill. At least it was blessedly dark in his room, the shades drawn to keep the room cool. As the door snicked shut behind him, Christof barely registered the room's overwrought opulence—all done up in that same emerald-green-and-polished-mahogany scheme—before cranking the thermostat down to whatever fifty-five degrees Fahrenheit converted to, gently setting his guitar down on the bed, and lying down alongside the instrument.

In that moment, he decided that if he could only speak to Gillian . . . if he could somehow be certain she was coming back and Nachtmusik wouldn't disband, everything would be fine. That was all he needed to feel better.

Tugging his phone out of his back pocket, he dialed.

Nothing.

He left another voice mail. Added another text message to the string of unanswered bubbles.

"Where are you?" he asked her still avatar image—a cropped head-shot from one of their first official band photos. He recalled that Gillian was the only one of the band who'd chosen to smile in that photo. That was evidence enough that she'd been happy—wasn't it?

He was half-tempted to call Gillian's estranged mother, if only to reassure himself that he'd tried everything to locate her, except he knew Gillian would hack off his balls if he dared get that awful woman involved.

"Deep breaths," he reminded himself, stroking the back of his hand along his guitar's smooth body for some sense of comfort.

He attempted to follow his own instructions, but it was like he'd forgotten how breathing worked. With every inhale before some repeating worry interrupted his focus, and with every exhale, he felt the urgent need to bolt upright. To pace. To *do* something.

Except he had no idea what he *should* be doing, because he couldn't make his band suddenly care about the album enough to prioritize it over all else, he couldn't write the entire album on his own, and above all, he was no magician, and he couldn't make Gillian simply . . . appear.

He gave up on forcing his body to relax, sat up, and turned on the TV.

And there she was.

CHAPTER 19

Gillian wasn't dead. She wasn't being held hostage by pirates, imprisoned by secretive government forces, or—God forbid—rapturously immersed in the Parisian underground punk-revival scene.

Gillian was at the *fucking* Eurovision Song Contest.

She beamed and waved at him through the screen, her halo of pomegranate ringlets bobbing in the shimmering lighting. The camera then cut back to a gaggle of long-necked men wearing . . . whatever the *fuck* one called the ruffled lion suits they wore, as they stepped offstage. To Christof's horror, the camera zoomed in as one of the spindly cat-men gathered Gillian in his noodle arms and smothered her in an open-mouthed kiss.

The announcer remarked, "And from Lithuania, it's disco sensation Pasididžiavimas, an early favorite. And that's lead singer Leonas, who's quite the international playboy, isn't he? Some of you rock and roll fans out there might recognize Gillian Dietrich of Nachtmusik—"

"Fuck!" Christof stabbed the power button. Missed. The screen flashed to the TV Guide Channel, but the torturous audio continued. "Fuck, fuck, *fuuuuck*!"

A female announcer chimed in with a giggle and a breathless "Wow, can't say I blame her after that performance. Who knew disco could be so . . . what's the word I'm looking for?"

"Primal?" the third host offered helpfully.

"Indeed."

He held up the remote and fired at the screen helplessly, but it wouldn't obey him. They were still *talking*. And now he'd somehow muted it, but the screen was back to the contest footage, and all he could see was a replay clip of three men in fur-trimmed bell-bottoms thrusting their hips directly at the camera, and then it cut back to Gillian, and she was *still* engaged in the face-devouring kiss with this Leonas nonsense. It hardly even looked like a kiss at this point, but Christof wasn't sure exactly *what* it was.

All he knew was, it didn't look like Gillian was about to pack her bags and hop on a flight to Las Vegas.

The sensation of helplessness—of drowning in a sea of fury—was suddenly so intense that he didn't even remember deciding to throw the remote. It simply left his hand and smashed into the screen. Thankfully, the screen didn't break. The remote bounced off the TV's flat screen, causing it to rock dangerously on its stand but only leaving an ugly purple impact crater in the middle of Leonas's face.

And then slowly, like in a dream, the oval banker's lamp behind the TV toppled over, hit the edge of the armoire, and shattered onto the plush emerald rug.

Stunned, he stared at the wreckage. He'd actually *broken* something. He never lost his temper like that.

". . . up next, it's the United Kingdom with something a little different."

Shaking himself, he found the clarity to stand up and turn the TV off by hand, just as a hologram of a mariachi band took the stage.

And after all that, all he could manage was a quiet "What the fuck?" Because how else did he grapple with what he'd just seen?

His girlfriend of over a decade—his *bandmate* for over *fifteen years*—had up and left him with no warning, abandoned everyone in Nachtmusik without a word, and sent his entire life into chaos.

For a fucking Lithuanian disco performer in a lion suit.

Well.

Well.

It was actually a bit funny, if you thought about it, wasn't it? All this time he'd been wrapping himself up in knots, desperately trying to hold his entire world together until Gillian's return, and it was all for nothing. Because she wasn't coming back. She was in Copenhagen with her new boyfriend, and she didn't even care enough about her band to let them know.

A sudden calm came over him. Carefully, he stepped over the broken lamp to get to the minibar. He took out a Kit Kat bar and slowly, deliberately ate it. Then he tossed the wrapper on the ground and found the M&M's and ate those. And when he'd finished eating all the candy, he opened the little vodka bottle and drank that.

It had been a while since he'd really chugged hard liquor, but he decided he liked the heat that swept down his esophagus. He liked the temporary dizzying rush of lightness that followed it. After the third mini bottle, he liked it even more, because suddenly the situation that had seemed only a little bit funny now seemed *hilarious.*

"I'm a fucking joke, aren't I?" His fist closed over the row of little bottles and came away with a handful. Slamming the fridge shut, he staggered to his feet, chuckling to himself at the absurdity of it all. "A rock star in Vegas, and here I am. Rocking you like a . . . a nothing." One by one, he shoved the bottles into the waistband of his pants, saving the last for the road. "Maybe Erika's right. I need to let go. I need to *be* the fire tornado. No, of course she's right. She's brilliant. Beautiful and brilliant. I should fucking marry her. I fucking *will* marry her. Sweep her right off her feet."

The thought made him laugh harder. Imagine! He proposing to Erika when they hardly knew each other? His band would think he'd had a mental break of some sort. He hadn't even proposed to Gillian after a decade together. He hadn't even considered it.

And good thing I didn't, yes? Considering.

Still cackling to himself, he swung his guitar onto his back, left the room, and positively *strolled* to the elevators, sipping his little bottle of gin all the while. Halfway down to the lobby, he recalled that he'd left his phone on the bed, and a spike of familiar anxiety made him pause.

He never left his phone behind. What if there was an emergency? What if someone in the band needed him?

The elevator dinged, and a group of high-heeled blondes got on. The youngest was technically old enough to be his mother.

"Well, look at you, handsome," one of the women purred, eyeing his chest, which was hardly covered by his unbuttoned shirt. "Are you one of the performers?"

Liquor-fueled confidence ran through him. He gave her his crowd-pleasing smile. "I am a performer, yes."

"Oh, Monica, he's not Australian. He can't be from down under."

One of the other women snapped her fingers. "Darling, he's quite clearly playing for the other team. Look at his gorgeous eye shadow."

"Doesn't he look a little like a young Bon Jovi?" Monica replied.

This elicited a collective sigh of admiration. "Oh God, *yes*. Hon, you have to come with us! We're going to see male dancers."

Fuck it. These women looked like they wanted to have fun, and Christof was on a mission to prove . . . well, he wasn't sure what he wanted to prove. But being impulsive seemed like an ideal place to start. Furthermore, there were still ten hours left before midnight—a wealth of time to kill before he could go to Erika's room and finish what they'd started last night in the costume closet.

"Christof Daae," he introduced himself by way of reply. He saluted them with his empty gin bottle. "Rock star, badass, and all-around fun machine. Lead the way, ladies."

She couldn't believe Christof had stood her up.

The bedside clock read 12:21 a.m. Beneath her hotel robe, the stiff lace on her new bra-and-panty set scratched her skin.

Erika paced back and forth across the golden carpet of her suite and debated the eternal question of *How dare he?*

He had to have gone back to Paris. There was no other explanation for it. She was clearly no match for his upstanding conscience, and that was his problem; it had nothing to do with her.

It was dark in the closet. Maybe he was weirded out by the scars by daylight. No, that made no sense; he'd seen her uncovered face before all that.

Did it matter what his reasons were? He'd made his choice, and it wasn't her—that was what mattered. The disrespect. She was over being tossed aside like the tissue paper in a gift bag. Couldn't anyone see she *was* the gift?

She'd thought Christof was different. Apparently not.

"Asshole!" Erika flung off her robe and jerked her new burgundy sequin dress up over her hips, ripping the tags off as she went. So what if she'd used Raoul Decomte's generous house credit to buy show tickets, promptly sold said tickets to a scalper, and then used the cash to go shopping and buy herself a few nice things? She deserved nice things.

A pang hit her when she thought of all the nice things she'd left behind in New York. All those designer clothes. The apartment full of minimalist-chic furniture. Fresh-cut flowers on her dining table. One of those little hockey-puck vacuums that cleaned her parquet floors while she was out drinking expensive martinis and being wooed by ineligible men. She'd lived the dream life, hadn't she?

Never mind that whenever she'd come home—usually the following morning—she'd often found herself slithering down her apartment door the moment it had shut behind her and collapsing into a puddle on those parquet floors. It hadn't mattered if they'd been cleaned, because she'd usually been too hungover and full of maudlin self-recrimination to care.

Dressed to kill and pissed off enough to actually do it, Erika had one foot out the door to go out and make deliciously irresponsible life choices when she received Sibylle's text:

Christof has been abducted.

Erika found Sibylle on the eleventh floor, outside the rooms she'd reserved for Nachtmusik with her own money. Technically, it was rent money Christof had paid in advance for the following week, which should have gone toward the theater's debt. But then Christof had acted so betrayed, and Erika had felt so guilty, and she was trying to be *good*, so throwing money at the problem seemed like the fastest way to fix it.

Little good that had done her.

"He's gone," Sibylle repeated upon seeing Erika, impatiently thrusting a cell phone in Erika's direction. The bassist wore an oversize Criss Angel T-shirt so hideous that Erika was momentarily distracted by the sight of it. "He left his phone! He never leaves his phone."

She shook herself. "Sorry, hold on. What did you mean, he's been 'abducted'?"

"I mean, someone's *taken* him."

"Is this a Liam Neeson situation? I thought he went back to Paris."

"No, he left me a message soon after we arrived, to say he got this room. He was very upset with me, as usual. But then I ran out of tokens, so I went to his room to ask for forgiveness, and he was not there. And look!"

Sibylle pushed open the door to the hotel room she stood in front of, and Erika realized it was already cracked open. Lodged between the door and the frame was a little minibar gin bottle.

That was odd. She hadn't taken Christof for the kind of man who'd pay minibar prices for his booze. He seemed more of the "we have perfectly good alcohol at home" type.

Tentatively, she pushed open the door. "Christof?"

When there was no reply, she flicked on the lights. The room was empty. The only evidence of Christof's existence was a rainbow of candy wrappers on the floor and a shattered lamp.

This *was* concerning.

She nudged the minibar door open with her foot, and her heart sank, even as her suspicions were confirmed. She'd wanted him to let go of the reins a bit—not drive the whole fucking carriage off a cliff.

"See?" Sibylle said from the doorway. "The only explanation is he's been abducted by netherworld revenants! Fucking spectral cuuuuu . . ." Seeing Erika's face, she amended, "Countrywomen. It's my fault. I shouldn't have substituted iodized salt during the séance. The dead despise iodine!"

Erika scanned the room a second time, then shook her head. "His guitar isn't here, which means he's still alive, because I think you and I both know that death is the only way he'd part with that thing."

When Sibylle didn't respond, Erika turned to find her gazing forlornly at the cell phone in her hand. In that moment, with her body swallowed by that giant T-shirt, Sibylle looked less like a scary Elvira-Catwoman impersonator and more like Christof's scared, worried, twenty-four-year-old little sister.

"Sibylle, he's probably *fine*. He's the most responsible, self-controlled person I've ever met. What's the worst thing he could be doing right now?"

"He never leaves his phone," Sibylle repeated in a small voice. "He says we can always reach him if we need help. But what if *he* needs help?"

Erika balled her fists and fought the instinct to do something horrifically touching, like go over and *hug* the poor girl. Here Erika was, dressed in her power-vixen finery, with an entire night of dancing and martinis and self-care via Vegas debauchery ahead of her . . . and she was considering ditching it all to go on a wild hunt for a German rock star who was probably in the midst of a personal crisis. And the fact Christof had decided the solution to his problems was to go on a bender rather than come up to Erika's room for sex was, quite frankly, insulting.

"Fine. I'll help you look for him for an hour, tops." Erika refused to acknowledge the warm fuzzies that Sibylle's grateful look set off in her chest. Joining Sibylle in the hallway, she let the door close behind her and added, "I'm only doing this because I feel partly responsible. I should have left you all back in Paris."

"Thank you, Erika! You are so nice."

Ugh. "Don't try to hug me or anything sappy like that."

Sibylle recoiled. "I would never."

"Good. Now, where do we start?"

Sibylle tapped the phone against her chin, thinking. "Whenever Waldo goes missing, Christof always calls the hotel security. They usually know where he is."

"Good idea." Erika dug her own phone out of her purse to make the call, then paused. She still had her meeting with Raoul tomorrow. If she alerted hotel security and they connected her with whatever shenanigans Christof had gotten into—beyond his minor lamp destruction—her free ride might get rescinded, and it might affect the financial offer Raoul made her. Not that she intended to sell the theater, for any price. But just in case . . . "Better idea—we find him ourselves. *Before* security does."

"I can channel the spirits—"

"You almost called them all cunts, remember?"

"Oh. Ja." A determined expression came over Sibylle's features. "Okay, then. We go."

CHAPTER 20

She found Christof at the roulette table. It was hard to miss him. For one, he towered over nearly everyone else in the place. And two, it seemed like half the casino floor was clustered around him, and anyone who wasn't actively watching him play was *talking* about it.

"I heard it landed on black thirteen times in a row. Do you know what the statistical odds of that are?" asked one onlooker.

"One in sixteen thousand, five hundred forty four," replied the onlooker's companion matter-of-factly. She held up her phone. "I have an app."

Erika pushed her way to the front of the crowd, drawing the ire of many. She didn't care.

Because there he was. His glorious mane of platinum hair cascading over his shoulders and into glittering eyes that stared dispassionately at the ungodly tower of chips in front of him. A young, well-muscled man and an older, well-dressed woman perched on either side of him, cheering him on along with the rest of the crowd. His guitar rested beside him on its own plush armchair. As she watched, a cocktail server brought him a glass of something amber and viscous in a snifter. "Rémy Martin Rare Cask. Compliments of the house."

Christof calmly plucked the snifter off its perch and tossed it back in one go. He replaced it neatly in the center of the tray, wiped his mouth with the back of his hand, and grunted a terse "Danke." To the dealer, he barked, "Black. All of it."

The croupier's eyes flicked off to the side before giving an infinitesimal nod. "No more bets," she called.

Erika shot off a text to Sibylle: Roulette. Very drunk.

The crowd gasped. "He's going for it again!" someone cried out.

Christof turned toward the source of the emission. "Of course I'm fucking going for it. I'm Christof Daae, and I'm a *fucking* rock star."

The mountain of chips in front of Christof had to be a lot of money. She shook her head. *Too* much money. The sign on this table stated the maximum wager was $5,000 for outside bets, yet somehow the casino was letting him gamble far, far more than that on each spin. Erika was no expert gambler, but she'd grown up among the wealthy and cutthroat Upper East Side elite, and so she did know that when powerful people "let" you do things, it was never really to your benefit.

"Christof!" she called to him from across the table.

His eyes rose and met hers. His lips slowly curled. "Erika. Meine Hexchen. You're here!" He gestured to the riches on the table—and staggered forward as he did it, catching himself with his other hand. Undaunted, he went on, "Look what I've done. I'm having *fun*."

"I can see that!" she replied, trying to stay calm. What was he *doing*? She could probably buy the opera house out of ruin five times over with the amount he'd accumulated. She pushed her way closer to him, but the beefcake at his left side blocked her way. Angling around a thick bicep, she called to Christof, "You need to cash out!"

"Nein. Don't you see?" Christof whispered something in Beefcake's ear, and suddenly her path to Christof was clear. She stepped in, only to find herself dragged firmly against Christof. His arm coiled around her lower back; his hand splayed open against her thigh. Bold. Possessive. She fought the desire to melt into his hardness, because someone had to stay in control here—and for once, it wasn't going to be Christof. "It's all a joke. All of it. None of it *matters*."

"Oh God," she whispered. "You've discovered existential nihilism." The situation was worse than she'd thought. Cynicism and ennui were her bread and butter—and look where they'd gotten her. She lived in the basement of a defunct brothel with two rats, and only one of those rats wanted to be there. Christof could not be allowed to succumb; he was too good, too pure.

"All bets in," the dealer called. Then the wheel began to spin.

Christof's hand slid up her body, trailing fire in its wake, and tangled in her hair. He held a cluster of locks up to the light and watched it fall, fascinated. "Black," he uttered confidently.

"My hair? It's actually a very dark brown."

"Your eyes, then."

"Also dark brown."

His brow furrowed. The wheel was starting to slow, and a hush fell over the crowd as the ball rattled slowly into place.

"Hmm." He leaned in closer until his lips brushed her ear. "Close enough."

A guilty shiver went through her. Christof was probably going to deeply regret this—and whatever else he'd done tonight—but she couldn't deny that a part of her loved seeing him in this state of decadent disarray. Especially when the full force of his seductive charm was trained entirely on her.

Clank. The ball fell into its slot.

"Twenty-one. Red."

The crowd collectively gasped. And just like that, all of Christof's winnings were scooped away.

Christof began to shake against her. She stole a glance at him and realized he was silently laughing.

"How much did you start with?" she dared to ask.

He doubled forward and began laughing out loud. Was there something hysterical about her question? Because if Christof had lost a lot of money, he was *not* going to find it funny tomorrow. Nor was she, when she no longer had a cash-flush band willing to pay $4,000 a week to stay in her subpar and slightly illegal venue-and-boarding situation.

"Christof," she hissed. "Answer me. What did you do?"

He pushed back from the table and threw up his free hand. As if he were wrapping up a set in a packed stadium, he called out, "Thank you, Las Vegas! Thank you! You've been fucking lovely! And you, Adonis, and you, Monica"—he pointed at Beefcake and his female companion—"it's been a real pleasure."

Adonis blew him a kiss. Christof swept up his guitar and started forward, dragging her along with him through the crowd. The masses parted for him like he was the rock star he claimed to be. When they'd cleared the densest part of the gathering, they found Sibylle waiting for them, her hands on her hips.

"Sibby!" Christof lurched toward her, barely managing not to trip over his own feet. Sibylle recoiled. "Join me! I'm having *fun*. It's fucking incredible. I should have—what's the word? I should have . . ." He swayed and held up a finger for pause. "I will think of it."

Sibylle gave Erika a horrified look. "I've never seen him like this."

Erika widened her stance and leaned into Christof's side, using her body weight to hold him steady and vertical. Well, vertical *enough*. "Help me out here? Based on my experience with drowning problems in alcohol, we have about twenty minutes or less before he pukes or passes out."

"Too late." Christof gave her an exaggerated wink.

"Jesus," Erika said under her breath. When had he *started* drinking?

Sibylle dutifully came around to Christof's right side and tried to relieve him of his guitar.

He clutched the instrument close to his chest, much like he had done to Erika. "No! Not my *precious*. I need her for the . . . for the karaoke. We're going to karaoke next, aren't we?"

"Absolutely," Erika assured him, subtly guiding his unbalanced, loping steps toward the elevator bank. Sibylle gave up trying to take his guitar and instead came around to his back and guided him from behind.

"Going to sing a power ballad." Christof began humming familiar notes.

"Ach, what a mess," Sibylle grumbled, gingerly using only the tips of her fingers to touch Christof's back.

Erika shook her head. Some help Sibylle was.

Somehow, they made it into the elevator and up to Christof's floor. "Where's your room key?" Erika asked.

Christof's lids lifted long enough to focus on her. His pupils shrank as he focused, and he gave her a slow smile. "Pocket."

Of course. Erika glanced at Sibylle for help, but the other woman was already shaking her head. "Igitt!" Not hard to guess she meant *gross*.

"Yes, you do it," Christof murmured into the crook of Erika's neck in a way that was awfully intimate.

Erika leaned away from Christof, and for Sibylle's benefit she added, "Whoa, cowboy. Don't forget about your *girlfriend*, Gillian." Erika patted his back pockets and found them empty. *Great. Front pockets.* If only there were anything at all sexy about this scenario.

"Gillian . . ." Christof bit out the name. "She left us. She left *me*. Forever. For a disco lion!"

Sibylle drew back as if she'd been struck. "What are you talking about?"

"Shhh." Christof drew in close to Erika's face again. His breath smelled like liquor and breath mints. "Can't let the band find out."

The only room card in his front pockets was hers. Where had his gone? More importantly, where was his wallet?

Sibylle slowly shook her head. "Gillian's really not coming back?"

Erika tried to deflect. "Drunk people say all sorts of untrue things—"

"Oh no, it's true," Christof announced. "Do you want to see her email? Sent it the morning after the Berlin concert. She left us and now she's at—guess where! I will tell you. Eurovision." He patted his butt, his brows furrowing. "Phone's gone missing. Have you seen my phone?" He began patting Erika's behind, as if she'd hidden it in a secret back pocket beneath her dress.

"Will you shut *up*?" Erika redirected his groping paws by shoving his phone into his grip. "Sibylle, can you help me find his wallet? It's gone."

"Gone. Like Gillian." Sibylle's eyes were round and glossy with unshed tears.

Oh, this was not good. Beside Erika, Christof swayed, his attention fully fixed on his phone. He seemed to be trying to turn it on, and she decided not to tell him it was out of charge. It would keep him distracted for a few minutes while she dealt with Sibylle.

Why couldn't I have minded my own business instead of getting involved in these people's problems? Erika sighed. Being a good person was a pain in the ass.

She snapped her fingers in front of Sibylle's face. "Hey! Bring it back."

"He *lied* to us."

"You totally have a right to be upset, but this isn't the time or place. I know Christof's always the responsible one in your group, but he's clearly out of commission right now, so it's up to us to step up, put our big-girl pants on, and handle damage control, okay?"

Sibylle nodded woodenly.

"Christof's wallet is missing, and there's no way the casino let him play on credit. Go find it before someone runs up that glorious black credit card of his and all of us are fucked. In the meantime, I'll take care of your brother."

"Okay," Sibylle whispered.

"And tomorrow morning, we'll get the Gillian situation sorted out. I'll make sure Christof shows up, but I'm counting on you to rent a conference room and get the rest of Nachtmusik together."

"Me?"

"Yes, *you*, Dummkopf."

The German insult seemed to knock Sibylle back to reality, because her eyes cleared, then narrowed. "You don't tell me what to do."

"I do if you want a ride back to Paris. Now listen to me very closely, Sibylle, because this is going to be hard to hear, but I know you can handle it." Erika lowered her voice, forcing Sibylle to lean in. "Christof has just been dumped by his long-term girlfriend. He's obviously going through a lot right now, and he's been holding it together for the sake of your band and the album. That doesn't excuse the fact he lied to you, but even good people make mistakes and do bad things sometimes, right? At least give him a chance to explain."

Sibylle crossed her arms and looked away. "Why do you even care so much about my boring brother and his silly feelings? You hardly know him."

A denial rushed to Erika's lips, but she swallowed it. Lies, which had once come so easily, now tasted sour in her mouth. "I don't know," Erika said quietly. "But I do, and it's really annoying that I don't actually find him or his feelings boring or silly at all. I think he's a good person, and good people deserve to be happy."

"I see." Sibylle's brows drew together as she ingested this information. "So, you are taking Gillian's place in the band, then?"

"Of course not. I have a theater to run."

Sibylle blinked. "But we need a keyboardist."

Erika gritted her teeth, wishing she were colder and deader inside than she apparently was. It would be easier that way. Couldn't the world just leave her alone and let her waste the rest of her life in anonymous peace? "Fine. I'll fill in for Gillian's parts. *For now.*"

Sibylle's morose expression morphed into a brilliant smile. But instead of acting honored and delighted by Erika's humanitarian largesse, Sibylle had the sheer chutzpah to say, "I suppose you will do. I hope you can keep up."

"I went to Juilliard, you peasant."

Sibylle shrugged. "We will see."

"Go find the wallet," she reminded Sibylle, flipping her off for good measure. The other woman gave the same loving gesture in return. Then, somehow, Erika managed to steer a nearly catatonic version of Christof back to the elevators and up to her room.

Erika helped Christof crawl onto her bed, carefully easing the guitar out of his hand to set it safely against the nightstand. Then, grunting with effort, she rolled him onto his back. Her skirt rode up as she did it, and he somehow had the presence of mind to growl in appreciation—as if he were in any state to do something about it.

Her irritation faded when he pressed his cheek against her knee and gazed up at her with heavy-lidded hazel eyes like she was personally responsible for putting the stars in the sky. He breathed in deeply against her skin. "I heard you," came his muffled voice.

"I should get you some water." She tried to pull away, but his hand closed over her bare thigh.

"You said you care about my feelings."

Heat rose up her neck. "So? Don't take it personally. I care about a lot of people."

"You're lying."

"No, I'm not."

"Who, then? Who else?"

She ran her hand over the gold bedspread. "Jean. Javert. All my other suitors."

Christof smiled lazily. "Lying," he repeated. His head tilted to look up her skirt. "Well, hello. Is that red lace?"

She snapped her thighs closed. "If you hadn't done whatever *this*"— she made a sweeping gesture to encompass his whole person—"is, then you'd already know the answer. But you had to go full Vegas, didn't you? Why?"

His chest rose and fell in a heavy sigh, but he didn't answer, and after several more seconds passed, she was sure he wasn't going to. But then he surprised her. "I think I'm lost."

"Put your foot on the ground. It helps the room stop spinning."

"No, no. I don't know . . ." Beneath his wavy bangs, his brows drew together. "Don't know where I'm going. Thought I did before. But now . . ."

She swallowed at the strange sensation of her heart ka-thudding in sympathy. "It sucks, huh?" she said. "You think you have your whole life planned. You're on top of the world, so sure you've got it figured out, and then—"

"Schwupp!" He wiped his hand through the air. "It's all gone."

"Yeah." In that moment, it felt like every hour of sleep she'd missed over the past two years settled on her shoulders and weighed her down. Carefully, she lay back on the bed so they rested side by side on the plush coverlet. They barely touched—upper arm to upper arm, her high-heeled sandaled foot lightly resting against his calf, his own feet dangling off the bed—but it still felt strangely intimate. She couldn't remember if she'd ever lain next to a man while fully clothed. The chill of the room's air-conditioning made goose bumps on her skin, but where her bare arm pressed against his cloth-covered one, warmth seeped through.

Was this what it felt like to date someone? To *really* date them—not just be ferried into someone's downtown apartment at two in the afternoon only to be dismissed into a rideshare before their girlfriend came home from work? Because if so, it was . . . nice. She might like to experience intimacy more often.

Ideally, with someone who wanted a serious relationship and who didn't, say, live on the other side of the world. Someone who was not only single (although that alone would be a step up from her spotty record) but actually in the right headspace for a relationship. Someone who wouldn't make her play understudy to his career ambitions.

But for now, it was nice to pretend, and it was okay to let her guard down a little, because Christof was too drunk to remember any of it.

She wasn't sure how much time passed while they lay there, side by side, but the steady inhale and exhale of his breaths made for soothing white noise, and eventually her eyelids started to droop. She'd almost drifted off to sleep when his drowsy voice stirred her.

"Erika?" His voice sounded close to her ear, and she realized without opening her eyes that he'd turned his head to face her.

"Mmm?" She refused to turn to look at him, because *that* was intimacy—and far too much of it for her comfort level.

"You are a very good person."

A bitter taste welled on the back of her tongue. "Sure I am. And you're the Goblin King."

"You let us stay with you."

"I needed the money," she reminded him.

"But you taught me to sing better."

"I was trying to seduce you." What was he trying to do here? If he was looking for a heart of gold, he'd come to the wrong girl.

"Yes, you did."

She turned to look at him. When she did, she found him grinning in that lopsided, lazy way that made her flush with heat, and she knew he was thinking of last night.

"But tonight, you rescued me," he went on. "Brought me home. See? Good person."

"You're drunk, and you have no idea what you're talking about."

"Why?"

"Why *what*? Why are you drunk? I'd also like to know that."

"No. This other thing."

"Why am I not a good person?" She pushed up to her elbow and glowered down at him. Why did he have to look so appealing, sprawled on her bed with that trusting expression on his egregiously handsome face and his angelic hair splayed out around his head like a cloud? "You never met the Old Erika. She—no, *I* was a selfish bitch who took what I wanted, always needed to be the center of attention, and didn't give a shit about anyone else's feelings."

"Ah. And now you atone. Sins . . . and so forth?"

"Reluctantly. And definitely not by my own decision. The whole Farmer Carla curse and dramatic-disfigurement thing got the ball rolling." She plopped back down onto her back.

His warm breath tickled as his nose came to rest lightly on her shoulder. Like a human dragon, puffing in and out. "You smell like roses."

"Yeah, well, I wear a lot of lotion. The air is dry in Nevada."

"When is it done?"

She gave him a puzzled look.

"Atoning."

"Oh." She pressed the back of her hand to her brow and drew out her sigh this time. "Never, I guess. I just accept this is my life now and make the best of it. The show must go on, as they say. Whether you want it to or not." She was despondency incarnate, yet so brave, so stoic.

Something pinched at her shoulder, and she realized he'd lightly nipped her. "No," he said gruffly.

"What the hell? Did you *bite* me?"

He stuck out his tongue. "You don't taste like roses."

"Stick your tongue back in your mouth. No sampling the buffet until you're sober enough to eat a full meal."

He did as he was told but made a show of scrunching his face in disgust. "Tastes of chemicals."

"Well, I'm sorry I didn't taste my lotion before buying it! And I didn't tell you to bite me. Why did you bite me?"

He paused to think. "Ah, yes! Because you can't give up. Pershish—persistence is key to success."

"Ugh."

"Why is this *ugh*?"

"I'm exhausted merely thinking about going through life with that much optimism. Don't you ever get tired of *trying*? It seems like it's a fucking lot of work."

He mumbled in a morose tone, "Ja. It is a lot of work."

"See? My way is better. Put zero effort in, expect the absolute worst, and you'll never be disappointed. Plus, you'll have the deep satisfaction of being *right* a good percentage of the time."

The way he looked at her made her feel a bit like she was being pitied, and that made her stomach clench defensively. At least he didn't make it worse by saying something, because there was absolutely nothing he *could* say that would make her feel better.

Something brushed against her fingertips. She tried to ignore it, but then it happened again. Was he trying to *hold her hand*?

A disgustingly wretched ache clutched at her heart. Longing, maybe. Or fear. Or both.

Probably both.

As if sensing her irrational stage fright, he tentatively hooked his pointer finger around her own index finger, leaving the backs of their hands lightly pressed together. A sort of modified, beginner-level hand-holding.

The ceiling was a generic white stucco thing, but suddenly the details of it were blurry, and if she didn't know better, she'd think she was getting choked up about this finger-twining business. Imagine! Her, the jaded New Yorker who only cried onstage (with the exception of that one time when she'd asked her hair stylist for bangs), losing her cool over something toddlers did to show affection.

She swallowed. Hesitantly, she scooped her hand beneath his and went all in, tangling their digits. His grip immediately adjusted and gently squeezed hers, as if he'd been patiently waiting for exactly this moment.

"I need to get up soon and brush my teeth," she warned him, though she wasn't exactly sure why, since the whole concept of moving was growing less and less compelling by the second.

"Stay . . . ," he murmured.

"Just for a few more minutes."

"No. Stay," he repeated, but his consonants were getting slushier, and now it seemed like he really was falling asleep.

"Okay, fine. I'll stay," she agreed in a soothing tone. What harm could a few more minutes do?

His hand gave another squeeze, though less firmly. "Mean it." Reflexively, she opened her mouth to say something about ex-girlfriend-induced abandonment issues, but he wasn't done. "Not now. Forever."

"I don't—"

"Marry me."

Erika's heart stopped beating, and in its place, hope became a star-burst in her rib cage, sparks of long-buried dreams shimmering through her entire being. Once upon a time, Erika Greene had longed for a whirlwind wedding. Something impulsive and cinematic and possibly ill advised, but they'd be so wildly, passionately in love that nothing else mattered.

"I now pronounce you married," Elvis declares. A passionate kiss. The music crescendos. Lights dim and curtain falls. Standing ovation.

"You're not serious," she said in a trembling voice. She was afraid to look at him.

He didn't answer.

She prompted, "Are you?"

When there was still no response, Erika sat up.

Christof's face was smoothed in sleep, his chest rising and falling in steady breaths. His plush mouth, slightly parted, seemed to Erika as if it were waiting for a kiss to awaken him again.

"Damn it." Sparks fizzled into nothing, leaving her insides cold and damp.

Quietly, so as not to wake him, she found a spare blanket and draped it over Christof's long body as best she could.

Later, once she'd washed off her makeup and changed into her nightgown, she slid under the sheets on the other side of the king-size bed. It was the first time in her entire life she'd actually slept in the same bed as another human being, but miles of distance and a thousand layers of chilled sheets separated her body from Christof's, and Erika had never felt more alone.

CHAPTER 21

Erika wasn't sure what she imagined Raoul Decomte's office would look like. Scrooge McDuck's mansion, maybe, done up in the same tacky *Great Gatsby*–meets–Monopoly aesthetic as the rest of the hotel. But when the art deco elevator doors whooshed open, Erika was greeted by cream hues, breathtaking views from sky-high windows, and the kind of tasteful modern furniture that suggested that even if the casino's owner didn't have good taste, he'd spent good money on an interior designer who did.

Maybe Raoul wouldn't completely ruin the Paris Opera House. What if she could convince him to renovate and reopen it as a more modern venue? Erika smoothed the skirt of her dress before stepping into the foyer, using the opportunity to wipe her damp palms.

She wasn't *really* going to sell the theater. This meeting was merely a courtesy—the price she paid for a free night's stay in Vegas. No matter how much money Raoul offered, she'd turn it down. Even if he agreed not to raze the building. Even if a lump sum payment might give her the freedom to explore career options, should she decide to return to performing. Or give her the opportunity to travel the world and go places her intensive Broadway schedule hadn't allowed.

Berlin, for example.

After a moment, a well-dressed Black man emerged from the glass-walled office and introduced himself as Raoul's assistant. "Monsieur Decomte's off-site meeting is running late. He apologizes for the inconvenience and invites you to order whatever you'd like to enjoy for lunch from Carte Blanche's selection of fine-dining options."

Maurice provided Erika with a tablet to browse through the menus, then waited politely while she scrolled down to the most expensive item she could find. "I'll have the absurd gold-plated thing."

"Très bien." Maurice moved to his desk to place the order, leaving Erika alone in the sitting room outside Raoul's office.

She drummed her manicured nails on the side table as she waited, finding that the clicking sound soothed her nerves. But it wasn't only this meeting she was nervous about.

Although it was already noon, Christof had still been sleeping when Erika had left. Given that she knew he'd been sleep deprived for weeks—if not longer—she'd been loath to wake him. That . . . and the tiny matter of the drunken proposal that Erika wasn't ready to address.

Would he remember it when he woke up? And did it even matter? It wasn't like he could possibly have been serious.

And what if he was?

Erika tapped a faster rhythm. Best not to bring it up, she decided, and she'd laugh it off if he mentioned it—it wasn't like she *wanted* to marry Christof Daae. The cold light of morning had been a refreshing wash of reality. She'd known him for three weeks! And what would she do with the rest of her life if she did marry him, anyway? Move to Berlin, even though she didn't speak a lick of German? Play keys in a hair metal band? She didn't even *like* hair metal. She only liked Nachtmusik's music because Christof sang it.

It wasn't like Christof would give up the band to support *her* career. For one, she didn't have a career anymore. And two, he'd said it himself: the band always came first. That fact was unlikely to change just because Erika gave a killer blowjob.

The elevator dinged, and an impeccably dressed light-brown-skinned man swept into the room flanked by two equally well-dressed security guards. Raoul wore his longer dark hair back in an old-fashioned queue, sported a dashingly Musketeer-like goatee, and pulled off a three-piece pin-striped suit like the look had come back into style specifically to be worn by him—and only him. He looked like money, smelled like money, and walked with the elegant, striding confidence of a man packing an enormous . . . wad of bills.

At least, she *hoped* that was merely a wad of bills in his front pocket.

Either Raoul Decomte had gotten bang-up plastic surgery, or he was still shy of forty—and looked nothing like the evil old man she'd envisioned. Erika reassessed the demure white linen dress she'd donned for the occasion. If she'd known Raoul was this young, foxy, rich playboy, she'd have worn something low cut.

"Ah, you must be Mademoiselle Greene." Raoul strolled over to kiss the air by her cheeks. Erika held her breath to avoid inhaling a mouthful of spicy cologne. It wasn't *bad* cologne, per se—it smelled complex and expensive. But it wasn't Christof's muted wood scent, and suddenly anything but that specific fragrance on a man made her want to gag. Raoul pulled back, sweeping his green-eyed gaze over her form. "Maurice, why did you not inform me what an enchanting woman awaited me here? I would have abandoned my meeting immediately! Come, come. You've ordered lunch, yes? We'll dine in my office. Do you drink wine? I've a lovely little bottle of Nuits-Saint-Georges I've been saving for a worthy guest."

She let him usher her into his office, where a linen-draped table was set up by the window. When she sat in the plush seat, she could glance to her right and see all of the Las Vegas Strip laid out before her in a stunning panorama.

Raoul approached with the bottle of wine, and before Erika could politely decline, she caught a glimpse of the label. *Jesus.* She couldn't very well let *that* get opened for no reason. "Just a little bit," she said with a wince of apology. "I have another meeting after this one."

"Of course." Raoul poured, and even the stream of rust-hued liquid in her glass looked elegant. Then he winked. "I confess, I was untruthful about the wine. I was going to drink this bottle today anyway. I believe one cannot truly enjoy life without good wine, and I own part of this vineyard, so to me, this is merely a drink for every day. Do not feel obligated to imbibe out of courtesy. It is nothing to me, see?" And with that, he took the bottle and poured the equivalent of a glass into the potted plant by his desk.

Erika couldn't tear her eyes away. "Is that . . . *okay*? For the plant?" A vision of the plant being swarmed with fruit flies was the first thing to pop into her mind.

Raoul laughed and patted one of the large heart-shaped leaves. "But of course Odette likes it. Though she prefers Beaujolais . . . she's still young."

Maurice entered with the food, whisked off the metal domes like a butler in an old movie, and discreetly vanished.

Raoul raised his glass of wine in a toast. "Let us toast to new beginnings."

His tone was innocent enough, but as Erika touched her glass to his, a pit formed in her stomach.

Raoul delicately forked a sliver of blue-rare meat into his mouth and groaned in pleasure. "Magnifique," he breathed. After finishing this rapturous bite, he smiled. "Naturally, that brings us to why I've been so eager to meet with you."

Erika poked at the gold-drenched lobster on her plate and suddenly felt very bad for the creature who'd died for this culinary atrocity. "I won't sell. Not for any price."

Raoul's smile faded. With a sigh, he set down his own utensils and steepled his hands. "Mademoiselle Greene, I fear you've gotten the wrong impression. I don't wish to buy the Paris Opera House."

"You don't?" She fought a wave of irrational disappointment.

"Au contraire. I already own it in all but name." From his breast pocket, he withdrew a folded sheaf of paper and handed it to her. "It appears that in early 2012, your grandmother took out a sizable loan from Paris Community Bank to finance this theater of yours. Unfortunately, it is my understanding that payments on that loan have been rather . . . irregular. And as I have some friends at that institution, it was my pleasure to purchase that loan from them at a delightfully reasonable price."

Erika clutched her dinner knife so tightly it hurt. "I'm still making payments on that loan."

"Why, yes! I have noticed this unexpected infusion of income. How lovely that you've found renters for the venue." Raoul leaned forward and lowered his voice as if they were sharing an intimate secret. "I am concerned, however, that your theater is not . . . how shall I say this delicately? Appropriately permitted. What will happen if you cannot pass your fire inspection in a mere few weeks' time?" He stroked his goatee as if deep in thought. "Things could become very difficult for you. I've heard imprisonment is a possibility in these matters."

"Is that a threat?" It didn't surprise Erika that Raoul had all this dirt on her. When powerful men wanted things, they usually got them—no matter the means. He had to have anticipated that she wouldn't say yes to a straight money offer; if Erika hadn't been so distracted with Christof and Nachtmusik, she might have thought ahead to this exact scenario. But instead, she'd been daydreaming about imaginary weddings and childish fantasies of Christof sweeping into her life to make her problems magically evaporate.

When had a man in Erika's life *ever* done anything but make her problems worse?

"You mistake me, once again." Raoul gave her a kind smile. "I only wish to be of assistance. It is within my power to make your personal liability in this matter disappear. My new property, Magnifique!, is in need of a star performer. A unique allure to draw guests out to Paris. Might you be interested in headlining a selection of rotating musical productions? A showing of *Les Misérables*, for example, is exactly l'esprit français our guests desire."

For the sake of them both, Erika forced herself to set her knife down. "I don't perform anymore. But if I wanted to, I could return to the real Broadway in a heartbeat. You're dreaming if you think I'm going to *give* you my theater so I can perform to tourists at a casino."

Raoul calmly sipped his wine. "I see," he said, finally. "That is indeed a shame for us both, then. I take such wonderful care of my star performers. Everything you'd ever desired could be yours . . . a salary in the realm of millions, your name and face on every Magnifique! billboard and advertisement across the nation, and the freedom to leave whenever you desire. Is this shambling theater of yours really worth so much to you that you'd turn this down?"

"The Paris Opera House has been in my family for over a century," Erika replied reflexively.

"Yes, it has." The look he gave her was pitying. "And it certainly appears that way to all who see it. A shame it was not more carefully maintained. A single spark, and . . ." He snapped his fingers. "Quelle tragédie."

Erika pushed back from the table and stood. "Were you the one who called the fire marshal on me?"

"What a terrible accusation, Mademoiselle Greene." He looked up at her calmly but didn't stand. So much for Old World manners. "Why would I do such a thing, when I've already changed the terms of your loan so the balance is due immediately? I believe you still owe near to one hundred thousand dollars. If this isn't paid within thirty days, well . . . the theater belongs to me."

"Oh, fuck off." Erika snatched her purse and strode for the exit. As if summoned, Maurice was there behind the glass, swinging the door wide before she could slam it open herself.

"I encourage you to change your mind," Raoul called after her. "I can be a fearsome enemy but an *extremely* valuable ally."

Without turning around, she gave him the finger.

She was nearly to the elevator when his voice came from closer behind her. He'd followed her to the door of his office. "Perhaps you might be more interested in seeing your friends in Nachtmusik nominated for a Grammy Award. Or might they be compelled by a *Rolling Stone* cover? A coveted spot in the Rock and Roll Hall of Fame, someday? There are precious few limits on my influence."

Erika's finger hovered over the elevator call button. "As if you could ever guarantee that kind of thing." She made the mistake of glancing over her shoulder, if only to see if he was laughing at her.

He wasn't. Raoul looked as cool and calm as he had the entire meeting. If he was lying, he was exceptional. "Consider my offer," he said. His green eyes swept her up and down. "I can make whatever you wish for a reality."

If only. Erika looked away and pressed the button, forcibly dismissing the image that had immediately reappeared in her mind. *I now pronounce you*—"I'll think about it," she bit out.

"Will you not stay to finish your meal?"

Erika shook her head. The longer she stayed here, the harder it would be to say no. "I think there's another meeting I need to get to."

She hoped Christof would be awake when she got back to her room, because getting him to Sibylle's band meeting while he was unconscious was going to be a challenge.

CHAPTER 22

He dreamed he was crowd-surfing.

It was a familiar dream, one he'd had often during the past year while on tour. He was soaring through the audience, hundreds of reverent hands pushing into his flesh and holding him aloft, and then someone's grip slipped, and he began to fall. He'd flail, struggling to stay up, because he knew if he could just keep moving forward, then he'd be safe, but the crowd began to disperse beneath him. As if the very act of him falling made them lose interest. They didn't want a rock star who fell.

It was his fault. It was always his fault. If only he'd tried harder . . .

Too late. The last pair of hands fell away, and he hit the dirty ground. He scrambled on the sticky, beer-cup-strewn cement, trying to get to his knees, but the crowd kept stepping on him, dirty boots leaving patterned dents on the backs of his hands. They didn't seem to care he was down there; a new act was taking the stage. His time in the spotlight was over. He could hear the first strains of a Lithuanian disco song. The crowd was going wild, and Christof was being trampled.

This was the part of the dream he hated. It seemed to go on and on forever—this fruitless, increasingly desperate struggle to get up. To be *relevant*. He was a nobody down here. Just some loser from a provincial town without formal schooling or any other applicable skills. He'd decided to be famous, and if he failed, there was no backup plan. He'd just be down here forever.

Then something new happened. A warm hand settled on his shoulder. "Hey. Time to get up." *Erika.*

"Ich kann nicht . . . ," he tried to tell her. Couldn't she see? He was being crushed by the crowd. They'd turned on him.

"Yes, you can. Come on."

"But—" He stopped, bewildered. The prints on the back of his hand were gone. He looked around and saw that although the crowd was still packed tightly, they'd cleared a little area for him. He pushed to his feet. No one stopped him. And now, standing, he could see over the tops of the audience's heads, and he realized that he'd been mistaken; there was no Lithuanian disco band. No one had taken his place. The rest of Nachtmusik was still onstage—Waldo, Sibylle, Sergei . . . even Gillian. Everyone was looking at him, and as if from far away, he heard his name. Over and over. Louder and louder.

They were chanting. Waiting. For *him.*

"Christof!"

He woke with a start.

His brain, as soupy and muddled as it was, took its time catching up. The first things he saw were the close-up grain of bedsheets that weren't his own and, beyond that, a blindingly bright view of a desert spotted with tall buildings.

Right. Las Vegas. He squinted against the yellow sunlight streaming in, trying to remember how he'd gotten here and why his head felt like he'd been beaten to death with his own guitar.

His guitar.

He shot up in bed—which his head didn't like one bit—and looked frantically for his love. Relief hit him when he found her resting comfortably in a nearby wing chair, her shimmering lacquer unscathed.

"Finally. Jesus, I thought you said you were a light sleeper," came Erika's voice, and it sounded irritated. She offered him a cup of coffee from the sideboard, which he gratefully accepted, even though he usually drank tea so as not to exacerbate his already high-strung demeanor—what little good that sacrifice did. "Hurry up. We're late for the band meeting."

He eyed her over the rim of his mug as he took a sip, and though the coffee scalded his throat with cleansing fire, it didn't help explain what was going on. All he was certain about was that Erika looked quite pretty this morning, with her dark hair freshly waved and her lips painted like fire. She wore white today—the first time he'd seen her in any color but black, and it suited her, brought out the golden tan of her skin. And since Christof knew that women appreciated compliments when they'd made an effort on their appearance, he told her, "You look exceptionally badass this morning."

Instead of thanking him for noticing, however, Erika looked away. "I know."

"What's wrong?"

"I met with Raoul, the casino's owner. I thought he was going to try and buy me out, but he doesn't have to. He purchased the loan Grandma Meg took out on the opera house, and now if I don't come up with a hundred grand by the end of the month, the theater's his."

"That is completely unreasonable!" He rubbed his forehead and tried to think. And yes—there it was. Like sudden earsplitting feedback from an overexerted amp, he inwardly recoiled from the assault of memory. Gillian. The drinking. The hedonism of the male-dancing revue. The unfettered excess that had followed, culminating in the bout of ill-advised gambling before the rescue by Erika and his sister. After that, though, it was all a bit blurry, and he had no recollection whatsoever of falling asleep. Erika's reluctant demeanor sparked concern, but the news she'd just told him was a higher priority than what he might or might not have done or said last night. "Is he giving you no other recourse?"

She hesitated. Then asked slowly, "If you had to sell your soul to the devil . . . let's say, someone offers you everything you ever wanted, but in order to get it, you have to record an album of bland, top-forty-style pop music. Would you do it?"

Christof narrowed his eyes. "Can you be more specific? Not all pop music is so terrible."

"I'm talking songs written by those cookie-cutter hitmakers. The kind of insidiously generic songs you hear at the dentist's office and at the grocery store. The ones that sort of annoy you, but they have really catchy hooks and get stuck in your head and make you want to claw your brain out."

"Never," he growled.

"Not even if it meant the people you love would have everything they ever wanted?"

The second denial froze on his lips. Would he? For Sibylle? For Waldo and Sergei and Gillian?

For Erika?

"I would consider it," he begrudgingly admitted.

"Yeah, well. That's what I told Raoul." Erika handed him his phone. "Here. I plugged it in last night, so it's fully charged. That said, you'll want to check your credit card statements this morning, since Sibylle had to retrieve your wallet from the lost and found."

"Thank you," he managed to grit out, even as a wave of terror swept over him. He pulled up his banking app and scrolled through to find what was undoubtedly a disastrous accounting of irresponsibility, holding his breath as he did so. What had he done? All his years of diligent accounting, of managing every last penny . . . had he undone all that careful work with a single night of excess? How would he explain this to the band? This was exactly why he didn't allow himself to lose control, ever. There was too much responsibility in his hands.

A dizzying nausea took hold. But when he got to the charges from last night, he stopped and stared.

"This is not right. It can't be."

Erika peered over his shoulder. "You spent seventy dollars on tickets to Thunder from Down Under? And what's this? Thirty-four dollars at a bar? Ouch, Christof." He could sense her amusement. "Ooh, scroll up! Yeah, that's the ultimate in excess, isn't it?"

$500.00—Carte Blanche Casino. He'd lost five hundred dollars gambling. He felt nauseous, and he wasn't sure if it was from relief or the multiples of Blowjob shots that Monica and her friends had bought for him.

"Over four hundred euros," he muttered, as if repeating it in his native currency would make it sound more dire.

"Disgusting," Erika agreed. "So, you had a fun night out, lost a paltry amount of money for someone who's supposedly an international rock star—"

"I *am* an international rock star."

"—and passed out before you could fuck me. It's not like you were completely reckless, like some people are when they go to Vegas."

"I suppose."

"It could be worse, you know. You could have done something ridiculous, like propose to a woman you barely know."

He grunted. "Right." He thought of Gillian, how she'd been horrified at the mere *suggestion* of a proposal after ten years together, and inwardly cringed. The rejection had stung, he realized, perhaps a tad belatedly. Perhaps that was why he'd been so furious when he'd seen her on the television, being so carefree with a veritable stranger. Was the idea of spending a lifetime married to him so repulsive?

Maybe it was. Maybe he was too boring.

After all, even in his attempts to be carefree, he hadn't *really* been carefree. Hadn't done anything that impulsive at all. Perhaps that was his problem.

"But even if you *did*, it wouldn't matter, because people say things they don't mean when they're drunk. Don't they?" Something in her tone knocked him out of his inner turmoil. She sounded almost . . . pleading.

He searched her face, trying to see what was going on beneath her fall of hair, but she was looking away from him again, her dark eyes shadowed by her long lashes. All he knew was that she was clearly upset, and it was his fault.

He grasped her hand and held it to his lips. Caught a faint whiff of her rose lotion—which nagged at a recent memory he couldn't quite retrieve—and gently kissed her knuckles. "Whatever I've done, I'm sorry. You are my savior, you know. My musical angel. And I will not let you down again. Today, I am New Christof. A cool, laid-back guy."

The look she gave him was skeptical, but she only withdrew her hand and moved toward the door. "Great. In that case, *Cool Guy*, you'll have no problem with Sibylle leading today's band meeting. Let's go. We're already a half hour late."

Christof had a vivid flashback to the time Sibylle had demanded to be in charge of their stage props; Waldo had subsequently spent the evening in the hospital because Sibylle had rigged his drum set with "pyrotechnics," which were not actually stage-certified pyrotechnics but rather discount fireworks she'd ordered from a website promising they'd been constructed by the ghosts of dead World War II soldiers who'd died by explosion.

He'd since learned never to put Sibylle in charge of anything.

He hurriedly grabbed his boots and guitar and followed her out into the hallway barefoot, sure he'd misheard. His head throbbed harder the faster he moved, reminding him he wasn't finished paying for his sins. "My sister is not leading today's meeting. I am the band manager."

Erika didn't seem to hear him. She called the elevator, stepped in, and spun around to give him a beatific smile. "Oh, and in case you don't remember, you blabbed the truth about Gillian in front of Sibylle, so I'd prepare to spend approximately half this meeting groveling."

He reeled back. *"What?"*

"And you should know I joined the band. Temporarily. You needed a keyboardist, and I can fill in for Gillian. For now."

He shook his head. "When . . . how . . . ?"

"Which part of that wasn't clear?" The elevator doors started to close, and he darted in.

"Who is making these decisions without me?" he sputtered, aghast at how quickly his ordered world had devolved into chaos.

It wasn't that he didn't want Erika's help. Erika was far more talented than any of them, and her expertise would only elevate their album. And they *did* need a keyboardist to even begin properly rehearsing songs. It made sense. All of it made sense.

But . . . Nachtmusik was *his* band.

"Sibylle approved everything," she replied calmly.

"But—"

She raised a brow. "Cool guy, remember? Deep breaths."

He forced himself to breathe. "Yes. Cool guy," he bit out. He could do this. He *could* let go of control.

And then, when it became abundantly clear to everyone that Nachtmusik would fall into disastrous ruin without his guidance, he'd graciously take back his seat at the helm.

He couldn't wait to see what nonsense the band had concocted in this meeting so far. No—that was foolish of him; it had only been thirty minutes. Surely Waldo wouldn't even have arrived yet, and Sergei and Sibylle would be arguing about something inane—their last band meeting had been derailed by a thirty-minute debate about whether Reb Beach's solo album, *Masquerade*, was worthy of inclusion in the hair metal genus despite his having left Winger a decade prior.

Christof quietly stewed in his smug certainty all the way down to the eighth floor, where Sibylle had rented a conference room for the occasion. It was only when he walked into said room and saw Sibylle standing in front of a neatly organized dry-erase board—with a list of titles on it that looked suspiciously like a track list—that Christof began to worry.

"Sit down. You're late." Sibylle pointed to an empty seat farthest away from the front of the overly lacquered mahogany table. The damn thing reflected beams of sunlight from the floor-to-ceiling windows directly into his sensitive eyes like radiant swords, and no one had seen fit to draw the blinds. For the first time in living history, everyone else in Nachtmusik looked well rested, and it was Christof who was nursing an unholy hangover and looked like he'd been returned from the grave by one of Sibylle's poorly translated summoning spells.

At least the brief vacation had done them all good. Good for them. Good for fucking *them*.

Sergei flicked a glance up and down Christof's disheveled appearance, pausing the sweep on both his unbrushed hair and his bare feet. "Hmm," said the guitarist. Was it Christof's imagination, or did it sound like he was being judged and found wanting? As if Waldo hadn't appeared at rehearsal for weeks in the same state of disarray—if he showed at all!

Waldo, meanwhile, wouldn't even look at him. Wonderful.

Christof made his way toward the only other available chair that was closer to the front of the room, but Erika slid into it first. "Sorry about that," she said to Sibylle. "What did I miss?"

Sibylle circled the top two song titles, "Riding America" and "Cowboy Ghost," and placed her hands on her hips. "We have to open with a song that sets the mood for the album. I propose 'Cowboy Ghost,' because it has more sinister vibrations yet still appeals to American nostalgia for western symbolism." He noted that Sibylle had painted her skin death white and worn her tallest boots today—a sure sign she was feeling particularly feisty. He could only be thankful Sibylle had been unable to convince airport security to allow her handheld scythe on an international flight.

"Ja, but 'Riding America' is mega geil," Waldo argued.

Sergei raised a finger. "And there is room for a second guitar solo after the hoof—ah, the drum solo."

Erika said, "Sibylle makes a good point, though. I think whichever song you open with should represent your entire album, just as the opening number of a musical sets the tone for the audience about what to expect from the rest of the production. 'Riding America' feels more like a single release . . . something playful to perk up the midalbum." Then she looked up at Christof expectantly. "Are you going to sit down?"

No. This wasn't how it was supposed to go. They *needed* him. They couldn't do this without him. He stared at the collection of serial-killer slashes that Sibylle passed off as handwriting and felt a vein pulsing in his temple in rhythm with his aching head. "Where is 'Fire Tornado'? That is our opening track. We already determined this, yet it doesn't appear to be listed."

Waldo muttered, "It is wherever Gillian has gone."

So long to the hope they might not address Gillian at all. Christof glared at his sister. "You took my best song off to punish me?" He seethed at the notion, even as guilt assailed him.

Sibylle dared to raise her brows. "Maybe. Is it true, then, about Gillian? She quit the band?"

He took a steadying breath. "Yes," he said simply. That truth—that simple word—was a boulder thunking into a still pond.

No one spoke for a long moment. Then, in a small voice, Waldo said, "You said we were family."

"We *are*," Christof said.

Waldo looked away. "You do not lie to family."

"If I could only have a moment to explain, you will see why I had no other recourse."

Sibylle said in a cold voice, "You had weeks to tell us the truth, and you didn't. Why?"

What was this, an interrogation? Even though Erika had warned him this was coming, he didn't feel ready. A jittery, unsettling sensation raced through his veins. "It was my personal business," he snapped, eyeing the air vents near the ceiling. This room was very small, and he couldn't feel any air-conditioning. Perhaps the air needed to be manually turned on? "Gillian ended our relationship rather suddenly, and I thought it best for the band's success if I handled the situation privately until matters were . . . confirmed."

"But it's *not* your personal business when it has to do with the band. Isn't that always what you've said to me? 'I am not your brother; I am your band manager,'" Sibylle reminded him.

"I do recall him saying that, often," Sergei added in a thoughtful tone. "And very good imitation. Sounds exactly like him."

"Ja, ja." Waldo nodded. "Really sounds grumpy."

Sibylle curtsied. "Thank you."

Christof clenched his fists, barely managing to stifle a childish roar of frustration. Sibylle made him sound like a crusty old man. He didn't sound like that. He didn't sound *anything* like that. He was badass and cool!

Erika gave him a pointed look. "Groveling, remember?"

Yes, yes. Groveling. Taking a deep breath, Christof said gruffly, "I am deeply sorry to have occluded the truth from you all."

Still in her mock-Christof voice, Sibylle continued, "'Professionalism is key to success.'"

"That's *true*." He'd apologized! Hadn't they heard him?

She wasn't done. "'Trust is key to success. Communication is key to success. Timely attendance is key—'"

The pounding in his head was suddenly intolerable. He slammed his hands on the table, and the room fell deathly silent. Then he stood and looked around at each of his band members. Sibylle was looking at him like she was projecting her soul into the spirit realm to plot his assassination. Waldo looked as if he were about to cry. Sergei . . . was Sergei: impossible to read.

Enough. They wanted the truth? *Fine.* "Do you know why I say these things all the time?"

Sibylle looked as if she had a clever answer, but Erika cleared her throat in warning. His sister's mouth snapped shut.

"I say these things because I am afraid," he said—and instantly regretted doing so. Saying it aloud made his stomach roil. The glare of the sunlight through the tall windows was too bright. The air in this room was too hot. Too still.

What was he *doing*?

Then Erika reached for his wrist, her cool fingers sliding over his skin. *I have you,* her touch conveyed. It grounded him enough that the tension in his gut loosened, making way for a full breath.

He swallowed a mouthful of saliva and forced himself to keep going. "I am afraid that if I don't say these things, Nachtmusik will fail. I kept Gillian's departure a secret for the same reason. In fact, I'm always worried about failing. Terrified. All the time."

Waldo's heavy brow knit. "But Nachtmusik is already very successful."

"But this success is so *tenuous*. So fragile. If we can simply ensure this album does well, then it will be more secure. Then I can stop worrying." But even as he said it aloud, the words rang false. His world had always felt precariously balanced—constantly a stiff breeze away from toppling over some invisible ledge and plummeting into a canyon brimming with his deepest fears. And it would all be his fault.

"The album may not do well," Sergei said. "There is a distinct lack of guitar solos, for one."

Christof ground his molars. "It *will* do well."

"What if it doesn't?" Sibylle prompted. "What are you going to do? Cut out your own still-beating heart and bury it someplace ominous? Go on a bloodthirsty killing spree? Unlock the gates to hell and unleash an army of mutant undead—"

"Point made, Sibylle," Erika said.

Waldo scooted his rolling chair closer to Sibylle and whispered, "Undead what things?"

Sibylle nudged her sketchbook closer to Waldo.

The drummer eyed the page, his eyes widening. "Extra cool."

Erika said, "I think what Sibylle is trying to say in her uniquely imaginative and morbid way is that there are some things in this world you can't control. You can do every single thing right, and bad things might *still* happen." Erika laughed darkly. "Trust me. For a while there, I'd convinced myself that bad things only happened to bad people, but now I'm realizing there's no correlation. I've tried for two years to be good, to do the right thing and save the theater. But Raoul's just going to get it anyway because he bought the theater's loan knowing I'll never come up with a hundred grand in time, and it *sucks*."

"No!" Sibylle held up the marker she'd been writing with as if it were a dagger. "The theater is a haunted treasure. On behalf of the vengeful spirits who reside there, I will make this man suffer!"

Erika held up her hand. "Love the enthusiasm, but let's talk about this later. We're talking about Christof's problems right now." She turned to look up at him, and the compassion in her dark gaze nearly undid him. "My point is this: Don't make the same mistake I did. You only have one still-beating heart—you can't cut it out every time something goes wrong. Gillian might not ever come back, and Nachtmusik's next album might fail, but life keeps going on afterward. You will continue to wake up every single morning, get out of bed, brush your teeth, put food in your mouth, and do something to make enough money to *continue* putting food in your mouth. And I promise—you don't want to face the rest of that life, morning after morning, with a giant hole in your chest. Does that make sense?"

Christof sank back down into his seat, suddenly exhausted. "So then if the album fails, what will we do then?" He looked to his bandmates, but they didn't seem to be concerned.

Waldo grinned. "Maybe we can be horse cowboys!"

"We could release an experimental album," Sergei mused, tapping his nails together. "All guitar. Five guitars."

"I have always wanted to learn the guitar," Waldo agreed.

Sibylle scowled. "I refuse to play guitar."

"Very well. Four guitars. One bass."

Christof wished he could share their enthusiasm. "Will you all please be serious?"

"Maybe we are," Sibylle suggested. "In fact, I think this band might benefit from much more communing and much less of you ordering us around and making all the decisions."

She was right.

Christof could deny it all he wanted, but the truth was written plain as day across each face in that room.

All this time, he'd feared Nachtmusik going up in flames, but his attempts to smother the others into submission had only made the coals burn hotter. And if he kept going, the band's demise would be his own fault.

Gillian's departure was, in its own way, a warning. He'd been so afraid of their relationship changing that he'd stuffed them both into an impossible box, the way one might grow a bonsai by forcing it to adapt to a specific shape. But it hadn't worked, had it? If he'd only let go earlier . . . accepted change before it was too late . . . perhaps Gillian might not have felt the need to run away.

He couldn't undo what he'd already done, but he could stop it from happening again. The people in this room—Sibylle, Waldo, Sergei . . . even Erika—they were everything he had left.

Christof knew what he had to do. He took a deep breath, and as if sensing he needed a small dose of reassurance, Erika tightened her grip on his wrist in a brief squeeze.

"I think," he announced solemnly, "it's time we hire a band manager."

For a moment, there was only silence.

Then the impossible happened: Sibylle smiled. Really smiled, her black-painted lips stretching into a gleefully demonic grin. "Fuck ja!"

Waldo and Sergei voiced their agreement. Then Waldo gestured to Erika. "And you?"

"Me?" She blinked. Her grip on his wrist disappeared as she crossed her arms tight across her chest. Was she somehow cold in this stifling room? "But I'm not really—"

"Yes, yes." Sibylle waved in dismissal. "We know this is temporary. But while you are in Nachtmusik, even for this short while, you are one of us."

Christof had never seen Erika look stunned before. For the briefest instant, her perfect composure broke. Her scarlet lips parted, and the expression of pure longing on her face left him winded. In that moment, Christof would have indeed raised an undead army if it meant never seeing Erika look so much like an orphaned creature longing for adoption. "Then yes," she said. "Let's hire a band manager to take extra responsibility off Christof's plate."

Christof barely heard her. He wanted to gather Erika in his arms and assure her that she would never have to be alone again. She could stay in Nachtmusik, if she wanted. Come back to Berlin with them. They could date properly, even, now that the rest of the band knew the truth about Gillian. But until the moment was right, he'd take things slowly. Carefully. Ensure he didn't frighten her off or make any mistakes—

It was that thought that unlocked the memory itching at the back of his skull.

Marry me.

Erika's odd demeanor toward him this morning suddenly made sense. No wonder she'd been distant. They'd had one sexual encounter, and now he was proposing? To a woman as worldly and experienced as Erika, he could only have come across as a bit desperate, certainly inexperienced, and—at the very least—extremely uncool.

Worse yet, everything after that moment was a black hole. What if they were now engaged?

What if they were now *married*, but he had no memory of it?

Or worse . . . what if she'd said no?

Gillian's face the night of their final concert flashed through his mind. The look of utter misery and dread. The way she'd run away, as if marrying him were the worst possible fate . . .

What had he *done*?

Oblivious to Christof's dawning horror, Sibylle swept an eraser across the board on the wall, wiping away all trace of the album. Instead, she wrote in block letters, her marker squeaking as she crammed it against the writing surface: *PARIS OPERA HOUSE EMERGENCY RESCUE.* "Our first order of business as the new Nachtmusik—we must save Erika's haunted theater. Who has ideas?"

"Bank robbery on horses!" Waldo said.

"A fundraiser, perhaps?" Sergei suggested. "My friend here in Las Vegas is a woman of great influence who happens to be fond of charitable causes, and she could doubtless sell every seat in the house with little effort."

"Who *is* this friend?" Sibylle asked.

The edges of Sergei's mouth curled. "She is a private person—rather prefers not to reveal her identity. I will say only that she is an ardent believer in love and the afterlife."

"It could work," Erika said slowly. "The loan balance is due in thirty days, though—not a lot of time to prepare and rehearse for an entire concert."

The nausea he'd fought earlier returned with a vengeance. *She hasn't run away yet,* he tried to reassure himself. But he'd had coffee on an empty stomach, and his hangover wasn't being kind to him after having survived the emotional turmoil of the last twenty minutes.

"Are you okay? You're sweating. Like, a lot," Sibylle noted.

He was not. He was absolutely, with utter certainty, *not* okay. "Going to be sick," he croaked. Without waiting for a reply, he burst out of the conference room.

He barely made it to the trash bin in time. Erika took Christof back to her room after that and urged him to shower, which seemed to help. A little.

After her back-to-back meetings, a cocktail of emotions simmered in her belly—anger and frustration with Raoul, hope about Nachtmusik and the theater, and when she thought of Christof . . .

Lust. Longing. Other L-shaped words that had no business loitering in her subconscious after only three weeks. If she let it continue, she'd be setting herself up for a motherfucker of a third act when Christof inevitably left her behind in Paris.

She'd thought sex with Christof would be harmless, but the way she felt now seemed dangerous. And when he emerged from the bathroom in his towel, terry cloth loosely wrapped around his waist, cedar-scented steam puffing around his hot and mist-slicked skin, his snake tattoo rippling along the rangy muscles spanning his rib cage . . . her mouth went bone dry.

Not so harmless.

Erika had been sitting on the end of the bed with her legs primly crossed. Now she tightened her thighs, pressing them together to relieve her fraying sanity. She'd already wiped all traces of vulnerability from her expression. "I told them you were hungover. I think they understood. At least, Waldo definitely did."

When he looked around, she pointed out where she'd folded his clothes and set them on the nearby chaise. "We should probably hurry up and get dressed. The front desk called while you were in the shower to inform me that due to a booking conflict, our rooms aren't available for a second night's stay, and checkout was an hour ago." Raoul Decomte had clearly decided to play the "suave yet underhanded villain" role.

Fortunately, Erika wasn't too upset about being forced to return to Paris a night early. Now that they had a plan to save the theater, she was eager to get underway. There hadn't been time to work out the details yet, but she did know that it meant a lot of rehearsing with Nachtmusik if they were going to pull off a mega fundraiser like the one she, Sibylle, Sergei, and Waldo had concocted.

Seeing his clothes in a tidy pile, color rose to Christof's damp cheeks. He cleared his throat. "I have realized belatedly I owe you an apology."

Oh God, no. She recognized that tone. It was the tone men used right before they dropped the other shoe—the one they'd been holding behind their back. And that meant Christof was going to tell her he hadn't meant to propose, and no matter how much sense she'd talked into herself already, she didn't want to hear Christof say it aloud. Not right now.

"For what?" Her face was bland. Expressionless. At least, she prayed it was.

"For the, ah . . ." He let go of the towel around his waist to make the circling "you know what I mean" gesture with both hands, and for a heart-stopping moment, the edges began to unravel. Erika caught the barest glimpse of muscle dipping into the crevice of his hip bone, and the desire to follow that indentation with her tongue became stunningly urgent. "The thing I said," he finished carefully.

Erika wrested her attention away. "I have no idea what you're talking about," she said sharply. "Do you mean your diva moment at the roulette table?"

"It was not a *diva moment*," he said gruffly.

She tried and failed to repress a teasing smile. "Oh, sorry, I didn't mean to threaten your masculinity."

He glowered at her. "My masculinity is impermeable, thank you. It is my magnificent ego that is wounded." Catching sight of his face in the mirror, he sighed. "Might you have mascara I can borrow?"

The tension in her shoulders eased. He wasn't going to keep trying to address it. For now, anyway.

Just one more night to pretend the fairy tale is real, she told herself. When they returned to Paris, she planned to finish what they'd started long before they'd first touched in the closet, even before she'd stroked herself to orgasm for his secret viewing pleasure. It had begun when she'd first seen him standing there at the apex of the twin sets of stairs in the theater's entry, gazing down at her like some immortal being from the heavens sent to tempt her into crawling out of her miserable belowground purgatory.

Tonight, she and Christof were going to fuck as if they really were engaged to be married. As if they actually had a future beyond the next five weeks.

Tomorrow, she'd be ready to face the music.

She directed Christof to her makeup kit, and without needing to be asked, she moved to open the curtains so he could see better. Bright afternoon light from outside streamed in through a triangle of sheer fabric where the heavier layer of curtains parted, illuminating them like a spotlight while the rest of the room lay in shadow.

When his skin was properly moisturized and his eyes were sufficiently sultry, Christof felt worlds more capable.

He was blinking at his reflection, inspecting his work, when Erika's snow-encased curves appeared next to his lanky body in the mirror. The weight of her gaze was an almost physical thing, as if he could feel it stroking along his bare skin. Instantly, he became aware that he was naked beneath the terry cloth around his waist.

Her hand came up toward his chin, and he froze. *Now she'll tell me she's leaving,* he thought. He'd scared her away with his proposal. Perhaps she hadn't let him address it in order to spare him the humiliation.

"Just a smudge here," she murmured, leaning over the desk to take his jaw in her hands and turn his face toward hers. Her thumb swept over his cheek, somehow firm yet gentle at the same time.

He was unable to resist leaning into her touch and closing his eyes. He'd been wrong; she wasn't running away. Erika was nothing like Gillian at all.

"My little witch," he said quietly.

Her thumb paused on his cheek. "Is that what *Hexchen* means?" Her voice had an odd tone to it.

Keeping one eye shut, he cracked the other and peered at her a bit guiltily. "It's meant as a compliment."

"Yeah, I got that from context."

Erika on her knees in the dark, his cock in her hot mouth—

Heat shot down his spine. He released a breath through his nostrils, slowly.

Voice rough, he said, "If you wish, I won't call you that." It was, admittedly, rather early in their relationship to start using custom pet names. Christof was certainly no expert on the matter. He'd never had a pet name for Gillian at all—she hadn't liked them. But perhaps there had been a small, overly romantic part of him he'd stuffed away in the darkness, and it had been desperately seeking the symbolic familiarity of that sort of thing.

Was that why he'd proposed? Was he merely an affection-starved fool who was now clinging to the first hot-blooded creature who darkened his metaphorical doorstep?

But Erika bit her lip. Thinking. After a moment, she swallowed and said, "No. I like it. I've always wanted . . ."

He waited.

She looked away. "To be someone's something."

It was like a punch straight to his solar plexus—because hadn't he always desired that, too?—and in its wake came another blurry memory from the night before. Of the warmth of her hand in his as the ceiling spun lazily above him. And talking. Sharing his secret fears; things he hadn't even told Gillian. He hadn't known Erika long enough to know her well, and yet he did. He *understood* her. And she understood him. Because beneath the skin they displayed to the world, and despite their wildly different life experiences, they were so very, very similar.

The word *love* was dangerously close to spilling out in some form or another. After all, he was an artist. A songwriter. And thus an utterly hopeless romantic by nature who had apparently gleaned no wisdom from last night. Thankfully, some responsible fragment of his former self was coherent enough to intervene.

He certainly felt *strongly* about Erika—if obsession, lust, worshipful admiration, and the keen desire for friendship could be rolled into a single emotion—but it wasn't love. It couldn't be. He'd been in love with Gillian, and it hadn't been like this at all. Love was sort of calm and reassuring—a soft, constant breeze, not a tempest. He'd thank himself for his restraint later.

There was *something* between them, though. Something magnetic and consuming, and her proximity made him painfully aware that it hadn't been remotely sated.

Her hand was still cupping his face, so he turned into it and pressed his mouth against the soft padding at the base of her thumb, tasting the salt on her skin, watching her all the while. Heat swept through him, flushing his skin, despite the cool air moving over his damp body. Even the smallest taste of her set him on fire. From the way her breath hitched, she felt it too.

Her eyelashes fluttered closed. "We really should head down," she said in a breathy voice. "Everyone will be waiting for us."

With her face angled the way it was, light from the window set half her face aglow while casting the other half in darkness beneath her long sweep of hair, and she was impossibly beautiful. Like some dangerous night creature who'd risked everything to be with him in his bright world.

He was unworthy of the honor—but he'd earn it.

Sliding his own hands into her silky midnight hair, he pulled her close and kissed her.

Christof's lips glided over hers, softly but with determined purpose, and it made her blood fizz with electric pleasure. He kissed like he did everything else: methodical, purposeful, and focused. He kissed like this wasn't merely foreplay to sex but like kissing *was* the sex. One hand cupped the back of her head, adjusting the angle with the subtle press of his fingers, and his other hand wove through the hair she used to shroud her face and swept it back, baring all of her face to him as he rose to his full height. Unable to resist, she curved toward him like a flower bowing toward the sun, drawing her fully clothed body flush against his nearly naked one.

God, what she wouldn't give for that towel to fall . . .

But when her hands strayed to his waist to unravel him, he caught her wrists and held them in place against his hot skin. As if to say, *You'll pay attention while I'm kissing you,* and the challenge behind it made her breath catch with need. A pulse began to throb between her thighs. She thought about tugging her wrists free—his grip was light enough that she could, if she wanted to—but his mouth was making a compelling argument she couldn't ignore.

He teased her by pulling away, again and again, only to brush his lips across hers so skillfully that the nerve endings in her own lips lit up, sending showers of sparks coursing into every other cell in her body. And just when she thought she couldn't bear the light torture anymore, he'd close his mouth over hers again, sealing their flesh together with a measured hardness that would leave delicious, invisible bruises on her lips. He kissed like he was branding her soul with the imprint of his mouth, like he never wanted her to forget what he tasted like—and in that moment, she was dead certain that even if she lived a thousand years, she never would.

To be the subject of his careful intensity was thrilling, and yet it wasn't enough.

The next time he pulled away, she reminded him breathlessly, "We probably don't have time for this. But it's only an hour's drive back to Paris. When we get back . . ."

"Yes," he said softly. "Then."

CHAPTER 23

Erika was leaning against her truck outside Carte Blanche, waiting impatiently for the rest of Nachtmusik, when a voice from her past called her name.

"Erika? Erika Greene?"

It was Misty, her old dressing room neighbor, careening toward her with the short-stepped armadillo gait of someone running in too-high heels.

Old instincts, honed by years of believing she was better than everyone else, kicked in: Erika pretended not to hear. *Maybe she'll go away if I pretend not to recognize her.*

"Erika! It is you!" Misty skipped up the steps like a manic-pixie whirlwind and squealed in delight, arms stretching in an alarmingly hug-like motion toward her. Only when she saw Erika's expression—probably looking as unenthused as she felt—did Misty's arms wilt down to her sides. "It's me? Misty? From *Les Mis* in New York? We used to sit next to each other in the dressing room? You know, the one who talked your freaking ear off?"

And just like that, the sheepish tone in Misty's voice struck something in Erika. As if in the last two years she'd acquired temporal glasses with which to see the world clearly, Erika realized that she was being a mega bitch to Misty—and probably always had been. *What's wrong with me?*

Misty had never done anything to hurt Erika. She'd never gossiped about her behind her back. She'd even sent several texts while Erika was in the hospital, offering to help with running errands or picking up takeout—texts Erika had ignored, because Misty was never going to have enough talent to be anything but a B-list performer, and above all, she'd dared possess the repulsive personality trait of being *talkative*.

Guilt and shame made her want to bolt in the opposite direction, but instead she forced herself to stay—and do better. She smiled. "Misty! Of course I remember you."

Misty's trepidation melted into delight. "Phew! I thought I was embarrassing myself in front of a total stranger. Wouldn't be the first time. You look *amazing*, by the way."

"That's sweet of you to say." Erika had never suffered from a lack of self-confidence, but she was a realist; being a Nevada ten now was not the same as being the New York City ten she'd once been. But Misty's tone was sincere.

"I mean it! You were always so pretty, but now you're like . . ." Misty drew curves in the air with her hands. "Bada *boom*, baby. You must be so happy! What are you doing in Vegas? Are you in a show?"

"Just visiting." Erika swallowed her pride. "I run a historical performance venue in a town a few hours north, actually."

Misty gasped. "No way! That must be unbelievably fun."

"It's definitely something."

"God, I've always wanted to have my own venue. Feature my own shows, sponsor indie productions, that sort of thing. I'm actually here to pitch my latest musical, *Justice Jane*. It's like *Legally Blonde* but if a time-traveling Calamity Jane got stuck in our present and became a lawyer for wrongly accused criminals, and she gathers evidence for her cases by time traveling to when the crimes were committed."

"How does she time travel to the crimes if she's stuck in our time?"

"Oh, it's totally explained in the show. Trust me, it makes sense by the end of the third act. It's five acts total, but the fifth act takes place a hundred years in the future."

Erika tried to make her expression encouraging. "Wow. What a really creative concept."

A sigh. "If only the money people felt that way about it. Best I've gotten so far is that it might make a good plot for the feminist Blue Man Group reboot show they're doing."

"I'm sorry, did you say—" Erika shook her head. "Never mind."

"I didn't ask questions," Misty said with a helpless shrug. "Didn't want to know."

"Probably a good call. Regardless, I hope you get funding for your play. You're a good person, and you deserve to live your dream of seeing your musicals come alive."

Misty blinked, as if stunned. "Really?"

"Really."

"That's . . . that's the nicest thing you've ever said to me."

Erika winced. "Yeah. I know. I was always rude to you, and I'm sorry. Thank you for thinking of me after my injury when no one else apparently did."

Misty's brows knit together. "Oh, Erika. Of course people were thinking about you. But after some of the other cast visited you in the hospital, they said you didn't seem to want people there, so I think we all thought you wanted space. Then you just disappeared, and someone said they thought you'd moved to LA to do movies, and Stefano said he'd heard from Yulia that you'd gotten a contract to do *Les Mis* in Tokyo, but no one really knew. We were all devastated by what happened, especially after the news came out about Carla, but we just thought you were living your best life and had moved on."

Was this what it was like to have an out-of-body experience? Her lips oddly numb, she asked, "What news about Carla?"

Eyes wide, Misty gasped and clapped her hands to her cheeks. "You didn't hear?"

Erika shook her head. She'd deleted her social media apps. Stopped checking her old email accounts. Buried her old life in digital oblivion and started a new one in a place that had shit Wi-Fi.

In retrospect, maybe she'd been a little too dramatic about the whole thing.

Just a little.

Misty lowered her voice—which wasn't saying much. "Carla's in *prison*. Like, actual prison. *Chicago*-style."

"What? Carla as in the Oklahoma Carla, the sweet girl from the farm who everyone loved?"

"Same one. Apparently, she already had a warrant out for her arrest in Oklahoma under a different name. She went full Glenn Close on some poor girl."

Erika gave a tiny gasp of dismay even though, internally, the scandalous gossip injected dual bursts of vindication and schadenfreude into her bloodstream, and—may her blackened soul dwell forever in shame—it secretly thrilled her. Unable to help herself, she asked, "*Dalmatians* Glenn Close or *Dangerous Liaisons* Glenn Close?"

"Worse."

"Not *Fatal Attraction*, bunny-boiling Close?"

"I was thinking more *Damages*-style Close—cold and premeditated. You know, the show where she played a successful lawyer who literally murdered people to win cases?"

"I can't believe goody-two-shoes Carla killed someone." She tried not to look delighted—as that would be extremely wrong. Just to be entirely clear on the matter, she added a half-hearted "How horrific."

"*Tried* to kill someone. Some rival for a local theater production. At first, everyone wrote it off as a tragic accident." Misty surreptitiously scanned the casino's valet drop-off area, as if any of the sweat-soaked tourists coming and going cared about their conversation. "She would have gotten away with it, too, if said rival hadn't woken up from her coma and recovered from amnesia with the help of a friend who'd apparently always been in love with her. He claimed to be her husband and nursed her back to health; then when they fell in love and went to file the paperwork to get married, she discovered her identity had been stolen! Turns out Carla had been impersonating her for over two years. Huge deal, FBI involvement—the works. I heard they're making it into a Lifetime movie."

"Unbelievable."

"Tell me about it." Misty rolled her eyes. "And they say *my* plots are unrealistic."

"I wonder if . . ." Erika wasn't sure if she should say it aloud—the obvious conclusion she'd drawn—but Misty raised a brow as if she knew exactly what Erika meant.

"Trust me, we all wondered about whether your accident was actually an accident. But I guess we'll never know, huh? After all, she's already locked up, and you seem to be doing great, so I guess it's best to let the past go, right?"

"Yeah, you're right. That's what's best," Erika said. Because Misty's words were trite but true. Knowing the truth about Carla didn't exactly bring closure, and it definitely didn't bring justice or any money from a civil suit. But Erika had been trying—and failing—to close this chapter of her old life for two years, so for now, it was enough.

Misty suddenly straightened in alarm. "Crap! I gotta go—I'm going to be late to my meeting. But we should catch up. You probably deleted my number, but I'll text you. If you want, I mean."

"I'd like that." *More than I thought I would.* Then some unfamiliar and gooey feeling spurred her to grasp Misty's shoulders and tell her, "Don't give up. Okay? No matter what 'they' say. Someday, you'll find someone who believes in your work. I know it." The sight of Christof emerging from the casino, right on time, made her lips quirk into a smile before she could stop it from happening. Absently, she added, "Remember, optimism and persistence are keys to success."

The moment Christof's eyes landed on her, a matching smile lit his own face. He eagerly started through the crowd toward her with his long-legged stroll, but he was stopped by a valet who acted as if he needed to speak to Christof urgently. Christof replied to something the valet said, confusion written all over his face, then reluctantly accepted a clipboard and pen.

Erika was so distracted by this exchange that Misty's hug caught her by surprise.

"Thank you," Misty said, tightening her hold for a split second before releasing her grasp. "Thanks for being so nice to me. It means a lot. You're basically my idol!"

Erika stifled the urge to tell Misty the truth—that her life was definitely not worth idolizing. That she was living in a dank basement (by choice), she had no friends (also by choice, apparently), and all she had to her name was a failing business—and if a hastily planned fundraiser didn't raise enough cash, she wouldn't even have that.

Which was not by choice.

But instead, she said goodbye and let Misty totter away, and then she let Christof come up to her and sweep the hair away from her cheek and kiss her in front of dozens of strangers.

At least she had Christof to look forward to. And this temporary thing with the band, which gave her some silly feeling of purpose.

For now.

CHAPTER 24

The ride back to Paris was by far more pleasant for Christof than the ride out. For one, he preferred riding up front with Erika to risking death in the back of the truck bed, and he enjoyed a playful debate with her about their differing musical tastes and performance styles.

Most important, though, was that due to the high back of the seat hiding most of their bodies from view of the truck's rear passengers, Christof had the freedom to do things like reach out and lightly stroke Erika's bare skin where the skirt of her dress stretched tight across her lap and mounded her plump, sun-gilded thigh like a tempting little hill. Or follow that hill down into the shadows, causing her to do things like quickly suck in air and bite her red-inked bottom lip and tighten her thighs around his wrist and accidentally jerk the wheel—the last startling him enough to tame his wandering hand before he became responsible for a catastrophe.

When they pulled into the dusty gravel lot behind the brothel, Erika placed a staying hand on his forearm, silently asking him to wait until Sibylle and the others had unloaded from the back of the truck. Waldo, who had chugged an entire thirty-two-ounce white chocolate mocha and then promptly fallen asleep for the entire ride, had to be physically roused from his repose, and it took all of Christof's restraint to stay where he was instead of tending to his bandmate. Thankfully, Sibylle continued her newfound devotion to responsibility by being the one to resurrect him from his slumber.

Christof unbuckled his seat belt, prepared to follow everyone inside, when her fingers slipped down his forearm to hold his hand.

"Relax," Erika murmured, and he realized he was tensing his grip too tightly.

"If they see us go in together, they might suspect . . ."

"What?" She sounded amused. "That you're a newly single adult who's fucking the hot theater owner who's temporarily filling in on keys for the next few weeks?"

He scraped a hand over his face. "What if they think it's too soon after Gillian? They've always looked to me as the responsible one."

She bit her lip, white teeth denting plush crimson. He wanted to feel that softness between his own teeth. "Do *you* think it's too soon after Gillian?"

Not soon enough. "No."

"Then stop worrying. They're adults who can take care of themselves. Besides, they don't need you right now." She guided his hand back to her thigh and locked her midnight eyes on his. "I do."

Her skin blazed under his palm, obliterating all other thought.

As soon as the brothel door closed behind Sergei, Christof undid Erika's seat belt. The clang of the metal latch releasing echoed in the hushed cabin, as if it signaled the start of something grave and important. And it did.

Tonight was the night he slept with a woman who wasn't Gillian. For the first time in his life. And it was *Erika*—a woman who could have stepped out of his darkest fantasies. She was the mysterious subject of every lusty power ballad he'd ever sung, long before he'd met her.

"Christof?" Her voice was low and raspy with need.

"Come here." He lifted her out of the driver's seat and onto his lap, and she eagerly straddled him. Her soft thighs closed over the outsides of his own, encasing him in her heat, inundating him with her rose-scented air. When she kissed him, her hair fell forward and shrouded their faces in dark shadows, even though it was barely four in the after-noon and the sun blazed with oppressive, blinding heat. It didn't matter that anyone walking by the empty gravel lot could see them or that it was a thousand degrees in this vehicle without the air-conditioning blowing at them; when Erika was in his arms, nothing mattered but her.

She tasted like glacier-cold water, and he wanted to drown in it. Her hushed gasps of air made his skin tingle with painful awareness. He was so hard he was sure he could feel the individual buttons on his jeans leaving imprints on his sensitive shaft, and yet the angle was wrong. She wasn't riding him close enough. He dug his fingers into her lush hips and tried to drag her closer against him, but her knees hit the seat back. No room.

She nipped at his bottom lip as she pulled away, and he felt it like a bolt of lightning shooting straight to his balls. "Take me inside."

He kicked the truck door open with her still clinging to him, her legs wrapped tight around his waist, and carried her into the building. She directed him down wooden steps to the cellar below.

The words *sex dungeon* echoed in his head, but he was beyond caring if that was where they were indeed headed. He'd have followed Erika to a French Canadian discotheque—or any other vile pit of hell she named.

He swept her down the steps into the darkness, where an onyx wood door met them on the landing and he was forced to set Erika down so she could retrieve her key and unlock it.

The door creaked open, and Christof squinted into the dark rect-angle. It was pitch black in there. Under normal circumstances, he'd question exactly what he was doing letting a woman he hardly knew lead him into a windowless basement room, where his screams might go unheard and his body might go undiscovered.

"Go on," she urged him in a husky voice, one of her little painted claws poking into the small of his back.

But these were not normal circumstances. Erika was his midnight witch, and she had him in her thrall.

He stepped into the inky beyond, and a second later, the door snicked shut behind him and her heels clicked against the hard floor. The only other sound was his breath. His pulse seemed to slow, his blood pouring like a viscous drug through his veins. Time disappeared.

The crack of a match snapped time back into place. Erika lit a standing candelabra nearby, illuminating the room in flickering golden light. He took in the threadbare carpets and the cracked plaster ceiling; the cobwebs stretching from wooden support beam to beam; the sprawling antique bed with its ornate velvet-clothed frame; the glass-enclosed display of whips and crops, covered in dust—

He slid her a look. "You said this wasn't a sex dungeon."

"Well, not anymore." Erika blew out the match and dropped it into a cup on a nearby dresser, then strolled toward him. "These used to be the late Mistress Giry's quarters, though, and I get the sense my great-great-grandmother did good business. Don't worry, it's a new mattress."

A metallic clang came from behind him, and he glanced over his shoulder to see a black rodent wrestling furiously with the door to his waist-high cage. And there was another one living there—a fat brown-and-white creature obliviously munching on a seedcake. The sight momentarily distracted him from the romance of the moment.

"You have rats?"

Erika wandered over to the cage and murmured something that made the squirrelly one relinquish his grip on the bars. "This is Javert and his brother, Jean," she told him. "They needed to be rescued, and

I needed the company. It's a solid deal we have going, although Javert forgets that most of the time."

He wasn't surprised to hear she'd done a kind thing; Erika struck him as the sort who thought of herself as much colder than she really was, like the grouchy old man who ran the corner shop in his home-town and had always looked the other way when he and Waldo used to sneak candy into their schoolbags. But it did make him wonder: Did Erika merely see him as another sad creature to be rescued?

Christof drew toward the cage and bent down to peer closer. The black rat scurried to the back of the enclosure, where he eyed Christof warily, nose twitching. "Not very cuddly, are they?"

Her shoulders drew inward. "That's not true. Javert's just a misan-thrope. But Jean is a sweetheart and likes to be held. Rats are really mis-understood, you know. They're actually very gentle and loving creatures if you can get past their appearance and reputation."

It clicked. He wasn't the rat in their dynamic—she was.

Erika was still watching him with an air of trepidation, as if she was waiting for him to make some disgusted proclamation about her choice of pets, so he pulled her into an embrace and squeezed her tight against his chest. Her head tucked securely under his chin.

"Erika . . ." Didn't she understand he was already lost in her? "Your rats are just fine. And you are perfect as you are."

"You barely know me."

"Nothing you tell me will frighten me off. You could sleep in a nest of bones and human hair, and I'd still want you."

He felt her smile press into his skin where his shirt opened and left his chest bare. "That's disgusting."

"Ah, well, I *would* suggest moving affairs upstairs to a more tradi-tional bed. At least for the first time."

"But then I have to drag your bones all the way downstairs afterward."

"I promise it will be worth the effort. I have excellent bones."

"One in particular." Her hand slid down his front and found the bulge of his cock. It throbbed under her touch.

Air hissed out through his teeth. "Do you want this to be over quickly?"

"Don't tempt me." Her hand moved to undo the buttons of his trousers.

He caught her wrist. "Not this time." *This time means something to me.* But she'd likely scoff at him if he expressed even half of what he was feeling.

She pulled back so he could see the playful pout she'd put on for him. "Don't be cruel. Let me touch it. I love having your huge cock in my hand."

"Cruel?" He captured her other wrist in his free hand, then collected her wrists together in one, holding her fists up like a bouquet. "You brought me to your sex dungeon and promised to do unspeakable things to me. And yet you haven't undressed for me."

"Let me go, and I will," she purred, but just like when he'd held her wrists earlier in the hotel room, she didn't try to free herself from his grip. An unfamiliar thrill lit up strange and new places in his brain.

Or maybe places that weren't new at all.

He firmly nudged her backward, and she willingly went with him, letting him guide her until they stood at the base of the bed. Then he stopped, unsure of what he was meant to do next. He wanted her naked. He wanted to be naked *with* her. But this other thing that was happening, this other role he was playing . . . well, he was wearing new skin, and he hadn't quite broken it in yet.

Her breath came fast and hot against his skin as she rested her cheek against their entwined hands, and she gazed up at him, her dark eyes glimmering with the reflection of candlelight. She asked softly, "Have you ever done something like this before?"

"Many times," he lied.

Her gaze didn't waver.

"No. Never." He released her wrists.

"Do you want to?"

He fought the inexplicable urge to lie again. This subtle undercurrent of shame shouldn't trip him up like it did. He was the modern sort. A mega cool rock and roll musician who was beyond comfortable with his sexuality. He didn't give a fuck about gender or tradition or genital equipment or labels or whatever the hell these things were called, as long as it was badass. He wanted to try everything, at least once.

But *wanting* and *doing* were oceans apart. He was thirty years old, and he'd only ever been with one woman. Only ever done things within the narrow realm of what Gillian had liked. And because he'd loved Gillian—or so he'd told himself—he'd never felt like he was missing anything.

Or so he'd told himself.

"Christof?"

"Yes," he choked out, almost desperately. "Do *you* want this?"

"With you? God, yes."

"Tell me what to do."

The corner of her mouth quirked. "I think it's supposed to be the other way around, you know."

"Right. *Right.*"

"Relax. It's easy. Just ask me to do things that turn you on, and I'll do it." She kissed the back of his hand and sidestepped so she could bend down and unclasp her heels, one by one. When she was done, she gently set them aside, her head a full four inches lower than before. She had to crane her neck to look up at him now, and it made him feel strong. Powerful. *Protective.*

"And if I ask you to do something you don't want?"

"Then I'll ask you to stop, and you will. Or if you want to get rough, we could choose a safe word."

Did he want to get rough? No. Yes. But not this time. He took a breath, and it was all rose-scented air. The muscles in his shoulders unknotted, and something else in him unlocked too.

He drew up to his full height and stepped back. In a voice he didn't recognize, he said, "Take off your dress."

CHAPTER 25

Christof's light-brown eyes were so much darker in the dim light. They reflected twin flames from the candelabra behind her and gave him a sinister appearance. It was thrilling to see him step into this commanding role—watching his tentative uncertainty bleed into sureness. Christof claimed he'd never been the director in the bedroom, and yet the speed with which he adapted made Erika certain he'd been born for it.

All that control he craved so badly that it twisted him into knots—this was where he could find it.

And Erika, naturally, was always meant to perform. To take her director's cues. To be the center of his world.

So when her breath trembled out of her lips and she reached behind her to grasp at the high zipper of her dress, was she slipping into character—or out of one? The line blurred.

The zipper hook was one of those slippery, teardrop-shaped ones, and it escaped her grasp. "Please," she said quietly, presenting her back to him. Facing this way, she could see their reflections in the mirror.

They were a study in contrast: his towering, rangy, black-clad frame hovering over her short, voluptuous, white-clothed one. She watched him lower his head as he inspected the zipper, and he looked like a spider closing in on innocent prey.

A wicked smile flickered over Erika's lips, but she wiped it clean before he saw. *The greatest trick of all—letting the fly believe he's the spider.* He was here in her web, after all.

His touch was feather light as fingertips pressed into the fabric at the top of her neck. Slowly, the zipper lowered, its metal casing being pressed into her skin just enough to feel like a single fingernail dragging down the right side of her spinal column. When it reached the end at the small of her back, the pressure of his fingers disappeared, and the linen parted. Cool air touched her back.

And that was all.

She waited. Was he deciding what to do next, or was he making her wait for direction on purpose? Erika swallowed as excitement flooded her bloodstream. The uncertainty of it was intoxicating. The knowledge that this was his show, and she didn't have to be in charge of or responsible for anything in his arms . . . the belief that Christof would take care of her . . . it was sweeter than any drink.

And with a bolt of surprise, she realized she really did believe that—in the bedroom and out of it.

She trusted him. Completely. With the uncanny certainty that made no sense and would have horrified her old self, who had trusted no one.

"Take it off," he repeated. His voice was soft, not cruel. But it didn't need to be.

Erika brought her hands up to the straps and slipped them off her shoulders, but the bodice stayed upright. Of course it did—it was lined with body-shaping material, because it was too sweltering to wear another layer, but she sure as hell wasn't fitting her abundant self into an A-line sheath without compromise. Taking the dress off would require a fair amount of wiggling.

Erika slid her hands between the fabric and her waist, letting herself enjoy her own touch as she forced the fabric down to her hips. If she closed her eyes, she could pretend they were his hands.

The dress caught on the widest part of her hips, and she huffed, shimmying side to side as she dragged the constricting ring down.

A sharp inhalation of breath from behind her made Erika's eyes flick to the mirror, and she saw what she looked like, her breasts overflowing from the nude balconette bra she wore, jiggling along with her soft flesh as she struggled. Her nipples were dangerously close to slipping free, the dark-peach half moons of her areolae welling over the top. No wonder Christof's face had drawn tight, his jaw clenching hard enough to throw his impossible cheekbones into stark relief in the candlelight's flickering shadows along his face.

"That's enough."

Erika stopped moving, but she didn't release her grip on the fabric. Did he want her to stop wiggling or to stop taking the dress off entirely? Like this, with her dress stuck under the swell of her bottom, she couldn't spread her legs, and walking would be difficult.

"Leave it there."

Heat tunneled under her skin. He wanted to flirt with light bondage, did he? *Well, well, well.* Erika found his gaze in the mirror and held it. The fevered, half-starved look in his eyes should have scared her, but instead it made wetness pool between her legs. "Now what?" she whispered.

"Don't move. I'm going to touch you now, and you're going to tell me exactly how you like to be touched. And then you're going to watch me do it."

Her breath shuddered out. "Okay." Her voice was barely audible. A gasp of smoke.

Strong, elegant hands fell on her shoulders, his long fingers closing over her collarbone. She could feel the delicious rasp of his calluses as he slid them up to her neck and brushed her long hair back. When his head lowered to feather his breath on her neck, her eyelids fluttered shut of their own volition.

He nipped at the skin on her neck, and a shock wave of white-hot sparks sizzled over her breasts and spread aching heat in its wake, turning her nipples into tight, coiled buds.

"Eyes open."

His eyeliner-smoked eyes fixed onto hers, locking her in his unrelenting gaze. With his mouth still closed over her neck, his tongue flicked out, gliding like a whisper over her sensitive flesh.

It was unbelievably erotic—but she needed more. Her nipples pushed hard against the constricting edge of her bra, and when she took a breath, the elastic edge dug in so keenly that it made her clit throb in need. If she was alone, she'd slip her breasts free of the cups and rub the aching tips with her own fingers.

She swallowed. When her voice came out, she barely recognized it. "Touch my breasts. Please."

A rough groan vibrated against her neck, and his teeth slipped over the skin again, grazing now. Without hesitation, his hands slid over her chest until he could slip his fingers under the edge of the fabric to cup the globes of her breasts. The beige lace showcased the ridges of his knuckles and the shadowed valleys between his fingers. His thumbs hovered mere millimeters away from her nipples. Close enough that if she squirmed, she could make them touch.

"Is this what you want?" he asked.

She bit her lip. Shook her head.

His lips found her ear. "I want to hear you say it."

"Touch my nipples."

His thumbs lifted the edge of the elastic, sending circulation rushing back into the stimulated tips, and gently brushed against them. Erika hissed, squeezing her thighs together against the fresh spike of pleasure. "Again." He did it again, and that spike came again too. But she needed to be more specific. "Roll them under your thumbs, like you're—" Her breath hitched as he did exactly that, and she had to force her eyes to stay open and not roll back in her head.

"Like I'm . . . what?"

"Plucking a note on the guitarrr—*yes, that*." He did exactly what she wanted, with the perfect pressure and rhythm. God, he was good. She should have known that a man that good at guitar could play her body like this. There was an intuitive nature to pleasure and music alike.

"Do you like that?" he asked, even though he was still locked onto her eyes, her face. He had to know already.

"I love it."

"Good." He jerked her back roughly against him so her soft form crushed against his impossibly hard one. The steel length of his cloth-covered erection jutted, hot and heavy, against the curve of her back. *"Good."*

Her head fell back against his chest, but she didn't dare let her eyes close, even when he brought his left thumb to her lips and lightly pressed, urging her to open for him. There was no question—she obeyed without thought, sucking his digit into her mouth and laving it with her tongue as if it were his cock. The thought made her whimper in want, and he used the opportunity to slip his thumb free with a wet pop. It came back to her nipple, slick with her own saliva, and swirled over the tip. A new pulse began throbbing between her legs, faster and more insistent with every swirl of his thumb.

Erika couldn't help it—he'd told her not to move, but she needed to. Needed *something*. Her bottom pushed back against his thighs, desperate for pressure to relieve the throbbing, but the bunched-up fabric around her hips cushioned her sex. Protected it from his hard ridges.

Had that been his plan all along, or was this little torture a byproduct of happenstance? Erika searched Christof's face, but it was hard to tell. The shadows were so dark, hiding the parts of him that she could normally read. "Are you sure you haven't done this before?"

Against her neck, she caught the slightest twitch of his lips. "I've gone into great detail in my dreams."

"You dreamed about doing this specific scenario? With me?"

"Yes." One hand strayed to her stomach and held her against him so his cock could press against her back with more pressure. She felt it pulse, then grow even bigger. His fingers clutched reflexively at the soft flesh of her abdomen before splaying wide, careful not to hurt her. "Yes," he repeated, more roughly now. "Even before I knew it was you."

Her lips parted on a quiet inhale. When he said things like that—

Don't think about the proposal. He didn't mean it.

She forced herself to the here and now. To what she needed right this instant that *wasn't* a lifetime of devotion or promises she couldn't have.

"Touch my pussy," she said. "I like what you did with my nipples, but I want you to do that to my clit."

Instantly, his right hand moved from its spot on her belly and shoved under the constricting fabric of her dress. It slipped over the smooth mound of her sex, and before he even parted her folds, he found the slickness that pooled there.

"Fuck." His harsh exhalation came right below her earlobe in a rush of hot breath, and his hips bucked against her, almost helplessly this time. "You're so . . ." He seemed unable to finish his sentence.

"Wet?"

His only reply was a pained grunt. His hand closed over her pubic bone, cupping her pussy so he could press with the base of his fingers into her clit. Then his middle finger slipped easily between her folds and tested her heat.

Pleasure coiled in the nerve endings behind her clit with every heartbeat, every pulse against his firm grip. And he hadn't even moved yet. His finger still hovered over the entrance to her pussy, even as she could feel the muscles around her opening clench helplessly, desperate to pull it inside.

Suddenly, it felt like she hadn't come in *years*. Like a single slide of his fingers would undo her.

"Don't tease me." In the mirror, she could see her skin flushing pink and blotchy, her eyes shimmering with the gloss of unfocused need. Her lips were parted, wet and swollen from being bitten by her own teeth.

"Are you sure?" The pressure over her clit lessened, his finger withdrawing.

She whimpered. "*Christof.* Come on. I've wanted this for so long."

"This?" he asked, sliding his finger back into her folds. Lightly, *oh so lightly*, he began to swirl his fingertip around her clit, just as she'd asked him to.

"Yes," she whimpered. But his touch was still so gentle. And God, her breaths were coming so fast, the pleasure coiling so quickly and sharply, she wasn't sure it would even take much more to get her to come. That was the problem. "No," she corrected. "Not this."

His finger stopped moving. "What, then, have you wanted for so long?"

"You." She didn't allow herself to look away. Not this time.

He stilled, his whole body going taut. Then it was he who broke their gaze in the mirror, his eyes falling shut as he inhaled, slow but shaky.

"For how long?"

"Ever since I first saw you standing there on that balcony, like you were some . . . some egotistical *god* who could bend the world in half by just asking it to fold."

His hand slid out of her thong, and he stepped back. For a brief instant, Erika was terrified she'd said the wrong thing and he was going to stop.

But instead, he picked her up and settled her on her back, crosswise along the end of the bed. If she tilted her head back, she could still see herself in the mirror, her dark hair pooling below her onto the floor like opaque smoke. Could watch the reflection of Christof as he came up over her on his hands and knees and tugged her dress free, and her panties along with it, so she was naked save for the bra around her rib cage, the cups shoved down to push her breasts up in an obscene tableau of spit-shined pink flesh and distended nipples.

And Christof . . .

Christof had shed his shirt and pants in record time, and now he was fully, gloriously naked in the candlelight. His pale, chiseled chest slicked with sweat and heaving with every breath. His full, unholy mouth parted, his cheekbones looking like he'd 3D printed his own skull from molds of an ancient Egyptian pharaoh, his eyeliner sooty and his gaze Vantablack. And his cock, as elegant and beautifully made as the rest of him, curving up toward his navel, its slick, reddened head pushing out of the velvet-soft skin around it with pulsing urgency.

He took her breath away.

"My gorgeous witch," he said in a low, rough tone. "I'm going to make you sing for me."

Yes. This was the performance of her lifetime.

He came up onto the bed with her. His hair fell forward, and candlelight cast him in looming shadow as he held himself up on his hands and knees. In the mirror's reflection, something shiny glinted in Christof's hand.

Erika raised her head to see what it was, and he held up the shimmering condom packet. "Hotel gift shop," he said in explanation, and Erika fought a smile at the thought he'd shelled out for overpriced condoms—just in case. She didn't tell him she'd bought some on her errand run in Vegas; he'd find out, eventually. Later tonight, if she was lucky.

"Preparation is key to success," she murmured, letting her head fall back again. There was something so . . . *reassuring* . . . about Christof's need to anticipate the future, especially for someone like her who often operated as if tomorrows didn't exist. His carefulness—the sense that she was now part of his circle of things to protect and care for—was so exotic and appealing to her that it was an aphrodisiac all its own.

I have you.

If only he'd always have her.

She let her legs fall open, sinking back into the haze of lust where she could stop thinking and merely feel, and watched as he used one hand to slide the sheath over his erection so he could still crouch over her. His eyes found hers in the mirror.

And as she locked onto his hypnotizing reflection, he pressed his hand into her wetness again, his thumb circling her clit as his first and second digits teased her opening. When she whimpered and lifted her hips for more, he gave her what she wanted, slipping his guitarist's fingers halfway into her tight channel and slowly pumping in and out, angling his movement just enough to feel the friction on the soft pad of her G-spot. She contracted around his fingers, aching for more, even as pressure built in dangerously jagged, unpredictable waves. Until she felt like she'd fall into an orgasm too soon, before he'd even gotten the head of his cock inside her, and that thought formed a spear of panic.

She pushed back into the mattress, as if she could escape his expert touch by squirming away from it.

"Christof," she panted, unable to form other words as his thumb pressed just so, just a little harder than before. Her breath caught, and she squeezed her eyes shut; it took every scrap of concentration not to come.

With seconds to spare, his touch disappeared, and even though she'd all but begged for this, her hips jerked up of their own accord. Desperately pleading for more.

"Watch me." His voice was strained. Rough.

Her eyes flew open at the command to see that he'd taken the hand that was slick with her moisture and bathed his cock in it until the latex gleamed wetly. Then he stroked his encased length with firm precision, until his cock was so hard it bobbed toward his flat stomach the moment it was released, and the base of it was dark and slick and straining against the condom's stretched ring.

"Ready for me?"

"God, yes. Please. *Please.*"

And then she felt the blunt pressure at her opening and the brush of his circled fingers as he guided himself against her pussy, and Erika's arms came up of their own volition to circle his neck and draw him down to her.

She wanted him against her for this. To feel his chest heave and feel his breath in her ear. He'd said this meant something to him, and in that moment, it meant *something* to Erika too. Something huge and unfamiliar that she couldn't name, but it made her throat close up and her lungs feel like they were too full of air—

He pushed the head of his cock into her, and she forgot how to think. There was only feeling. The initial tightness, the sting of discomfort that came from going two years with only her own fingers and a dildo that now seemed laughably inadequate—it had not prepared her for this. Nothing could have. He felt so hard, his shaft so unforgiving, her inner muscles could only clamp down helplessly. Yet at the same time, she was so turned on, her body so primed, and his cock so slick from her wetness . . . there was no stopping this. Nothing she could do but clutch him against her as he worked his way in, his breaths coming out in ragged bursts as if he were in pain.

When he was hilt deep, she slid her hands up through his soft, ice-white hair and held the base of his head. "Give me a second," she gasped.

He followed her guidance, stilling his hips but bringing his forehead to hers so they were nose to nose. His woodsy cologne surrounded her like a dark forest. His eyes were shut, as if he was concentrating with all his might, but she stared at the iridescent dark shadow on his lids as her tight pussy adjusted to accommodate him. It was her own eye shadow—the same stuff he'd applied this morning—and he was devastatingly gorgeous in it.

For a brief instant, she imagined sitting side by side with him in the mornings as they applied their makeup, and it sparked a keen longing for kinship that she'd never thought to want before. The loneliness she'd lived with for so long suddenly felt like slow poison, and this temporary fling with Christof was a drop of a cure she was forbidden to drink in full.

Stay with me forever, her body pleaded as it finally began to relax and open for him. *Be beside me, always.* But she couldn't say those words aloud, because even in the throes of what was shaping up to be the most earth-shattering sex of her life, Erika was self-aware enough to know how clingy she'd sound, smart enough to know her problems couldn't be solved by latching on to the first man who was kind to her, and cynical enough to believe he'd break her heart anyway. So instead, she ran her thumbs across his cheekbones to memorize the feel of his silky skin and guided him down to a kiss.

With their mouths meshed together and Christof's tongue sweeping into her mouth, he began to move again, rolling his hips with a languid pace that matched his tongue and lips as he consumed her—and holy shit, could that man roll his hips. He eased into her and dragged out of her with the patience and flexibility of a man who did yoga every morning, and with the raw sexiness of a performer who could grind against a microphone stand for two hours straight and never once bore the crowd.

Her hips began to roll in response, first with intention to match Christof's beat, and then because she couldn't control herself. Every time he slid into her, her ass lifted to meet him and grind her clit against the hard base of his cock, and as he withdrew, her pussy tightened to battle the loss.

Stay, she wanted to cry out. *Be inside me, always.* But he was still kissing her, and it felt intimate and magical and like everything she dreamed of in secret, so she stayed silent in the hope it wouldn't ever end.

She tried to be as graceful about it as Christof was, but it had been too long since she'd last done this—and far too long that she'd waited to do it with Christof. The need had built beyond her limit and then kept climbing. The things he made her body feel were too sharp, too intense, *too much*. Her thighs began trembling. Hushed exhales solidified into hot moans. And then, despite hours in front of a metronome, despite the fact that Erika had never once missed a cue or mark, her rhythm broke, and her hips jerked unsteadily, and her moans turned ragged, and her hands transformed into claws, clutching at his skin and long hair.

As a rule, Erika did not come merely from penetration. It was a matter of personal principle, she'd decided, and not mere physiology. But now, with her hands clinging to Christof's neck and shoulders, and his own arms busy supporting his weight to avoid crushing her, there was nothing but his thrusts that could be responsible for the spiraling knot of impending orgasm.

Just as she thought maybe—just once—she was going to break her own rule and shatter into a thousand pieces of glass, Christof ripped his mouth off hers and grunted, *"Fuck."*

His hips stilled at the base of his thrust, buried hilt deep in her, and she whimpered in dismay, the orgasm hovering mere millimeters out of reach. She lifted up against him, her clit throbbing for contact. "Don't stop." It wasn't enough. Couldn't he see it wasn't enough? The weight of his hips pinned her to the bed, limiting her movements to helpless contractions of her thighs as she sought friction against him to no avail.

Christof hissed through his teeth. "If you don't hold still for a moment, I will come."

Blood suffused her flesh at his words, as the heat in her core was flooding through her and rising to the surface of her skin. Erika wanted him losing control over how good her pussy made him feel. It was the greatest tribute she dared ask for.

"Do it," she snarled, surprising herself at the vehemence of her tone. He'd offered something she hadn't known she wanted, then told her she couldn't have it—which made her want it all the more. She wriggled under him, intentionally squeezing her inner muscles tight.

Taking what she desired even when she wasn't supposed to, like she always did.

He reared back right as his hands shot out to seize her hips and pin her immobile—impaled on his thick, slowly pulsating cock, unable to move. She moaned, but she wasn't sure if it was a complaint or a reaction to the intensity of the position as his girth shoved up against her G-spot.

His hazel eyes narrowed. "I thought I was giving the orders."

"But I'm so close—"

"As am I," he bit out, but it was a warning. "Now, *stay still.*"

It was commanding and asking, all at once. She heard the words, and then in her heart, she heard the echo: *Tell me I'm in control.*

He needs this, she realized. Christof needed to have this power, if just for this once, and only for the here and now. To feel what it was like to have things be entirely and utterly perfect. She couldn't fix the parts of his world that were crumbling, and she couldn't take away his worries, as much as she dearly wanted to.

But she could give him this moment. This magical, private space, separate from reality, where she was loved and cherished forever and he was the ruler of his universe.

"Okay," she whispered, her body melting into his grip around her hip bones. "I trust you."

Her back arched and her arms splayed out against the coverlet so she could once again watch in the mirror. Except this time, a different Erika and Christof stared back at her from that mirror universe. These reflections were phantoms from a different timeline where there were no bills to pay or albums to record—only this.

Only pleasure.

She saw when he recognized what her capitulation meant, saw it a split second before he snapped and gave in to his dark side—she'd been waiting for it. His face changed: that constant line of worry between his brows smoothing, his hard jaw going slack. And then a wicked, unchained demon rose to the surface, free from its prison where Christof had kept it locked up tight, and it was magnificent.

His teeth flashed white in the shadows as he growled, "Now, we dance."

And then he was fucking her in earnest, grinding his cock into her in short, purposeful thrusts that rattled the mattress in its ancient wooden frame, grunting and making guttural, inhuman moans that were so fucking feral and sexy and uncontrolled that the sound of each one slammed on a chord deep inside her and made electricity sizzle through her veins and capillaries until every blood vessel lit up in white-hot sparks and the very act of breathing burned.

And she was making sounds, too, but they were incomprehensible. Helpless, unchecked cries that came so fast with every thrust that they began to blend together into one long, earsplitting cry.

It was almost too much. He drove her to the edge of pleasure and kept her there for long enough that she was afraid her impending orgasm wouldn't come at all. That it would remain tantalizingly out of reach, even as his cock grew impossibly bigger and harder inside her, even as his fingers clamped tighter on her hips and he snarled, "Fuck, I'm coming," and his entire body tensed, the tendons in his neck straining into ropes.

Yes, she wanted to cry in encouragement, but her voice only made another garbled cry. It didn't matter if she came. He was beautiful when he was unleashed like this. She wanted to revel in his pleasure.

Then his grip changed, and even as he shuddered over her, his thumb found her clit and kneaded in taut circles. Gifting her that last little bit she needed to plummet over the edge, because he was *Christof,* and even in the throes of his own pleasure, he was unable to be selfish. And there it was: an orgasm slamming into her like a silent implosion. It stole her voice and, along with it, the breath in her lungs. Her back bowed. Stars danced at the edges of her vision. And her feet drummed on the bed as waves of pleasure pummeled her with relentless force.

They collapsed together into a tangled heap. He should have been too heavy for her, but Erika didn't care. She didn't really need to breathe, anyway. In the mirror, a drugged woman stared back at her, her face reddened, her lips swollen, and her eyes glazed. Silvery strands cascaded forward from Christof's limp head and tickled her cheeks.

"Mein Gott," she heard him croak out. The sound was muffled by her breasts.

She sipped air in through her mouth. "Yeah," she managed to wheeze out.

He pushed up on unsteady forearms and looked over her with a concerned expression. "Are you all right? Was that, er . . ."

She raised her hand to cup his cheek, and it was like moving through heavy water. Her whole body was spent. Exhausted. "I've never, *ever* been better."

His shoulders unknotted, and he let his head rest on her cupped palm. His relieved exhale tickled her wrist.

Another impossible thing was happening: she was getting sleepy. In the middle of the goddamn day. After *sex*. Normally, she was the one lying wide awake while her lover snored peacefully by her side. But now her eyelids were heavy and she had no choice but to let them fall shut. For a second, while she caught her breath. That was all. Then she'd be up for another round or two—at least.

Vaguely, she felt herself being lifted; then something plush settled under her head, and warmth cocooned her.

Maybe she imagined that she heard Christof softly singing another power ballad to her. Maybe she'd already fallen asleep and merely dreamed that he sang to her about surrender and fantasy and darkness, but also of love and devotion and eternity. The kind of music one whispered at night, while their lover slept, when no one could hear. She couldn't be sure.

But Erika wished she'd been awake to sing with him.

CHAPTER 26

Erika could count on one hand the times she'd felt genuinely happy. The moment she'd first gotten a standing ovation. When she'd been cast in her first Broadway show. When she'd gotten the role of Fantine.

But all those moments had been temporary and fleeting. She'd always woken up the next morning feeling slightly adrift, like she'd conquered Everest's peak but still had to climb all the way back down. Sure, she'd gotten her dream role, but she'd still had to show up every day for rehearsal, and she'd lived alone, and she'd been the mistress and never the girlfriend, and her friends had bored her, and the critics hadn't always been kind, and her feet had blistered in her summer heels and frozen in her winter ones, and she'd *constantly* been hungry and tired and hungover. The temporary blip of happiness she'd experienced when she'd gotten The Call from *Les Mis*'s casting director hadn't fixed the rest of her unhappiness. It was like dumping a cup of clean water in a poisoned pond and expecting the entire thing to be potable afterward.

The following two weeks with Christof, however, Erika was really and truly happy, down to the last drop. Or at least, she thought she was.

She wasn't very familiar with the feeling.

"Stay with me," she'd asked him after the first night, and so he'd stayed until morning.

She awoke to the smell of coffee, because he'd gotten out of bed and called for breakfast delivery from the diner—and she hadn't even known Paris *had* a food-delivery service. "No one's ever brought me anything in bed before," she told him. "Unless you count news that the Horrible Wife is on her way home and I need to leave out the fire escape."

He feigned horror. "Your wife is on the way home? I must hide!" He pretended to peer under the bed. "Too narrow. Perhaps you've a hidden passage somewhere?"

"Yes, right behind that mirror." She pointed at the floor-length antique on the wall they'd used last night, and if she wasn't mistaken, that was a *blush* filling in over Christof's cheekbones. "That's where all my clandestine lovers come from. Return to your ethereal form and begone before daylight breaks, baby."

He kissed her, morning breath and all. Thoroughly.

After breakfast, he patiently waited for her to get ready and didn't even complain about how long it took to dry her abundant hair with a round brush. She'd been nervous about him seeing her postshower, without a drop of foundation to cover her scars, but he didn't seem to notice.

He was more focused on the contraption she'd set up to wire electricity down to the basement—a cluster of loosely joined power strips hanging from the hole she'd drilled into the ceiling. "This looks dangerous."

She eyed her work and shrugged. "Probably."

He glowered at her in the mirror.

"What? Do you have any idea what a licensed electrician would charge to come out and do it properly? I'm on a budget."

His dark look didn't abate. If anything, her words made him even more resolved. "When the album is finished, I will ensure these problems are fixed."

As if Christof would have any reason to stick around after the album was done. A stab of sadness slid between her ribs, searching for her well-guarded heart. Her only defense was to deflect. "Don't bother. I doubt Raoul will appreciate me living in the basement of his new theater."

"We won't let that happen. This fundraiser will be a success."

What if it wasn't? Would she have to go back to New York and beg for scraps from her family? Whore herself out like Fantine, singing in Raoul's knockoff Broadway shows and filling her shamelessly empty soul with piles of money?

Or an even more daunting prospect—stay with Nachtmusik as a permanent band member?

Think of all the power ballads. Her pride wouldn't allow her to sing one in public. In private, however . . . well, one night later that week, Christof hummed a power ballad while simultaneously performing oral sex on her. After that, Erika was a wholehearted convert.

Still, it was one thing to sing power ballad duets in a claw-footed bathtub with her lover. It was another thing to get up on a public stage and sing them in front of an audience. To the public, she was still Erika Greene, former Broadway legend. If she were to make a comeback—*if*—hair metal wasn't how she'd envisioned doing it.

Even if she was having a ball rehearsing with Nachtmusik. And for some reason, the band seemed to like her too. She'd been worried that when Sibylle and the others learned she and Christof were sleeping together, Erika would be seen as stepping into the wicked-stepmother role. But after a week of sharing her bed, Christof grew tired of sneaking upstairs to his own room before dawn.

They lounged in her tangled sheets that particular morning, Christof idly coiling a lock of her hair around his finger and then releasing it to marvel at its silkiness. "I will tell them today that you and I are . . ." He glanced at her, and then his forest eyes darted away. "Together."

"Are we?" Her pulse fluttered like mad. He still hadn't brought up the proposal again; neither had she. Everything had been too perfect to ruin with the prospect of rejection. This was the only role she was being actively offered: temporary girlfriend, substitute band member, and doomed theater owner.

"What else do you call this?" He gestured to their entwined naked bodies. "Or what we did last night?"

"Introductory pegging?"

Christof's face flushed. "We don't need to go into details."

"Are you sure?"

He rolled over so he could push up on his elbows above her. "Little witch. There was nothing *introductory* about last night."

Her arms came up to coil around his neck. "So, we're together, then." Some old, self-protective instinct made her add, "For now."

The sparkle in his eyes dimmed a little. "Yes. For now."

But before they entered the auditorium that morning, he glanced at their linked hands for a beat longer than necessary. Erika fought the urge to let go. Christof squeezed tighter.

"I'm not ashamed of you," he said.

She didn't answer. How to explain the acid swirling in her gut? She didn't *want* to care this much. It shouldn't matter if his bandmates liked her or if they thought of her as the home-wrecker who'd moved in on Christof when he was still fresh off dating their beloved Gillian. Being the Other Woman was familiar, but the way Christof was treating her wasn't familiar at all. He made her feel treasured and safe and desired, in a way no one—unless one counted faceless audiences—ever had.

Despite Erika's trepidation, the band accepted their newfound relationship status with indifference. Exasperation, even.

"Yes, we *know*," Sibylle said when Christof told them before rehearsal began. She made a disgusted face. "I am overjoyed my miserable brother seems happy for once, but you two are very loud. It disturbs the restless spirits haunting my attic room."

Waldo applauded. "High five!" he called to Christof. Christof reluctantly complied, and before Erika could roll her eyes, Waldo turned to her. "And for you, higher five!"

"You want me to high-five you to celebrate sleeping with your best friend?"

"Ja! Sex is super geil!"

She looked at Christof for confirmation, who only shrugged. "He's not *wrong*."

So Erika high-fived Waldo. It might have been her first high five . . . ever. She didn't hate it.

Sergei was the only one who didn't have anything to say about their announcement. He only looked up from his guitar maintenance with an impatient expression. "Your assignations do not interest me. Are we rehearsing now? I have perfected the guitar sequence on 'Fire Tornado.'"

"No one minds that I have moved on so quickly after Gillian?" Christof asked.

Sibylle crossed the stage to the primary mic and intoned in a dour voice, "Do you think you are somehow the main characters in this tale? Because you are mistaken. I am the main character! The bassist medium will now regale you all with how I have solved the mystery of Mistress Giry's chandelier murder—"

Everyone else groaned, and Christof clapped his hands, rescuing them all from another one of Sibylle's rambling ghost theories. "Okay, let's begin rehearsal! Waldo, lead us in on the first track."

As Erika settled onto her stool behind the keyboard, she marveled at how quickly this had all become normal. Waking up every morning and spending hours playing this instrument that didn't belong to her, for a band that wasn't hers. Laughing and joking with these people who were passing through her life temporarily. Every night, falling asleep in the embrace of a man she couldn't keep. It was easy to close her eyes and pretend that this dream would go on forever.

That she wouldn't wake up three weeks from now and realize that she was, once again, entirely alone.

CHAPTER 27

Christof was proud of himself. Over the past three weeks, they'd begun interviewing potential band managers over the internet, and in the interim, he'd begun distributing his responsibilities among the other members of Nachtmusik. Despite how difficult relinquishing control was for him, he'd only lost his patience with the new democratic decision-making process exactly sixteen times.

He credited Erika for his exemplary behavior. Although she'd been reticent to fill in on keys at first, she seemed to enjoy herself at rehearsals.

Better yet, Erika was an incredible teammate to have in his corner. She conspired with him to step in as the villain when it was time to crack down on Sibylle's or Waldo's penchant for unrelated distractions, allowing Christof to play the hero for once. And whenever his anxiety began ratcheting up as a result of the often chaotic energy his bandmates brought to meetings, Erika stayed him with a knowing look or a gentle touch on his arm.

"Have you ever seen *Avenue Q?*" When he shook his head, Erika explained, "There's a funny line where Christmas Eve is talking about how people need to learn for themselves. To paraphrase, if a mama bird pushes her fledgling out of the nest and it doesn't fly properly, it'll get eaten by a cat. So next time, the baby bird knows what not to do."

Christof's brow furrowed. "But the baby bird is dead."

"That's why it's funny."

As skeptical as he was, he trusted Erika, so he forcibly tamped down his protective instincts and let Nachtmusik fly. Against all reason, it worked.

When Sibylle insisted on including the pipe organ on a track, Erika stopped Christof from intervening—allowing Sibylle to discover how impractical it would be to both learn to play and get an authentic pipe organ into their Berlin recording studio.

When Waldo came to rehearsal with a fifty-two-minute track he'd composed while under the influence of a psychedelic, Erika had insisted Waldo's song be heard in its entirety so that he could learn on his own that sober individuals couldn't see the rainbow of colors he'd seen come out of his cymbal the night before.

And when Sergei's guitar solos got out of hand during certain numbers, Christof stepped back and let it continue—until *Waldo* was the one who eventually cut him off.

Christof had to admit, Erika's influence on Nachtmusik was transformative. In only three weeks, they'd written and nearly perfected an entire album. By next week, they'd be on track to perform in front of a sold-out audience at the fundraiser. Christof hadn't thought such a thing possible.

After rehearsals, Erika was there for him. First, with the mind-blanking things she did—and allowed him to do—with her lush body, and then afterward, as they lay in exhausted, sweat-slicked bliss in her bed. Or in his bed, because they no longer had to keep their assignations a secret. Or some nights, on the foldout chaise on the roof of the opera house where Erika occasionally sunbathed during the day, moonlight cooling their bare skin under a ribbon of stars.

Like tonight. The nights were short this time of year above the equator, and the searing heat of the day had decided it wasn't worth leaving only to return in a few hours. Although Erika's cellar was cooler, he liked making love to her on the roof. Of all the new sexual proclivities she'd introduced him to thus far, the thrill of getting caught was one of his favorites. Even if the winged statues guarding the rooftop—and the lack of taller buildings anywhere nearby—made the rooftop as private as a public place could be.

"Sibylle is being completely irrational," he vented to her, and Erika hummed in sympathy. "She cannot build a trapdoor in the stage so she might enter the stage by 'emerging from the underworld.'"

"She can if she finds a contractor who's willing to come out to Paris before the show next weekend," Erika murmured, tracing a lazy pattern on his bare chest. She lay half-sprawled across him on the lounge chair, her gloriously lush naked body bare to the 2:00 a.m. sky. "Because I haven't been able to find anyone to replace the fire sprinklers, which I'm pretty sure is Raoul's doing. If we can't get that fire permit, we're not having a fundraiser anyway. So I'm inclined to let Sibylle give it a shot."

"We'll find someone." It made him feel helpless that he couldn't do more to help. He'd offered Erika money, but she'd turned it down.

And if Erika lost the theater, Nachtmusik would have to head home. There would be no reason to stay in Paris beyond his own selfish desire to spend more time with Erika. The album was almost done, and the next step was to record it in their Berlin studio.

The band always came first. It had to.

Come with us, he wanted to say. But something made the words catch. A sense that he could only ask once, and if she said no, he'd never get a second chance.

He wanted it desperately. These past three weeks had been the best of his life, and a deeply ingrained part of him insisted he could cling to this happiness if he tried hard enough and planned everything to precision. How hard could it be to convince her? She claimed to like him well enough. Moreover, she enjoyed playing with his band, and Sibylle and the others had warmed to Erika quickly. And perhaps their music wasn't her favorite, but surely it was beginning to grow on her.

Really, he didn't have to do much at all, did he? If the fundraiser couldn't happen, or if it failed to raise enough money, Erika would lose the opera house, and then she'd have nowhere to go. She could choose to go to Berlin with him because it was the easiest, most practical solution.

Like Gillian, who stayed with you for ten years because it was easier than leaving? a voice whispered in the back of his mind.

Erika's thumb rubbed at the space between his brows. "What's wrong now? If you keep scowling like that, you're going to need Botox before you score your first *Rolling Stone* cover."

He forced a smile. "Ah, nothing. Merely worrying about things I have no control over, as always."

"We've talked about this," she said, and Christof realized Erika thought he was talking about the email he'd gotten from Gillian earlier that day. Every week, he'd taken to updating Gillian with a brief summary of the band's progress on the album—in case she decided to return. This morning, she'd emailed him back and said simply, I'll have an answer for you soon.

Erika continued, "If you love something, you have to let it go. The harder you push, the less likely it is Gillian will come back."

If only he could confess what he was really thinking: He didn't want Gillian to come back—he wanted Erika. For the band, and for himself.

He knelt on the chaise in front of her and took Erika's hands in his. Her lips were still swollen, her hair askew, her neck stained pink where he'd worshipped it with his mouth earlier. Her makeup had long since melted and rubbed off, and if he looked closely, he could see the exhaustion tugging at the delicate muscles around her eyes, because they hadn't bothered much with sleep. She was everything he'd ever been afraid to dream of, everything he'd secretly wanted. She'd helped him see his own weaknesses and strive to become a better person. And even though she was flawed in her own right, and she could still be vain and dramatic and haughty and, at times, deeply melancholy, he didn't care. She was his perfect little witch, just as she was.

He was hopelessly, helplessly in love with her.

CHAPTER 28

Three weeks after the fateful trip to Las Vegas, Erika hung up with the last plumber on her list and quietly sang to herself, *"Then it all went wrong . . ."*

The fundraiser was doomed.

Even though it seemed like Nachtmusik might actually pull this concert off on short notice, and Erika had moved hell and earth (and promised unholy sums of money) to get the opera house repaired to code in time, none of it was going to matter if she couldn't get the fire marshal to sign off on her inspection—which was scheduled for the day before the concert. And unless a miracle gave a qualified plumber within a three-hundred-mile radius a sudden schedule opening, the theater's fire-sprinkler system wasn't going to pass muster.

The solution came to her in the most unexpected way: while shopping for stage costumes with Sibylle and Waldo at the eclectic thrift store the next town over.

Christof and Sergei had chosen to stay behind to fine-tune several guitar duos, and Erika had been handed the Black Credit Card of Power and instructed to ensure nothing "unrelated to the concert" was charged to it. Although Christof's controlling attitude had subsided since he'd stepped down from the band-manager position, he'd still retained responsibility for the band's finances—and from what Erika had seen of Sibylle's and Waldo's spending habits, it was the right choice.

"Guck mal! A crystal ball!" Sibylle held up an opalescent orb the size of a soccer ball with a hook protruding from the top. "I need this for the concert."

Erika rubbed her temples. "I think that's a lawn ornament."

"Ja?" Sibylle eyed it skeptically. "What is it for? The Christmas season?"

How to explain this facet of Americana to a foreigner? "No, it's like a . . . year-round suburban thing. I believe it's considered highly desirable to complete the look with ceramic animals, pinwheels, and wind chimes."

Sibylle cocked her head, examining the ball. Then she handed it to Erika to put in the shopping cart. "I need it."

"For *what*?" Erika crossed her arms. "I already said yes to the old wedding dress. And the creepy doll. And the black cat plushy."

"I need the ball," Sibylle repeated, a glint in her eye. "It is that or the coffin."

"You can't have a used coffin!" At Erika's outburst, the ancient storekeeper frowned in their direction, her wrinkled face scrunching in suspicion. Erika lowered her voice to a whisper. "Why do they even sell something like that here? The term *used* implies it's housed a dead body before, Sibylle. Doesn't that make you suspicious?"

Sibylle did not look suspicious. Sibylle looked *delighted*. "The coffin or this crystal ball. This is my final negotiation."

Erika begrudgingly jerked the ball out of Sibylle's hands and set it into the overloaded cart. "You're going to get me in trouble with Christof."

"You? I don't think so." Sibylle smirked, then continued to inspect the dusty shelves along the aisle.

"What? You know he's going to want to see an itemized receipt, and he's gonna be pissed when he sees how much money we spent on nonconcert stuff." Erika pushed the cart to keep up.

"That is why I invited you. Because you are immune to his anger."

Waldo materialized at the end of the aisle, his arms laden with red, white, and blue clothing. "Ja. He is . . . how do you say? Geschlagen?" Before he could hear the answer, something caught his eye in another aisle, and he disappeared again.

"Smitten," Sibylle translated for Erika, twisting her face in a way patented by younger sisters across the globe.

Something in her chest twisted in longing. "You're reading it wrong. We're very casual. A temporary vacation fling."

"So you say." Sibylle studied a rusted dinner knife with too much interest.

Don't ask. Don't ask . . . "Why? Did he say something?" Erika winced. "Pretend I didn't ask that."

Sibylle looked away, but not before Erika glimpsed a slow, satisfied grin creeping across the other woman's face. "Ja, okay. Secret's safe with me." She tossed the knife in the cart. Erika waited until Sibylle turned around before removing it.

Waldo reappeared from behind them and heaved his pile of clothing on top of Sibylle's haul. "What secret?" He glanced back and forth between Sibylle and Erika. "Did he ask her?"

"Ask me what?" Erika couldn't stop herself from blurting, even as equally unwelcome sensations of hope and dread battled for control of her psyche. *Marry me. Marry me. Marry me—*

STOP.

Nothing good could come from dwelling on that. If she'd been smart, Erika would have brought up the drunken proposal right after they'd gotten back from Vegas. Mercilessly uprooted the fantasy before it blossomed into full-blown delusion. But she hadn't wanted to ruin the life-changing sex they were having, so she'd told herself a few days couldn't hurt.

And a few days more.

Suddenly, three perfect weeks had gone by. Now, it was too late, because her heart was a hot, vulnerable mess. And it didn't matter that she *knew*, with every fiber of her jaded, bitter soul, that Christof had been blackout drunk and couldn't possibly have been serious. He didn't even remember it. The fact that she was still dwelling on it was desperate and pathetic. She was better than this, damn it.

Erika had her pride to retain. Hell, if—*when*—she lost the opera house, her pride was all she'd have left.

But what if he really did mean to propose?

It was too soon. Erika wasn't the type that men proposed to. And even if he did, she wasn't going to say yes to someone she'd known for a month. Besides, what would she even do with her life? Would she follow him around on tours, like a groupie? Live in his shadow until his fame petered out and they could *both* be aging has-beens, longing for their glory days of yore?

Still, hope fizzed merrily in her stomach. He wanted to ask her something. What else could it possibly—

Waldo, oblivious to Erika's internal angst, cheerily answered, "Invited you to join the band as permanent! He already asked us what we thought about it. I said, 'Yes, Erika is mega geil!'" He beamed at her. "So that is why I need all of these blouses, please."

Erika stared at the pile of hideously patriotic clothes, unseeing.

"Erika? These are for the concert."

Her lips felt numb. "Yeah, sure."

"It is A-okay?"

"Mmm-hmm." She released the cart and let it roll toward Waldo. From the corner of her eye, Erika spied Sibylle wandering toward the furniture aisle. *She's going to get the buy tag for the coffin,* some vestigial, coherent inner voice warned, but Erika couldn't make her mouth form the words to stop her. Even her limbs felt heavy and unresponsive.

"I'll be right back." Without waiting for a response, Erika drifted out the door and onto the sidewalk.

The midsummer heat was breathtaking, but even as she stood on the sidewalk in the direct sunlight, she fought the urge to shiver. Was she feverish?

Erika pressed the back of her hand to her forehead. Was her skin too warm? Had she contracted a zombie disease from Sibylle's sketchy coffin? Did death lurk moments away? Hard to tell.

I'm being dramatic. But how else to react to the idea that Christof was more interested in her as a keyboardist than in any romantic sense? Or that for a split second, she'd seriously considered being excited about being asked to join Nachtmusik? Playing in a European hair metal band was so far removed from what she'd wanted to do with her life. At least with the opera house, Erika had been able to convince herself she had a clear purpose: saving the family legacy and making up for a lifetime of selfishness. But if she joined Nachtmusik, she'd be abandoning her own journey solely to follow Christof on his.

Old Erika would *never*. Not in a thousand lifetimes.

Then again, Old Erika had never been in a position where the alternative might be accepting Raoul Decomte's offer to sing show tunes in an off-Strip casino.

How sad. How far she'd fallen. She was like Fantine—

Erika shook herself. What was she doing? She wasn't Fantine. Thanks to that chance encounter with Misty, Erika knew she *wasn't* the victim of a retributive supernatural curse. And maybe Christof was partially right about his insistence that he could forcibly imprint his will on the universe through something as simple as *trying extremely hard*—not always, but sometimes. She didn't have control over the cards she'd been dealt, but she did have control over how she played them. Feeling sorry for herself wouldn't change a thing.

Maybe if she wanted things—Christof, the opera house, a less miserable future for herself—she could try fighting for them instead of abandoning all hope and flinging herself into full-blown despair at the first sign of adversity.

A white van rolled to a stop at the stoplight in front of the thrift store. The green logo on its side sparked a glimmer of familiarity, and Erika shaded her eyes with a hand, squinting to read the words: **WEATHERFIELD & SONS WATERWORKS . . . TOILETS, POOLS, SPRINKLERS, AND MORE! "IF IT'S WET, WE'LL FIX IT!"**

That was the company Jackson Weatherfield's family ran. Jackson, as in the *Benjamin Franklin* Jackson, whose mediocre and unfaithful dick had kicked off events that had resulted in Erika's tragic fall from grace.

Like the low gong of a replica Liberty Bell in her head, Erika had an idea.

The way she saw it, Jackson Weatherfield owed her—in a lot of ways, but *especially* for having called out Ben Franklin's name when he'd orgasmed (a fact she'd tried and failed to *Eternal Sunshine* from her permanent memory). Jackson had also inherited a giant plumbing company that happened to operate all over the Southwest. Therefore, Jackson had the connections with which to supply her a sprinkler-repair technician.

And by God, he would fucking do it for her, or she'd unleash upon him a diva's wrath like no mortal had ever seen.

She pulled out her phone and scrolled down to the *F*s, where she'd categorized all her former fuckboys, and queued up his number. As she did it, her spine seemed to lengthen. The dregs of unease in her stomach dissipated. And for the first time in two years, she felt a glimmer of that preperformance "fire in her veins" excitement. As if she might look forward to getting out of bed tomorrow, because there were bright, shiny things in her future if she chose to fight for them.

She was going to war for the opera house—not only for her own benefit but also to avenge her great-great-grandmother on behalf of wronged mistresses everywhere.

And after she'd won that battle, she'd campaign for Christof's heart—because she deserved a good man like him, and she shouldn't have to settle for a mere fling.

And then . . . who knew? Maybe she'd move to Los Angeles or Paris or some other metropolitan city that appreciated the performing arts and get her career back.

It felt magnificent simply to not give in, for once.

She pressed the call button.

Six days later, Erika watched Jocelyn Song scrawl her signature on the fire-inspection certificate.

"I have to say," Jocelyn said as she tucked the certificate into a tidy folder and handed it to Erika, "I didn't expect you to turn this around so quickly. I was going back through reports from the previous chief, and I couldn't find a thing on the Paris Opera House. You said Hank came through here every year?"

Erika gave Jocelyn an indulgent smile. "That Hank . . . he always was misplacing his notes when he was around Grandma Meg."

"Right." Jocelyn looked around the foyer, where drop cloths reeked of fresh paint and dusty boot prints crisscrossed the marble. Jackson's crew had finished with minutes to spare—but they'd finished. She was going to send that man a bouquet of flowers. Bluebells, maybe. Or bellflowers. "Well, your sense of urgency is appreciated." Jocelyn's face softened. "I know these codes seem draconian, but I've been doing this long enough to see the consequences of lax enforcement. I'd rather play the hard-ass than lie awake after a tragedy, wishing I'd been tougher."

"Like you said, it's fire season. Safety is my utmost concern."

"To be clear, this certificate is for the opera house only. I can't certify the . . . er, the attached building yet."

"The brothel?" Erika supplied helpfully.

Jocelyn cleared her throat. "Yes, that wooden contraption. It's a damn fire waiting to happen. I understand you've offered tours to the public in the past, but it'll need to stay closed for now. Understood?"

"Absolutely. Not a soul goes in or out of the brothel until I have your seal of approval." Erika walked her to the door. Good thing she'd had the band move into rooms at La Rose ahead of this final inspection, even though it had required a substantial damage deposit to get Waldo's visit approved by the hotel's management. The rooms cost a pretty penny, but it wasn't particularly difficult to persuade Christof to part with pennies these days, and it was only temporary, after all. "Will I see you at the fundraiser tomorrow? It would be my pleasure to set aside seats for you."

Jocelyn narrowed her eyes. "That sounds an awful lot like a bribe, Ms. Greene. I'm not my predecessor, and I should hope you're nothing like yours."

You're right. I'm much better at this than Grandma Meg. "My goodness, I didn't intend for it to come across that way. I wanted to show my gratitude for what you do for the Paris community. The seats are here for you if you change your mind. Bye now!"

When the door swung shut behind Jocelyn, Erika darted up the steps and ran out to the front of the balcony seating, holding the certificate aloft. "We did it!" she announced to the band onstage below.

Sibylle sat up from where she lay in her center-stage coffin and cheered, and Christof, Waldo, and Sergei echoed her joy.

They'd cleared the second-to-last obstacle. Somehow, all the pieces had fallen into place: Sergei's mystery friend had come through and sold every ticket, rehearsals were going beautifully, and now they'd been approved to open to the public.

If Erika had a sense of lingering foreboding in the back of her throat at the thought of what Raoul Decomte might do to ruin their plans, the rest of the band didn't need to know that. She'd gotten a letter from him that morning: an honest-to-God handwritten note on actual stationery, enclosed in a monogrammed envelope with a *wax seal* on the back side. The note had read, simply:

It is my understanding that Box Five is still available. I believe it would be in your best interest to leave it open for me. I look forward to attending your concert.

À vendredi,

Raoul

There was nothing inherently threatening about the letter, save for the idea that Raoul knew she hadn't sold seats in Box Five. Until earlier this week, she hadn't finished the necessary repairs on that box. He'd most likely learned this information through contractors Erika had tried to hire, but it still unsettled her that he knew exactly which box to ask for.

Christof leaned forward into the mic, which was still hot from running through dress rehearsals all day. "Tonight, we celebrate! I'll make dinner reservations someplace very nice."

Waldo asked, "Le Dennis?"

"He means the restaurant at La Rose," Erika called down to them. Christof shook his head. "You ruined my surprise."

"You said 'someplace nice.' This is Paris—you kind of narrowed it down," Erika said, fighting a smile. "But make the reservations for a late seating, because I want to run through the set at least two more times."

Sibylle groaned and flopped back into her coffin. "If Waldo and Christof wouldn't have dropped the coffin during 'Crowbar,' with me inside—"

"Not too late to get rid of the coffin," Christof reminded her.

"No fighting!" Erika called. "We already voted that the coffin stays. We've been at this all morning without a break, so why don't we get some air and come back in thirty? Christof, meet me in my office, please."

She could see the heat spark in his eyes from here. Into the mic, he gave her a throaty "Gladly."

Sibylle muttered something, quietly enough that Erika couldn't hear from the balcony.

As Erika walked away, she heard Christof tell his sister, "We're all adults here . . ."

He beat her to the office and was sitting in her desk chair when she arrived. Being the diligent planner he was, he'd already twisted the blinds shut for privacy. She closed the door behind her and pressed her back to it. "It's not that kind of meeting," she said, although the low hum in her voice suggested otherwise.

It was hard not to get turned on in Christof's presence. They'd spent too much time together these past few weeks; her body was primed to melt in his proximity. It didn't help, the way he sprawled decadently in her chair like some underworld god, his steely thighs encased in black leather and spread wide, his glossy black shirt open to the navel in heathen disregard for propriety. He'd done his full stage hair and makeup for rehearsal, too, and it was sinful how good that man looked in full eyeliner.

"Don't look at me like that," she warned him. "I mean it."

"Mmm." He caressed his own lips with his thumb. Obscene. "Then what's this meeting about?"

"I'm worried about Raoul," she confessed, unconsciously drawing closer to him. As she approached, he pushed back from the desk, creating ample space for her. "I feel like he's not going to let me get away with paying off the loan so easily. As of this Monday, he's bought every other building on this block."

Christof patted his thigh. "Have a seat, and I'll address these concerns."

"You're giving orders. I know what that means."

A corner of his mouth curled wickedly. "Yes? What does it mean?"

She sat primly on his left thigh, tucking her hands in her lap. "I'm serious! Don't distract me with sex."

"That doesn't sound like me."

"No, it doesn't sound like you from a month ago. Now you won't shut up about sex." She traced his long nose down to the tip and tapped firmly with her finger, lightly reprimanding. "I've created a monster."

He pretended to snap at her finger.

Lightning fast, she spun to straddle him, using her palms to push his shoulders back into the chair. A low growl of pleasure came from the back of his throat as he rose to meet her lips, and she shoved him hard against the seat. "Behave. I'm talking business. That used to be your favorite subject, remember?"

"Hmm. Vaguely." Light as a feather, she felt his fingertips begin trailing up her calves. "Now, *you* are my favorite subject."

Ugh. *Ugh!* His words made her heart twist with pure, unadulterated joy, and it made her miserable. Why was he doing this to her? Why make her feel these hopeful, pathetic feelings, when she *knew* he wasn't ready to offer more than mere placeholder spots in his band and his bed?

And here she was, the loser who would have said yes to a proposal that he didn't even remember making. It was so laughable she wanted to cry.

"Erika? Did I say something wrong?" He looked at her in confusion, and she realized her expression must have shown part of what she was thinking.

Swallow your fucking pride and tell him how you feel. She'd promised herself she'd do it—that she'd start going after what she wanted. So why was she still hesitating?

"It's nothing. Sorry . . . I'm just worried about all the things that could go haywire tomorrow," she said and convinced herself it was only partially untrue, so it wasn't a lie.

His hands slid higher, under the hem of her skirt and up her thighs. "A witch once said to me, it's better to worry about problems that can be solved, rather than imaginary ones."

"Careful. Witches are trouble."

"Tell me more."

Her hands slid down from his shoulders, slipping across fabric until she got to the bare skin of his chest. She closed around the edges of the shirt and jerked upward to free the hem from where it was tucked in, then splayed the lapels wide. "They'll capture innocent guitarists wandering lost through their woods. Tie them up . . . feast upon their flesh with venomous fangs." Her claws stroked down his rib cage, and the flat of his abdomen shuddered under her touch. "Use their victims' bodies for . . . depraved . . . feminine rituals." She closed her mouth over one of his nipples and lightly nipped the bud with her teeth.

"Fuck." His grip tightened around her thighs. Dragged her hard against him so she could feel the iron press of his cock through his pants. His words came out jagged. "What if a victim refuses to submit and struggles in her hold?"

She flicked with her tongue before pulling back to catch a glimpse of his deliciously tormented expression. "Even better."

"Do you really think your evil powers can overcome my badassery?" he warned. "You've chosen the wrong guitarist to bake into your gingered bread."

"Have I?" Her hands fell to his belt buckle, and he didn't resist at all. Not even a little bit. If anything, his hips bucked against her touch. She tsked. "A good actor says his lines with his whole body."

"Fuck me, witch." He thrust against her again, this time rolling his hips slowly enough to let her know it was deliberate.

"Good enough," she managed on a shaky exhale.

As she wriggled out of her underwear, she vowed to herself, *Tonight*. She'd tell him how she felt tonight, after dinner.

No sense in ruining a good thing too soon.

CHAPTER 29

"I wish to say a few words for a toast." Christof stood up from the round table at La Rose's fine-dining restaurant, where he and the band had reserved their celebration dinner. "Tomorrow, we will play our first show as the new Nachtmusik. This will be the first time an audience hears this album. What we have found here in America is not what we expected, but it is even better. As we reach the end of our journey here in Paris, I am grateful to each of you for helping us become what we didn't expect to be."

As he raised his glass of champagne, he looked at his bandmates, one by one. He held his notebook in his other hand, where he'd written what he'd wanted to say, but he didn't require it for this part. He'd rehearsed the speech the night prior, until Erika had ripped the notebook from his hand, tossed it away, and insisted he join her in bed with an argument so persuasive that his pulse skipped at the mere memory of what she'd done to him.

There was only one part of the speech she hadn't heard him rehearse, because he hadn't dared speak what he'd written aloud. Not even to an empty room.

"Waldo," Christof said with a nod in the drummer's direction. Waldo, wearing his chosen formal wear—a bolero tie and a screen-printed American-flag shirt featuring a glaring eagle head in the center of the chest—leaned his chair back on two legs and grinned back at him. "You were the most excited about this adventure. And although this enthusiasm has taken many years off my life, I cannot help but be thankful to you for your creativity and your energy and your kind nature."

Waldo flashed him the rocker hand sign. "Danke, brother. Nachtmusik forever!"

To Waldo's right, Sibylle leaned forward, chin propped on her hands and a smug expression plastered across her face. "Next, you will speak of me. Your perfect sister. I await your praise."

Christof pretended to scan his speech before shaking his head. "No, I see nothing here about you."

"*Wie* bitte?"

"No, no . . . here is about Waldo, Sergei, Erika, myself . . . ah, wait!" He snapped the notebook shut and raised his eyes to the ceiling. "I'm receiving a message from beyond! The spirits are saying . . . what's this? They're saying you did very nicely with taking on more leadership in the band? I must be mishearing them."

"You did not mishear." Sibylle stood and raised her own glass. "To me, the greatest visionary Nachtmusik has ever known—"

"Second greatest," Christof corrected. "And sit down; this is my speech. You may do a speech after."

Sibylle begrudgingly sat, though not without muttering, "My speech will be better."

"If you would stop being a nuisance, I would like to continue lauding my darling sister."

She waved him on with an impatient gesture.

"All those years ago, when you first insisted on joining our band, I was uncertain. You were a strange little demon, and I thought you would ruin the coolness of what Waldo and I had created. But," he rushed to add, seeing Sibylle's murderous expression, "I was wrong then, and you're still proving me wrong now. You continue to push

Nachtmusik to the edge of creativity, testing the boundaries of our sound and ensuring that we always sound mega badass. And you do your best to keep my ego and controlling ways in check . . . these days, more than ever. I am indebted to you, and I am proud of you." He had to clear away a lump in his throat at that last bit.

Sibylle scrunched her nose. "Blech. So sappy."

Erika jerked in her seat across from Sibylle, and whatever she'd done to Sibylle under the table made his sister yelp. Erika said in an overly sweet tone, "Sibylle meant to say, *Thank you for those touching words, Big Brother.*"

"*Thank you for those touching words,*" Sibylle mimicked, before muttering something under her breath that sounded a lot like a variation on her favorite insult, which was invariably something about farts and his fat head, and it made him smile. From Sibylle, it might as well have been a declaration of sisterly love—she had a strict personal rule against displays of emotion. He couldn't wait for her to find a partner who smashed her rule book to pieces.

He instinctively caught Erika's eye, and she winked at him over her wineglass. Under any other circumstances, he'd have glowed inside and out from her regard. But tonight . . .

Two days ago, he'd booked Nachtmusik's departure tickets. He hadn't told Erika yet.

When the concert was finished, it would no longer make sense to stay here. This stage of their album was nearly done, and they couldn't go much further without being in the recording studio. As it happened, the Berlin studio where they preferred to record had an open slot available that was perfect for their album's timeline.

But recording the album meant choosing someone to play the keyboard and sing backing vocals. They'd have to audition for a new band member when they returned to Berlin. He'd even drafted the text of the posting that advertised tryouts, and Sergei had mentioned he had a few candidates in mind they might wish to consider first. It was by no means dire—if anything, he saw now how Gillian's departure had been an opportunity for the band to evolve, not the end of his entire world.

No. The end of his entire world hadn't been Gillian's departure—it was the idea of leaving Erika. Because he was hopelessly, entirely in love with her, and yet he couldn't stay here.

Even if he'd been willing to give up Nachtmusik—his dream, his life, his creation—he knew he couldn't live with himself if he abandoned the band now. It would be selfish of him, after all he'd asked of his bandmates, after all the effort and sacrifice they'd made, to abandon them so soon after Gillian had done the same. Deep in his gut, he knew that Nachtmusik wouldn't survive if he left too. Perhaps someday, but not now.

The band had to come first—and for once, he wished that weren't true.

But if Erika agreed to join Nachtmusik . . .

He'd bought her a ticket, though it was refundable. And he'd had Sibylle casually inquire as to whether Erika's passport was current. Sergei had even put him in touch with a contact in Vegas who'd offered to coordinate a theater manager to take care of the Paris Opera House while Erika was away. All the pieces had fallen into place so smoothly that it was hard to believe this wasn't the ideal scenario.

All he needed was for her to say yes.

This is it. His stomach clenched, and he wished he'd waited until after the food had arrived before downing half his champagne. Thank the heavens above that he'd memorized his speech, because his mouth managed to recite the words he'd written about Sergei even as his body tried to convince him he was standing at the edge of a cliff with a strong breeze at his back.

Christof wrapped up Sergei's portion of the toast, then fumbled for his notebook. Expectant stares reminded him he was still supposed to be speaking, but his hands shook as he turned the blank pages, searching for where he'd hidden the portion he'd written for her, secreted away in case she accidentally stumbled upon it.

"And last but not least, to Erika," he heard himself say as if from far away.

Why couldn't this be a song? He could easily put his feelings into music; this was so much harder.

Something wet sloshed on his wrist, and when he glanced down, he realized champagne had sloshed over the side of his glass. Hoping no one had noticed, he set the glass down and inhaled air through his teeth. Cleared his throat. "First of all, I must thank you on behalf of all of Nachtmusik for this album, for it would not have begun to take form if you hadn't welcomed us to stay at your Paris Opera House, even though you took a risk in doing so. Tomorrow night, we hope we will be able to begin repaying the generosity you have shown us . . . at least, more than the four thousand dollars a week the band's credit statement would argue we have paid."

The table's occupants spared him polite laughter, even though he knew his comedic delivery was flat. He didn't dare look up. Tried not to feel Erika's dark gaze cutting directly to his quick.

She knows. Erika was too intuitive to not suspect what he was about. Surely, she already anticipated this, and if he dared to look her in the eyes, he'd already know her answer before he asked.

What was he thinking? It was selfish, to ask her to leave her theater after working so hard to save it. To ask her to go with them to a country where she didn't speak the language and expect her to adapt entirely to his way of life. But he was desperate. All his life, he'd sung power ballads believing that the passionate sentiments expressed in them were fantastical tropes, exaggerated for maximum angst. Now that he'd found his muse, his fantasy witch, and his best friend—all wrapped up in one woman—the idea of giving her up seemed impossible. He'd give up *anything* to keep her.

Almost anything.

He focused on his notebook. *Maybe she'll say yes.*

"But I must next thank you on a personal level. I came to you when I was lost. When my world was crumbling to pieces around me, and I'd still thought I had the power to hold it together with my will. But you . . ."

His throat was too parched to go on. He fumbled for his water glass and took a gulp—and nearly inhaled it. *Fuck.* He tried to stifle his cough, to play it cool, but that only made it worse.

"Sorry," he croaked, when he'd finished hacking into his sleeve. He cleared his throat again, buying himself time to find his place on the page. "But you . . . you helped me learn to let go. And now it is I who cannot let go. I cannot imagine a future without you. And so I wish to ask—"

She's going to say no. The thought came out of nowhere, seized control of his body, and paralyzed him.

Why now? He'd been so close—

If he could simply explain why she should stay with him forever—

If I do everything exactly right, nothing will go wrong—

His own heartbeat was so loud he couldn't think. His blood roared through his veins. Spots danced in his vision. *Fuck, fuck, fuck.*

"Tof?" Waldo's voice came from far away. In German, his drummer continued, "You don't look so good. Maybe you should sit down?"

He tried to focus on Waldo. Concerned eyes peering at him from under a mop of hair. A hand landed on his sleeve, and Christof ripped his arm away. He had to finish. He had to ask. He had to *know*.

"I'm fine," he bit out.

In a low voice, Erika said, "Why don't we go outside and get some fresh air?"

He managed to look up then and find her beautiful, bitter-chocolate eyes locked on his, and for once they weren't shadowed by her hair, because she'd pulled it back tonight in a low twist to boldly bare her scars to the world, and somehow she was even more gloriously bewitching than when he'd first laid eyes on her.

The room grew blurry behind her, but she remained in focus.

"Come on," she said, rising to slip an arm around his waist. To the rest of the table, she announced, "We'll be right back."

And then he was outside, in the landscaped courtyard, sitting on a low stone wall in front of an artificial fountain, with the night breeze cooling the sweat on the back of his neck. He stared at the shiny casino tokens wavering at the bottom of the pool of water, winking at him. Why did people believe throwing tokens into the pond would bring luck? What a waste. Those tokens could be exchanged for real dollars and invested wisely, put to practical use.

"That's it. Breathe. You're okay." Her hand ran circles on the small of his back until his heartbeat slowed, and when the tension finished leaching from his flesh, exhaustion took its place.

He attempted a wry smile. "That was not very badass, was it?"

"What are you talking about? You're the most badass person I know." Her hand slipped around the back of his neck, and she rested her forehead on his. Her rose scent enveloped him, and he let his eyes fall shut so he could remember the smell of her more precisely. "It takes a lot of badassery to stand up there in front of your band and give a heartfelt speech like that. I know those people in there mean everything to you."

"Not everything," he said roughly. *"There's you."*

Now. She had to confess her feelings now, before it was too late.

Erika took a steadying breath, filling her lungs like she might before hitting an impossibly high note. "I've been meaning to talk to you about something."

He stilled, as if he were tensing for something unpleasant. "What is it?"

Oh God, I know that tone. Cool. Distant. That was how they always sounded before they informed her that she was mistaken—that the relationship wasn't all that serious. But Erika had promised herself she'd give her dreams a chance, so she had no choice but to power through. She'd accept relegation with dignity, just like she always had all the times she'd been disappointed before. "How much do you remember from that night in Vegas?"

For a split second before he looked away, panic splashed across his features. "Is this about the car?" he asked, inspecting the water rippling in the fountain below them.

"What?"

"Ah . . . do you remember those gold coins you gave us?"

What in the world was he talking about? "Christof, you *proposed* to me."

"Oh." A long, tense pause followed, in which he still refused to look at her. "Yes. I did."

"People say all sorts of silly things when they're drunk. I know you probably didn't mean it. Did you?" Her heart awaited the answer by lodging in her throat.

"I . . ." He grimaced, then finally looked at her. The submerged fountain lights cast illuminated patterns on his beautifully sculpted cheeks. A golden god, devastated at delivering bad news to a mere mortal such as Erika. "I'm sorry."

"You're sorry for asking?" she forced herself to say. "Or sorry you pretended you didn't remember?"

Another wince. "Erika, I was very drunk. I'd never ask such a thing of you so soon. But I do care for you very much. I'd really like to continue seeing you after our time here. And tonight I'd hoped to ask—"

"Whether I'd join your band as a permanent member?" she finished before he could say it. Better to break her own heart than let him do it.

He lit up. "Yes!" He clasped her hands in his, and it was so much like the proposal he *hadn't* offered that Erika reflexively slipped her hands free. Undaunted, Christof continued, "I bought return tickets for this upcoming Tuesday, and there is a ticket for you, if you want it. The band already agreed—there is no one we'd rather have to replace Gillian. And you and I, we could keep dating. What do you say?"

Erika swallowed. "Wow," she said, but her voice sounded hollow, so she forced a smile for his benefit. "What an offer."

"I know it will be a big change, but Waldo has this great phone app you can use to learn German. We'll have someone take care of the theater, and you can still manage it part time, and we can all come back to visit very often . . ." Christof went on, lauding the majesty of this life he was offering her, but Erika couldn't focus on his words. He seemed so animated compared to a few minutes earlier. It was like she'd given him exactly what he wanted.

At her own expense.

This isn't what I want, her heart shrieked, and that was when Erika realized she was angry. *I want everything. I deserve everything.*

". . . and we can find you a flat in the same neighborhood—"

Erika bit out, "Is that all?"

The smile died on his face. "What else do you want?"

I deserve your love. I deserve the chance to fulfill my own career dreams. I deserve to have a role in your life that doesn't make me feel like I'm Gillian 2.0!

"I want something you clearly aren't ready to offer. And that's not your fault. I just need some space to . . . process." She stood as calmly as she could manage and gathered her purse. Tears threatened, and she knew there was no going back inside the restaurant now. Not if she wanted to cling to any dignity, anyway. "I'm heading back to the opera house to make sure everything's ready for tomorrow. Tell the band I'm sorry I couldn't stick around for dessert."

Chin held high so her eyes wouldn't leak, she strode stiffly through the courtyard toward the parking lot where she'd parked the truck. It was a nice night—a reasonable eighty-six degrees at ten o'clock. Nevertheless, Erika found her arms wrapping around herself to ward off an intangible chill.

"Erika!" His footsteps drew closer, and several other guests meandering in the tranquil courtyard stared. "Stop. Talk to me. Don't run away without explanation—"

She dodged out of the way before he could grab her arm and whirled to face him. "Don't cause a scene. Only I get to cause a scene."

"Must there be a scene at all?"

"Yes! My heart is breaking as we speak, and a dramatic exit is my goddamn right as a practitioner of theater!"

"Erika, listen to me. I think we've had a misunderstanding—"

"I understood *perfectly*." She spun and charged forward again. And for the second time, he darted in front and cut her off.

"Stop. If you give me one moment—"

"You've had a month's worth of moments to address your drunken proposal, and you didn't!" To her horror, the lush green surroundings had gone wholly blurry, and now people were *definitely* watching. But it was too late. She was too deep in the emotion of the moment to pull back from the cascading drama: a moth to the flame. Her voice shaking, she continued, "I would have said yes. If you'd meant it, I would have married you. I would have found it the most thrillingly romantic thing in the entire world. To imagine that you'd fallen so in love with me that you were willing to throw caution to the wind and take me to the altar right that instant. How naive and silly of me, right?"

"Fuck . . ." He scraped a hand down his face, smearing his eyeliner. "This is going poorly."

She barked a laugh. "You think? This is exactly why I didn't say anything."

"Don't go," he pleaded. "Come to Germany with me. If marriage is what you want, we can get married. We can plan a small ceremony for as soon as the album is done, wherever you like. Please . . . just . . . don't leave me."

"That's not *enough*." The tears were flowing now, undoubtedly ruining her mascara, yet she couldn't help but notice she had everyone's attention. There was nothing left to do but commit fully to the performance. They wanted a show? She'd give them one. "I know I'm not perfect. I've been selfish and vain and shallow, and I've done things I regret. I lived a charmed life for so long, and I didn't even appreciate how lucky I was because I was so busy feeling sorry for myself for all the things I didn't have. I *know* this. And I know that I still have a lot of work to do if I want to be a good person. But I'm *trying*, you know? I'm not so bad anymore. I'm doing better."

"Erika, you *are* good. To me, you're perfect."

"To *you*. But that's not enough, Christof. When I look in the mirror, I need to see someone I like. Someone I admire." She squared her shoulders. "A part of me bought into the idea of being cursed because it was easier than acknowledging that I was unhappy because I treated myself the way I'd treat someone I hated. It wasn't until I met you that I understood how happy I could be. How happy I *deserve* to be.

"I deserve to be loved, thoroughly and unconditionally, and I also deserve more than just a backup role in someone else's band, and I shouldn't have to choose between those two things. I deserve to *actually* be proposed to in a Vegas hotel room, in the middle of the night on a whim, while you're in the middle of an existential crisis. I deserve my fairy-tale, shotgun wedding. I deserve to be, as Sibylle calls it, the *main character* in this story. I deserve all that and more! And I'm not asking for you to give me all of that, but I have the right to hold out for—"

"Erika, I do love you." His voice was quiet, yet sure. "I've loved you since that first moment in your office when you helped remove my splinter. And I did want to marry you that night in Vegas. I meant every word of it. The only thing holding me back the next morning was my fear that you'd run away and I'd lose you."

The courtyard was so silent, all she could hear was her own ragged breath and the trickling of water from the fountain. His words unbalanced her. That wasn't his line. He was supposed to apologize and beg and bargain and do everything *but* declare his feelings so he could maintain the status quo that benefited him until he was ultimately ready to cast her aside.

She took an uncertain step toward him. Maybe . . . maybe she'd been hasty.

Maybe there was a future for them, after all.

Maybe she'd actually find happiness in his band. It was better than wasting away here in Paris, wasn't it? And if it meant—

"Tof?" came a lilting voice from behind her.

Erika froze. She watched Christof as he stiffened, his skin blanching as he looked past her at the newcomer, and every square inch of her body seemed to dissolve into the ether. Erika Greene ceased to exist.

And before Christof even said a word, Erika *knew*.

From far away—from whatever dimension her soul had gone to when it had left her body in abject humiliation—she heard him speak. "Gillian, what are you doing here?"

CHAPTER 30

Christof stared at Gillian. Her fuchsia curls had been dyed blue, and she wore a set of enormous silver earrings he'd never seen before, but her heart-shaped face and dainty body and quizzical expression were the same as they'd always been. He could even smell her perfume from here—a citrus concoction that she'd dab on her wrists and then press her wrists to her neck and chest to distribute. He could picture it so vividly, having watched this ritual on a daily basis for most of his adult life.

Eight weeks wasn't such a long time, relative to how long he and Gillian had known each other. A minuscule scratch leading to a single skipped note on an LP.

And yet as he stared at her, he had the disconcerting sense that she was a stranger. Or maybe *he* was the stranger—having jumped from one world to another so seamlessly that he'd become someone else while she'd been gone.

"I came back," she said in German. "This hotel is where I'm staying. I didn't expect to find you here." There was a roller bag gripped in her fist, and she set it upright as she looked back and forth between him and Erika. Likely taking in Erika's tearstained face and his own distress, as well as the crowd of onlookers, and piecing together that she'd walked into something rather fragile and important. Her brows slashed together. "Who is this?" Her tone was curious, not that of a jealous lover, but Erika visibly bristled.

"English, please," he said. It seemed vital that Erika not feel like the intruder in this conversation. It was Gillian who'd intruded.

"We should talk in private," Gillian returned, but at least she'd done so in English. "I think I owe you an explanation about . . . a lot of things. And an apology. But I'm ready to come back to the band. If you'll have me."

Fuck. "This isn't the best time—"

Erika thrust out her hand toward Gillian. "Erika Greene. Proprietress of the venue where Nachtmusik has been rehearsing, and your temporary replacement. In both the band . . . and Christof's bed. And you've managed to walk in at the worst possible cinematic moment, because he's attempting to declare his love for me before I storm off in dramatic fashion."

Gillian blinked at Erika in surprise but accepted the handshake. "You are bold. I appreciate that."

"And you abandoned Christof and Nachtmusik without explanation. I don't appreciate that at all," Erika said coolly, somehow managing to look imperious with mascara bisecting both cheeks. "Your skin's incredible, though. What moisturizer do you use?"

"Clinique."

"A classic. Good choice. You have a lovely soprano range, as well. Excellent work on 'Wish You Were Here.'"

"Thank you." Gillian's tone matched Erika's tersely polite one. "And of course, my gratitude for filling in on the album in my absence."

"It was a surprising pleasure." Erika smiled, but it was full of teeth and didn't look quite as friendly as a smile should. "And now you're back."

"I am." Gillian raised her brow as if to say, *Will there be a problem?*

"Gilly," he warned.

"Ja?" Gillian asked innocently, never taking her eyes off Erika.

As small and demure as she appeared, Gillian had never been a delicate flower. But she hadn't an inkling what sort of ferocious demoness she was dealing with. Erika could devour Gillian alive if she wished—and God help him, the thought aroused him. After all his history with Gillian, he should have been ashamed.

Should have.

Then again, he *was* hurt about what Gillian had done. Had she any clue what kind of hell he'd gone through in her absence? As long as he never voiced his secret schadenfreude fantasy aloud, surely it wasn't wrong to imagine Erika sundering Gillian into metaphorical pieces.

Somehow, a wiser part of his brain prevailed and reminded him that watching Erika and Gillian rip each other's clothes off in the decorative fountain was neither realistic nor conducive to his ultimate goal of persuading Erika not to leave him.

"The rest of the band is inside the restaurant. Perhaps you should say hello to them. I will join you all shortly." Despite everything, Gillian *was* his oldest friend aside from Waldo. He cared about her—it was impossible not to—and he owed her the chance to explain herself.

Gillian gave Erika one last long look. "That might be best."

He watched Gillian make her way through the courtyard toward the restaurant. Then he turned back to Erika and found her already striding away.

He darted after her. "Where are you going?"

She kept walking. "Back to the opera house."

"We need to finish talking."

"Do we?"

Christof followed Erika to the truck, matching her increased pace. "I'll go with you," he insisted as she fumbled for her keys. His stomach had hardened to lead, and he had the absolute certain notion that if she left now, he'd never win her back. Desperation tinged his voice, and he didn't care. *"I love you,"* he said again, but this time it had no effect. Hadn't she heard him?

"I love you too," she snapped, wrenching open the door. She held it open, her right hand curled around the frame so tightly he could see her knuckles go white. "So what? You want me to fight Gillian for her spot in the band now? I didn't even want it that badly, and now you don't need me."

He wanted to slap himself, because she was right. He hadn't had time to think this through. His entire plan had hinged on convincing Erika to join him in Berlin as a member of Nachtmusik, and now that wasn't necessary. And he couldn't very well throw Gillian out, could he?

He didn't know. That was the problem—because the band now had the power to vote on these matters, he couldn't make unilateral decisions anymore. He was once again adrift, his meticulous plans blown to smithereens.

He scrambled for purchase on anything that would stop him from losing her. "Come with me anyway."

She laughed bitterly. "Abandon the only thing I have left of my life to . . . what? Wait for you after your shows with the rest of the groupies? Keep your apartment clean while you're recording all day long?"

"You make it sound much worse than it would be."

"Do I?" She climbed into the seat and keyed the ignition. The truck coughed to life with a squealing rumble, and over the noise she raised her voice. "Would you do it for me? Give up Nachtmusik and abandon your whole life to be with me?"

He wanted to say yes. More than anything. But his throat wouldn't let the word out.

She watched him with an expression that made him want to shrivel and die of shame. "The band always comes first, doesn't it?"

"I . . ." He didn't know what else to say.

The band didn't just come first—the band was *everything*. Or it had been, for over half his life on this earth. Every single thing he'd done, every sacrifice he'd made, had been in pursuit of ensuring that Nachtmusik became world famous and that they could spend the rest of their lives doing what they loved. It wasn't just about him—it was about Waldo and Sibylle and Sergei. Even Gillian. They were so close to achieving their dream. He couldn't walk away in this critical moment.

Not even for love.

"See, that's the thing about power ballads," Erika said. "They're all talk. All this exaggerated, bullshit sentiment about eternal love and devotion. But how many of these world-famous 'rock gods' are actually in healthy, committed relationships?"

"I believe Jon Bon Jovi is still with his secondary school sweetheart."

She rolled her eyes. "Okay, name another one."

"Ozzy."

"Does he count?"

"Very well . . . Alice Cooper, then. He's been married since the early seventies. And then there is Pat Benatar and Keith Richards—"

"Never mind." She scowled at him. "That question was meant to be rhetorical anyway."

He thought it very wise not to argue.

She went on, "The point is, I don't want to hear overblown promises. Do you have any idea how many men promised me the world and never delivered? I'm sick and tired of it. If you mean it, put your money where your mouth is."

"What does this mean?" American expressions were so strange sometimes.

"It means put up or shut up."

Put what up? He wished he had Waldo's app to translate these colloquialisms. "Ah. I see."

She sighed and threw up her hands. "If you really want to be with me, *prove it!*"

There was a too-long silence while he stood there like a helpless oaf, unable to form the magic words required of him. "I'm sorry," he said, finally. She had no idea just how sorry he was.

"Yeah. Of course you are," she snarled. With that, Erika slammed the door shut and peeled out of the parking lot, exiting out the one-way entrance lane with apparent disregard for the stop sign posted there.

"I'm sorry," he repeated to the empty air in front of him. Useless words were all he had to give.

He waited a long time in the parking lot, staring at the oil stain her truck had left behind.

La Rose was located fifteen minutes away from Paris, nestled in its own narrow valley oasis between two narrow hills—removed enough from the town itself that if one looked out from one of La Rose's balcony-equipped suites, one might see the stars and think oneself all alone in the desert. As Erika drove along the dark, winding highway that would spit her out of the hills into downtown Paris at the end, she wondered why she felt so . . .

Good.

As good as a woman whose heart had been slit open and left to bleed out in the middle of the parking lot of an overpriced hotel, casino, and spa could feel.

Maybe because she'd finally respected herself enough to demand what she was owed in a romantic relationship.

The truck cleared the hills, and Paris revealed itself half a mile below her in a splattered electric grid centered on a single main road. And at the end of that main road, lit up against the sickly eggplant sky, was a smear of orange flame. Exactly where the Paris Opera House was located.

No, no, no . . .

She squeezed her eyes shut. Then remembered she was driving and forced them open again, swerving hard to avoid veering off the highway entirely.

The Paris Opera House wasn't burning down. It couldn't be. Fate wasn't that much of an asshole. The curse *wasn't real*.

"It's not real," she whispered aloud.

Had Raoul . . . ?

No. No, that was arson. He wouldn't commit a *felony* because he couldn't have her theater—would he?

Then again, rich men had committed worse crimes for far less reason. Her great-great-grandmother had likely been murdered over petty jealousy.

She didn't remember the rest of the drive. Only that as she drove down Main Street, the door of the firehouse was open, and people were coming out of their buildings to catch a glimpse of the fire. The cooks and servers at Le Dennis stood on the sidewalk, staring up at the billowing plume of smoke like it was a late Independence Day fireworks celebration. As she drove by in her recognizable truck—Grandma Meg's truck—heads turned.

A block away from her destination, the sheriff's car blocked the street to give Paris's only fire truck full access to the two-lane road, forcing Erika to park and get out. The crowd of onlookers parted to let her past as she stared, unseeing, at her home. Her business. Everything she had left.

The fire engine blocked most of her view from the front, but she could see ugly glowing smoke billowing from behind gargoyle wings near the back of the theater. The front of the theater appeared pristine.

"Ms. Greene!" Jocelyn spotted her and dashed over in her fire marshal uniform. Her face was sweaty and streaked with ash, and she had to raise her voice to be heard over the din of the gushing fire hose and crackling flames and shouts of the fire crew. "I'm glad to see you're safe. Is there anyone inside the building?"

Erika forced her voice steady. "No. No—the theater is empty."

Jocelyn nodded, expression relieved. "Good. Appears the fire started inside the . . . er, back building, and we may have caught it in time to contain it to that structure thanks to the sprinkler system suppressing most of the flames in the rear portion of the opera house."

Erika's heart skittered to a stop. *The brothel.* "I need to get into the basement." She launched forward, but Jocelyn held her back with an outstretched arm.

"It's not safe! We managed to get the fire out on the theater side, but the brothel is still burning. The entire structure could collapse at any moment."

"My rats!" Her eyes stung from the acrid smoke. "I need to . . . I need to get my rats."

"What?"

"My rats!" Erika repeated, furiously shoving Jocelyn's arm aside. What was wrong with this woman? Why was she just standing there? Didn't she understand? "They're inside. We can't just leave them there!" She stumbled forward, tripping on the marble steps she'd effortlessly walked over hundreds of times before. Her hands smacked against the dirty stone; her knee slammed into the edge of a stair, and pain radiated up her leg.

"Ms. Greene—"

"Fine, send your firefighters, then! They're in a cage in the basement. Jean is brown and white. He'll be easy to find. He's probably eating. If you don't see him out, check under the plastic igloo; he might be hiding. Javert's fur is dark gray—he looks like a common subway rat, but he's actually a deluxe breed, and his coat is much softer than it looks. He might try to bite you, so you should wear gloves—but of course, you're wearing gloves anyway. Please don't drop them; they'll be scared and try to run away, but you can't let them . . ." She trailed off. Jocelyn wasn't moving but rather gesturing over Erika at someone behind her.

Something warm settled over her shoulders. A blanket. She turned. A light-brown-skinned man in an EMT uniform stood behind her.

"Hey, why don't we get you over here and check out that knee, okay?" he said in a soothing tone.

Knee? She glanced down and saw a rivulet of inky blood dribbling down her skin.

Vaguely, she realized they must have called for medical help from the next town over where there was an actual hospital, in the event anyone was inside the building and needed treatment.

"Can you do CPR on rats?" she asked him, numbly. She let him help her to her feet. When she tried to straighten her injured leg, it screamed in protest. "They're going to get my rats from the basement. Jocelyn? You're going to get them, right?"

Jocelyn's expression was grim. "We're doing everything we can to get this fire out. But I cannot in good conscience risk my team's lives to go in there right now. I'm sorry . . . I truly am."

They're only rats went unspoken as Jocelyn rejoined the fire team around the back of the theater. But they weren't only rats. Not to Erika. Jean and Javert were her only companions, and they were all she'd have left once Nachtmusik went home. Without them, she'd be truly alone.

Cold resolution settled over her, and Erika waited. Minutes later, a firefighter approached with what looked like a minor head wound, and the EMTs abandoned Erika to tend to their new victim. Amid the chaos, Erika went unnoticed as she crossed the street to slip through the front doors of the opera house.

CHAPTER 31

It was dark inside with the electricity having been cut off, and the stench of burnt wood carried a smell marked by metallic, plasticky fumes. The air was hot and heavy, and something about it made spots wiggle at the corners of her vision. Stuffing the emergency blanket against her nose and mouth with one hand, Erika made her way to her office by the light of her cell phone screen.

The hallway swam around her. Warped floorboards groaned under her feet. Her pulse fluttered in her temple.

What was she doing? She'd done a lot of reckless things in her life, but this had to take the cake; maybe she should sit down and rest. There was always more oxygen close to the floor, right?

The only thing driving her forward was the panic that if she passed out and died from smoke inhalation after the fire was already out, she'd look absolutely ridiculous in the news bulletin about it. Unbidden, she heard Christof's voice in her head, reminding her that preparation was key to success.

I wish he was here right now.

A sob escaped. Had her office always been so far away from the lobby?

I'm going to die, aren't I? My wish came true . . . ha ha! It finally happened. You're welcome, Carla. Also, fuck you for trying to murder me. Over Jackson Weatherfield, of all people! Really? Couldn't we both have done so much better? Wait, I really am dying, right? Or am I being dramatic? Oh God, I don't think I actually want to die—

The hand that had been guiding her along the wall hit air, and she was finally inside the office.

She fumbled for the crowbar crammed in the bottom drawer of her desk, then jacked the ancient window up with the almighty crackling of decades' worth of latex paint busting loose. She stuck her face into the opening, eagerly sucking in fresh air.

Better.

"Okay," she gasped into the empty room, as soon as she felt steady again. "Let's be smart about this."

She found a half-empty plastic water bottle in her trash can and dumped it on her blanket, soaking the navy fabric through. Then she dug out Grandma Meg's tool kit and found a flashlight and a hammer. She wasn't sure why she'd need a hammer, but it seemed like the right thing to bring. It was either that or the screwdriver, and what the fuck were screwdrivers even *for*?

Then she got down on her hands and knees and began to crawl. She probably looked outrageous, scuttling along the filthy hallway in her skintight white dress and heels with a blanket wrapped around her head while clutching her flashlight and cell phone with one hand, the crowbar and hammer in the other.

The end of the hallway seemed so far away. Halfway down, the heel of her hand scuffed across sharp grit, and she hissed in pain. *Fuck, broken glass.*

She picked the sliver out of her skin as best she could with her hands shaking in the wobbling beam of the flashlight, making sounds that were halfway between laughter and hysterical sobbing. Christof still owed her a new sconce. Well, technically, it was Raoul's sconce now, wasn't it? She'd never raise the money to pay off the debt now.

After a thousand years, she reached the door that would take her to the brothel's back entrance. It was already cracked open enough for her to squeeze through. Tentatively, she peered into the stairwell—or what she could see of it.

It was dark on this side, and the smell was thicker here, but there was air movement: searing, bone-dry air rushing across her face and sucking upward. Fire on the floors above was gorging itself on whatever oxygen it could find. Her eyes burned as if she'd gotten flakes of mascara in them, but a thousand times worse than that, and even her own watery tears failed to soothe the stinging. And God, the *roar* of noise. The crackling and popping and the groaning of wood, heaving in ways solid objects should never heave. Why was wood that had been dead for over a century seemingly coming to life? It was the most malevolent cacophony of sound she'd ever experienced.

Through a blurry haze, she glanced up to where the stairs leading to the first-floor lounge went and glimpsed the smallest triangle of orange flashing ominously from behind inky smoke. The stairs were gone—collapsed into a heap of smoldering wood, piled high with whatever had caved in on top of it. To her right were the stairs down to the basement; they were half-concealed by the smoking detritus that had fallen to the landing, but they were still intact.

Breath gusted out of her. There was a way down.

She came off her hands into a stoop and inched forward, testing each step with a tentative heel before putting her full weight on it. The wood creaked with each step, but it was nothing compared to the shuddering of the structure above her. Looking up was out of the question. She didn't need to see the way the ceiling slanted—what was left of it—or how chunks of . . . *building* . . . seemed to shift on their own.

The image of the brothel collapsing around her, burying her in rubble as she suffocated beneath its crushing weight, was suddenly so vivid, so tangible, that she couldn't breathe.

You can breathe down here. The fire is above you, she reminded herself.

As if summoned by her thoughts, something thudded above her, which was followed by a gruesome crack, and her eyes squeezed shut and her body seized in anticipation. And then . . .

Silence.

She opened her eyes. The building hadn't collapsed. Nothing had fallen. No thousand-pound stage light slamming into the ground, molten-hot glass exploding up into her face.

She swallowed. Jean and Javert were down there, and she was too afraid to save them. She'd thought she was brave. So tough, so jaded, so unafraid of her own mortality. But she wasn't. She was a vain, selfish diva. Still a helpless coward with a victim mentality who gave up as soon as shit got tough. She'd thought she'd changed for the better since meeting Christof, but clearly she hadn't.

Two hot tears spilled out and dribbled down her face.

No. *No!*

She'd come this far. She had to keep going. Christof would have kept going if he were here instead of her. That man would walk through a . . . a *fire tornado* if one of his loved ones were on the other side, wouldn't he? He really was that badass. Or just hopelessly, relentlessly determined to protect what mattered to him.

"I can be badass too," she whispered.

One step at a time, she tiptoed down to the basement landing and closed her hand over the door handle. Triumph coursed through her—and then immediately dissipated. It was locked. Because of the fire inspection. Had that really been only this morning? It seemed like an eternity ago.

And Erika had no idea where her keys were. Probably in her purse, which was still in her truck. She glanced down at her tools: crowbar, hammer, flashlight, cell phone. She'd left the screwdriver in the toolbox, because why on earth would she need a screwdriver when there had been a hammer?

Fire. Tornado.

She dropped everything but the hammer, spread her stance as wide as she could in her constricting skirt, and swung at the door handle. The first time, it missed. She swung again—*clank!* Her forearms reverberated with the impact, and it hurt, but the handle was unmoved, so she did it again. And again. Until the handle bent and then, finally, broke, leaving a stubby end poking out of a wooden hole. She flipped the hammer around to the clawlike side and thrust it into the hole to knock the base free, then shoved at the door with all her might until it burst open so suddenly that she fell forward into the pitch-black room, collapsing onto the scratchy weave of her great-great-grandmother's once-luxurious carpet.

Adrenaline kicked her back onto her feet before she could register the bruises she'd acquired. She dashed back out into the hallway to scoop up her tools before hurrying to spin the flashlight's beam toward the cage. *Please, please be okay . . .*

The cage was empty, its door ajar.

"No . . ."

She stumbled toward the cage, unwilling to accept what she was seeing. Her beam zigzagged over the shredded newspaper lining the cage bottom, as if its light could make her rats materialize in the fluffy mounds, but the enclosure was still and silent.

They were gone.

Javert must have escaped, leaving the door open for Jean to follow. Rats' noses were sensitive; they'd have smelled the smoke and known something was wrong. But to where could they have escaped? The only way out was under the door and up the stairs, and it was the only place Javert had ever tried to go.

A desperate search of the room came up empty. Her brain refused to connect the dots, to allow herself to understand what had happened.

Every last ounce of energy she'd summoned evaporated, leaving her boneless and hollow.

Erika slid down to her knees and pulled out her phone. There was only 5 percent battery left; the screen was dim from the automatic battery saver, but she could see her blinking message notification. Christof had called twice, then texted her four times since she'd left, asking if she was okay, pleading for her to return, and begging her to simply let him know she'd gotten home safely. His last text was simply, I love you.

She began to sob in truth. Gross, ugly crying, with snot that dribbled over her upper lip. How like Christof, to only be concerned about her well-being. Any of the other men she'd fucked would have blown up her phone, begging for forgiveness and pleading for her to listen to their increasingly desperate excuses. But Christof *cared*.

If she could hear his voice, everything would be okay, and Javert and Jean wouldn't be—

She dialed. *Please answer.*

The phone rang. And rang. But of course, he was probably busy talking to Gillian, which made sense. But he *should* be hovering by his phone, tormented by heartbreak—why wasn't he answering?

His voice mail greeting was in German, and she didn't understand a word of it. *Beep.*

"Christof. It's me. Erika. I . . ." Her voice, so steady and sure for the first few words, broke as her phone beeped a low-battery warning. A wrenching sob broke free, and then the rest poured out in a tearful rush. "The brothel is on fire, and the firefighters wouldn't go in the basement to get Jean and Javert because they said it was unsafe, and

I thought I could go in to rescue them, but now I'm down here and they're gone, and it's so dark and I'm afraid it's going to collapse on me, and no one knows I'm down here. I know it was stupid, I'm sorry, I . . . I didn't want to be alone again when you left me. I don't want to be alone . . ."

A sixth sense told her to pull her phone away from her ear—the screen was black. She had no idea how much of the voice mail had gone through.

Another shuddering groan came from the stairwell. She should leave. It really wasn't safe down here. Yet she couldn't seem to find the motivation to move. Her limbs felt heavy. Her hand throbbed. Her knees ached. Her head was cloudy with sleep deprivation and whatever other toxic things she'd breathed in on her way down here. What if she just lay down on her bed for a bit . . .

A thunderous crash jolted her back to reality. Something slammed into the ground hard enough to make the earth beneath her vibrate, and suddenly the flashlight beam, which had been aimed toward the door, went opaque as the room flooded with a burst of ash and particles.

The building really was collapsing around her.

"Another café, sir?"

Christof nodded and wordlessly handed their server the empty cup from his third espresso, ignoring Sibylle's narrow-eyed glare.

Waldo leaned over and, in what sounded like a failed attempt at a whisper, suggested, "Maybe after this, no more?"

Christof didn't dignify the idea with a response. He'd drink as much fucking caffeine as he wanted. Maybe after this fourth shot, he'd start to feel something.

They'd been here for close to an hour catching up with Gillian and discussing what to do next, and he suspected the service staff of the now-empty restaurant was eager for them to finally vote on Gillian's role with the band. His phone was faceup on the table; Erika hadn't answered a single one of his texts.

Leave her alone, he told himself. *You'll see her tomorrow morning for the final preshow run-through.*

But that wasn't how it was supposed to be. Erika was supposed to stay here with him tonight, in his hotel room. He'd planned to surprise her by preordering the pain au chocolat from room service for breakfast. A bag of dark-chocolate pretzels with a bow lay upon his pillow—a congratulatory gift he'd brought and would now be eating alone at four in the morning, weeping into his chocolate-stained bed linens like a little child.

"Let's get this over with," he snapped, interrupting a heated discussion about other hair metal bands that had *two* keyboardists.

Gillian wanted to rejoin Nachtmusik. Sibylle wanted Erika to take Gillian's place. Waldo and Sergei had suggested either letting them both be keyboardists or finding a new role for one of them. Never mind that Erika hadn't agreed to anything yet—or that Christof would be damned if he'd let Gillian waltz back into the fold after all this time.

"Maybe we should think things through tonight," Gillian gently suggested. "It sounds like these past few weeks have been . . . a lot. For all of us. We shouldn't make any rash decisions."

"Ah. Gillian Dietrich, advising us on rash decision-making." He'd tried to be diplomatic. Patient. *Understanding.* But in his numb, heartbroken exhaustion, a cold smirk found its way to the surface.

He looked around the table. At these people who'd been so dear to his heart that he'd been willing to sacrifice the one fucking thing he wanted that was solely for himself, all in the name of their collective success. He loved Nachtmusik. He loved his sister and Waldo and Sergei and even Gillian. But in that moment . . .

He resented them with every badass particle of his being.

Gillian stiffened. "I suppose I deserve that."

She'd been unhappy for quite some time, according to her tale of woe—years, even, though Gillian hadn't been able to pinpoint exactly when her disquiet had begun. Perhaps as early as when she and Christof had moved into the Berlin apartment and he'd insisted on the spare bedroom being used for a sound-dampened practice studio rather than a guest room to host Gillian's assorted menagerie of friends and foster animals. Or perhaps it was that he'd always remembered their anniversary, but he'd gifted her only musical books or accessories instead of intuiting that she'd prefer some sort of fucking yarn to spin into whatever the hell teapot regalia she'd bookmarked on their shared browser in the hope he'd get the hint. (The problem was, Christof unilaterally decided, Gillian *had* the ability to intuit things, and Christof was as dense as a fucking Devin Townsend album about everything except music and the business of music.)

Yet her sense of displacement hadn't come solely from her lackluster relationship with Christof, she'd rushed to explain to everyone at the table, after having laid out their personal issues like a gruesome crime scene for their bandmates to behold.

Gillian had been uncertain about her direction as an artist, unsure if hair metal was the right genre for her. Unsure if she even *enjoyed* playing keyboard and singing backup. Did she want to record a solo folk album? Was she wasting her God-given choreography talent with a band that didn't perform dance routines during shows? Did she want to go back to school and become a veterinarian?

These questions had swum in her head until she couldn't stand it any longer. At one of their final tour stops in Lithuania, she'd met a man who'd said he understood exactly what she was going through, and they'd hit it off. Leonas had given her his number. (And where had Christof been during all this? He hadn't the faintest fucking idea, except if he'd venture a guess, it was that he'd been in their hotel room, reviewing expenses for the slightest error or practicing guitar segments he knew by heart but could stand to further fine-tune or folding his luggage into the most efficient configuration so as to ensure successful unpacking at the following stop.)

The night Christof had proposed they go to America, her unease had reached critical mass. Gillian had gathered her still-packed bags, boarded a plane, and run away to discover if any of her questions had answers.

"You could have fucking called," he had accused, and Gillian had supplied a rambling excuse about being ashamed at first and then feeling like she could only reach full soul freedom by severing all lingering bonds that imprisoned her. For whatever reason, this had received nods of sympathy from his bandmates, and Sibylle had chastised Christof for the outburst, which rankled. Did no one besides Erika comprehend what he'd gone through those first few weeks?

His chest squeezed. Erika *understood* him. She hadn't judged him. He could tell her he'd committed murder, and she'd calmly help him sort out where to dispose of the corpse, with only a wry suggestion afterward that perhaps he should refrain from doing it again.

And that was true success, wasn't it? It wasn't to be in the Rock and Roll Hall of Fame, to grace the cover of *Rolling Stone*, or to perform to sold-out stadiums when his skin was liver spotted.

The ultimate success was simply to be known and loved without condition. To have a partner who would ride into a fire tornado for him, knowing he would do the same. A partner who would have been willing to *join a hair metal band* to be with him—even when that choice was far, far from what she wanted and deserved.

Erika *was* success. Without her, nothing else mattered.

The server came by with his espresso and set it down in front of him—along with the bill. An unsubtle hint.

He fumbled for his wallet, withdrew a stack of cash large enough to cover the meal twice over, and tossed it on the table. "Very well. If we're not going to decide anything tonight, I'll be on my way." Who cared if he didn't get a receipt for his expense records? Suddenly, things that had once seemed very important now seemed laughably inconsequential.

Gillian caught up with him at the valet stand. "Tof, wait."

Irritated, he turned. "What?"

She held his phone and his guitar out to him. "You almost left these behind. Are you all right?"

He stared at the light shimmering off the iridescent blue opal embedded in his Galaxy Dragon guitar. This had been so important to him, once. Now, he'd trade this thing a thousand times over if it would take him back in time so he could undo the hurt he'd caused Erika.

And just like that, he knew what he had to do.

He took the instrument and slung it over his shoulder. Then Christof turned to the valet and handed him a ticket from his breast pocket. The young man's eyes widened when he read the number on it. "We wondered whose car this was! It's been waiting for you here for weeks, sir."

He shrugged. "I wasn't ready to drive it yet, and Carte Blanche offered to transfer it here for a reasonable fee. Seemed safer than parking it downtown."

When the valet darted off to retrieve his ride, Christof turned to Gillian. "Tell the others I went after Erika and I won't be back tonight. I will do this concert tomorrow and finish recording the album with Nachtmusik, but after that, I'm done."

Gillian reeled back in shock. "You're done with the *band*? But the band is everything to you!"

"Gilly, I'm madly, hopelessly, desperately in love, and I need to do something dramatic to prove it." He gently clapped his hands to her narrow shoulders and stared deep into her faerie-creature eyes. Despite everything between them and all the apologies and explanations still unspoken, he knew there was still genuine caring. Whether their friendship could ever be salvaged was uncertain, but their past couldn't be erased in only eight weeks. He hoped she felt the same. "Please . . . take care of them for me after I leave."

With tears in her eyes, she gave him a stiff nod. "I will."

It wasn't until he'd slid into the driver's seat and tucked his phone into the cup holder that Christof saw he'd missed a call from Erika.

CHAPTER 32

Erika opened her eyes. She wasn't dead. If she were, it would be a lot hotter in here.

She swung her flashlight toward the doorway and swore. She wasn't dead—yet—but whatever had collapsed was now blocking the exit with wood and plaster piled high. The top of the doorframe had buckled under extreme weight and taken a portion of the ceiling with it, so now the ceiling above Erika was bowed, sloping farther and farther toward the earth as it neared what had once been the doorway.

Reassuring.

If she tried to dig her way out, she might get buried under the rubble. If she sat here and did nothing, praying someone would come rescue her, she might get buried anyway.

"I'd like a third option, please," she told the dusty room. Carefully, she inched her way toward the bed. Her velvet coverlet was covered in crusty bits of ceiling and whatever else, but she shook them out and slipped under the bottom sheet, where it was blessedly clean, and curled into a ball. Then she began to laugh, and she couldn't stop. She was probably suffocating on carbon monoxide or something. When she was done laughing, she did the only thing left: she began to sing "Memory."

Maybe Christof would hear her voice mail and come to rescue her in time. It wasn't entirely hopeless, was it? La Rose was only fifteen minutes away.

A dull thud came from somewhere above her. More shaking. Bits of plaster rained down around her.

Only *mostly* hopeless.

She kept singing.

And then, against all hope, something soft brushed against Erika's cheek.

Erika bolted upright, throwing the coverlet back and fixing her flashlight beam on the small creature next to her on the bed. It was Jean. The white spots on his brown coat were gray with soot, but his eyes were clear, and his sides rose and fell with steady breath.

"Jean," she whimpered. She picked him up and cupped his warm, cinnamon-roll body against her chest. "You're *okay*." She shuddered with relief and heaved in breaths between sobs, swallowing acrid tears and not caring about what the smoke would do to her singing voice if she ever made it out of here.

Then Jean began to wriggle in her grip. "Hey, calm down . . . what are you—"

He popped free of her cupped hands and landed on the floor, absorbing the leap's impact with his legs splayed like a starfish. Shaking off the fall, he glanced back at Erika before darting toward the mirror.

"Jean! Where are you going?" she called. This was unlike him. Unlike Javert, his escape artist compatriot, Jean could be held for hours without complaint. Was he sick from the smoke?

Erika stood to chase after him, pointing the flashlight in the direction he'd gone. Except Jean was nowhere to be seen. For an instant, her stomach bottomed out in panic. Then she saw it.

In the dirty air, tiny whorls of particulate matter were being sucked into a small space at the corner of the giant mirror on the wall.

Erika stooped down, angling the flashlight at the bottom corner of the mirror's ornate wooden frame. Air seemed to be escaping through a tiny opening there. The mirror was so long that it hung only two inches off the ground, but now that Erika was down here, it was clear that a large chunk of the corner had been gnawed off.

As if by an extremely motivated rodent.

Erika held the light up to the hole and saw only blackness. But blackness wasn't the wall behind the mirror. There was a *space* there. Was something back there?

She stood and locked her fingers around the right side of the frame, then pulled as hard as she could, but the mirror didn't budge. The other side was equally recalcitrant. Erika shook out her hands, frustrated. Was this thing glued to the wall? Was there some secret unlocking mechanism she was meant to discover?

Well, screw that. She'd brought a hammer, and she'd damn well get use out of it. With a cathartic yell, she swiped her hammer off the ground and swung. The reflective glass cracked, and so she did it again and again, until jagged shards crashed to the floor and cool, blessedly *clean* air funneled into the room, and Erika could plainly see the passageway beyond. It looked like an old mining tunnel, but air seemed to flow in here, and that meant there was a way out.

When she'd cleared most of the jagged pieces out of the frame, she gathered the blanket around her and stepped through, her heels crunching on broken glass and gravel. Her flashlight illuminated a curve in the tunnel, and she followed it until she got to a small room, no larger than the size of her walk-in closet in New York, with another tunnel branching off it. The tiny area was packed with crates, from dirt floor to ceiling, but a relatively modern camping lantern propped on the nearest box suggested someone had been here in the last decade.

Erika started forward, continuing through the tunnel toward what she hoped was the way out, then halted in her tracks. She was exhausted and bruised and bleeding and possibly suffering delusions from inhaling toxic air . . . but she had to know.

"What were you up to, Mistress Giry?" she murmured, returning to the room with the crates and setting her flashlight on the ground like stage uplighting. There was only one box that wasn't stacked, and that was the one with the lantern on it. She'd open that one, and then she'd get the hell out of there.

She moved the lantern to the ground and paused on the brown paper envelope that had been sitting beneath it. The paper was crispy and fragile under her fingers, so she was careful as she slid the contents out and crouched next to the light. It looked like some sort of handwritten ledger. Erika frowned at the pages of faded, nearly illegible scrawl. Just as she was about to set it aside, she felt a sheet of paper come loose from the back of the packet. She slid it free. The texture of this sheet was thicker, like vellum.

Erika read the words on the paper twice, unwilling to believe what she was seeing.

It is hereby certified that the property located at the Township of Paris Lot 5 Block 17 otherwise known as the Paris Opera House has been paid for in full by Mme. Antoinette Giry for the sum of 1,000 dollars.

Her great-great-grandmother hadn't been gifted the opera house—she'd *bought* it, fair and square. But how? A thousand dollars had to have been a fortune in the early 1900s. And Erika had always wondered how this place had stayed in business all these years, considering that it seemed to bleed money out of every outlet—especially after the brothel had closed down.

Erika suspected the answer was inside the crate in front of her. Using her crowbar, she pried the lid off and peered inside.

Christof tore into the Paris city limits at a velocity so reckless and irresponsible that even Waldo would have been alarmed.

His heart thundered in his chest as he cleared the final hill leading into town and saw the waning smoke plume and emergency vehicles crowding the street outside the Paris Opera House. With one hand, he gripped the leather of the steering wheel hard enough to leave indents, and with the other, he hit redial. Again.

Erika's familiar voice, sharp and precise, played after a single ring. "You've reached Erika Greene. I don't check my voice mail, so don't bother." *Beep.*

He hung up. In the last ten minutes, he'd heard those words so many times he could recite them with precise accuracy. They haunted him.

A billboard greeted him with a cheery BONJOUR! BIENVENUE À PARIS, NEVADA! He was so close. But would he make it in time? He blew past the first stop sign and slammed on the brakes to avoid barreling into another car.

Sibylle and the rest of the band had taken Gillian's rental car and rushed to follow him to the opera house the moment he'd gotten off the phone with emergency response, so he knew they weren't far behind.

He careened around the corner onto the town's main street.

A sheriff's car angled itself across both lanes of traffic in front of the opera house, attempting to block the road. Christof slowed only enough to avoid ramming through the other car, then maneuvered up onto the sidewalk to go around it. He slammed to a stop directly in front of the opera house's steps, jammed the gearshift into park, and exited the car without bothering to kill the engine.

He ignored the crowd silently gaping at him as if he hadn't broken several driving laws on his way to arriving in a brand-new vehicle worth nearly as much as Nachtmusik's entire album advance and looked around, as if Erika might materialize before his eyes. A crowd of approximately fifty locals gathered behind street barriers and multiple emergency vehicles with their lights flashing—but not a single glimpse of his raven-haired witch.

The short-haired woman he recognized from the fire inspection stood next to the man in the sheriff uniform, and their equally dour expressions turned his blood to ice.

"Where is she?" he demanded. "Why are you standing there and doing nothing?"

The fire chief sighed. "Sir, I have several crews working to excavate the collapsed area. We've dedicated every available resource from Paris County to this, and we have teams from nearby jurisdictions en route. We've put out the fire, but rescue crews can't go any faster than we're going without risking further damage to the basement structure. If she's alive under there—"

"She is." With that, he stormed around the side of the building toward the pile of charred wood that had once been the brothel.

"You can't go in there!" the fire marshal shouted. Several emergency workers looked up in alarm as he strode by, and one even tried to stop him when he reached the collapsed building.

Christof roughly shoved the hapless man aside and reached for a smoldering piece of wood near the top of the jumbled stack of debris. It shifted under his grip but refused to move. *Erika is under there.* Somewhere under the rubble. Alone.

"Sir, this is an active emergency scene; you could be seriously injured. If you attempt to trespass, I may have to detain you."

He whirled to face the man who'd dared stop him. It was the sheriff: a kindly-looking fellow with a blocky head, a graying mustache, and a prominent six-pointed-star badge, like in Waldo's western movies.

"You cannot detain me. I am not an American. I will do as I please."

"That's . . . er, that's not exactly how the law works."

"Do I look like I fucking care how the law works?" he snarled.

The sheriff's eyes bulged. "Uh . . . sir . . ."

"The woman I love is down there. Helpless and frightened, and I will reach her!" He turned back to the plank of wood he was working on and shoved at it with his boot. It shuddered under the impact but remained intact.

They are wasting precious time! Why was no one helping him? Erika could be injured. She could be bleeding out at this very moment or gasping her final breaths! All while everyone stood there behind him, frozen. Useless.

He didn't think about what he did next. All he knew was that he had to save her; he had to get this wood out of the way, and he had no tools to break through. Only his guitar.

Gripping the neck in his hands, he raised the guitar over his head, widened his stance, and readied a mighty blow.

"Sir, please stop!" someone else called from behind Christof. "You don't have to do that!"

Could they not see he was *busy*? Gritting his teeth, he lowered the guitar and turned to face the crowd. Then he raised his voice so all could hear and toed a line in the ash and debris in front of him. "This is the point of no return. Anyone who dares cross it to try and stop me will see their blood race in the streets!"

When no one moved, he spun back around—and stilled.

Erika's ghost stood in the ruins, wavering in the low clouds of white smoke. Her skin was as white in death as her pale dress.

His legs gave out from under him, but he didn't feel pain as his knees hit the sidewalk. "No . . . ," he choked out. He'd hoped . . . believed that if he only drove fast enough, he could make it in time . . .

But it was too late.

Then the ghost spoke in a tremulous voice that sounded so, so very much like Erika's. "Blood in the streets? Really? I thought I was the dramatic one."

He blinked. *What*—

"Ma'am! Are you all right?" The stillness of the moment broke as chaos descended, medical and emergency personnel dashing toward her. "Ma'am!"

Bewildered, Christof looked around and belatedly realized that Erika's ghost wasn't hovering over the ruins of the brothel, after all, but standing a fair distance behind it. And as she staggered closer, he saw that she was very, very much alive. Her dress was torn and stained, her knees bloody, and her face swollen and streaked with soot and tears, but she was alive. In her arms, she clutched a bundled blanket as if it were a child, and when the crowd of helpers approached her, she drew inward around it—protecting her cache.

"Does anyone have a cage or a box or something? I have two really scared rats in here," he heard her say, but he was still too stunned to move.

She's alive.

Nothing else mattered.

"Erika . . . ," he called hoarsely, but his voice was drowned out by the commotion.

A hand fell on his shoulder. It was the sheriff. "Sir, why don't we get you on your feet and get you all looked over by our guys here, and then you can say hello to your little lady. How does that sound?" His tone was slow and wheedling, as if speaking to a volatile individual undergoing a crisis. But he wasn't undergoing a crisis—not anymore, at least. In fact, Christof had never been more calm and certain in his entire life.

Erika was alive, and he was going to marry her.

He grunted as he pushed to his feet, ignoring the assorted protests directed at him as he shoved his way through the crowd. He stopped in front of her, ignoring the medics buzzing about like harried flies, and searched her wide, glossy brown eyes for any sign of pain. Despite the surface wounds and grime coating her trembling frame, she appeared unharmed, and yet his brain wasn't ready to accept what his eyes saw as true. He half suspected he was in a horrible dream from which he'd wake to find she was gone for good.

"I drove as quickly as I could." His voice came out gravelly with emotion. "I thought I was too late. How?"

Someone ran up with a hard-sided storage bin, and Erika paused to help unload her wriggling bundle into the container, eliciting promises that her rats would be taken to a veterinarian and given a thorough checkup.

Finally turning back to him, Erika swallowed hard, and when she spoke, her voice was equally raspy. "Either I was tripping balls from toxic gases, or my rats led me to a hidden mining tunnel behind the big mirror in my bedroom." Erika pointed at the rusted garden shed on the far side of the brothel's dusty parking lot. "There's an exit in there, but the tunnel keeps going . . . probably up into the hills where the abandoned gold mines are."

It seemed like an impossible story. But who was he to pass judgment on what was possible? Just four weeks earlier he'd gotten drunk on mini bottles of vodka, dropped a token into a slot machine on a whim, and won a Rolls-Royce Phantom. That same night, he'd proposed to the woman of his dreams—and been too much of a coward to follow through on it.

He shook himself. Why was he wasting time like this? Careful of the rubble beneath them, he went down to a knee. Vaguely, he heard someone whoop and several onlookers gasp, but the crowd's reaction didn't matter.

Not as much as the way Erika's eyes went wide, her shaking hands coming up to clasp at her chest as if her heart were about to leap out like one of her rescued rats.

"You don't have to do this," she warned.

She was trying to give him a way out. He didn't want it. "Marry me," he demanded gruffly. When she frowned, he inwardly winced at his own ineptitude. "Forgive me for not beginning with a romantic speech. All I know is that I love you enough to give anything to be with you. I'm leaving Nachtmusik, and I'll stay here in Paris with you if that's what you want. It doesn't matter, as long as I'm with you. I love you with a fire that burns hotter than . . . than . . ." He racked his brain for an acceptable lyric.

"Volcano!" shouted Waldo. The band had arrived behind him in time to witness his declaration.

Sibylle supplied, "The eternal bonfires of hell!"

"Holy water!" This last came from Sergei.

But it was Erika who said, "An early-twentieth-century brothel?"

Someone in the crowd gasped, but Christof smiled. "It's a bit soon, yes?"

"The joke or the proposal?"

"Well . . ."

"I told you. You don't have to do this." She returned his slow smile. "My answer is yes. It was already yes four weeks ago. And it'll be yes if you stay with the band, and it'll be yes if you leave. No matter the how or when or where . . . my answer will be yes. Forever."

Relief flooded him, so fast he thought he might pass out. In its wake came delight, then a desire to kiss Erika so thoroughly they'd drive everyone else away.

"Let's go." He stood and pulled her roughly against his chest. She came willingly, twining her arms around his neck like they'd choreographed the moves in advance, and then he swept her into his arms.

"Where are we going?"

"To get married," he answered without hesitation.

The crowd cheered, although as he began walking away with his prize, several emergency personnel attempted to stop him. "Sir, we should really take her to the hospital."

The sheriff added, "And we have some questions for Ms. Greene."

Erika tilted her head back to glance at the sheriff, her expression serene. "I'll call you, darling."

"Does no one here understand how this works?" grumbled the sheriff.

Erika blew him a kiss.

He rounded the building, and Erika caught a glimpse of his ride. "Where did you get *that*?"

"Las Vegas," he hedged.

"You won this while you were on your existential bender?"

He carefully lowered Erika to her feet and opened the car door for her, ushered her inside, then joined her in the driver's seat. The door shut behind him, drowning out the noise of the crowd. He gave her a sheepish glance. "I wasn't sure what to do with it at first, but then I decided I was going to sell it and anonymously donate the money to save the opera house, in case the fundraiser didn't work. We still can. I've only driven it this once."

She nibbled her bottom lip. "About the theater . . ."

The back door opened, and Sibylle thudded into the plush seating behind them. "What the fuck, Big Brother? Did you really plan to get married without me as witness?"

The car shuddered again as Waldo flung himself in next to her, nudging Sibylle to slide in farther. "Wedding party! Woooo! Oh, what is this?" A loud pop sounded, and Erika and Christof flinched, only to see that Waldo had discovered the complimentary champagne bottle and flutes that had been included with the car.

Sergei gracefully slid in next to Waldo. "If we are all going, then I will attend as well. My friend and I will have to discuss arrangements for rescheduling the concert."

"That may not be necessary," Christof said at the same time as Erika replied, "I don't think we'll need that."

Erika and Christof shared a glance, and her dark eyes glittered with excitement. "I may or may not have found the title of ownership and, like, twenty crates of gold bars in the tunnel under the brothel. Guess we know what happened to all that stolen gold from the Leroux mine."

Sibylle snorted. "I could have told you all this, but *noooo*. No one wanted to listen to my ghost murder theories."

"So you knew? You knew that Mistress Giry was running a gold-smuggling ring in the old mining tunnels beneath the brothel?" Erika raised her brows.

"Not . . . specifically. But it was *alluded* to." Sibylle slunk down in her seat and held out her glass to Waldo, who held the champagne bottle. "Give me some of that."

Gillian peered into the open back seat door. "Is there space for me?"

"Ja!" Waldo exclaimed. "Space for everyone!"

Christof fought the instinctive urge to proclaim that there weren't enough seat belts for everyone, regardless of how spacious the back seat was, but Erika's hand squeezed his thigh, and he bit his tongue.

"We'd love to have you there," Erika said smoothly. "Let's put the past behind us, right?"

Gillian flashed a brilliant smile and agreed, giggling as she clambered in to lie down across three separate laps. "Just like the old days when we sat in the back of Waldo's mother's station wagon with all the instruments!"

Sergei pulled the door shut just in time to cut off the protests of the sputtering sheriff. Something about seat belts and laws and the sort of nonsense he used to care passionately about, back before he'd thrown his caution into a fire tornado.

Christof gestured apologetically through the window: *Can't hear you!* He revved the engine, reveling in the vehicle's powerful purr.

Erika shot him a sly look. "Can I drive?"

"Absolutely not." There was a limit to how *much* caution he could throw into the fire tornado.

"Fair enough."

He pulled onto the highway and glanced at the sign marking the eighty-mile distance to Las Vegas. That was how long he had to change his mind, if he suddenly awoke from this fugue and decided he was making a monumental error.

Erika had been fiddling with the touch screen stereo controls, but now she snagged his gaze before it returned to the road and fixed him with a beaming smile so wicked he forgot, for a moment, how to breathe. "Are you ready to rock?" she asked, as the first familiar strains of "Rock You Like a Hurricane" filtered through the speakers.

"Always," he vowed, and he knew then that he was absolutely certain. As long as he had Erika by his side . . . *always*.

EPILOGUE

Ten months later

It was a sold-out show, and the crowd in the auditorium was loud and restless. The air reverberated with fervent anticipation.

As Christof peered out from behind the backstage curtains, nervous energy sizzled in his veins. This was it. The night it all either came together in perfect, electric harmony—or crashed in a spectacular conflagration of failure.

Except he knew it wouldn't fail. He wouldn't allow such a thing to happen.

Sibylle appeared at his side, craning her neck past him to catch a glimpse of the audience. "They're bloodthirsty tonight. The spirits will be pleased."

"Ultraexcellent!" Waldo exclaimed, spying the same view as Sibylle from Christof's other side. "This crowd is the best one I have seen since the Amsterdam show from our tour."

"You don't even remember Amsterdam," Sibylle shot back.

"Ja! You are right. But I remember the awesomeness!"

"Psst!" Gillian signaled to the three of them from the backstage stairwell. She was wearing a green tulle skirt tonight with a Pasididžiavimas concert shirt tucked into the waistband. Against all odds, the infamous

Lithuanian playboy and Gillian were still dating, and Gillian had spent her time over the past ten months commuting between Berlin, Paris, and . . . wherever disco was happening, apparently. Christof tolerated Leonas's occasional presence only because it seemed to make Gillian happy, and also because Erika had made him promise to be civil and not to make any more disparaging remarks about disco in Leonas's company. "Come on, the show is starting in three minutes." Gillian waved for them to follow her up to their reserved box.

With one last glance out at the audience, Christof reluctantly released the curtain. As the fabric fell, he caught a glimpse of one of the scorch marks hidden behind it on the wall. They never had determined the cause of the fire, though everyone had a pet theory; as with the mystery of Mistress Giry's murder, the Paris Opera House kept its secrets.

When he was settled in his seat, he felt a nudge in his side. It was Gillian again. "Don't be nervous. She's going to be incredible."

"I know," he said. "My wife performs flawlessly." Still, he rubbed his damp palms on his velvet pants to dry them. It wasn't Erika he was worried about. What if the audience didn't connect with the songs that Nachtmusik had helped write for the show?

With the help of their new band manager and agent, Christof had worked to renegotiate Nachtmusik's contract with the label in order to delay their album release so it coincided with the opening of Erika's show. The performance of *Sporeceress: A Rock Opera* would directly impact Nachtmusik's success, since they were credited for collaborating on nearly every musical number.

The lights dimmed, and Christof's pulse ratcheted up a notch. Even though it wasn't Erika who strode to the spotlight in center stage but rather Erika's old stage daughter and newly reacquainted friend, Misty, who was the show's producer—and the Paris Opera House's new co-owner. Thanks to the hoard of gold beneath the brothel, Erika had been able to pay off the theater's remaining debt, repair the fire damage, and outfit the entire building in new, state-of-the-art performance equipment and safety features. Then Erika had sold half her owner-ship share to Misty at an enormously reasonable price—in exchange for right of first refusal on starring roles in her future musical theater productions.

The brothel was gone for good, but a part of Erika's family legacy would live on in Paris. Thrive, even, now that Magnifique! had opened and was bringing in droves of tourists every weekend. The Paris Opera House was one of the only local businesses left on this side of town, so visitors adored it. The fire and the tale of Christof's so-called rescue had even made the rounds enough times to become recent urban legend.

Best of all, Erika now had the freedom to choose where she spent her time. Whether that was touring with Nachtmusik—not as a key-boardist but as his partner—starring in any productions she might choose to pursue, or living at home in the new flat they'd bought in Berlin. They'd gotten a two-story loft in a midsize condominium—far away from the basement level, and with a spacious spare bedroom for bigger and better rat castles. But for now, while Erika prepared for her role as Madame Morelle, the Dark Sporeceress, they lived in a rented RV they could drive anywhere they wished.

Correction: *Christof* could drive anywhere they wished. Erika was still working on passing her driving test. She'd explained it was quite normal for Americans to fail a minimum of seven times, and Christof hadn't had the heart to argue because he liked driving anyway, and Erika made an excellent road-trip karaoke-duet companion.

As Misty approached the mic, the audience quieted. "Thank you all so much for coming here tonight. I'm delighted to share this heart-warming and totally *badass* musical story with you all, but before we begin, I want to thank some very important people. First and foremost, our star, Erika Greene. A brilliant, talented, incredibly *good person*. She is also my mentor and role model and, I'm proud to say, my friend. This theater has been in her family since the early 1900s, and I'm honored she chose to open it up to independent theater productions."

The audience applauded, and Misty went on, "Many thanks as well to our anonymous sponsor who funded this entire musical. Thank you for your generosity to the musical arts." Christof stole a glance across the theater at Box Five, where Sergei sat next to a tall figure who wore a dense black veil. If he looked closely, he thought he could make out pale skin and long, straight black hair.

Sergei had promised to introduce them after the show, and Christof was nervous as hell. He suspected he was going to be rather moonstruck by the encounter.

But not even that prospect could distract him as soon as the curtain rose.

Erika stood at center stage in a simple black column dress—a darkly ethereal pillar among technicolor mushroom set pieces and glitter falling slowly from the rafters, the simple white lighting casting her in a magical cloud. Her lips were scarlet, her scars left uncovered and plain to see in the stark lighting. In that long, silent moment before she began to sing, he could *hear* the audience holding its collective breath.

She was utterly, heart-stoppingly magnificent. If it were possible to die of love, he would've been buried with the rest of the Paris Opera House's phantoms long ago. Thankfully, he lived on.

When Erika's voice rang out, angelic yet thrillingly seductive all at once, hushed gasps rose from the audience. Christof knew that the show would be successful. With her voice and his band's music combined, they were an unstoppable team. A powerhouse of musical creation.

All his life, he'd torn himself apart searching for the key to success. Persistence, determination, preparation, efficiency . . . all these careful rules he'd tried to abide by. As if he could use sheer willpower to simply pry open the future he dreamed of.

Yet in the end, it was love that had unlocked the door.

ACKNOWLEDGMENTS

I wrote my debut novel, *The Astronaut and the Star*, during a pandemic. So I thought, How hard could it be to write a *second* book during a pandemic? Sure, I had to go back to my day job at the restaurant, but the writing part would be easier this time, right? Because I knew what I was doing now . . . right?

Ba-dum tiss!

Cue audience laughter.

Suffice it to say, this book wouldn't exist if it weren't for my support network of friends, fellow writers, and family holding my entire life together with metaphorical emotional glue. I wish I could bottle their collective love and support and sell it, because then I'd be rich and I could buy a vast swath of land and rescue one hundred sad animals who would live upon this land in bucolic harmony! Don't steal my business idea.

To make emotional glue, my crit partners, Alexis, Jo, Kelly, and Kate, are always the first ingredient in the mix. They carry *weight*, from providing the usual motivational chats and emails to dropping everything to read my hot mess of a first draft in record turnaround time, sending me the kindest care packages during hard times, and—in Jo's case—taking on the great and noble responsibility of being my writing dom, which involved regularly texting, YOU BETTER BE WRITING RIGHT NOW!!! as my deadline loomed. As always, my gratitude to all the incomparable Ponies—my fellow romance writers and all-around incredible human beings—Alexis, Jo, Kelly, Lin, Elle, Mel, Jas, and Chris.

Shout-out to Virginia—my personal Sibylle—who inspired a whole character without either of us knowing it. And to my friends who've been my champions during the rough stuff—Anna, Anchi, Tara, Kimiko, Sara—thank you for the phone calls, the advice, the wine, and, mostly, being there for me when I needed it. Bonus thanks to Demelza, my manager at my day job, who's been beyond understanding about my writing schedule and deadlines.

I'm also in deep musical debt to my two musical consultants, Kyle and Alexis, since I'm the least musically adept person I know (trust me: my elementary school choir teacher assigned me to the xylophone rather than have me sing—then assigned a second person to play xylophone with me, since I couldn't keep a rhythm on my own). Kyle, my roommate, super talented jazz guitarist, and classically trained musician, went through and painstakingly corrected my musician lingo and answered questions like, "First of all, what's an amp, and second, how do I make it catch fire?" Alexis was my musical theater consultant, because at the start of writing this book, the only show I'd ever seen live was *The Phantom of the Opera* (which has nothing to do with this book at all), and Alexis made the brave sacrifice of offering to watch a lot of musicals with me, as well as being on hand to help me make pop-culture musical theater jokes that would have flown over my head a year ago.

And then there are the absolute geniuses who actually made this book happen while I spent months lurking around my writing lair in the sweatpants that I definitely washed at least once. Eva, my impeccably badass agent, who creates time out of ether and always believes in me, even when I'm hopelessly behind schedule on sending her my drafts and they're filled with a thousand instances of the word *just* (and that's an improvement, I tell you!). My editor at Montlake, Alison, who heard my half-formed pitch for the book and without any further information was fully on board, despite this book being so very different from my first one in tone and premise—thank you for trusting me to take on this ambitious, slightly far-fetched idea for my sophomore book, when even I wasn't sure I could pull it off! To Krista, my developmental editor, who, once again, implicitly *gets* what I'm trying to do and knows exactly how to tweak things so the finished product nails it—plus, she (and her mom!) helped fix my horrendous German so I don't embarrass the German side of *my* family. To Riam, my copy editor: I'm glad we got you for this book, too, because you understand how the English language and the concept of linear time work in fiction—when I clearly make do with *guessing* how those things work—and you're so patient about explaining these concepts to me. I promise by the next one, I'll retain this knowledge! Sylvia, the proofreader who has the supernatural power to detect every errant typo, made this finished manuscript shine like Christof's gold pants. And none of you would have heard about any of my books if Ashley, sorceress of public relations, hadn't performed her secret magic arts from the dark school of marketing to supplement my mediocre attempts at promotion—which mostly involved unsuccessful attempts at photographing my pets posing with my book covers. Karah, this book's production manager, gets bonus thanks for keeping track of all these moving parts and making the finished product worthy of the spotlight.

To my parents and family: thank you for your encouragement and support. And to all my human loved ones who moved on from the state of corporeal existence this year—I'm grateful for the time I had with you.

Finally, to my furry family: Taiga, my best friend; Zero, my cuddle buddy; and my new kitten, Kitana, who dreams of nothing but murder and destruction yet has brought so much joy into my life in a time when I didn't expect to find it. Last of all but never the least, to Leo, my big, softhearted cat who was always in my lap when I wrote . . . I can still feel your warmth as if you were here. In my heart, you always will be.

ABOUT THE AUTHOR

Jen Comfort is originally from Portland, Oregon, and dabbled in astro-physics before spending a decade working in restaurants in New York City and Portland. Now she writes romantic comedies about hot nerds with very cool jobs. She spends her free time growing plants destined to die before their time, playing video games, and encouraging her cat and malamute-husky dog to become internet famous, with zero success.